STILL LUCKY

Book Two

C.J. BAILEY

NUL AUTRE
an imprint of
pronghornpress.org

For Stephen...still my inspiration!
Sinceriously!

For thou not farther than my thoughts canst move,
And I am still with them, and they with thee;

—Shakespeare, *Sonnet 47*

Table of Contents

The Past as Prologue

For those of you who have decided to start in the middle of this trilogy—this being Book Two—I don't expect you'll find yourselves too lost since this book begins right where Lucky Girl *left off, with one half of our astonishing couple leaving for three months in Europe and the other half housesitting (along with her friend) in his absence.*

Richard and CJ met one night at an opening in his art gallery. He knocked her off her feet, literally, and that's how it all started. CJ jumped in with both feet and Richard did everything he could think of to convince her that they belonged together. (Little did he know she didn't need much convincing!)

Suffice it to say that the breadth and depth of their commitment to each other grew at an amazing rate in the weeks before it was time for him to leave. He did invite CJ to make the trip with him, and though tempted, she chose to stay behind and finish the project she's been working on for several years, while taking advantage of a rent-free summer and Richard's business connections.

And so the lovers are forced to part. What remains to be seen is if absence will make their hearts grow fonder or if their ardor will cool as Richard fears it may. But CJ has found her man and she has a few tricks up her sleeve to keep those internal fires burning. For CJ long distance love is merely another creative challenge!

STILL LUCKY

STILL LUCKY

1
So Long and Thanks For All the Fish

Sunday, July 14

Note of the day, slipped into his briefcase:

> *True love is like ghosts,*
> *which everybody talks about and few have seen.*
> — François de La Rochefoucauld

I see it in your eyes!   XXOOJ

As I turned back to the house, my phone rang. It was Steph.

"I wanted to say goodbye to your Magic Man."

"You just missed him. He's on his way to the airport. Antonio's driving, you can give him a call."

"You OK?"

"Yup. I'm imagining he's just off to work. It won't really catch up with me 'til tonight. Meanwhile, I'm gonna get my week laid out so I can keep busy. Will you be here for dinner?"

"I should be home 6:00-6:30. I'm gonna give Michael a chance to recover."

I laughed. "Thoughtful of you."

"I've got to make myself a schedule, too. Maybe we can do that together tonight. And we can talk about the yoga and the trainer."

"Have a great day. And get in some good licks—if you catch my drift." I couldn't help but wink, though of course she couldn't see it.

"Perv!"

"Yeah, like that's not *exactly* what you're going to do!"

I laughed as I went back in and headed for the kitchen. I wanted one more cup of Marie's coffee to take with me to the library.

It was getting close enough to lunch that I started wondering what Marie had on the menu when my phone sang out Richard's *Magic Man* ringtone.

"Hey, Handsome, miss me already?"

"Do you have to ask?"

"Hmmmm. Probably not. I, on the other hand, am pretending you hard at work at the gallery and this is just another day slaving over my desk."

"I haven't spent any time at the gallery on a Sunday since I met you," he reminded me.

"Details…they don't always fit into my alternate universe. I prefer not to start missing you until dinnertime. So what's up?"

"Well, not me. I just got through security and am ensconced in the VIP lounge until they invite me to enjoy fourteen or fifteen hours on the plane followed by a trip through Rome's traffic."

"I'm not sure I can feel sorry for you," I said skeptically.

"Think about me wandering the streets of Rome, alone, sad, wishing you were with me."

"*Really* hard to imagine. You'll be meeting great people, enjoying fabulous food and seeing some great art. Who knows, maybe you'll even do a little shopping."

"And what will I be shopping for?"

"Hmmm…maybe a little souvenir—and I do mean *little*—for the girl you left behind. Just to let her know you were thinking of her."

"You don't think she doubts that, do you?"

"Did you remind her how you felt about her before you left?" I asked with no hint of irony in my voice.

Richard let out a huge laugh. It was a sound I'd loved since the first night we met.

"I certainly hope so. I was starting to wonder if maybe I overdid it a little. You know…too much of a good thing…"

"A very good thing," I assured him. "And never too much."

"Good to know. So what are you doing?"

"Organizing my week. Steph will be home for dinner and we're going to get ourselves on a schedule so we can stay focused. Easier for me than her."

"I have a feeling she can handle it. She called on the way to the airport. I told her to keep an eye on you for me."

"Not sure if I should be flattered or offended."

"Flattered."

"OK," I agreed happily.

"You're easy."

"Depends on who's doing the persuading."

"Lucky me."

"Lucky *me*!"

"Seriously, Sweetheart," he said softly, "I want you to know how much I appreciate everything you did to make this as painless as possible for me. I confess I was worried about how I was going to react if you went all weepy on me."

"Have you ever seen me weepy?"

"Only in a good way."

"Then you had no reason to expect anything else." I said it dismissively, but I wasn't fooling him.

Richard laughed again. "Is this your business don't-fuck-with-me mode?"

"Maaybee...I have to practice for when those multi-million dollar offers start rolling in."

"It won't be long. I'm absolutely certain of that."

I confessed it was a little hard to think about at that point.

"Just follow the path Ben and Jerry laid out for you and you'll be fine."

"Still can't help thinking 'ice cream' whenever I hear their names. I want to try that new *Coffee Coffee Buzz Buzz Buzz* flavor."

"Tell Marie," he said. "She'll get you some. Sounds like a motivational tool. Might be deductible."

"Is that how you one-percenters stay in the one percent?"

"Every little bit helps," he admitted playfully.

"There oughta be a law."

"That's what accountants and tax attorneys are for."

"I'll keep that in mind."

"They're calling my flight," he said. "Take your phone to bed with you tonight. I should get to the house in time for your wake-up call."

"It won't be the same without you, Magic Man. Travel safe and remember who loves you."

"You've made it impossible to forget."

As he hung up, the house cell let me know lunch was ready.

After dinner Steph and I settled in the library to make our plans. It was where Richard and I had enjoyed our postprandial (Remember? I have words!) cuddles and a glass of wine as we compared our calendars. I realized how much I missed him just then.

"What's that look?" Step asked as she sank into the opposite end of the overstuffed couch.

"I think Richard's absence just poked me. We used to cuddle in here after dinner and go over our schedules."

"Well, schedules I can do. Michael gets all my cuddles."

I laughed. Good old Steph. After three years together as roomates while we finished school, I knew she'd get me through this.

First on my list: *Training*.

"So, I'm thinking I want the trainer to give me an idea of what I should be doing, with an eye to him coming…maybe once a week. Are you interested in that?"

"Sure. You and I both have a pretty full summer planned. I think some strength training will help. I really would like to have a schedule to stick to. I think it'll help me focus and not get distracted too much by my hunk."

"Don't rub it in," I whined.

"Turnabout's fair play."

"I know. And I know how hard it is not to flaunt happiness. So go for it. I'm hoping I can figure out how to keep my own torrid affaire going long distance."

"Dr. Hunter is a pretty creative guy," she reminded me. "He'll come up with something."

(Steph had given Richard the "Doctor" title when he'd helped her think her way through the decision to take a chance on her career as an artist.)

"I'm depending on it," I told her. We just have to work out the timing. The distance between us kind of goofs up the schedule." I glanced at the fancy chronograph Richard had gotten for me before he left so I would know what time it was for him. He was in the air somewhere over the Atlantic.

"So, are you still good with a morning swim?" I asked. I was determined to force myself into that water early in the morning. At least Richard had told me I could set the temperature for a slightly warmer experience. "I'd like to sort of follow Richard's schedule, only maybe cut the times a little. Maybe up at 6:00, gym 'til 6:30, swim and then breakfast and at my desk by 8:00."

"Yup. And don't forget to warm up the pool a little," Steph reminded me. "Despite my tough Frontier Gal upbringing, another ten degrees will make me very happy."

Next on my little list: *Yoga.*

"And what are you thinking about the yoga?" I asked. "Any interest? I'd prefer to do it in the early evening, before dinner. Maybe 5:00 or 6:00 p.m.? I feel more relaxed and bendy at the end of the day, rather than the beginning. What kind of studio hours are you thinking about keeping?"

"I'd like to be in the studio and ready to work by 8:00 or 8:30. I'm going to see if Marie will fix me a lunch to take with me. I don't want to waste time to try to figure out where to get food. Of course I'll paint until it's a good time to stop, so the end of my days may be a little irregular. And I'm planning on spending Wednesday nights at Michael's and then most weekends with him."

"I hope you'll bring him here some weekends," I told her. "You guys can play with the goodies and each other and keep me company at the same time."

"I know Michael would like that. We should try to have Mark and Sam come to dinner, invite some of our friends. Richard reminded me he wanted us to enjoy the house and to be honest, I think he wants me to keep you from missing him too much."

"I'm sure we can keep busy and become the superwomen our new careers demand. I intend to present my Magic Man with the new and improved version of me by the time he gets home. Meanwhile, I'll give his exercise gurus a call and see when they can come."

At 5:00 a.m. the next morning *He's a Magic Man* sang out from my phone, which was in bed with me near my pillow. I opened one eye only long enough to reach for it, then brought it to my ear.

"My Prince, do your tender feet once again tread *terra firma* among us mortals?

"Well, my ass graces the seat of an Italian taxi currently snarled in the chaos of Roman traffic."

"I'm sorry, Charming. I pictured you at home, relaxing with a nice glass of wine as you choose the words to help me greet the day. You're running a few hours late, aren't you?"

"We sat on the runway and ended up nearly two hours ` late leaving L.A. That screwed up our landing slot here and then there was some slow down through customs. All that put me in the middle of this rush hour mess." Richard sighed. "So, my sweet Sleeping Beauty, I'm afraid the words you long to hear cannot be uttered at the moment."

I sighed with hammy disappointment. "Then I shall wrap my damp thighs around the pillow that took your place in my arms last night. At least it's warm and smells like you."

Richard laughed. "What?"

"I perpetrated a clever ruse to procure some of your unlaundered Tshirts, one of which Marie thoughtfully stretched over the kingsize pillow I found waiting for me in bed last night. I closed my eyes and imagined your arms around me."

"I'd love to hear what else you imagined, but I'm afraid that will have to wait until I get to the house. So what's your schedule like today?"

"Gym, swim, shower, breakfast and at my desk by 8:00 a.m."

"Really?" He sounded surprised.

"Really. I'm on a schedule and I intend to stick to it. Can I pencil you in, Mr. Hunter?"

"How about a lunch date?" he suggested hopefully.

"Fine. I'll eat at my desk and we can go over some computer things. You'll need your laptop." I was sounding all business and efficiency. It threw him off, as I hoped it would.

"Uh, OK…Maybe all that technical instruction will make you tired and you'll want to relax, you know…maybe take a nap?"

"Maaybee…"

He laughed. He knew I'd been expecting a little bit of more personal communication when he called. Despite my pretense, he had no reason to doubt I was anxious to do a little sharing, albeit delayed.

"Until lunchtime, Sweetheart. I'll FaceTime you."

"I'll be waiting."

"Now get that beautiful ass of yours out of bed and onto the treadmill."

"You are a cruel man!" I complained.

"Sometimes we must be cruel to be kind," he said with conviction.

"Really? I may remind you of those words one of these days when you least expect it."

"That could be interesting." Then he threw my line back at me as he said goodbye. "Just remember who loves you."

2

When in Rome...

Monday, July 15

Note of the day:

> *Welcome to Rome. I will omit no*
> *opportunity that may convey my*
> *greetings, Love, to thee.   XXOOJ*

The extra ten degrees of pool temp made a difference, but the cold water was still a shock. Steph seemed to appreciate the change more than I did, but I forced myself into laps beside her and then we both hit our showers. Imagine my surprise when, rather than what I'd programed for my morning inspiration, my friend Zarathustra (the high tech shower) greeted me with Leonard Cohen singing *I'm Your Man*. I didn't realize Richard could do remote programming. That cheered me right up! I loved a hot wet message from my man in the morning and this was second best!

I showered quickly, braided my hair (not taking time to fool with drying it) and met Steph on the balcony for our breakfast by 7:15.

"So far, so good on our new routine." We toasted with our pink grapefruit juice.

"To continuing discipline," Steph added.

"I suppose one day does not a new life make, but it's a start. I really want to try to turn this into a habit. What are you doing today?"

"I'm going to start laying out my workspace. Mark says my

boxes will be here on Wednesday so I want to get organized, order canvasses and shop for additional supplies. Next Monday the paint will hit the canvas and we'll see what happens."

"I hope you'll give me a tour," I told her. "I have to meet with Ben and Jerry Thursday, so maybe we can get together and have lunch. The trainer will be here at 3:00 this afternoon and then we're supposed to go to the yoga studio at 5:00. Richard said we can have her come here if we want, but I thought if we went to the studio first, we could see which we prefer."

"Works for me. Living this high life ain't half bad, eh?"

I admitted I was finding it pretty easy to get used to. "I have to keep reminding myself what a privilege it is. I don't want to take any of this for granted. It's an amazing gift."

"Exactly," Steph said. "And when you talk to your hunk, thank him again for me."

"He called this morning for my wake up but was still in a taxi in Rome. I was hoping for a more personal connection, but we'll have to wait and see if he can make up for it at lunch."

Steph shook her head. "I'm anxious to hear how you two work out this long distance thing and at the same time dread it may involve TMI."

I laughed. "I can keep it on a need-to-know basis, though I suspect we'll both get a kick out of some of the things he comes up with. And I may have to enlist your help on this end. Have to keep him interested."

"Somehow, I can't see that being a problem, it's pretty obvious he loves you as much as you love him. But feel free to engage my choreographic talents and any others I have that might be helpful."

"Be careful what you offer." I glanced at the time. It was a quarter to eight. "Here we go," I said as we both stood up.

I followed Steph into the kitchen where Marie had left an insulated lunch bag waiting for my friend on the counter and a carafe of her coffee (already creamed and sugared!) for me. I walked with Steph to the front door, gave her a hug and then went on to the library.

I was actually feeling pretty energized after all the morning activity and that pleased me. I set the computer to let me know when it was 11:30 and flew through my email, tossing all the ads and setting aside the things that needed a response for later. I did decide to take a look at my bank statement, something I hadn't paid much attention to over the past three weeks since I'd moved into Richard's house. I wasn't spending any money. I'd paid my credit card bill and hadn't seen any statements from American Express, probably because I had yet to use the card Richard had given me through his gallery.

I clicked into my online banking and stared in disbelief at my accounts page. What do you do when the numbers don't make any sense? I looked at my name on the page, at the account numbers and balances (checking, savings and Visa). Yup, my accounts, but why was there such a high balance in my checking? It was eight *thousand* (!!) dollars more than it should have been!

I smiled as I clicked into the account details. It was very obviously some mistake, but it's funny how your mind immediately wonders if they'd catch the error. In an instant my brain began thinking of how I could spend it—you know, all the possibilities. Eight grand would pay off three-quarters of my student loan balance! Should I tell them or just wait and see if they noticed? Surely, after a certain amount of time they couldn't take it back? All these thoughts zoomed through my mind in the seconds it took for me to open the details of the account.

June 25, deposit—$6,000.00. July 5—$1,000.00. Last Friday, July 12—$1000.00. I clicked on the first one to see the deposit info and saw *LCLLC. Louis Chasseur, LLC.* It took a minute to register, then I realized that was the corporation under which the gallery operated! I needed to call Christina and get to the bottom of this. It would be another half hour before they'd be in the office, but I decided to try anyway. If no one was in yet, I could leave a message. Much to my surprise, Mark answered.

"Hey, CJ. Everything OK? Have you heard from the boss?"

"My lover was stuck in traffic when he called me at 5:00 this morning. They were delayed leaving LAX, which screwed up their landing and there was some slow up in the line at customs. He was not a happy camper."

"The jet lag can be a bitch and he really doesn't have much patience with delays. He keeps threatening to charter flights but never gets around to it."

"I don't suppose Christina's in yet?"

"Actually, she is. We're going to have a meeting as soon as Lynda gets here. Do you want to talk to her?"

"Please," I said and suddenly found myself wondering what I was going to say. It's not something I'd ever had to do—you know, complain about someone giving me money.

"Hey, CJ. What can I do for you?"

"Uh, I just looked at my bank account. I'm confused."

"Has there been a problem with the deposits?"

"Well, I don't know what to say. It's seems like there are way too many zeros involved."

Christina laughed out loud.

"I feel quite stupid for asking," I admitted, "but what is all this money for, exactly?"

"I know. It is a little overwhelming. The initial deposit, $6,000, is your signing bonus."

"Is there some sports commitment I'm not aware of?"

"Noooo...at least I hope not. I'm not much of an athlete, myself. You get a signing bonus because you are a hot new graduate with an impressive array of computer skills and we had to be sure no other company would snatch you out from under our noses."

"Yeah, right. Offers were flooding in. I'm sure that my personal association with your boss had nothing to do with it."

"Don't be offended. The boss convinced us we all deserved a signing bonus when he hired us. You can ask Mark. You know our Hunter is far too classy to offer that as payment for...uh..."

"Personal favors?" I offered. But I was laughing. I knew Richard would be hurt if he thought I felt that way.

"Exactly...as in exactly *NOT* that. The next two checks, each for a thousand, represent your weekly retainer so we can keep you on call in case we have any problems. You will see a deposit every Friday."

For a minute I didn't know what to say. "I guess we never discussed a salary, since I always assumed he was just making me an 'employee' so he could give me the insurance and the Amex. It's a little overwhelming."

"I know," she said sympathetically. "But you'll just have to learn to go along with the flow. It makes him happy and it makes us all happy, too, so we try to focus on gratitude."

"Life in Richard's alternate universe?"

"Exactly! Ain't it grand?"

"I guess I'm still adjusting. But thanks. I hope you don't think I'm an ingrate."

"We think you're the best thing that ever happened to the boss," she assured me. "We all love you, so relax and enjoy!"

Well, that was enlightening! Another shift in my universe. I could almost feel that energy moving around me, even though my sweetie was halfway around the world. It nearly brought me to tears.

Back to work.

I popped up Ben and Jerry's outline with the steps I needed to complete before our meeting on Thursday, and started writing.

I was completely engrossed and it surprised me when the computer informed me it was 11:30. I picked up the house cell to let Marie know I wanted to eat in the library but would come grab a tray in the kitchen in about fifteen minutes. Then I went upstairs to survey my meager wardrobe and see if I could find anything that might be suitably tantalizing for my Prince when he called.

I pulled out a little ring of stretch jersey that could either work as a skirt (very short, usually worn over tights) or as a bandeau top. I figured if I took off my panties and rolled it up a bit it would give him a view he had no doubt imagined sometime in the last twenty-four hours or so. I needed to find some innocent pretense to bend over and give him a clear look at the goods.

Now, what top? I had a very thin red Tshirt that said *INSPI(RED)* with a ripped out neck that was very low and could easily "slip" to one side and expose a breast. I pulled the skirt down below my belly button. The shirt was long enough to cover my belly so I hoped I wouldn't scandalize Marie, and off I went to get my lunch.

Marie was nowhere to be seen, but my tray was on the counter waiting for me. I picked it up and returned to the library. I rolled my skirt up as short as I could without exposing myself completely and sat down at the computer. Five minutes to twelve.

I took a bite of my salad and spread some brie on my piece

of baguette. (I swear I could live on Marie's baguettes with butter or cheese.) *Yummmm...*

Of course I had a mouthful when Richard's FaceTime came through. He caught me and I started laughing.

"Ah, the elegant woman I remember!" he said, smiling at my awkward self.

"Sooorry," I said between chews. "I started without you."

"What's so irresistible?"

I presented my bowl of greens and then my chunk of baguette with a spokesmodel flourish.

"I understand. I've been gorging on pasta, myself."

"So how are you feeling, my Prince?"

"Much better. Relieved to finally be able to relax and put my feet up. How's your day going?"

"Good, actually. I've already gotten a lot done."

"Wanna do me?" he asked.

"Absolutely! But first things first. Do you have your laptop?"

"I do."

"Get me your IP so I can connect."

"I've got your connection..." he mumbled grumpily as he fingered his keyboard.

"Discipline, my love."

With a sigh he read out the number sequence and within a few seconds I was on. I reduced the window showing me, freeing up his desktop.

"Hey! I want you big and in my face."

"What part of me, exactly?" I asked even as I began opening files for him.

"How quickly they forget," he said with a sigh.

"Focus, Mister. You'll be glad you did."

"Promises, promises."

"Now, pay attention. You see where we are here? I'm in your personal files and see this one labeled *MHP_In_Out*?"

"Yes." I heard the change in his voice. He was still smiling, but he was paying attention.

"This is a private file I set up for us. It can't be accessed through your network, so no one else can get in there and it won't show up on your history. It's also password protected. See?"

I clicked the file and it asked for a password.

"It's three capital letters followed by an exclamation point. Care to guess?"

I could see he was enjoying the idea that we would have a spot on there to exchange anything we liked privately.

"*GTF!*?"

I laughed. He'd quickly guessed the reference to the shorthand we'd shared since the night we met: *Good and Thoroughly Fucked.*

"*Biensur, mon amour!* Go ahead, enter the password."

He typed it in and the file opened with a screen saver image of me in that necklace—the photo from the gala that Giano had given us a copy of.

"My beautiful girl," he said softly. "Have I mentioned recently how much I love you?"

"It has been far too long, but just another few minutes and you can explain that in detail. Now see these two folders? *2J* and *4R*. To me, Juliet, and For you, Richard. Self explanatory, no?"

"*Ouais.*"

"Now just one more thing. Open your iTunes." He did. "You can check in "Recently Added" to find things I want to share." Then he asked how to do the same thing coming my direction.

"Done?" he asked when we'd finished a few more housekeeping details.

"Done. You can supersize me now."

"That, my love, is the least of what I want to do to you."

"Care to elaborate?" I asked innocently.

"Oh, yes. But what's that shirt you're wearing?"

"This?" I pulled the neck of my shirt down as if to read it and one of my breasts popped out. "It says 'inspired.' One of the Project Red pieces raising money for AIDS in Africa."

"I see," he said slowly.

"What do you see?" I asked as I sort of gave my breast a squeeze and tucked it back into my shirt.

"I see something I'm very fond of."

"Oh?" I said, as if I were curious. "Fond in what way?"

"In a way that makes me long to caress it, to rub it gently. I want to lick that little hard spot in the center. I need a taste of that just now."

"You have a very talented tongue but I fear the distance is too great." I shook my pen in his direction and pretended it flipped out of my hand to land on the floor beside my chair. "Oops!"

I turned and got up on my knees in the chair and bent down over the arm to get the pen. I swiveled the chair to be sure he got a straight-on view of something now quite wet. I heard a groan behind me and looked around with a completely innocent expression.

"What?"

"Now you've done it," he said.

"Done what?" I asked as I sat down in the chair again and reached for a banana from my tray. It was out of camera range as I held it in my lap.

Richard stood up, and pulled his sweats down, exposing that beautiful penis, as anxious for me as I was for him.

"Oh, dear," I said. "What are you going to do with that?"

"What would you like me to do?"

"Hmmm...let me think," I said as I slowly brought up the banana and began to peel it.

"You are a very naughty girl."

"*Moi*? I'm just eating the food I was served." I ran my tongue very slowly up the banana. Richard groaned. I was having trouble keeping my face straight as he sat down again. It was obvious there was some hand action going on. I continued to lick the banana and slide it in and out of my mouth very slowly. A little twirl of the tongue on the end, occasionally.

"What are you thinking about?" I whispered.

"You and that hot wet mouth of yours."

I heard his breathing shift and I worked my banana faster and deeper. I could tell he was ready to come and I gave my sexy fruit a good long suck, imagining he was in my mouth. (Not easy, mind you—it was a small banana!)

"Save a drop for me," I whispered.

He stood up again and offered his penis to the screen at close range. A gob of semen remained. I ran my tongue slowly over my camera and heard him groan again. I wiped the lens off with a tissue.

"And here I thought you wanted to lie down beside me for a nap," I said with disappointment as I presented a pouty lip.

"I absolutely do. Get thee to thy bed, sweet Juliet. Take the iPad and I'll FaceTime you back in five."

I picked up the house cell and texted Marie that I was going to take a short nap. Then I grabbed the iPad and headed for our room.

Marie had made the bed, of course, and I hurried to turn the covers back down. I piled up the pillows and tossed my king-size surrogate Richard pillow with his Tshirt into the center. Then I pulled Bob (my Battery Opperated Boyfriend) from the drawer in my nightstand and slipped him under one of the pillows. I kept my skirt and shirt on, waiting to see if my hunk wanted me to shed them slowly or just bare it all immediately.

The iPad zinged and I punched him up.

"I missed you, Handsome. It's been minutes, *and in a minute there are many days*," I reminded him, quoting my namesake.

"So there are. But you threw me off with that tempting display of your dripping thighs!"

"You mean this?" I asked as I lowered the tablet and lifted the edge of my skirt just enough. "Or is it the rear view you prefer?" I held it behind me as I bent over.

"Sweet girl, the sight of any part of you, from head to toe is what I prefer. Any and all of you."

"And how would like me right now, my love?"

"Take off what little you're wearing."

I went over and propped up the tablet on the tansu chest.

"Can you see?"

"Step back just a little." I did until he said, "Can you close the west drapes? Too much backlight."

"Picky, picky, " I mumbled as I walked to the wall west wall of windows and pressed the button to close the drapes. There was still plenty of light from the south end of the room.

"I just want to be able to see you. You are so beautiful."

"Here?" I asked as I returned to the spot where I'd been.

"Perfect."

I proceeded to do a very slow striptease for him. I threw my head back and pressed my breasts together and rubbed them as my nipples responded. I pulled the shirt tight against myself, released it, then slipped the neck down exposing first one breast, then the other. I turned my back to him and with swaying hips slowly pulled the shirt up and off over my head. Shades of my *Full Monty* performance.

"Remind you of anything?" I asked as I turned around, my hands crossed over my breasts.

"One of the most amazing nights of my life."

"Me, too." I slipped my hands down under my breasts and lifted them toward him. I bent my head to give one nipple a slow lick, my eyes on his, and then moved to the other. I gave them a gentle squeeze and released them.

I pushed the band of fabric that passed for a skirt down to my bikini line and offered some belly rolls as I slowly turned. When my back was to him I gave my ass a shimmy shake until the skirt slipped to the floor, just as it had that night.

"My thighs are dripping, Magic Man."

"Get in bed and give me a taste."

I held the iPad in front of me while squeezing my breasts together as I went to the bed. I crawled in and settled into the pillows.

"Show me how wet you are," he said and I spread my legs and offered him a clear picture. "Where shall I touch you?" he whispered.

"Here, " I said softly as I spread myself and pointed.

I couldn't manage to hold the iPad and deal with an orgasm at the same time.

"I want to look into your eyes as I come, my Prince." I propped him on the pillows and pulled my surrogate pillow to me as I reached for Bob.

"Let me in," he whispered.

I know he heard that telltale sigh as I slipped Bob into myself. Paltry as Bob was, he would have to do, so I cranked up my imagination and let Richard's words carry me into believing he was there with me.

"You feel so good, Sweetheart. I'm far from home and yet I'm back where I belong. Is this what you want?"

"Yes." I stroked myself slowly.

"Can you come for me?"

"Yes," I said breathlessly and I felt my orgasm begin to build. More?" he asked.

"Faster," I said. "Yes, exactly."

I let the wave crest and as I was slipping down the other side as he whispered, "Again?"

And, as I always did, I answered, "Yes, please."

I watched him on the screen. The love radiated from his eyes. Even at the incredible distance I could feel the energy.

"Come with me?" I urged and heard his breathing shift again.

We finished together and I pulled my big pillow closer inhaling the scent of him.

"Ah, Charming, you never fail to please."

"I promise to do everything I can to make sure you always feel that way."

I smiled, awash in the afterglow and imagining him there beside me.

"And thanks for the note," he said. "It was a wonderful surprise."

"It's the least I could do."

"It means a lot that you took the time. Anything handwritten is rare these days and your words are always special. I'm also enjoying that whiff of your perfume. May take it to bed with me tonight."

"Awwww…You know I'm a sucker for that sweet talk."

"And you know how I feel about the way you suck," he whispered.

"All the better to please you, my love. So are you ready for bed?"

"I am. Need to do a little reading for tomorrow's meeting first."

"Can you exercise there in the morning?"

"Yup. We've got some equipment—treadmill and weights—and a lap pool so I'm sticking to my schedule."

I thanked him for the shower music that morning. "Had no idea you could do that from there."

"Just want to remind you who's thinking of you."

"It would me hard for me to forget."

"Good. Part of my master plan. Now you, Miss Mogul, had best get back to your desk."

"Slave driver!"

"Just trying to be sure you don't stray too far from the path of success."

"*Now* you say that…after tempting me down a nearby rosy trail!"

"Oh…well…"

"One last look at what you've left behind," I said as I picked up the iPad, and stretched provocatively while slowly running it down the full length of my body."

"Temptress," he scolded. "And the girl of my wildest dreams."

3
Gee…Maybe…

Still Monday

I mopped up a little, slipped into a Tshirt and my yoga pants and went back to my desk. Unfortunately I was not thinking about business, I was thinking about ordering a bigger vibrator. After Richard, Bob just wasn't up to the job anymore. If I was going to be required to overwork my imagination in the absence of my lover's physical self, I wanted all the help I could get.

Just to prove I could exercise some discipline if I had to, I went back to work on the project instead of scouring sex toy websites.

At about five minutes to three the house cell buzzed to tell me our trainer had arrived and would be coming through the service entrance on the lower level. As I started down the stairs to go let him in, I heard Steph come in the front door upstairs.

"Perfect timing," I shouted up at her. "He's just coming to the door down here."

By the time I reached the entrance between the window wall and the kitchen area, Steph was with me. A few moments later we greeted the most amazing black man I'd ever seen! Gobsmacked again.

I couldn't stop staring but tried to recover by saying, "Hello!" and extending my hand. "I'm CJ, and this is Stephanie."

I could see Steph was having the same reaction.

"I am Ji," he said.

(He pronounced it "Gee" and I thought, *exactly!*)

"That is spelled J-i. I am most pleased to meet you ladies."

He had a deep voice and lilting accent that I assumed must be African. He was about six-four and totally ripped, of course. His skin was very dark and he was flat out beautiful. He reminded me of Peter Mensah in *Spartacus*. His muscles had the most exquisite contours, enhanced by his coloring. I badly wanted to run my hands over his arms but managed to restrain myself.

"We're so happy to meet you," I said. "I hope you don't find working with us too much of a challenge. We're just starting to try to lay out a routine we can stick to."

"I can see that both of you are in very fine shape. Shall we go into the gym and discuss what sort of program you would like me to prepare for you?" He gestured for us to lead the way.

We talked for a while, telling him our vague ideas about what sort of things we thought we wanted to do. We were obviously clueless and hoped he could come up with a plan for us.

He tested us on the weights to see what range we were in (don't ask!) and questioned us about the treadmill and how much swimming we were doing. He asked if there was any exercise we enjoyed and Steph and I just looked at each other and made a face.

"I think dancing, swimming and yoga are the only things we can actually say we've *enjoyed* so far." I was embarrassed but thought it best to let him know what a slug I was from the get-go. Steph was more active, but not all that much. I did tell him we planned to start a new yoga program.

"This is very good. Yoga will keep you flexible and this is very important. It is good for your body and for your mind, also."

I had to ask if there was any chance I could work up to the salmon ladder. I explained I didn't have any delusions of grandeur but was just wondering if it was possible I could manage one step on it by the time Richard came home. I confessed I didn't even know if it was an exercise that a woman could do, meaning a non-*American Ninja* woman.

Instead of laughing at me, Ji took me over to it and placed the bar on the lowest rung where I could just barely reach up and grab it.

"Take hold of the bar and show me how far you can pull yourself up."

I struggled but managed a chin-up.

"Let me show you," he said, taking hold of the bar and swinging forward, then back as he used the momentum to lift himself above the bar, so it hit him just below his waist. He held himself there and crossed his ankles. It seemed more like a gymnastic move when done that way. Richard went more straight up.

"Now, you try."

The third time I almost managed to get up there and stick.

"Very good. This, I think you will be able to do. You must build up your muscles a little but if you persevere, you can surprise Hunter when he returns.

"Now watch me and see how the pull up moves me to the position where I can raise the bar up a step. You will begin this way, though it is more vertical to do the ladder. If you can truly see the movement in your mind, you are halfway there. You must exercise your mind along with your body in order to achieve true results."

He worked his way up the rack slowly, explaining as he went, letting me see. Steph had never seen a salmon ladder (the kind without the fish!) and watched with her mouth hanging open as Ji went up slowly for the first six rungs and then finished quickly and came back down. It was a joy to watch. I was thinking of putting in for a slot as a man in my next life. It must be wonderful to have that kind of strength.

We decided Ji could come at 6:30 a.m., starting the next day, for the rest of the week. We would be easy on ourselves in the beginning and just go for thirty minutes. Then he would prepare a video workout for us and come only once a week to check our progress and update the videos. I was surprised he was available, but he told us many of his regular clients, like Richard, were out of town. He assured us he was happy to be working with us.

After we bid Ji goodbye at the door, we turned to each other exchanging an expression of amazement.

"OMG!" Steph said. "Is there anyone in your hunk's world who isn't gorgeous?"

"Richard insists it's just their inner beauty that shows on the outside, too. Whatever it is, eye candy is eye candy. And what a nice man. Exercise is beginning to seem more appealing."

Steph gave me a high five. "If we get lazy we can just watch his videos and drool."

C.J. BAILEY

At a few minutes before five we found ourselves a parking space across the street from Maybe Yoga. There was a young man behind the desk who greeted us with a broad smile.

I introduced myself. "We've got a five o'clock with Ms. Arnott."

"She'll be with you shortly," he said. "The 3:30 session is just about to end."

We took a seat and a few minutes later a small woman with dark hair pulled back into a single braid and wearing a tank top and shorts joined us. She looked to be in her forties and just glowed with an energy that was peaceful and at the same time radiated good health.

"You must be Hunter's friends," she said with a bright smile. "I'm Maybe."

I know I gave her a funny look and she laughed.

"Yup. Maybe. My parents named me Mable, if you can imagine. They never could explain what they were thinking. Fortunately, I was always called Mabie with an 'i-e' as a child and by the time I was in my rebellious teen phase I changed it to M-a-y-b-e. Then I ended up marrying Jackson Arnott. Hard to believe I'm Maybe Arnott, but I am."

We all laughed.

"I'm CJ Bailey and this is Stephanie Sheperd."

"Nice to meet you. How's Hunter?" she asked.

"Off for the summer in Europe."

We discussed options and decided we would go for the package that allowed us to drop into any of the classes up to five times a week. Once we could tell how we were dealing with our new routines, we'd think about private sessions. Then we joined the group that was about to start.

"What do you want to do about dinner?" I asked Steph after the yoga class. Marie knew we'd feed ourselves that night.

"Wanna go for Chinese? Do you remember the name of the place where Richard ordered for us that night? I really loved that honey walnut shrimp."

"I do, it's only a couple of minutes from here. Shall we eat there or get an order to go?"

"Let's take it home. Will Marie mind if we use the fridge in the service kitchen, you know, to keep a few things around for nibbling? I'm having a hard time adjusting to all my meals being served to me, fantastic as they are. I need a spot for occasional grazing and I hate to bother her."

"We can ask her at breakfast. I can't imagine she'd care. What did she give you for lunch?"

"It was amazing, as you might expect. A ham and brie sandwich on a chunk of baguette with sunflower nuts and sprouts and some amazing mustard. There was yogurt and sweet potato chips and a perfect peach. Fortunately, there's a fridge at the studio—a whole little kitchen in fact—so the peach and yogurt will be waiting for me tomorrow. We may start being hungrier when we get on our schedules, but until I know, I'll have to tell her to cut back. In fact I'd be content with our Chinese leftovers for tomorrow."

I laughed. I knew what she meant. We were so used to eating, catch-as-catch-can that having beautifully prepared and delicious meals served to us three times a day was kind of hard to get used to. I didn't want to hurt Marie's feelings, but I thought I could let her know we needed some time to adjust to our fancy new lifestyle.

I decided to give Magic Man a wake-up call and went outside to do it while Steph waited for our food.

"Are you up yet, my love?" I asked when he answered.

"Actually, I am. Just thinking of how I'd wake you this morning if you were here."

"I'd be sleepy and wet, ready for you as I always am. Wanna slip in for a quick one?"

"Where do you want me?" he whispered.

"I feel you hard against my bottom. Just slide in gently as you always do." I offered the sigh of satisfaction he was familiar with and could hear his appreciation in the soft groan that followed."

"My Sleeping Beauty, I'm in a state of wonder and gratitude every time I find myself here."

"Will you come for me this morning, my Prince?" It was the question he usually asked me.

"How could I not?" he whispered.

"Oh…" I said softly. Not much chance for a *When Harry Met Sally* moment with the people on the street nearby. Still, I hoped that and some heavy breathing were enough to help him along. And then I heard him come. "You beautiful man," I sighed.

"I love you," he whispered. After another minute, during which I could hear his breathing slow, he asked where I was.

"I'm standing in front of Kung Pao. Steph and I just came from yoga and we're waiting for a to-go order.

"You, sweet girl, should reconsider your line of work. You may be meant for the stage, after all." He laughed.

"And you may just be particularly susceptible to my sighs."

"No argument there. How was your day?"

"You could have warned us about Ji. What an unbelievably beautiful body!"

"Uh…should I be worried?"

"Well, I'm happy to say I managed to restrain myself and not touch him, but it was a struggle. I so wanted to run my fingers over the contours of his arm. Where do you find these people?"

"I can't fault you for appreciating him. He is flat-out sculptural. I think you'll enjoy getting to know him. He's a truly nice man. Be sure to ask him about his name. And tell him you want to touch him. He'll be flattered."

"Sure of yourself, aren't you?"

"I'm pretty sure you love me as much as I love you."

"Pretty sure?"

"Ask me again after you touch Ji."

Steph came out the door with a shopping bag full of takeout.

"Our food's here…" I told him.

"Wait," Steph said, grabbing the phone out of my hand. "Dr. Hunter?" she said as she put him on speaker.

"Hey, Steph."

"Just wanted to thank you again for giving me a life I was having trouble imagining."

"You're welcome. Imagine hard and then live it."

"Will do. Here's Miss Hot Pants. Don't let her cool off."

"I'm doing my best to keep her warmed up for you. I admit it doesn't require much effort on my part."

She handed the phone back.

"Have a wonderful day, my Prince, and remember what's waiting for you at home."

I was drying my hair that night and feeling quite happy as I reviewed the previous twenty-four hours. Steph and I had one day of our new life under our belts and we were both in a positive frame of mind about being able to stick to it. Funny, I know, but I was full of yummy Chinese food and rosy thoughts of the future.

We were excited about working with Ji (and he was the *only* reason we were excited about training!) And I was encouraged that Ji thought I could manage a rung or two of the salmon ladder by the time Richard came home. We'd really enjoyed Maybe's class. I'd actually managed to join Steph in the pool that morning and was convinced I could force myself to it until it became a habit.

I was busy enough not to be longing for Richard (unless I thought about him too much) and I'd had enough contact with him to ease the distance between us. It was a different dynamic with him so far away. I was focusing on my project and with my mind occupied, I had less time to allow my body to express its deep longing for him. It felt like my sweet Prince was being pushed onto the back burner, though I would never let him know it.

I got into bed and pulled my pillow-surrogate into my arms and was surprised at the small aftershock that came with the scent of him. I smiled and cuddled it as I whispered, "Sweet dreams, my love."

I was hovering at the edge of sleep when my phone sang out with *Magic Man*.

"I was almost asleep in your arms," I said softly.

"Would that you were, Sweetheart. I just called to say goodnight, I wish I could rock you to sleep, but I'm just ready to leave the house and head for the countryside and one of our vineyards."

"Have a wonderful drive. You'll have to take me along next year for a tasting."

"You know I love the taste of you and I have no intention of waiting until next year!" he scolded.

"As if I'd expect you to. But you know what I mean. I'm looking forward to traveling with you."

"I'm counting on that. Until then, your wake up dose of love will come during siesta, so I should be able to help you greet your day properly. Until then, sweet dreams."

"Always dreams of you, my love," I whispered as he hung up.

Tuesday, July 16

Note of the day:

> *As soon as I saw you, I knew a*
> *great adventure was about to begin.*
> — A.A. Milne, *Winnie the Pooh*

I was sound asleep when his call came but found myself smiling as I felt around for my phone.

"Open those beautiful eyes, sweet girl, I have something for you."

He was on FaceTime so I punched my camera on and smiled for him. I knew he loved me with my hair a mess, looking like I'd just been Good and Thoroughly Fucked (even if I hadn't!)

"How can you look so beautiful when you wake up?" he asked.

"I don't. You're usually half asleep and doing more poking than looking."

"I'm not half asleep now. Feel like a little 'poking'?"

"Yes, please. What do you have for me this morning?"

He moved the phone down to display his erection. He was dressed, apparently sitting in a chair with his feet up on an ottoman. His pants were open and his penis and balls exposed. He was stroking himself but let go in order to demonstrate his penis was perfectly capable of standing on its own. It nodded with his pulse and waved a bit as if searching for me.

"Hmmmm….that looks delicious. I want a taste." I put the camera closer and wiggled my tongue at him.

"Sorry, Sweetheart, you'll have to satisfy yourself a little farther south."

I rolled the covers off slowly and took the phone down, first to one breast, nipple to camera, then back farther and on to the other for a second close up.

"Here?" I asked innocently.

"Sadly, no. Down there between your legs."

I slid the phone down, lingering at my belly button but then moved down my landing strip…very slowly. He groaned but I held my legs together and stopped at my knees.

"Here?"

"Nooooo…I think if you just open your legs and then move up to that nice warm wet place…"

I spread my legs and cocked my knees to give him a clear view.

"You must mean here."

"That's it. As our friend Leonard says, 'The cave at the tip of the lily…'"

"Now what?"

"I need to watch myself slide in there. Can you manage that?"

"Hmmmm…hang on…" I propped the phone on a pillow and got up on my knees to rearrange things, making sure he had a tantalizing view from the rear. Didn't want him to forget what he was after.

I climbed into the pillows with my hips elevated, thinking I could slip Bob in there and keep the cell above it all, at an angle so he could see the in and out but not my hand holding the vibrator.

"How's that?" I asked as I started to tease my clit with Bob.

"Perfect. But are you comfortable?"

"Comfort is not at the top my list at the moment. Fuck me, Richard." I slid Bob in fast and couldn't repress a little squeal. Richard groaned (rather more loudly than he would have done if he'd been there with me, I might add!)

I stroked myself slowly. "You feel so good," I whispered breathlessly. I speeded up my movement and heard the change in Richard's breathing. "Come with me…please!"

"Now?" he asked.

"Now," I said as my orgasm exploded. I continued to stroke

myself gently, twitching with the slowly fading sensations. I pulled Bob out to rub my clit, then back in. In and out. Finally, I let go of Bob, though he remained inside me, and brought the phone back up to my face.

Richard was smiling.

"Show me," I whispered.

He turned the phone toward his lap, where he was gently stroking his penis. He'd spread a towel over his legs.

"Now who's the tidy one?" I asked.

"I'm still at the vineyard. We have another meeting this afternoon and then I'll be here for dinner. Not the time for a Lewinsky."

"You, my Trained Professional."

"So what are your plans for today?"

"We're swimming first and then Ji comes at 6:30 for a half hour. Shower, breakfast and off to our respective work stations."

"Discipline?" he asked.

"You bettcha. A new woman is in your future."

"Just remember how fond I am of the old one."

"You make it hard to forget."

"Good. Now get yourself out of that bed and into that refreshing water."

"Refreshing, my ass!"

4
Leisure Suit

Thursday, July 18

Note of the day:

The Crossing

I dwell upon your love
through the night and all the day,
through the hours I lie asleep
and when I wake again at dawn.

Your beauty nourishes hearts.
Your vice creates desire.
It makes my body strong.
"He is weary," so may I say
for there is no other girl
in harmony with his heart.
I am the only one.
                    —anon. Egyptian

Around 8:30 on Thursday morning, Richard rang in via FaceTime. I was at the computer, going through my emails, so it was a welcome interruption.

"*Buona sera, Bello! Come sta?*" I greeted him.

"Your Egyptian poem came today. Where do you find these things?"

"Vee haf our Vays…" I assured him in a cheesy German accent.

"Seriously, these notes from you are something I look forward to. I don't know how you've managed to coordinate them, but I love receiving them. Thank you, Sweetheart."

"I just want to remind you that you're always in my thoughts—you know, in case some beautiful *signorina* wobbles into your arms."

"Hmmm…must be working. I haven't caught a single woman since I arrived. Maybe I should worry. Do you think my charms are fading?"

"Look deep into my eyes," I instructed, that time with a sort of Carpathian tone as I turned the phone sideways and brought it close.

He did the same and zapped me long distance. *Aftershock!* I know he noticed when the phone jumped in my hand. *Those amazing grey eyes…*

"Nope, you're mojo's still working."

"Good to know," he said with a self-satisfied smile. "What's your day looking like?"

"I'm meeting Ben and Jerry at 10:00. And by the way, the *Coffee Coffee Buzz, Buzz, Buzz* ice cream is delicious. Then Steph is going to show me the studio and we're going to lunch. A few errands in the afternoon then home."

For a moment he just looked at me.

"What?"

"I love you."

I cracked up. "I depend on that, you know. But you're distracting me from my work and I need to finish these things for the Ice Cream Boys. I promise to give you the attention you deserve next time we talk."

"I'll dream of it."

"Dream big!"

My meeting went well. Ben and Jerry were pleased with my progress and we discussed the projected revenue streams from the portal I'd designed when it was up and running. They were stunned when they realized how broad the scope of that income would be.

Part of what I'd done for them that week was to chart that, so they could understand what was different about my idea and how vast the possibilities were. I'd also made them a little PowerPoint presentation to go with the text.

I got to Steph's studio at just after noon. It was about four blocks from the gallery and a block off the main drag, on the ground floor of the commercial building where Richard's storage facility was. It reminded me I still had some things in boxes there.

"Wow!" was all I could say as I followed her into the center of the space. "I see why you're so excited. This is flat out amazing!"

It was huge! And the entire north side was a bank of windows looking out on a courtyard that was about thirty feet wide and took up the space between that building and the bigger warehouse next door where Chasseur's wine was stored.

"I told you you'd have to see it to believe it."

It was one main room, open up to the beams that must have been thirty feet above our heads. There were more windows high along the upper north wall, above a sliding door at least twenty feet tall.

"Does that go to the alley?"

"It does," she said. "I could do some gigantic pieces in here, though the biggest canvasses I ordered are only eight foot. I did order three four-by-eight-foot sections for a triptych, though."

We turned back toward the front entrance hallway and faced a kitchen wall with a sink, dishwasher, stove and fridge. There was plenty of counter space with cabinets above and below. Behind the kitchen area Steph opened the door to a good size room with utility sinks for clean up and shelves for storage. The next door closer to the entrance disclosed a large bathroom. I checked out the big walk-in shower and noted the jets and control panel. One of Zarathustra's little cousins, no doubt. The door closest to the front door revealed a bedroom!

"So is this for a little afternoon delight or in case you need a nap after working too hard?" I asked eyeing the king-size bed.

"Nothing in my contract designated specific use of any part of the facility beyond the dangerous materials clause, so I guess it's artist's choice." She laughed. "I haven't mentioned that room to Michael yet and don't intend to. I have to stay focused!"

I gave her a hug. "I can only imagine how exciting this is for you. Are you feeling intimidated?"

"Not even a little bit. Like Richard said, I'm dreaming big and really looking forward to the freedom to do anything I can conceive. I thank goddess daily that you and your hunk dragged me into this."

"Kicking and screaming," I reminded her.

"Yup. But I'll never be able to thank you enough for not giving up on me and letting me go."

"I could hardly go on without my personal choreographer!"

"Well, you're choreographer is hungry, so let's get a move on."

We had lunch at Flauta near the gallery, where we'd gone to dinner that first night with Mark and Richard. Afterward, I dropped the week's messages for my Prince at the gallery and then made a stop to see Giano—world famous jeweler and second father to Richard—who greeted me with open arms when I arrived.

"Cressibella!" He gave me a hug and kisses on both cheeks. "You are lonely for the boy and have at last turned to me?"

"Not lonely yet. Even from a distance he remains a tender and thoughtful lover." *Damn!* I could feel myself blushing.

"That is good. Riccardo loves you. But come," he said as he ushered me down the hall. "Tell me what it is I can do for you."

His office was as low key and beautiful as the rest of his store, the same taupey-grey walls, surrounded on all sides by a row of photographs of stunning jewelry pieces, the pictures as perfectly lit as the actual pieces in the cubbies that ringed the room where we'd selected my earrings and watch on that first visit with Richard. I couldn't take my eyes off the photos and stepped up to them to take a closer look. The work was amazing. Gobsmacked, me.

"You like these?" he asked. "They are my own designs, each one special for the memories that came with the making of them."

"So exquisite. It must give you great pleasure to create such beautiful things."

"Exactly!" he said with a smile. "Not everyone understands this. They think it is about the money that comes when someone buys them, but is it about the joy of bringing the elements together into something new and beautiful."

"I want to have you make a ring for Richard," I said as I took one of the chairs in front of the desk.

"Of course. This I can do."

"But I want to pay for it out of my own money and I need to know that I can afford it before we begin."

Giano smiled. He was probably thinking there was no way I could afford his work, but I forged ahead.

"I would like it to be similar to mine, without the diamonds."

Richard had given me an exquisite ring with *VOUS ET NUL AUTRE* engraved around a band edged with diamonds. At the time—a few short weeks after we'd met—I mistook it for a proposal and was horrified. He assured me it wasn't an engagemnt ring but that if I ever decided I wanted him for a husband, all I had to do was ask. He'd told me about his history with a disasterous proposal and if I hadn't been so shocked by the sight of a ring box, I probably would have had a better reaction. Anyway, back to Giano…

"I want the poesy ring words in the center," I told him, "with a band on the bottom and a crown on top." I pulled a sketch from my purse. I'm no artist, but he could see what I had in mind. I passed it across the desk. "It would be gold. Do you know his ring size?"

"I do. And this I can do for you. When would you like to have it?"

"You're getting ahead of yourself, my friend. While the boy may not need to consider the price of your beautiful things, I do."

"You will pay only for the gold. This will be…maybe $1,500."

"Are you telling me the truth?" I knew the price of gold was sky high and I was envisioning a pretty heavy chunk of it.

Giano laughed. "How could I lie to a beautiful woman?"

"For you, I suspect it's a habit you're unable to break."

"Bella! I am hurt," he said with mock dismay. "But truly, this is the price I will pay for the gold in the ring. When it is finished, I will weigh it and tell you exactly, if you wish."

I couldn't suppress a smile. I could manage the $1,500. Considering what I was saving on rent alone for the summer, it was the least I could do for Richard. I would take it out of my own savings, pre-"employment" at the gallery. Still, I suspected there was some sort of family discount going on.

"When do you think I can have it?"

"I will give you a sketch next week. This is soon enough?"

"Perfect. I'm not in a hurry." I hadn't decided when I wanted to give it to him, but I wanted to have it in case the moment arrived. (Gees, I sound like a nervous suitor, don't I?) I wasn't thinking of proposing, just sharing the message of the ring he'd given me.

I stood up and reached out to seal the deal with a handshake. Giano laughed as he took my hand.

"It is easy to see why the boy loves you. It is also one of many reasons why I love you," he said as he took my hand in both of his, then lifted it to his lips and kissed it.

I assured him I was a very lucky woman to be loved by two such amazing men!"

I went to yoga before I went home and called to let Steph know I'd gone to the earlier class. I swam when I got to the house and enjoyed a snooze in the afternoon sun. I was feeling both pleased with myself for all I'd accomplished and mellow from the yoga and meditation by the time Steph and I sat down to dinner.

Marie had made us a lovely salad with avocado, interesting greens and strips of very pink (Yes!) filet mignon and sprinkled with walnuts and pomegranate seeds. Beautiful and delicious and accompanied by a warm baguette and some Roquefort-y cheese. The wine was a rosé—*Chasseur* label, of course. Steph and I were both in heaven.

"I have to say the only thing that could make me happier than I am at this moment is if you-know-who were here," I told her.

"Funny, I feel exactly the same. Totally content and excited about what tomorrow's going to bring."

"Are you ready to start painting?"

"Almost. I'm sketching and deciding what I want to start with. I'm even thinking about preparing three canvasses, in different sizes, so I can move between them if I feel like it. With luck, that will keep me from getting stuck if something doesn't work. It's a luxury

I've never before had the space for, so I'm anxious to see if it works for me. How did your meeting go today?" she asked.

"I think the boys were gobsmacked when they realized that I wasn't exaggerating the revenue my project could produce. Me telling them that in the beginning was one thing, but now that they can see it in black and white on the page and in color via my PowerPoint, I think it hit home that there is a great deal of money to be made. I felt their enthusiasm tick up another notch or two."

Steph laughed. "They still have no idea who they're dealing with, do they?"

"Sometimes it's good to be underestimated. So what are your plans for the weekend?"

"Michael's coming here for dinner and to spend the night tomorrow and then Saturday we're going to MOCA and I'll spend Saturday night at his place. Home in time for dinner Sunday."

"Feel like a movie tonight?"

"Sure. And maybe a dip in the spa after?"

"This is the life, eh?" I said, laughing as we left the table.

I was drying my hair around 11:00 p.m. when my lover called. I answered but didn't turn on my camera, just set the phone on the counter and put him on speaker.

"What are you wearing?" he whispered suggestively.

I laughed. "Oddly enough, a suit."

"Really? At this hour?"

I knew that would throw him off. "Yup."

"Funny, I don't remember seeing a suit of yours in the closet. Is it new?"

"No, I've had it quite awhile. You've seen it. Kinda of light pinky beige, double breasted…"

"Show me," he said. I could hear the suspicion in his voice.

I held the phone close to my face as I turned on the camera. "I'm hurt. You don't believe me?"

"Show me," he repeated stubbornly.

"Alright, let me go where I can show you in the mirror.

Men…" I grumbled as I went to the closet, keeping the camera on my face. "Care to wager, Mister-World-Traveler?"

"Hmmmm….if you're wearing a pinky beige double breasted suit I will send you something from Italy."

"Something *small*," I insisted.

"Something small," he agreed.

I turned the phone so it caught my naked reflection in the mirrored wall.

"Tah dah! I win!"

Richard completely cracked up. "Is this the Emperor's newest fashion statement?"

"No. It's my Birthday Suit! I told you it was double breasted." I put my hand and forearm under my breasts to emphasize them, lifting them slightly. "See?"

"Forgive me for repeating myself, but you really *are* something Miss Hot Pants!"

"So, what are you wearing?"

"Not a thing."

"What?" I'd expected he would be getting ready for his day and might be leaving the house soon.

"Just got out of the shower. And now I can't get dressed."

"Why?" I asked without thinking. He sucked me in on that one. *More the fool, me.*

"I don't know what to do with this." He kindly pointed the camera at the obvious.

"I know what to do with it."

"You do?"

"Yes. But why don't you tell me what you'd *like* to do with it," I suggested as I went toward the bed. I grabbed Bob from the nightstand, thinking (again!) that I really needed to get a bigger vibrator. I wasn't convinced puny Bob would give him the visuals he was hoping for and Bob's "modest" size no longer cut it on my end. (Spoiled, I was.)

"Well, it feels like I want to push against something, or rub it somehow."

I watched as he slowly stroked himself.

"Hey…my eyes are up here," I reminded him. "You seem to be rubbing that just fine."

"Well, it must require something else because it isn't getting any smaller. Just harder. Look."

Richard's cock was standing at full attention. He bent it down but it sprang back up when he let go.

"Let's think this through," I suggested reasonably as I laid the phone on the bed and sort of moved around over it to arrange the pillows. I propped myself against them, knees cocked and spread. "See anything here that you'd like to push against?"

"Maaybee…"

"There's this spot here," I said as I used Bob like a pointer, running him down my folds and holding my vagina open a little with the tip of him. "It's all wet and slippery. I don't know if you'd like that part of it." I pushed Bob in a couple of inches and then pulled him out all shiny. "See what I mean?" I brought the phone back up to my face. And our eyes met.

"I would love that part, just like I love the rest of you. I can almost feel you around me, hot and wet." Richard looked into my eyes and zapped me long distance.

I gave a little squeal and the jolt of energy made me shove Bob deeper.

"Oh…" I breathed.

" 'Oh,' what, Sweetheart?" Richard asked softly.

"Oh…I need a bigger vibrator!" I said breathlessly.

Richard cracked up. "Your little friend Bob there not up to the task?"

"You've spoiled me, Magic Man. No other man or tool will ever be a match for your beautiful self."

"Close your eyes, Cress. I can be there. Listen."

I was breathing faster as Bob stroked me slowly.

"Can you hear?" Richard whispered. "The sound of us together? You're so wet and you feel so good to me. Do you hear the sound we make as I slide in and out of you?"

I put the phone down there where it could pick up the sound, though it was nothing near the way we sounded together. I was also giving him a close up of the penetration action, but my orgasm was building and I wasn't thinking of visuals. I was listening to his voice.

"You hold me so tightly, Cress. You squeeze me as I move inside you. And you're hot, so hot…"

I heard the shift in his breathing.

"Don't come yet," I whispered. "Wait for me." I was nearly there.

"It's hard, Cress. I've been thinking of you since I woke up. I want this."

"I want you, all of you…" And then my orgasm broke and I cried out softly, even as I heard him groan.

"Fuck me, Richard. Don't stop, not yet." The sensations enveloped me as I felt another orgasm coming. "Don't stop."

"I'm here. Come again for me, Sweetheart."

And I did.

"My Magic Man," I whispered moments later.

"I wish I could touch you," he said softly.

"I wish I could suck you. I love that friendly drop you save for me. I miss the taste of you."

"I know. But we both have to remember how much fun we'll have making up for lost time when I get home."

"I think of that every night as I fall asleep holding my pillow."

After a couple of minutes he said, "Do you have any plans for Saturday?"

"Nope. Michael's here Friday night, then he and Steph are off to the contemporary art museum and she's spending Saturday night at his house."

"How about we share a meal? If you had an early lunch at 11:00, it would be my dinnertime and we could spend your afternoon together. I have a very special surprise for you."

"You are so good to me," I said with a sigh. "No wonder I love you so much."

"Ditto."

5

Ooh La La!

Friday, July 19

Note of the day:

> *You are the finest, loveliest, tenderest*
> *and most beautiful person I have*
> *ever known—and even that is an*
> *understatement.*
>
> —F. Scott Fitzgerld

Friday morning when Ji arrived I asked him about his name. (Honestly, I was so mesmerized by the sight of him, it had taken me that long to remember!)

He laughed. "Hunter has told you to ask me this, yes?"

"As a matter of fact, he did."

"My name is Jibada Adeyanju. It is Nigerian, as am I. I am of the Youruba people. Hunter appreciates the sense of humor of my parents. You see, Jibada has meaning, which is 'born close to royalty.'"

"And were you?" Steph asked.

"Actually, though I grew up in Nigeria, I was born in London where my father was teaching. The hospital was quite close to Buckingham palace so this is the name they chose for me."

Steph and I laughed.

"There's something else Richard said I should ask, but I confess I'm embarrassed and don't want to offend you."

Ji became concerned. "We are friends now, are we not? I cannot be offended by my friend."

"Would you mind if I touched you? You are so beautiful I really would like to see what you feel like."

Ji let out a huge laugh. "How could I refuse such a request from a beautiful woman? But first tell me, does Hunter not worry about this?"

Ji put down his bag and held his arms out to the side, inviting me to choose a spot. I took his hand and then ran both my hands up his arm slowly, feeling the warmth and smoothness of his skin and the incredible shape of his muscles."

"You are an extraordinary man, Ji. Thank you."

"I am happy to oblige you. Stephanie, do you also wish to touch me?" He offered his arm.

"Well, since you ask…" She stood in front of him and traced the outlines of his muscles from his shoulders to his wrists. "You are amazing. I may ask you to model for me sometime."

"I am a good model. The artists like me. They say my definition is something they like to draw. But come, let me show you the workout video I have made for you. I will come next Thursday to see how you have progressed and if you are ready to move on from the first sets."

As he went over the video with us, I realized Steph had hit the nail on the head when she'd suggested that if we got lazy we could just watch the video and drool over Ji!

"*Bonjour, Marie!*" Steph and I called out as we came into the kitchen.

"*Bonjour, Mademoiselles.* You had a good workout this morning?"

"We did," Steph said as we headed for the balcony. "Ji is an amazing man."

"*Homme splendid, non?*"

"Tray splondeed," Steph assured her, mimicking the French.

"Alright," I said as we sat down to our breakfast. "I need your artistic expertise."

"For?" Steph said, giving me a suspicious look.

"I've decided I want to send Richard some visual aids and I need you to take the photos."

"Why do I have the feeling you are leading me down the slippery slope into the world of pornography?"

"Uh…maybe because I am?"

Steph just looked at me.

I sighed. "It's not like you'll be looking at anything you haven't seen before."

"Really? Is that a promise? And Bob won't be involved?"

I cracked up. "I don't know what *you're* thinking but I was thinking more tease-y tits and ass. Maybe coming out of the pool or spa naked, full Monty outfit, stuff like that."

"Gees…" she whined.

"Come on, I can hardly ask anyone else to take them."

"Aren't you worried about them being found and shared somehow? Embarassing for you but not at all good for Richard, either."

"My plan is to crop them all so my face doesn't show. Shoot some from the back, maybe with my head turned but my hair covering my face or something. In the trenchcoat with the hat, collar turned up and just my eye showing. Hopefully they will be enough to help him recall the details on his own."

"I suspect he doesn't forget the 'details.'"

I laughed. "So far, he hasn't forgotten anything, but he's only been gone five days." I gave her a calculating look. "Just remember who's responsible for your wonderful new life…weedle, weedle, guilt, guilt."

"I had a feeling I might be more in debt to you than you've been telling me."

"Of course you're not…*reeeally*. So instead of guilt, how about if I bribe you with a shopping spree? Richard insists I spend money and surely you'd like some new outfits to wear for Michael? We could go select some secrets from Victoria, too. Pleeeze?"

"And just to be clear, I prefer wearing nothing when I'm with Michael." Steph gave me a speculative look before relenting. "Oh, all right," she said with a sigh. "But I reserve the right to refuse to participate if I think you're getting too pervy."

I gave her a high five. "So when can you do it?"

"Michael has to go to San Francisco again next weekend, so I'll be around." She rolled her eyes. "I hope I won't regret this."

"You won't, I promise. Just think about how happy you'll make Richard."

"I'm not sure I want you to tell him I took the pictures!"

"I don't think it would please him to think some stranger was doing it!" I reminded her.

"OK, OK. Shopping a week from tomorrow, then photo session on Sunday."

"Perfect. It will be harder for you to back out if your hands are full of shopping bags! *HA!*"

By 11:00 the next morning Steph and Michael had gone and I was settled into the couch in the library, facing the flat screen. I'd hooked it to my laptop as a monitor so I could enjoy a more lifesize version of Richard when he showed up on FaceTime. The connector was long enough that I could give him a close up of me if he wanted it. I didn't know if he knew how to connect his computer to the TV.

Just as Richard clicked on, Marie arrived with the smoothie I'd asked for for my lunch. Easier to chat and sip than chew and talk, I was thinking.

"*Bonjour, Marie!*" he said when she appeared in camera range.

"*Bonjour, Monsieur! Ça va?*"

They exchanged a few words in French and he asked her if I was behaving.

"Hey, I heard that!" I complained. "And *mon ami Marie* would never rat on me, would you?"

"*Non!*" she said very seriously while shaking her head.

We exchanged a high five.

"Uh, oh…" Richard said. "It looks like one of my spies may have defected."

Marie blew him a kiss and left, closing the door behind her.

"I convinced Marie there's strength in numbers."

"Well, as long as I'm not actually there, I guess you can't gang up on me."

For a moment, I just looked at him. Smiling.

"What?" he asked.

"It is so good to see you. It feels like you at the other end of the couch. I'm using the flat screen as a monitor."

"Great idea. When I finish eating I'll go in the other room and do that. I like the idea of you being bigger while we spend the afternoon together." Richard smiled and just looked at me. "I miss you. I loved your F. Scott Fitzgerald quote that arrived today."

"So true and spot on. And nothing I haven't told you already. Nice to know F. shared the sentiments." I smiled, thinking how perfectly it expressed my feelings.

"Wish I were curled up on the couch there with you."

"Me, too. But tell me…now that you're sorta up close and personal, it looks like you might have lost your razor in your travels."

Richard smiled as he ran his hand over his stubbly cheek and chin. "What do you think? I decided to try to grow one of those Euro-trash beards. You said you like 'em and I thought by doing it while we're apart, you could avoid the growing out, scratchy period."

I studied him. "It looks promising. We'll have to wait and see what the final results look like. You're not very hirsute. Do you think it may take awhile?"

"*Hirsute*, is it?"

"You've only been gone a few days. Have you already forgotten I have words?"

"Hardly. Some of your more memorable lines consistently thread their way in and out of my consciousness. Some times they cause an aftershock, others a stiff response."

"Good. Can't have you forgetting me."

He laughed. "I think that would be beyond even my carefully crafted powers of concentration."

"I'm hoping you'll never have the desire to give it a try. So my Prince, on what are you supping this evening?"

He turned the camera toward his plate.

"Simple and delicious little pizza and a salad. I've been dining out a lot this week and needed something lighter for a change. And a nice Chianti from the vineyard where I was."

"Both sounds and looks delicious. Certainly more interesting than my smoothie, but I'm in training."

"How's that going?" he asked.

"Well…I…I…" I acted unsure and embarrassed. "Richard, I touched Ji."

"And?"

"I put my hands on him and… I ran my fingers slowly over every curve of his sculpted…" I closed my eyes as if heating up over the memory.

"And?" he prompted.

"When I closed my eyes…"

"Cress…"

"It made me feel…" I sighed dramatically, then opened my eyes and looked at him. "…like I was touching you." I smiled.

Richard shook his head.

"Did I have you going, even for just a second?"

"I'm afraid I'm feeling pretty sure of myself as far as your affections are concerned."

"Funny, that's what Ji said. He thought you should be more afraid that his beauty might tempt me from your arms."

"Nope. You said you love me. I've already told you, you can't take that back."

I sighed dramatically. "OK."

"So how *is* the training?"

"Actually, we've had a good week. We're quite proud of ourselves for sticking to our schedule. And as Steph pointed out earlier, if we start flagging, we can just lay around and watch Ji's videos and drool."

He smiled.

"So tell me about your week," I suggested.

He'd sent a PowerPoint and he led me through the images of where he'd been and what he'd seen. It was same old, same old to him, I'm sure, but it was thoughtful of him to take the shots so he could share. He'd included lots of funny pics along with the beautiful countryside, the winery, some pieces from a gallery he works with and some from a sculptor's studio. There were some pictures of the locals, every one of them smiling broadly as they basked in his energy! He had also been to a bronze foundry nearby and took some pictures there.

"I can hardly wait 'til next summer. While you do your work, I'm going to have fun exploring. Can I expect to be pinched or is that just a Wishful Wives' Tale?"

"I have a feeling you'll be able to handle any unwanted attention quite successfully."

"The key word is 'unwanted,' Handsome."

"If we're together, I expect I'll be giving you all the attention you desire."

"I confess, you're doing a pretty impressive job so far, even at a distance. Still, I wish I could feel your arms around me. Alas, I must content myself with a rigorous schedule and losing myself in my work."

"And how is the project going?"

"I'm keeping up with the plan Ben and Jerry made, but I have some questions and I need some feedback. Feel like thinking about that?"

"Sure. Let me take my wine in the other room and hook up to the TV. If I lose you I'll FaceTime back."

"OK. And I'll send you the PowerPoint I showed the boys last week. I could use an hour of your laser focus, if you're sure you don't mind."

"Give me a minute."

Richard got disconnected, which was fine. I sent my file to his laptop. I slipped into my nerd glasses to give him the impression I meant business. Of course he cracked up when he saw me again.

"Miss Don't-Fuck-With-Me, is it?" he asked.

"Actually, I wish you were here to fuck with me, but since you're not able to share your body at the moment, please share your magnificent brain."

"I intend on sharing much more than that before I go to bed tonight. I have a surprise for you."

I assumed he was referring to an erection, though I didn't know what I'd done to encourage it.

"Focus, Mister. There are millions to be made here and if you're hoping I will keep you in the manner to which you've become accustomed, you must think about penetrating the labyrinth of my programming genius and not my nether regions."

"Yes, ma'am. I am at your service."

So for the next hour and a half Richard was all business as he applied himself to my questions and came up with some hugely insightful suggestions. I actually recorded the conversation so I wouldn't miss anything. I intended to listen to it again and get some notes into my file. It never ceased to amaze me how he was able to see the big picture along with complete awareness of the details. His questions were targeted and specific and led me into other perspectives, time after time. *No wonder I'm so madly in love with him!*

"Anything else?" he asked when I'd run out of questions.

"Nope. Can't thank you enough. You have no idea what a tremendous help this was."

"Cress, I have to tell you how impressed I am. Your PowerPoint really lays out the potential of this thing. I'm surprised Ben and Jerry were able to control their reaction."

"Well, they were gobsmacked, but hid it pretty well."

"They're probably still reeling with thoughts of their own potential profits when they find you some funding!"

"They'll be more than welcome to it. They've made it obvious to me that I could never do this without them…and more importantly, not without you! My Magic Man, you're the one making all of this possible."

"Hardly. I've just provided you with some space to make it easier to concentrate and a couple of mentors to help with the legal end of things. This is your project, Sweetheart. You're the one who came up with the concept and figured out how to build it and make it work.

"Just one more thought," he added. "Why not invite some people over for dinner and brainstorming? Mark and Sam, Lynda and Bill, Christina and Rebecca, Michael, Steph—people you can trust. I suggest you leave your computer geek friends out of this, just in case. Anyway, put together a PowerPoint with optional menu choices and do a survey. There's a big screen in the storage space at the rear of the pool house that you can use. Antonio will set it up for you. And Marie can either cook or have it catered as suits her. You'll be able to see what's most logical for users and your guests will no doubt be happy to spend the evening with you."

I just stared at him.

"What?" he said.

"I don't know what to say."

"It's just an idea. You certainly don't have to do it. I just thought some user feedback might be helpful. Logic varies from person to person, so it might help you get a feeling for what the most common choices would be."

"It's perfect, of course. I just don't understand how you zero in on these things when they never occurred to me."

"I suspect you would have come to that same conclusion in the next twenty-four hours. You've just been focusing on other aspects. Now that we've talked about the logic of the menu sequences, you'd have decided that other input would be helpful."

"Damn! Logic...whodda thunk it?" I laughed.

"By the way, I don't want to forget to thank you for the two pieces from Goldfrapp. I've never heard of them."

"The *Ooh La La* came via Michael. He's using it in a presentation for a new commercial he's working on. I loved it, so punched them up and found *Beautiful*. It seemed perfect, since I am already wearing your star." I raised my chin so he had a good view of my necklace, the diamond star he'd given me for a graduation gift. I was wearing a white V-neck tee and no bra (for his edification and enjoyment!) I sat up straighter and pulled my shirt down. My nipples perked up under Richard's unabashed gaze.

"You certainly are. I like those two perfect little pearls on your chest, too."

"*Magic maker, wish me one wish, hold me to your light...*" I sang. "Seemed to fit."

"I'd kiss you if I were there," he assured me.

"If you were here, I hope you'd do more than that."

"That's a given. We might want to turn our minds to another subject for a little longer. I hope we can go to bed together in a bit."

"Looking forward to me rocking you to sleep?" I asked.

"You have no idea...then again, maybe you do. When we have more time together like this—you know, a chance to just talk about all sorts of things—it seems like a much deeper connection than the quickies. And don't get me wrong, I thoroughly enjoy sharing that, but it's all of you I want, Cress. All of you, not just that warm wet home base."

"Hmmm...sports references is it now?"

"I speak to thee, sweet Juliet, of the quivering sheath thou holds for the sword of my desire. Better?"

"You know I love the Willie Shake references," I told him.

"I assume you are referring to Master Shakespeare rather than a trembling penis?"

"Would that yours might soon pierce the fearful hollow atop my thighs."

"Soon, Sweet Juliet. Stay but awhile. Your reward is yet to come."

"OK, be that way. You may regret parrying my amorous assaults."

"Really?"

"Well...maybe not, but I need to see you naked."

"That, too, can be arranged. I still have some tricks up my sleeve. I think you're going to have a very pleasant afternoon if you can turn down the flame for a little while longer."

I crossed my arms and tried to look stern, then said, "So, may I request a subject for the next PowerPoint you send?"

"I'm not sure I should say yes."

"You told me you'd do anything for me," I reminded him.

"You're right. I did and so I will. Tell me."

"I'd like a house tour. No hurry, but I'd like to imagine you in your current surroundings."

He cracked up. "And me envisioning a porn video."

"Now whose mind is traveling down the forbidden path?"

"Not forbidden, just temporarily requiring a detour. You'll be glad you waited, I promise."

"And?"

"I'll be happy to give you a house tour before I leave Rome."

"So you're off to Venice tomorrow?" Visions of canals and gondolas danced in my head.

"Yup. I changed my flight to the afternoon. Then I'll drive back with stops along the way. I never know where I'll run into some artist I might be able to exploit."

"You mean some artist you can shine a public spotlight on to change his or her life."

"I can always hope."

"Well, your artist in residence gave me a studio tour," I told him. "She is incredibly excited and so grateful. It was an amazing gift. Thank you from both of us."

"Has Steph started painting?"

"She was waiting on canvasses she ordered and unpacking her boxes when I was there on Thursday, but I know she got some sketching done before she left yesterday. She's decided to try to have three ready at the same time. She thinks that will distract her if she gets stuck—she'll be able to turn and work on something else."

"Good planning on her part," he said. "I know several artists who work that way. Saves time and by changing focus lets them come back to the problem later with a fresh eye. Sounds like Steph is keeping her nose to the grindstone."

"No telling where it is at the moment—she's with Michael. They were supposed to be going to the contemporary art museum."

Out of the blue he said, "Show me your breasts."

"*What?*"

"I'm pretty sure you heard what I said."

I pulled my shirt up and over my head so my arms were still in the sleeves but the front was on the back of my neck—like the jocks do. I spread my arms wide and just stared at him.

"OK."

"OK, what?" I asked.

"It's time for your surprise."

"How can you tell?"

He unzipped his fly and pulled out his penis.

"Was it something I said?"

"Nope."

"What then? Surely not the talk about Steph in the studio?"

"Nope."

I started to rub my breasts, just staring at him. He massaged his penis very slowly.

"Take off your clothes," I dared him.

"OK. But you need to get the iPad, go to my office and FaceTime me back. Let Marie know you're going to take a nap."

I pulled my shirt back down as he disappeared from the screen. I texted Marie, put my laptop to sleep, then grabbed the iPad and headed for the stairs.

6
New Friends

A few minutes later…

I hurried into the bedroom and shucked my shirt, panties (yes, panties!) and jeans and went on into Richard's office in that double-breasted suit of mine. I was hoping he would be similarly attired when he answered. I sat down in his desk chair and held the iPad on my knees, providing a closeup of my landing strip as I punched him up. A picture of his penis filled the screen.

"Great minds, eh?" I laughed.

He cracked up. "Well, pervy minds, anyway. Or maybe just two people in love and missing each other."

"Awww…you're a man after my own heart."

"Uh…I thought I already had it."

"Well, yahbutt…"

"*Yahbutt* what?"

"Yahbutt, my mind is on that familiar penis" I explained.

"Then you're bound to appreciate the surprise I have for you."

"Isn't that it?" I had sort of expected the sight of him to be my surprise, though I couldn't think of a reason he might send me to his office. *Maybe he has some visual aids of his own stashed in here somewhere.*

"You see the guy on the desk? The one you thought must be me in the morning in the shower?"

"I love him, though I wish you'd been there to model for the genital endowments. The abs look like you. And that nice round ass."

"Is he holding something?"

"There's a key on a ribbon hanging over his arm."

"Take it and go back to our bedroom. And by the way, nice suit."

I laughed as I followed his instructions.

"Now what?"

"Go over to my side of the bed. The key opens the bottom of my nightstand. But before you open it, I want you to prop the iPad up against the lamp so I can see your expression. You have no idea how much I wish I were there to give you this in person."

"If you were here, there's something else I would want first."

"Maybe, maybe not," he said, deepening the mystery.

I knelt on the floor, sitting on my heels and positioned the tablet. "How's that?"

"Perfect. Now, would you like to guess what's in there?"

"Porn?"

He laughed. "Not yet."

"Well, knowing you and Giano, I'm going to guess jewels."

"Sort of, but Giano had nothing to do with this. It's a family piece. One more guess."

"A picture of your beautiful self to put on my nightstand?"

"Nope, but if you want a picture, take one of the party ones and blow it up, then use your plastic to get a fancy frame."

"Can I open it now?"

"Go ahead."

I put the key in the lock and turned it, then opened the cabinet door. Standing tall and proud was a *very* impressive dildo with balls (!!) and a big red bow tied around it. I squealed as I reached for it.

Richard was laughing. "Look familiar?"

As I wrapped my fingers around it and pulled it out, I marveled at how lifelike it was. The texture of the silicone or whatever it was made from and the testicles…they moved inside the stretchy, flexible scrotum. *How did they do that?* There was even a little pubic hair along the top and then I realized it was Richard's penis!

I looked up at Richard. I'm sure my mouth was hanging open.

"Gobsmacked?" he asked.

"Waaay beyond gobsmacked!" I breathed as I untied the bow. "How on earth…?" I turned it around, watched the scrotum fall to one side. I cupped the balls in my hand—the weight even felt right. And the shaft of it was about as flexible as the original. It was flat out amazing, right down to the coloring. I ran my tongue over the tip, hoping it wouldn't have that strong chemical smell and taste that some of the "realistic" dildos have.

"Hey!" Richard groaned.

"Sorry. Sometimes these things taste chemical-y or smell really terrible. This one is totally neutral." I opened my mouth for it. It was very hard to resist when the screen was still focused on the live model and the hand gently stroking it.

"Wait," Richard said. I saw him tighten his grip.

"That's asking quite a bit. I've been missing the taste of you." I laid it against my cheek and ran it up and down as I slipped my tongue out the side of my mouth to touch it. Then I got an idea. I pushed the tablet back a bit and turned it horizontally as I rested my chin on the top of the cabinet, smiling. Richard moved the picture to his face. His smile was as broad as mine.

Very slowly I moved up, letting my stiff nipples catch on the edge of the nightstand so my breasts bounced when they let go! Then I moved back down, shelving my breasts on the surface as I slowly slid that lovely penis up between them. When the tip appeared Richard groaned again and I could tell he came moments later. It must have caught him off guard. (I bet there was no towel in sight!)

"Did you save a drop for your Juliet?" I asked as I bent my head and began to suck the cock still between my breasts. His eyes were fixed on me, but I could tell there was still some hand action going on. I smiled, tonguing and kissing my new toy.

"Cress…"

"What?" I asked innocently. "Isn't that part of the reason you gave me this?"

"Yes. But I guess I wasn't prepared to watch you 'bond' so quickly."

"Let me turn down the bed and we'll see if we can't do some more 'bonding'."

I rotated the iPad so he had a good look at me as I folded back the covers and then went around to my side of the bed to do the same. I slipped my hand into my nightstand drawer and unobtrusively grabbed Bob and pushed him under the closest pillow. I wasn't sure I was quite ready for a first time encounter with my new toy while

Richard watched. I wanted to experiment on my own and be sure that when I shared it with him, it would be all he must surely be hoping for.

I crawled across the sheet, giving my breasts some extra sway as I reached for my new penis surrogate and the tablet.

"I'm naming him 'Zoor,' by the way," I announced.

"Zoor?"

"Yes, like you sign your texts and emails—*XXOOR.*"

Richard cracked up. "Zoor, it is."

"So now tell me how this came about. I swear it looks like you modeled for it…which is sort of hard to imagine."

"Do you remember the night I told you I had a meeting at Universal Studios?"

"The bad news night?"

"Yup. I have a friend there who works in props and SPFX and she made it for me."

"She?"

"She. Chris. She did a mold and then cast the piece. She promised it would be made of their highest grade material, non-allergenic, not smelly and would last a long time."

"A woman made a mold of your erect penis?" I said, skeptically.

"Yes, ma'am."

"And this didn't embarrass you or her?" It was hard for me to imagine. "Doesn't it take a long time to make a mold?"

"It does. And it's not easy. I had to stay in that shape for a little over an hour."

"Good grief! How did you manage that?"

"Well, if you remember, I promised you I'd be thinking of you that night. I had some of the party pictures…and I put a ring on it."

"What?"

"A cock ring. Not entirely pleasant when you can't move, but the casting gel heats up nicely."

"So now tell me if Chris was also heating up as she ran that vaseline-y stuff all over your penis, to keep the gel from sticking."

"You seem to know a lot about this."

"The 'extras' section of the *Spartacus* Blurays. They showed Andy Whitfield having a head cast made. It looked quite unpleasant."

"All for you, my love."

"Yeah, yeah. Tell me more about Chris and your penis."

Richard laughed. "Jealous, are you?"

"I'm not sure how I feel about some woman rubbing slippery stuff on my lover's erection."

"Nothing to worry about. Chris is gay and also not very fond of penises. In fact she said she'd always thought they were ugly. She also said that mine made her rethink her position. She told me that if they all looked like this, the world would be less aesthetically challenged."

"She must be my kind of girl, after all. I've been trying to convince you your cock is beautiful." I was fondling Zoor's unbelievably realistic scrotum—right down to the wrinkles and the little "seam." I gave the testicles a gentle squeeze. "Would you like to elaborate on how she got the testicles so perfect? The weight and texture…"

"How do you think?" he said with exaggerated indignity, then laughed. "You've heard of Neuticles? The fake balls they make for neutered dogs?"

"Euwww….." That was downright creepy! Still…they felt exactly right.

"I thought you'd appreciate the realism."

"I'm overwhelmed that you would go to so much trouble." I couldn't stop fondling those balls.

"I assumed you'd be missing me, and as you've said since we first got together, Bob just isn't up to the job. Also, full disclosure: I admit the visuals will also benefit me."

I was mesmerized by Zoor and didn't respond.

"Maybe this wasn't such a good idea, after all," Richard said very pointedly.

"What? Sorry…I mean if I remember correctly, you're one orgasm up on me and having Zoor right here in my hands is making it difficult to focus on you so far away."

"I see," he said skeptically.

"Why don't you tell me what you'd like to watch Zoor do?"

"At the moment, I think I just want to watch you play with him," he said.

"Show me where you are."

Richard turned his camera toward his lap and wagged his half-hard penis a little. *Signs of life.*

"I see. Well, I'll play, you watch and we'll see where we go. I need to focus if I'm going to accommodate my new friend."

"Is that a problem?" he asked.

"Don't know yet. It's a little different when you're not actually here."

I pulled a bunch of pillows into a pile so I could prop up the iPad. Then I got my Magic Man pillow with the Tshirt and pushed it up like it was sitting, leaning against the headboard. I put Zoor in his proper location and settled down with my cheek against the shoulder of the Tshirt. I stroked Zoor slowly.

"Can you see?"

"Oh, yes," Richard said softly.

"So much like you..." I watched myself fondling my new friend. "...but he's a little cold."

"Chris said you can soak him in hot water...he'll retain heat. Maybe if you keep him in bed with you while you sleep, you can have a pre-heated wake-up call."

"If you think he won't be sleeping with me tonight, you, sir, are delusional." I slid down in bed, resting my cheek on the pillow that would have been Richard's thigh. My eyes remained on Zoor. I jiggled his testicles, still amazed by how realistic they were.

"Can you see?" I asked.

"Move your camera just a little farther south."

"Better?"

"Perfect."

"Good, because I have to have a serious taste of you." I scooted over to kneel between my imaginary lover's imaginary legs. I turned to arrange the pillows, surreptitiously slipping Bob out from where I'd hidden him and into me. I purposely turned my head away, hoping Richard wouldn't notice that sound I just couldn't seem to stop myself from making. I turned to smile at him. I was so hot that even my little friend Bob offered relief.

"Are you ready?" I asked.

Richard gave me a brief view of Zoor's double, standing every bit as tall as the one I grasped. Very slowly, I leaned forward and tongued Zoor as I watched Richard and smiled. He groaned softly. I performed a variety of oral gymnastics, then backed off and stroked him very slowly, palming Zoor's head a little.

"Do you remember the night of the party, in the gym?" I asked.

"I remember you wouldn't let me touch you anywhere but on your shoulders."

"Do you remember how anxious I was for a taste of you?"

"How could I forget? I love what you do with your mouth."

"Can you imagine how my mouth feels on you now?" I leaned over and sucked the tip again. Lots of tongue for Richard's enjoyment, albeit long distance. From his ragged breathing and soft noises I was sure it was having the desired effect.

Meanwhile, the lower portion of my anatomy was being stroked by my friend Bob. I didn't want to come until Richard did, but also wasn't sure I could wait. I grasped Zoor with both hands, while moving up and down on Bob. I closed my eyes and threw my head back, still working Zoor. *Good grief, so many penises, so hard to know where to focus…I think I'd be very confused if I found myself in the middle of an orgy!*

"Cress?"

My eyes were still closed. I bit my lip, trying to listen to Richard and come at the same time.

All I could do was emit a sort of strangled, "Hmmm?"

"Are you about to come?" I could hear the amusement in his voice.

I nodded my head and kept moving, hands on Zoor as I slid up and down on Bob. I was breathing faster.

"You know how I love to fuck you, Sweetheart," he said softly. "Come for me…"

"Yes…" I breathed. And then my orgasm exploded, surprising me with the force of it. My hands tightened on Zoor as if they were around a pole. (I suppose they were!) I continued to ride the sensation and my puny pal.

"I need more. Come again," Richard demanded.

I fell forward onto Zoor, sucked the tip of him a couple of times and quickly took him as deep as I could. Richard cried out. I'd surprised him again. I surprised myself as I started to come one more time. I sucked Zoor through the contractions I imagined my lover was having, finding it difficult to catch my breath. I forced myself to stop moving on Bob and focus on Zoor, for Richard's sake. I finished him off with some licks and sucks.

STILL LUCKY

I slid over and laid my head against my pillow's chest, one arm around it, the other hand still gently caressing Zoor. I smiled at my Prince. He looked happy and content, exactly the same way I was feeling.

"Me and Leda," I sighed. "Lucky girls."

"Lucky swan," Richard said softly. "Or are you simply saying you find me godlike?"

"Don't tell me flattery has made your head swell?"

"Only one of them," he said laughing, "And thankfully that's intermittent."

He had such a beautiful smile.

"Is it okay for me to say I miss you?" I asked.

"Is it making you unhappy?"

"Well, I'd be happier if you were here, but I'm really excited about how much I'm accomplishing, my new schedule and all the ideas around the project that keep my mind occupied. I'm happy, truly. I'd just like a 3-D chance to share it. And that being said, the 2-D sharing has actually been a lot of fun. You're too good to me." I leaned down and gave Zoor a little kiss.

"You know I miss you, too. And for me, it's been wonderful having you there to share things with. The sex, of course, but I really enjoy how often I find myself thinking of you throughout the day."

"Don't tell me your laser focus is flagging?"

"No. At least I don't think so. It's just that now there seems to be a Cressida thread running parallel to my other thoughts. I see things and immediately want to share them with you. It's why I take the photos. I imagine what it will be like when we're here together next year. All the things I want to show you."

"Pssst…" I whispered. "I think you're in love."

Richard laughed. "Not the slightest doubt in my mind. I also hope you don't doubt it."

"Nope. It's my stillpoint."

"That's my beautiful girl. I love you, Sweetheart. But I think you need to get back to work and I need to get some sleep. Keep Zoor warm tonight and I'll give you a wake-up call in the morning around 7:00 a.m."

"*Goodnight sweet Prince and flights of angels sing thee to thy rest,*" I quoted.

7

Somebody's Knockin'

Sunday, July 21

Note of the day:

> *You mould my Hopes,*
> *you fashion me within;*
> *And to the leading*
> *Love-throb in the Heart*
> *Thro' all my Being,*
> *thro' my pulses beat;*
> *You lie in all my many Thoughts,*
> *like Light…*
> —Samuel Taylor Coleridge

I experimented with Zoor Saturday night, first in the shower (to warm us both up!) and again before I went to sleep. He did heat up nicely and by exercising my imagination vigorously (and with just a little KY!) I could accommodate him as successfully as his older brother. He was just a lot to take in, if you know what I mean, as opposed to a run of the mill Prince substitute like Bob. I was anxious to see if the addition of Richard's voice with my wake up call would set my thighs to dripping and make way for Zoor. After all, with my lover halfway around the world, I wasn't in a constant state of readiness to welcome whatever he might offer!

So I snuggled down with my pillow and Zoor at attention and went to sleep.

When my call came, I woke enough to realize Zoor was pressing against my thighs and he was warm! I reached down to stroke him and marveled at how much he felt like Richard.

"My Prince," I mumbled sleepily, "you are very warm and quite insistent this morning."

"Am I?" Richard said.

"Well something is trying very hard to slip between my legs." I reached down and fondled Zoor's balls. "Those balls, " I sighed. "I'd like to suck them, but I think I need you inside me just now."

"No place on earth I'd rather be, sweet girl," Richard said softly. "Are you ready for me?"

I rubbed Zoor's smooth head against my clit and then down. He slipped partway into me. The sound I made was a little startled. I was surprised.

"What, Sweetheart?"

"I think you may need a little more determination."

"How about we take it slow this morning? Help me just tease you a little."

I lifted my leg over the pillow and worked Zoor slowly in little short strokes, sort of knocking gently at the door to my body.

Richard seemed happy to be talking me through it and his words fired my imagination.

"You seem to want to tease me a little this morning. You know when you just take the tip of me into you and move yourself around me, it feels like your mouth on me, your tongue circling me and I can imagine your smile. Treat me like a toy, Sweetheart. I love every wet minute of it. It feels so good I could come right now."

"No, please...no. Don't. Let me savor you here. It's times like this that I can't imagine how I will ever be able to take what you're so ready to give, and yet the thought of you inside me makes me so hot I can't wait for those long delicious strokes."

Words—both his and mine—were carrying me along and I could hear the moisture starting to snap between Zoor and me as he continued to make gentle little assaults.

"Somebody's knocking, should I let him in?" I sang softly.

Richard chuckled, "Well my eyes are sort of blue and I am wearing blue jeans, but I promise you I'm not the devil."

I sort of whisper-sang the next verse. The talk was heating me up fast. "*Well somebody's talkin', he's whispering to me, 'Your place or my place? Well, which will it be?' I'm gettin' weaker and he's comin' on strong...*" and then Zoor slipped in just like his namesake would have. The sound I made was loud and coupled with surprise because, just as it had that first time (and only a few times since!) my orgasm exploded.

"Sweet girl, it's good to be home," Richard said as I heard the shift in his breathing. "See what magic we can make?"

"Make me some more," I breathed as Zoor continued to stroke me, long and deep.

"Like this?" he asked.

I introduced Zoor to the clit stroke Richard was so skilled at and quickly came again.

"Feel like one more?"

I could tell he was close. "Come with me, Handsome, I want to feel you pulsing inside me."

We came together and it was no stretch to imagine his contractions as I squeezed Zoor tightly with my own.

For a moment neither of us said anything. I was savoring the weight and size of Zoor and how much he felt like Richard.

"Thank you, my Prince. Zoor makes it so much easier to imagine you're here with me."

"I am there in every way that matters, save one," he reminded me.

"Have I told you yet how much I love you?"

"Nope. You neglected to mention that."

"This much!" I said, throwing my arms wide, not caring that he couldn't see me.

Richard laughed. "So, tell me how you know a song that surely came out before you were born."

My turn to crack up. "It was a favorite of my Gran's. We used to dance to it when I was really small. Then it became a family one-liner, used any time someone knocked on any door. I even did a routine to it in my pole dancing class. It was a big hit, though most of the class had never heard it before."

"Now that's something I wouldn't mind seeing."

"Maaybee that can be arranged. I'll need a pole."

"We can talk about that when I get home. Meanwhile, you'd better get your hot little ass out of bed and into that pool."

"Uh, there're just two problems…"

"Being…?

"For starters it's Sunday," I reminded him, then defiantly added, "I can sleep in if I want."

"You've already gotten an extra couple of hours. And?"

"And the thing about Zoor…"

"Yes?"

"He feels like he's ready for more. No sign whatsoever that he's had enough."

"Uh, oh…I may have created a monster."

Trying to distract myself from the idea of urging Zoor on I asked, "Are you in Venice?"

"Yup. Meetings tomorrow and Tuesday, then I start the trip back. I should be in Rome by Saturday.

"Why don't you call me when you get in bed tonight? Bet I can make you sleepy," I teased.

"Bet you can, too! I'm staying with friends so I may be later than usual, but I'll call."

"Have a wonderful evening, Charming, and remember who loves you!"

Marie and I had decided that we'd do breakfast together on Sundays. It gave us a chance to discuss the schedule for the week and for me to get to know her better. And I wanted to talk to her about Richard's idea of having a dinner for my "focus group." I was hoping maybe we could do it on Friday. I needed to see if I could get everyone together and I was wondering if Michael would be available. Steph didn't say if he was leaving Friday or Saturday. And that reminded me that I had to decide what photos I wanted Steph to take. I thought I'd do some sketches, a picture being worth a thousand words and all that.

Gees…I decided I'd have to forgo another round with Zoor—despite the temptation—and give him a quick wash-up and put him away. I wasn't sure he was something I could stand to think of

Marie dealing with! (While she may have inadvertently seen Richard's penis over the years, I sincerely hoped it wasn't ready for business at the time!)

Around 9:30, when I finally sat down at my computer to do some work on the next batch of notes for Richard, I found an email waiting for me:

Sonnet 29

When, in disgrace with fortune and men's eyes,
I all alone beweep my outcast state
and trouble deaf heaven with my bootless cries
and look upon myself and curse my fate,
wishing me like to one more rich in hope,
featured like him, like him with friends possess'd,
desiring this man's art and that man's scope,
With what I most enjoy contented least;
Yet in these thoughts myself almost despising,
happ'ly I think on thee, and then my state,
like to the lark at break of day arising
from sullen earth, sings hymns at heaven's gate;
For thy sweet love remember'd such wealth brings
that then I scorn to change my state with kings.

— XXOOR (the original!)

That, of course required a reply and I sent:

STILL LUCKY

Ditto. Remember:

> *You take two bodies and you twirl*
> *them into one—their hearts and their*
> *bones—and they won't come undone*
> *—Paul Simon, Hearts and Bones*

> *PS/ Keep your boots on and avoid a*
> *cry to heaven! (Not the Rice book,*
> *it's great!)*

A few minutes later I received:

> *Looking forward to doing a little*
> *twirling tonight.   —XXOOR*

I replied:

> *You're not the only one. Now leave me alone,*
> *you're distracting me.*

Dissuading my Prince was sometimes difficult. And he could never resist an opportunity to test me. Next came:

> *Wouldst thou withdraw your love? For what purpose?*
> *— XXOOR*

Did he seriously think I didn't know my namesake's words?

But to be frank and give it thee again.
And yet I wish but for the thing I have.
My bounty is as boundless as the sea,
My love as deep. The more I give to thee,
The more I have, for both are infinite.

HOWEVER, while my love for you
is infinite, my time is not. Get thee
hence, knave, and tend to thy duties.
                                    —Juliet

I have but one duty, sweet Juliet, and
that to love thee well.   —XXOOR

And so you do, Charming, but I must
not tarry, for this woman's work is
never done. I bid you adieu until
the moon floats in the sky amongst
a sea of stars, when you shall once
again find me in your arms... sorta...
you'll close your eyes and....well, I'll
elaborate LATER!!!   —J

Very well. Parting is such sweet
sorrow, yet I shall say goodbye 'til it
be...later!—XXOOR

Now be honest, who wouldn't adore this man? I closed my
eyes and focused on sending him a big wave of love. Couldn't help but
wonder if he felt the aftershock!

STILL LUCKY

Monday, July 22

Note of the day:

> *There is only one happiness in life:*
> *To love and be loved.*
> —Georges Sand

Monday morning I called Mark and talked to him about doing the focus group.

"It's a great idea, CJ, and we'd love to come, but I'm attending a business dinner with Sam this weekend."

"Well, it is sort of short notice."

"I don't know if this would be of interest, but sometimes the boss has us come Saturday afternoon and stay overnight. It might give us more time to talk about your project, just relax and have fun."

I think I had a pretty good idea where that was coming from.

"OK, tell me the truth. Is this Richard's idea?"

Mark laughed. "Am I so transparent?"

"I know he's worried that I'll be lonely."

"Well, you don't seem lonely to me, but he did mention I should suggest an overnight with us gallery folk to remind you how many of us care about you. Your focus group seems like the perfect opportunity."

"It's hard to resent him when I know how good his intentions are," I admitted. "I'll have to talk to Marie and call Christina and Lynda and see if they're free, but meanwhile, pencil it in for a week from Saturday for dinner and an over-night. OK?"

"Done. Looking forward to it, whenever it happens."

I talked to Steph about the party plans that night at dinner. By then both Lynda and Christina had confirmed for a week from Saturday and I was toying with the idea of us doing the cooking.

"I thought it might be fun to give both Marie and Richard's catering budget a break and we could cook up one of our Mexican feasts," I said. "There will only be nine of us if Michael can come, so it's not that much work. I haven't had a chance to do any cooking since we moved in here."

"Our usual south of the border menu?" Steph said, getting onboard. "The sour cream spinach and chicken enchiladas, *refritos*, salsa and then all the makings for tacos and burritos and everyone can create their own plate."

"Exactly. Then maybe we can talk Marie into making us some flan," I added. "For drinks, Margaritas and prickly pear iced tea. I can make some green chili and posole and you can make your salsa."

"It would be fun," Steph agreed. "We won't be stepping on Marie's toes, will we?"

"I'll be sure she's okay with it. And I'll double check with Mark, but I don't think we've got any picky eaters in this group. I'll get a grocery list together and you and I can go over it to make sure I didn't miss anything. Marie will get us whatever we need."

8

One Redeeming Trait

Tuesday, July 2

Note of the day:

> *The heart is a thousand-stringed*
> *instrument that can only be tuned*
> *with Love.*   *—The Gift*, Hafiz

On Tuesday morning when I got out of the shower, I found three purses sitting on the island in the closet. (Marie must have spirited them in!) They all had tags in Richard's handwriting tied to them with gold ribbon. One was a good-sized shopper in a dark teal leather that felt like butter and smelled wonderful. It had gold hardware and lots of zippered pockets, three compartments on the inside (my preferred arrangement…but how did he know?) and was labeled *Mogul Bag*. The next, a smaller size, was a more modest convertible satchel in a warm shade of yellow-gold with a pebble texture, also squashy and just delicious to touch. It had both a detachable shoulder strap and handles. It was labeled *Lady Bag*. The third was a small evening bag that could be a clutch but also had a silver chain so it could become a shoulder bag. It was silver leather stitched in a quilted pattern. My Prince had designated it *Princess Purse*.

I couldn't stop fondling them. They must have cost a fortune if the quality of the leather was any indication. I could only conclude that Italian leather apparently deserved its reputation.

I pulled on my shorts and a top, then punched up Richard.

"Sweet Juliet, I just now received your quote of the day. You can't begin to understand how much these mean to me."

"I'm so glad, but things of much more magnitude are happening here. It seems the elves have come and made purses in our closet. And one of them has handwriting just like yours."

"Did they do a good job?"

"They did indeed. They are just beautiful. But…"

"Unh uh. No objections. Brace yourself because there will be more to come."

"Richard…"

"Cress, just relax and indulge me. And let me indulge you. I see things I think you'll like and I'm going to send them to you. Allow me the pleasure of that."

Then he zapped me with a shot of that remarkable energy of his and ended with a sincere, "Please?"

"What am I to do with you?"

"Uh…if you need a list…"

"Let's save that for when I run out of ideas."

"I hope that won't be any time soon." He laughed.

"So far, so good," I replied.

"So far, so *very* good."

Wednesday, July 24

Note of the day:

> *And I will love you, baby—Always*
> *And I'll be there forever and a day—*
> *Always*
> *I'll be there till the stars don't shine*
> *Till the heavens burst and*
> *The words don't rhyme*
> *And I know when I die,*
> *you'll be on my mind*
> *And I'll love you – Always*
> —Jon Bon Jovi

STILL LUCKY

After dinner on Wednesday, when it was time for Richard's Thursday morning wake-up call, I was on the couch in the library. I FaceTimed him.

"Good morning, Sweetheart," he said softly when he answered.

"Good morning to you, my sweet Prince. How may I please you this morning?"

For a moment he just smiled at me.

"I would suckle at your breast sweet Juliet, and be reminded of thy love."

"Then have it of me, for I would offer it to no other." I pulled off my shirt and brought up the camera in the cell until my nipple filled his screen. I flicked it but it was already hard. I caught my breath, imagining his mouth on me.

"This, also is for you alone," he said a moment later as he gave me a view of his penis. *Aftershock!*

"I beg you, let me taste what you have. Would I might make a meal of it."

Richard chuckled and offered a close up of the tip, already wet in anticipation.

"Eat then and satisify us both."

I licked my lips salaciously and leaned in. I surprised him when I pulled Zoor from under the cushion where I'd hidden him. Richard caught his breath when I ran my tongue over Zoor's head. I continued until I heard the shift in his breathing, then sped up and finished him off. I continued to kiss and tongue Zoor.

"Art thou satisfied, my love?" he asked a couple of minutes later.

"I am. Nectar of my god." I licked my lips and smiled.

"Cress. How can you love me so?"

"Well, as you can imagine, it's really difficult," I said suddenly, sounding quite practical. "You are *so* unlovable, but I do what I can."

"Have I no redeeming traits?"

"Let me see…oh!" Then, earnestly I said, "One of the things I most admire you for is the fact that you don't seem to find farts amusing."

Richard laughed so hard I thought he might roll out of bed.

And he couldn't seem to stop laughing. He had tears on his cheeks. When he finally managed to regain some measure of composure I was giving him a very serious look, having slipped on my nerd glasses.

"You find my observation humorous?" I said, sternly.

He started laughing again. Finally he said, "Who could ever have imagined that I would somehow find you among the more than seven billion people on this planet?"

"Life would hardly have been this much fun for either of us if you hadn't."

"*Exactly.*" For a moment he just looked at me. "There is no way I can explain to you how much I love you."

"Are you suggesting my intelligence is limited, Mr. Hunter?"

He started laughing all over again. "Noooo…I wouldn't dare!"

"I assure you I know exactly how much you love me: just a hairsbreadth less than I love you."

"Well, we could argue that point but I, sweet girl, must get on the road. I'll call later to say goodnight."

"Travel safe, Handsome."

Thursday, July 25

Note of the day:

> *Many waters cannot quench love,*
> *neither can floods drown it.*
> —Song of Solomon 8:7

After my Thursday morning meeting with Ben and Jerry I stopped by the gallery to give Mark the week's notes to send on to Richard and to take him out for coffee.

"I need to pick your brain," I told him as we walked up to the counter to order.

"How can I help?"

"I hope you don't find my plan involves a little TMI," I said as I reached for my gallery AMEX card.

"Let me…" he said.

"Nope, I'm the one asking the favor. And more importantly, your card or mine, I think your boss is the one picking up the tab."

"You have a point." He laughed as we took a table to wait for our order.

"So, I'm missing Richard. No surprise. And I want to send him some visual aids. I'm thinking photos of me presented like those 'dirty French postcards.' You know, rather graphic images that are specific to things between the two of us."

Mark smiled and shook his head. "I swear, you two are so unbelievably perfect for each other. Something like that will mean the world to him. I'm sure he's enjoying your daily notes, too."

"He is. He has a surprisingly tender heart. I don't know if you ever get a glimpse, but I see it all the time."

"I'm sure you see it more often than we do, but I know it well enough to want to guard it. Can't help myself. I'm half in love with him myself."

"Hey now! He's mine, and don't you forget it!" I shook a warning finger in his face and tried to look stern.

Mark chuckled and went to get our coffees when the barista called our names.

"So what can I do?" he asked when he came back.

"I have no idea how to find a photographer."

"Have you asked Steph to do it?"

"I have and she's agreed to do a few, but she thinks the more 'intimate' (and yes, I made the little quotes gesture with my fingers!) shots would be a little too much for her. She says there are a few things she doesn't want to know about my love life."

"She's probably right. I'd feel the same way."

"I intend the pictures won't show my face, because most of them will be well…akin to porn. I don't want any images going public. I wouldn't take a chance on something like that harming Richard or his businesses. So whoever it is, they have to be completely trustworthy and willing to sign a contract assuring me I have the only files. And it has to be someone I can trust to have come to the house."

Mark just looked at me.

"I'm sorry. Is this too much? Maybe I've gone off the deep end with this idea?"

"No. It's perfect." Mark smiled. "I'm just stunned that the boss's universe seems to be working in our favor, as usual."

I waited for him to go on.

"Recently I reconnected with a friend from school—Seiji McGreggor. He's a photographer who does a lot of artsy commercial work…in fact I ran into him again at Michael's office a couple of months ago. The first time I'd seen him in about six years.

"Sam and I had him over to dinner and it turns out he's trying to break into the fine art market and was interested to hear about the gallery. He's working on a series but didn't want to tell me about it yet. He's hoping I can get him a meeting with the boss when he's ready to show it. At any rate, I think it might be worth talking to him."

"I guess I was thinking of a woman, to avoid most of the awkwardness. Do you think he can handle it?"

"Can you?" Mark laughed. "Seiji's gay. Loves women and finds them aesthetically beautiful but not sexually interesting. Want me to put you in touch? It could be good for you and for him, and in the long run, for the gallery as well."

"Sure, I'd love to meet him. I'm just hoping something like this isn't going to be vastly expensive."

"He may consider it worth his time because of your connection. One thing I would suggest, just to avoid any problems, is to provide and then keep the card from the camera and also, if there's any way you could shoot at his studio, it would be better than the house. Seiji's reliable, but he might have to bring an assistant to handle equipment if they go on location, and the fewer people involved, the better. He can probably work alone in his studio. You should certainly discuss it with him, or whoever you choose. And if you need help interviewing photographers because you're not comfortable with Seiji, I'd be happy to be a masculine presence for you."

I leaned over and gave Mark a kiss. "You're the best, you know."

"Don't let the boss hear you say that!"

After dinner that night, Steph went to catch up on her email and I settled in to the couch in the library for Richard's wake-up call.

"This is the nightingale," I said softly when he answered.

"I fear it is the lark," he replied.

I could hear the smile in his voice, but he didn't sound like his usual perky morning self.

"Late night, my Prince?"

"Very. These Italians don't approach the dinner table until eight or nine…or ten…and then the talk continues 'til after midnight. They don't get up at five. And they have that essential siesta."

"No siesta for you?"

"I was driving all day yesterday. Needed to get here in time for the gallery opening."

"How was it?"

"Promising. I took some pictures of the work. I'm interested to hear what you think."

"Really? Me, who doesn't understand string and suitcases?"

Richard laughed. "This, I think, has a much broader appeal."

"I look forward to seeing the photos. Anything *you're* looking forward to this morning?"

"Surprisingly, no. I'm going to sleep another couple of hours if the woman I love will let me off the hook. Then breakfast with my host before I hit the road."

"Want another wake-up call? I can dial you up when I'm ready for bed, myself."

"Hmmmmm…I like the sound of that."

"You're gonna like the feel of it, too," I assured him.

"No doubt in my mind."

"Is 7:30 your time more like what you have in mind?"

"Let's make it 7:00. That'll give me time to rock you to sleep."

"Rest, my Prince. Dream of me."

"I always do."

Friday, July 26

Note of the day:

> *Truth is a deep kindness that teaches*
> *us to be content in our everyday*

C.J. BAILEY

life and share with the people the
same happiness. —Khalil Gibran

On Friday afternoon when I went upstairs to shower after my swim, there was a surprise waiting for me on the bathroom counter. It was a bronze sculpture of a hand, life-size, and in the palm was a glass heart, deep red and flecked with gold. Beside it was an envelope with my name written in Richard's hand.

For my Sweet Juliet—
Take my heart,
for in truth 'tis no longer mine.
I gave it thee when first we met.
                    XXOOR

I picked up the sculpture. It was heavy, a solid cast I guessed, and seemed to be molded from a real hand because it was three dimensional, though it was stable when sitting palm up. It was the hand of someone reaching out to take another hand. The detail was amazing. Then, as I turned it over I realized it was Richard's hand!

How did he do these things? Zoor was one thing—hardly something that could be out where everyone could admire it, but this…I was thinking I would keep it on my desk.

My sweet Prince…I kissed the palm, replaced the beautiful heart and jumped in the shower, wishing he were there with me so I could thank him properly.

After dinner, I decided to make Richard's wake-up call from our bed. I mussed up my hair into a semblance of GTF-bed-head and set my iPad on the pillow next to me, hoping I could wake him sort of face-to-face.

"Good morning, Beautiful," he said sleepily.

"Good morning to you. How does this day find you, my love?"

He smiled and turned on his side. "Wishing you were here."

"Me, too. Thank you for the sculpture and the reminder that I have your heart."

"It is yours. That particular version of it came from Murano."

"Ah! The glass island."

"Wow! She's beautiful *and* she knows her geography."

"You know how much I enjoy exploring your geography," I reminded him.

"The feeling is mutual—I hope you've noticed."

"I have. I also noticed that the hand is your hand. Any plans to cast any other body parts?"

Richard chuckled. "I think maybe you have the two most important ones. Any other suggestions?"

"Nope. But I confess I'm looking forward to the return of your living breathing self."

"Me, too.

"Meanwhile, any thoughts on how you want to start your day?"

Sunday, July 28

Note of the day:

> *God gave us memory*
> *so that we might have*
> *roses in December.*
> — J.M. Barrie

When we'd finished our Sunday morning crepes I said to Steph, "OK, I've bribed you with shopping, now it's time to return the favor."

We were still at the breakfast table, enjoying a second cup of coffee. I handed her my little drawings of what I was thinking of for the photos.

"These should all be tame enough for you to handle. I don't

know how I'm going to get some of the more intimate shots I want, but I'll worry about that after I see how interested Richard is in visual aids."

Steph shook her head and smirked as she paged through the sketches my ideas.

"I think I can stand it. Where do you want to start? Shall we do the inside stuff first and maybe the pool and spa after lunch? At least there's so little wardrobe involved that changing time won't be a factor."

On the way upstairs we decided to start with the more clothed shots and work down to the bare ones. I really don't know why Steph was so squeamish about taking the pictures for me. We'd seen each other naked and it wasn't as if I was asking for shots employing Zoor! Gees…suddenly she was concerned. She drew naked people in her life drawing classes all the time! I said as much to her.

"Yahbutt, I don't have to imagine what those models are doing with each other or why their partner likes the way they're posing!"

"Come on, there's nothing kinky here. No chickens, no feathers," I insisted.

"For you maybe."

"Hmmm…" I mused. "I've never asked my hunk how he feels about chickens…"

"Well, if you do, keep his answer to yourself, will ya? I'm not sure I want to know."

We started with my outfit from the *Full Monty* striptease, the performance I'd done for Richard. She took a shot of me in the hat and trench coat, with my collar turned up so all that showed was my eye. One from the back with the trench coat off my shoulders. We did a couple of shots in the red dress from that night—one breast exposed, both breasts exposed, one from the back with me bent over. Steph groaned loudly over that one!

"Get over it. That's one of his favorite views so there will be more." I was cracking up as my photographer continued to roll her eyes.

When we'd exhausted that outfit, I put on the blue dress from the graduation party Richard had thrown for us. I had her take one of me glancing back over my shoulder but with my hair covering enough of my face to make me unrecognizable. Another shot from the back (and in the highest pair of heels I owned, rather than the more modest pair I'd actually worn that night!) with me lifting the skirt just enough on one side that you would wonder (as Richard had) if I was wearing my thong or not. He'd enjoyed that tease.

Then I picked up one of the towels I'd brought up from the gym and tucked it in the front of the dress like a bib.

"You can get part of my face in this one. I'll crop it so only my mouth shows."

"What's with the towel?" Steph said as she adjusted her position for the right framing.

"Don't ask."

Then it hit her. "Really? The night of the party? While people were still here?"

"Yup. Snuck off to the gym for a little taste. You don't call me Miss Hot Pants for nothin'!"

"A bib?"

"A Lewinsky would have been a dead giveaway."

"I hope your hunk knows how lucky he is," she said, shaking her head.

"He does, or so he leads me to believe. But you and Michael must be doing some things to switch it up."

"He's pretty creative, himself. We just haven't been in a group situation that demands stealth…yet."

"Your turn will come. I'd bet on it. Things are still hot between you, aren't they?"

"Oh, yes," she laughed. "I swear it gets better every time, even though that makes no sense."

"I know. I just had no concept of this intimate level Richard and I have reached and I still don't understand how we could get there so quickly. I repeat myself, but I love him so much, Steph. He's such a special guy and I spend all of my waking hours grateful that he chose me."

"Bet he feels the same way."

"He sure makes me believe he does. And it's interesting to me how my life revolves around him while at the same time somehow making me feel completely free to do my own things." I was saying this as I put on the garter belt and stockings from my "nooner" outfit. I shook myself into the little demi bra, making sure my nipples peeked over the top evenly, then stepped into my heels and tossed a folded towel over my arm. I stood in the same spot I'd been standing that day when he came home.

"And what was this occasion?" Steph asked as she focused.

"Out of the blue he called and asked if I fancied a nooner. It was the first time that happened and this is what I was wearing when he arrived. I told him I was his server." I laughed. "He told me he had something for me, and sure enough, he did!"

We tried that with several facial expressions and even one with me bending forward with the scoldy finger. That gave a sort of 1940s pinup flavor (*sans* panties!) to the composition.

We did a few more odds and ends—zipping up his cashmere hoodie with one breast visible, my smile and the star at my throat with breasts (!), a closeup of one of my earrings piercing my lobe (I knew that one would make him laugh!), my head on the pillow with messed up hair covering my face, the Ali BéBé dress from the night we met—several angles, including bending over to show my breasts, as I'd done then. I told Steph I really wanted to get a shot on his desk at the gallery. (Eye roll from her on that one!)

We even did one shot of me in the pretty sage green silk set I'd worn the night we stayed at Giancarlo's. When I put water on the crotch of those panties Steph just shook her head.

"What?" I asked innocently. "Get yourself a pair of real silk ones like these and invite Michael for a taste through the fabric. Trust me," I urged, wiggling one eyebrow at her.

I led her into the bathroom. "OK, now I want you to do a few of me in the shower, under the lights."

"Really?"

"Yup. Sometimes I dance for him, but it never lasts long. We do dance together in here, though." I smiled thinking how much I missed sharing showers with him. "I'm really happy that he's as silly about this stuff as I am."

"I know I've said it before, but you two really are a perfect match. It's interesting to me that he can be focused and relaxed when he's talking business, then so comfortable among strangers like he was at our party, or exuding that mysterious energy when he's trying to help me see the error of my ways. And yet, from what you say, he's apparently uninhibited in the way he is when he's alone with you. I saw that side of him after the party when I was in the spa with Michael."

"Boy, did you ever! I was embarrassed for him but it didn't bother him at all."

"And," she added, "none of it seems forced or unusual for him."

"As I've told Richard, I think he exemplifies that 'comfortable in his own skin' thing. I've never known anyone so open and centered. He consistently surprises me."

"I suspect he feels the same way about you."

"I hope so. As you know, I'm pretty candid. As you also know, I can be pretty silly."

"I think I'd say downright funny—as in, I really love your sense of humor."

"Aw, Steph. No wonder we're friends. You're one of the few people who 'gets' me."

I'd been punching up a shower program while we talked.

"Do you think we should just go with the lights and not the water?" I was thinking the water might blur the pictures.

"We can try it both ways. Maybe if you just use the water in the very center it won't splash on the glass. Let's try some dry first and then go for wet."

I started to step into the shower, but Steph reminded me that even if we were going to shoot it dry first, my hair should still be wet so it would seem as if the water was on.

We finished and I put on a bikini and one of the shirred cotton cover-ups while Steph went and changed into her suit and then we went down to lunch. Afterward, we did a few shots in the pool and spa, mostly with me naked. Then we both went back and swam some laps.

"Now that wasn't so bad, was it?"

She laughed. "I have to admit, it wasn't as embarrassing as I expected it to be. I do want to see the pictures when you get through with them. And I have to say you may have even inspired me a bit. I'm thinking of letting Michael catch me in the studio with just my apron on."

I laughed and high-fived her. "You go girl! But don't show him that nice bedroom too soon."

"Nope. He can have me somewhere in the main room. Just a

quickie. I can't be distracted from my work. Fame and fortune are just around the corner for me, too!"

I gave her a hug. "Whaddaya think, will we make good rich girls?"

"Remains to be seen, but I'm anxious to find out!"

9

Ready for Your Closeup?

Tuesday, July 30

Note of the day:

> *...we lie a long time looking at each other.*
> *I do not know what he sees,*
> *but I see eyes of surpassing tenderness*
> *and calm, a calm like the dignity of matter...*
> —Sharon Olds, *The Knowing*

On Tuesday morning I FaceTimed Richard, hoping that he hadn't yet gone out for the evening.

"Hi Sweetheart. What's happening in your world?" He was sitting at his laptop, a glass of wine in his hand.

"Curiosity, the never ending exploration of mind and body."

"Hmmm...sounds interesting. You know how much I enjoy exploring both your body *and* your mind."

"Good, I'm hoping you'll feel like sharing because I have a question for you, my Prince," I said.

"Ask and receive answer."

I laughed. "What's that, the *Spartacus* influence?"

"Great show, by the way, but 'When in Rome...'"

"Sparty and the boys were in Capua," I reminded him.

"So, you saw the series? I'm surprised."

"Seriously, you're asking? All those naked hunks? Steph and I have our priorities, if you remember."

Richard chuckled. "Of course you do. So what's your question?"

"What do you think about when you masturbate?"

Richard nearly choked on his wine and then when he caught his breath, burst out laughing.

I slipped on my NGs and looked over the top of them at my screen with a serious expression—sort of a psychiatrist-evaluating-a-patient look.

"Inquiring minds want to know," I said slowly.

That brought a second wave of laughter.

"You find this amusing?" I continued in a clinical tone.

"What on earth makes you ask?" Richard said, wiping the tears from his eyes.

"I'm doing a study."

"A private one, I'm hoping." He was still chuckling and shaking his head.

"Yes. You're the only subject."

"That's reassuring."

When he didn't say anything else, I prompted, "Well?"

"You're serious?"

"I am. The more I know about what turns you on, the better I can please you, my love."

"Cress, when I feel the need to masturbate, what I'm thinking of is you."

"I was sort of counting on that. What I mean is, do you have a specific fantasy or scenario or memory?"

I watched as Richard shifted his focus into problem solving mode. *Fascinating!*

"It depends. You've given me so many options that I tend to go for variety and skip through more than one image."

"Would you mind if I watch sometime?" I asked.

"Only if you'll return the favor."

"Of course," I assured him. "You know how I love to share. So when do you want to do this?"

"You know me, Sweetheart, ever ready to satisify the woman I love."

That surprised me. I had been thinking it was something we

would do one of these nights, not necessarily right away. But I'm nothing if not adaptable.

When I didn't say anything, he offered, "Want to do it now?"

"Only if you want to."

"I could never turn down a chance to show you how much I love you."

"You know nothing pleases me more than looking at you. So, what if I turn off my camera but you leave yours on? And if you can narrate your thoughts and actions, that would help."

Richard laughed. "Help who?"

"Me, at the moment. You, in the future."

"Hmmm…So how do you want me to start?"

"From scratch. Do you usually just go for a quickie or do you enjoy a longer session more?"

"Depends on my schedule and the urgency. If thoughts of you create a…shall we say 'pressing need?'…a quickie serves the purpose. If I want to really enjoy myself with the imaginary you, I take my time."

"I think the longer version will be more informative, and since you're more verbal than most men, I'm counting on learning a lot."

"Have you forgotten? I'm a Trained Professional."

"How could I forget? It's just one of so many things I love about you."

"So, Madam Director, where do you want me?"

"Where are you most comfortable?"

"If I'm going to take my time, it's usually when I'm in the shower or in bed."

"Feel like a nap?" I whispered suggestively.

"Since you're involved, that sounds very appealing."

Richard picked up his laptop and carried it to a little table that he pulled over close enough to the mattress so that my view should provide an adequate image for my "study."

He sat down on the edge of the bed where I could see his face if he ducked down a little.

"That should work. Are you ready?"

"Ready, Ms. deMille."

"Looking forward to your close-ups. I'm turning my camera off, and I won't say anything until you're done. This is a solo performance. Wow 'em in the back of the house, Magic Man. I love you!"

I clicked off the camera and curled up on the couch to watch.

Richard stood up. His crotch was at camera level and filled the screen. He caressed himself, with a little squeeze of the whole package and a little rub.

"I'm not hard yet, but just trying to choose an image of you." As he pulled his Tshirt over his head he said, "Ah, I see you in our room, bending over the tansu chest and looking back at me with that smile, inviting me to explore your hot wet cunt."

He unzipped the fly on his khakis and let them fall. The bulge in his underwear was all I could see. He clutched himself and squeezed lightly, but I could see movement beneath the fabric.

"You're so wet and just begging me to slide in there."

He pushed his shorts down and released his already tumescent penis. All I could think of was how beautiful he was and how I longed to touch him. I also thought I should have brought Zoor downstairs with me instead of Bob!

Richard stepped away for a moment and reached for what must have been lubricant. I'd have to remember to ask him if he kept it handy.

"I'm picturing the dripping slit between your legs. You can see the effect it's having on me. I need a little help to replicate that wetness. This heats up so it enhances my experience of you. You're always so hot and wet." He poured a generous amount into his hands, rubbed them together and then ran them lightly over his penis and his testicles.

I was surprised by how gently he touched himself.

"I'm imagining rubbing against you, the temptation of how wet you are. I'm teasing you, knowing how much you want me, even as I want to be inside you."

He turned to the side, offering me a view as he held his thumb and forefinger together tightly, making sort of a slit, and with his other hand guided the head of his penis up and down against it.

"I'm feeling you. All wet and slick, begging me to fuck you."

He rubbed against his fingers…again lightly… and moments later was fully erect. He had to press his penis down and hold himself perpendicular to continue.

"I'm going to get in bed now. And I can imagine you wanting to be on top. You're smiling as you climb onto the bed after me."

He piled his pillows together so he would be half sitting and pulled a towel from somewhere. He placed himself close enough to the edge of the bed that now my view went from his head to just above his knees. Perfect! He checked the image on the screen.

He settled back and held himself with one hand while he massaged his balls gently with the other. He slid his scrotum up, pressing it against the shaft of his cock and slid it down again with a little tug. He pushed one hand against his belly, just above his penis, as his other hand held him up, as if waiting for me to lower myself onto him. Then, very slowly, he ran both his hands down his cock and I heard that little satisfied sigh that came every time he slipped into me. *Aftershock!*

"You feel so good, Sweetheart, so hot and slick and wet. I could come right now but I want to watch you come. I'm waiting for you to ask me to come with you."

He stroked himself slowly, still very lightly. I couldn't help but wonder if maybe I was too rough with him when I handled his penis. He'd always seemed to enjoy it, but maybe he'd prefer this.

"I love the way you move. I love us together like this."

I noticed that on some of the strokes he made a light pass with his palm over the head of his cock, with just a subtle twist. He reached for his testicles and gave them a gentle pull.

"I love it when you give my balls a little tug. It enhances the sensations."

He continued the rhythmic stroking with one hand while the other massaged his pubic bone. He ran his fingers lightly up and down the little strip of hair between his navel and his cock, then up to caress his nipples. Again, with surprising tenderness.

"It's getting harder to describe because the images of you run together and I see flashes of you getting ready to come."

He gave himself just a few rapid strokes, as he did to me when I came.

"I want you to come again. I love it when I can help you come a few times before we finish together."

He slowed the strokes.

"More, Sweetheart?" he whispered. "And you always say,

'Yes, please.' Sometimes I hear you whispering those words just as I'm falling asleep. But now I feel you're ready to go again."

And he sped up with a few quick strokes and then slowed again. I heard his breathing shift and I knew he was close, himself.

"And now I want your mouth, sweet Juliet…"

He paused for a moment, giving imaginary me time to shift position, then slid both hands down his cock and pressed his head back into the pillows as he came. The multiple bursts of semen shot up with a force that surprised me. It's one thing to feel it in your mouth, or the pulsing inside you, but to see the results of those contractions on a vertical trajectory was something else. After the first three he let his penis move closer to his belly as he held himself a little more tightly, pulling on his penis as he slid one hand up to the tip with a little rub and a soft pinch.

"When you suck me…"

And he ejaculated two more bursts and continued to finger the head of his penis as more semen followed in diminishing amounts. He kept stroking himself lightly for several minutes as his erection began to fade.

"You're a miracle, Cress," he said softly. Finally, he reached for the towel. Another minute passed as he mopped himself up and before he said, "Is that what you wanted, Sweetheart?"

I turned my camera back on just as he reached for his laptop and set it beside him on the bed.

"Do you remember the Rumi I gave you the night of the party? *I asked for a kiss, you gave me six. From whom did you learn such mastery? Full of kindness, generosity—you are not of this world.*"

"Of course," he said. "I still have it. It's in my wallet. It means a lot to me."

"Just remember it's true."

For a minute, we just looked at each other.

"Can I have one more look at your penis?"

He slid the computer down the bed until his softer self filled the screen. So beautiful and completely amazing to me. I noticed the skin on his scrotum was sort of squirming around.

"Does that always happen?"

"What?" he asked as he brought the laptop back up.

"Your scrotum seems to be undulating."

"*Undulating?*" He laughed.

"Remember: I have words. But maybe that's not the right one. The skin seems to be crawling around. Can you feel it?"

"Yeah, muscles relaxing, blood flowing again."

"I can't believe I never noticed."

He laughed. "At this point in the process, we're usually kissing. You're not studying my balls."

"Just you wait!" I threatened.

"I'd be honored to be your science project."

"I'll hold you to that."

"Just so you hold me."

"Always. So. In the interest of scientific research, can I ask you some questions?"

"Of course." He was amused.

I could see a gob of semen still on his throat. I pointed to that spot on my own.

"I see you left a drop to help me after. Wish I were there to catch it on the tip of my tongue. I long for a taste of you."

Even as I said it he twitched.

"You haven't lost your own magic, sweet Juliet," he said as he wiped his throat with the towel. "And FYI, normally I would have used the towel to avoid the mess, but I assumed you wanted to 'study' the complete process."

"I did. Hope you won't have to sleep in the wet spot."

"This is only a nap for me. I can have clean sheets before I go to bed tonight."

"Wish I could be there, between them with you."

"Ditto."

"First," I said, "A question I've been meaning to ask: I'm curious as to why you use 'cunt' instead of 'pussy.'"

He smirked. "It was the word you used first. And I'm glad. I've never liked the word 'pussy.' It may also be that the French slang is '*con*,' so it comes more naturally to me. I don't use it very often."

"You don't. And I've never liked 'pussy', either. It seems too precious. Maybe it's the old English or even the *Spartacus* influence!"

Back to the situation at hand. I took a deep breath.

"So, regarding my observations…I notice you handle yourself much more tenderly than I do when I have my hands on you. Have

I been too rough with you? Would you prefer a lighter hand on the 'throttle,' so to speak?"

He laughed. "I love your hands on me however they hold me. It's actually a turn on when you hold me more tightly, or tug at me a little. It signals that you want me and you need me…sometimes that you might even be desperate for me, and that means a great deal. It's very exciting and makes me feel bigger and harder, though I doubt there's any difference, externally, in my cock."

"I'll have to torment you with a light and slow version next time we're together and see how you feel about it."

"Can't wait," he assured me. "Now I have a question for you: Did watching me turn you on?"

"Just looking at you turns me on. But I admit, Bob buzzed me off as I watched you."

"Bob, not Zoor?"

"Zoor demands my total attention and commitment, a long fantasy with many delicious details and provides so much visual stimulation. I didn't want to be distracted from watching. And Zoor needs to be warmed up."

"Hmmm…I think I may make you show me with Zoor *and* with Bob."

"Oh, goodie, then I can make you demonstrate a quickie!"

Richard laughed. "As I've often said, you're insatiable."

"*Au contraire, Cheri*, you can satiate me, always and often, if only in my mind these days. I'm actually glad that the energy is still there that suddenly hits me with a incomprehensible wave of need for you. I'd be very sad if it started to fade."

"So would I, Sweetheart. My desire for you is as steady as a rock…and sometimes just as hard."

It was my turn to laugh.

When I went back to work I texted Richard one of my favorite *Spartacus* quotes:

STILL LUCKY

*"Do you know what it is to love? To
be filled with light and hope? To see
that blessing returned in kind in the
eyes of the only one who could ever
know the true depth of your heart?"*
—*Spartacus:Vengence*, Ep **8**

I do! XXOOJ

C.J. BAILEY

10
You Oughtta Be in Pictures

Thursday, August 1

Note of the day:

> *"If one day I was taken away...*
> *would you wait for me to come back?"*
> *Concern moved across his face.*
> *"Where are you going?"*
> *"Just tell me, please. I need to know,*
> *without telling you anything else."*
> *"No."*
> *I swallowed and blinked back tears.*
> *"I'd go after you," he said.*
> — Kelly Parra, *Invisible Touch*

On Monday, I had called Seiji and he invited me to his studio in Santa Monica that Thursday, after my weekly meeting with Ben and Jerry. Mark had told him about my idea and he seemed interested.

The building was windowless on the street side with just a simple (and graphically beautiful!) sign that said *seiji's* with a lighted pie-slice logo in an orangy-yellow next to the industrial glass entrance. I pressed the buzzer and a moment later a good looking Asian guy with a dark purple buzz cut appeared and unlocked the door. His mixed heritage showed in the few freckles scattered across his nose and his green eyes.

"CJ?" he asked as he reached for my hand. "Come in."

"Great hair!" I said by way of greeting. (I could hardly fail to comment!)

Seiji's smile could light a room. I sure loved the citizen's of Richard's universe, even the ones he hadn't met yet! And I was expecting Seiji would be no exception. With both Michael and Mark recommending him, how could I go wrong? But then there were details to work out. Maybe my idea would be too kinky for him.

He showed me around the studio, a huge open space with hanging paper backdrops, a few with set ups. There were lights scattered around and some of those umbrella-looking things...diffusers maybe? There was a long table in the center—three tables pushed together, actually—holding a variety of cameras and lenses. (I also noted how carefully the equipment was arranged!) I wasn't familiar with all of it, but I could see there was enough variety to indicate he must be pretty successful.

After the tour he invited me into his office.

"Can I get you something? Coffee, tea, water?"

"Actually, coffee would be great if it's not too much trouble."

"Easy. I've gone Keurig. Cream and sugar?"

Please."

I sat down facing his desk while he dealt with the coffeemaker that was on the credenza behind it. There were several large photos on the walls—product shots—two of which I recognized. Seiji must be doing well for himself. I was beginning to think he'd be way beyond the scope of my budget.

"I love your sign out front. Is that pie-section shape some sort of Japanese symbol?" His first name was Japanese and he was obviously part Asian, so I didn't think I was out of line asking.

Seiji cracked up. "It's a hunk of cheese."

"What?" I was confused.

"*Seiji's,* possessive, sounds like *'say-cheese'.* Common photographic quote, yes? I did a lot of wedding and graduation photography to get by in the early days, so it was apt. Now, I suppose I've outgrown it, but it's something my clients remember."

I laughed. "It went right over my head, sorry. And the sign is so graphically elegant. It didn't click for me. I guess I spend too much time in front of the computer."

"You look very familiar," he said as he brought me my cup. "Are you a model?"

I laughed. "Hardly. I'm a computer geek."

He shook his head. "I know I've seen you somewhere. Jewelry, maybe?"

"Jewelry?"

"An ad for jewelry?"

I shook my head and then I remembered Giano's photos from the event in San Diego. I had signed that release for him.

"There were some pictures taken of me wearing a very expensive necklace at a charity event, but as far as I know, they haven't been used."

"Well, if I can remember what I saw, I'll let you know. So tell me about this project of yours."

"I'm hoping you won't find this beneath you and if you are willing to take it on, that I can both afford you and count on your discretion."

I reached into my purse and pulled out the sketches of what I was hoping to get shots of. He smiled.

"Posing like this wouldn't embarrass you?" he asked as he shuffled through the sketches.

"No. Though I'm hoping it wouldn't make you uncomfortable. Mark probably told you that I need to be absolutely sure that the pictures remain private."

"I understand," he said. "I'm hoping to be able to meet Mr. Hunter when I have some work to show. I'm more than willing to follow your guidelines with an eye to you putting in a good word for me."

I smiled. "I think these photos might go a long way toward a favorable impression, though perhaps not for the reasons you imagine."

He laughed. "I'll take the good will any way I can get it."

I was really enjoying Seiji. He had an easy way about him. Business-like but friendly and comfortable. I took a deep breath.

"And now I have to ask…what do you think it might cost? Mark suggested I supply you a memory card, which I would keep to be sure there aren't any copies around. You can understand I have to protect Richard. And I can deal with the printing myself, since I assume you work digitally."

"That would be fine. The low end of my rate scale starts at $600 an hour and I think that you're looking at at least a half-day."

I know he could read the disappointment on my face.

"I'm sorry, I had no idea. I'm sure you're more than worth it, but despite the company I keep, I'm currently more or less unemployed. Do you think we could do two or three in just an hour? I'm afraid that's the most I can manage."

"Would you consider a trade?"

I must have looked shocked because Seiji laughed.

"Beautiful as you are, I'm not interested in your body, CJ. Well, actually, I am interested in your body...as a model. I might be able to trade you my time for yours."

"What did you have in mind?"

He proceeded to explain the series he wanted to shoot, the difficulty he'd had finding a woman uninhibited, willing and with the right look to get the shots he wanted. They would be very explicit and at the same time visually abstract in a way that the viewer would not know what they were, but rather see the organic nature of the shapes. I was both flattered and intrigued.

"Would you like to see the work? I've shot as much of the male anatomy as I need and so I'm starting to think 'female.' It's sort of perfect timing that you called."

"I'd love to see what you've done so far," I told him, thinking it was another example of the synchronicity of Richard's world.

He led me back out into the studio and to the countertop along the far wall. He woke up his computer, which was connected to what must have been a sixty-inch flat screen on the wall. He was using it as a monitor.

The first image was amazing while at the same time incomprehensible. Even knowing it was part of a man's body I couldn't begin to identify it. There were exquisite shapes, all planes and shadows and curves. Seiji watched me as I studied the picture.

"It's beautiful, but I have no idea what it is."

He moved on to the next shot. It had the same image, overlaid with the photo of the same portion of anatomy from farther away. It proved to be an extreme closeup of that spectacular delineation I still hadn't learned the name of, the line that arcs over a well muscled man's hips and drops down on either side of his penis. This was a portion halfway between hip and penis, no sign of any hair, just smooth curves.

"It almost looks like sand dunes or wind polished ice."

The next photo really did look like sand—those wiggly lines the wind makes.

"I'd have to guess scrotum," I said, "because I can't think of any other skin on a man's body that looks like that."

Seiji didn't say anything but popped up the next shot, which was the larger overlaid with a more distant shot. I was right.

"It's beautiful," I said, "And no offense, but it isn't the prettiest part of male anatomy. I think turning it at that angle makes it less easy to identify, which is probably a good thing."

"You have a really good eye, CJ. How about this one?"

"You've got me there. But, wow, that is outstanding!" That picture turned out to be the dip between the deltoid and bicep muscles. It was fascinating.

"Do you feel you'll find as many interesting shapes on a woman's less-muscled body?" I asked.

"There are so many curves and I think the smoothness and shadows will work. I won't know 'til I try some shots."

"Are you also thinking vulvas and clits?"

He smiled. "You really aren't shy about this, are you?"

"Not at all. And I'm really interested in what you're doing. Personally, I think all kinds of bodies can be beautiful and it must be inspirational to work with them as an artist."

He punched the computer off. "Do you think you'd be willing to participate in the project?"

"I'm up for it, but we'd have to agree that there would be no way to identify me as the subject. Again, I'm thinking of Richard and his businesses. I can't take any chances of damaging him."

"I understand. And it wouldn't do me any good as a prospective artist, either. If you'll forgive me, I will have to see you nude to be sure you're the right model, but when we shoot your photos, I'll know."

"And if I don't seem right, how will I pay you?"

"Let's agree to three shots for $600.00, the amount to be waived if you suit me as a model, in which case I will give you a half day of photography in exchange for a half day from you."

"And you'll sign the non-disclosure agreement?" I asked.

"I'd have to read it first, of course, but I can't imagine having problem with that."

We set a date and I promised to email a confidentiality agreement on Monday. I was excited and at the same time wondering if I might be too trusting. I'd talk to Steph and call Michael. I had no misgivings about posing. We all know I'm short on inhibitions as far as my body is concerned. And to be honest, I liked Seiji's ideas. It would be fun to see if my body was what he was looking for.

As I got in the car Richard called me.

"My Prince! How was your day?" I asked, admiring his beautiful smile. His beard was coming along nicely.

"Considerably brightened by your note."

"Good, that is always my intention, though I hope you understand that I do them a week in advance to be sure they arrive for you daily. Consequently, they may not always be a perfect match for where we are."

"I *would* go after you," Richard insisted, referring to the day's quote. "Never doubt it."

"How could I? Plus, I'd like to see someone take me away from you. They'd have a fight on their hands. I will only be parted from you if you ask me to go."

"And I never will, so I guess we're stuck with each other."

"Guess so. Are you leaving Rome tomorrow?"

"I am. Are you still expecting to be free next Wednesday?" he asked.

"Yup. Just sweating over my desk at the behest of the Ice Cream Boys."

"Want to spend the afternoon with me?"

"Yes, please."

"Good. 11:00?"

"I'll miss you on Saturday."

"Have fun with your focus group and enjoy the house party. Is Marie cooking or are you having it catered?"

"Ooooh, listen to Mister Moneybags wondering how we're spending his money."

Richard laughed. "I just hope you *are* spending some of it."

"Sorry. Steph and I are cooking. Marie is temporarily demoted to *chef de partie*...until it comes to dessert. We've tasked her with making the flan."

"What's the menu like?"

I explained our plans for the Southwestern buffet. (I think he was impressed!)

"I had no idea you cooked," he said.

"Confusicius say, "Man sit for long time with mouth open before roast duck fly in.""

Richard laughed.

"Cooking sort of goes along with eating for those of us in the 99%. Particularly, us girls. And you know how much I like to eat."

"Well, I will put you in an apron and force you to make me some of those enchiladas when I come home."

"Just an apron? Sounds pretty sexy to me. What else will you force me to do when you get home?" I wondered.

"To make love to me in as many ways as you can imagine."

"You'd better keep up your strength, Handsome. I have a pretty big imagination."

"Good. In the meantime, you should get a DHL from me today. I sent a copy of Italian *Vogue* for you. Be sure to read through it carefully, there's something in there I think you'll enjoy."

"Well, the 'reading' part may be a little difficult. You know I'm not that fluent yet." Even as I said it I realized I hadn't made any moves toward including my language training in my new regimen! I made a mental note.

"You'll recognize it when you see it, I promise." For a moment he just looked at me.

"What?"

"I'm so happy you're you."

My turn to laugh. "Who else might I be?"

"No clue."

"Well, barring a severe blow to the head, I expect to remain myself. Good thing it's something you like."

"Your self is something I love. But you know that."

I looked at my watch. "I've got to get a move on. I'm on my way to yoga."

"Tell Maybe 'hi' for me and meditate on how much I love you. I'll wake you up in the morning."

"I love you more," I reminded him as he hung up.

I headed to the gallery to deliver my week's notes for Richard. They included the first of the pictures that Steph had taken. I was planning to start slow and work my way up to the sexier ones, so the first "naughty" image Richard would get was me in the fedora and trench coat with the collar turned up. I was anxious to get his reaction. I figured I'd send one every three or four days. After he received them, I could put the images he'd seen into his private file on the computer. He could hardly carry the hard copies around in his pocket!

When I got home there was a DHL envelope waiting for me on the table in the foyer. Marie usually brought my mail to my desk, but she must have wanted to be sure I got that one as soon as I returned. I left it there and went upstairs to put on my suit. I wanted to get some laps in. Steph and I could look at the magazine over dinner.

I was asleep by the pool when Steph joined me.

"There's a DHL from Richard for you in entry."

"I saw it. He sent a copy of Italian *Vogue*. There's something in there he thinks I'll be interested in. I thought we could look through it while we eat."

"I hope it doesn't depend on me reading anything in Italian," she said just before she dove in.

I laughed.

We showered and when we came downstairs for dinner, I grabbed the envelope as I passed. At the table Steph opened it and started flipping through the pages.

"Do we know what we're looking for?" she asked.

"Nope. He just said there was something in there he thought I'd enjoy. I warned him that if it required a lot of reading I might not get it."

"OMG!" Steph squealed.

"What?"

"Well, reading doesn't seem to be required," she said as turned the open pages toward me.

There was a double page spread, with the picture of me in the necklace, the one where I had just looked up to see Richard. The only words there were *BARSANTI,* Giano's logo and *ROME • PARIS • LONDON • NEW YORK • BEVERLY HILLS • PALM BEACH.* I took the magazine from her.

I was gobsmacked. I didn't know what to say. The photo was gorgeous. They had adjusted the background and blended it into a nondescript brown-gold-y color that popped me out and made it easy to focus on that beautiful necklace and the earrings. My arm was extended and resting on the back of the empty chair next to me, so the bracelet and ring showed, as well. Wow! I looked beautiful, so beautiful it was sort of hard to believe it was me.

"You look amazing," Steph said. "And it doesn't look like they over-photoshopped you. You look exactly like yourself glammed up. What were you looking at?"

She'd seen the pictures Giano had given me from that night but hadn't asked.

"Richard. He'd just come back to where I was sitting."

"Well if anyone wants to know what love looks like, there it is."

I checked my watch, picked up my phone and sent Richard a text:

GOT VOGUE. FOUND PIC.
GOBSMACKED!!!
SOON...XXOOJ

"Did you know they were going to use your pictures?"

"I signed a release but I never thought they'd find something like this to do with them. I don't know what to say."

"I guess now you're officially a model."

"That's what you said on Sunday," I reminded her.

"If millions of people are going to be looking, I think it's for the best that this is the photo they see!"

11
Home Within A Home

Friday, August 2

Note of the day:

In your eyes are my secrets that I've never shown you.
In my heart I feel I've always known you.
In your arms there's a comfortthat I never knew.
You're what I've been waiting for,there's no one like you
    —Lyrics to *There's No One Like You*

Marie worked with me in the kitchen on Friday morning, putting the beans to soak for the refritos and getting the green chilies roasted, chopped up and into the pot. Chopping onions, crushing garlic. It smelled good already!

Around 11:00 Antonio appeared and asked where I wanted the big screen set up. I decided that under the covered portion of the patio was probably the best bet and I had him put it against the house so the view and ambient light wouldn't be a distraction. The seating there was comfy and I hoped it would help my focus group focus!

He mentioned there were also canvas drapes to block off the covered area if light or weather was an issue. He suggested I have him hang them on that end, just in case I decided to do my program while it was still light.

Brilliant! I could do the presentation before dinner without worrying about the Margaritas affecting anyone's judgment.

"Do you have any interest in participating, Antonio?" I asked.

"I will be your bartender tomorrow."

This surprised me…when Steph and I entertained everyone just served themselves!

"You can still participate. I'd love to have your feedback, unless you'd rather not. I've already talked Marie into it."

"I would be honored," he said, flashing that gorgeous smile.

I checked on my pots and then went upstairs to get my lunch. Marie was going over our lists.

"Steph should be home around 2:00, so I can take her salsa ingredients down."

"No need. Everything is down there already."

I was dismayed. I never intended this to keep Marie running up and down the stairs for us.

"Marie, let us do the toting up and down. We didn't mean to make more work for you."

She laughed. "We have a lift. Two, actually. Come see."

I followed her and just around the corner of the kitchen, she opened a cabinet and there was an impressive-sized….well, I'd always called things like that (which I'd only seen in movies!) "dumb waiter."

She came back toward the dining room and pressed a button. A wide section of the butler's pantry paneling slid away to reveal a large elevator! I clapped my hands together in delight.

"I had no idea. Where is this upstairs?" I hadn't a clue. (Remember, I'm not snoopy.)

"It opens at the top of the stairs, just outside your bedroom. This is how we move furniture, cleaning equipment, art…everything."

"I am so relieved! I've always felt so guilty for running you back and forth between the floors."

"Monsieur Richard allowed me to design this to suit myself. He said I was the one who needed to use it and I should have it the way I wanted it."

"It must be awfully quiet, I've never heard it."

"This one is very quiet. *Très réservé.* I tested six different types before choosing. And the architect also insulated the shaft very well. We were all pleased."

I shook my head. "So many things I still don't know about this house."

"Would you like to see my home?" she asked.

"Do you want to show me?" Of course I was curious.

"Come," she said, as she led me back down the hall and opened the door at the end.

The entryway opened into a large room. On the east wall was a small kitchen with an overhanging counter and bar stools. The south wall was all glass, with a balcony, just like our bedroom above. She had a dining space with a table and four chairs and the west end was the living area, again with glass looking west and the balcony that ran all along the west side of the house on that floor and the floor above.

It was beautiful. The furnishings, which included some antiques and some artwork, was perfect and worthy of any decorating magazine. It seemed Marie's taste was as impeccable as Richard's.

She led me into a little hallway and showed me her bedroom. Again, glass and the balcony. There was a large bathroom that had a second door that opened onto the hallway.

"Marie, do you also have a WATTOR shower?" I asked, noting what looked like Zarathustra's little brother.

Marie laughed. "You have the big boy upstairs, but this is the more practical model for me. It is very nice. I enjoy it."

"I'm still amazed by the mega version upstairs. I love the music Richard programs for me. He can be very funny."

"It is because he is happy. This, you have done for him."

"You know how happy he makes me. I am so lucky."

"You are both lucky to have found each other. I know you are missing him."

"I am, a little. But he's so good about staying in touch and I'm so busy with my own work that so far, we're doing OK. And thank you again for saving those Tshirts. They're a comfort."

She smiled and patted my shoulder, then led me out into the hall and showed me the second bedroom that she was using as an office.

"This couch becomes a bed when I have a guest."

"Do you have company very often?"

"No. But sometimes one of my friends comes from New York or my nieces visit from France."

"Oh, Marie, you must tell me more about yourself. You are such an amazing woman."

She laughed. "Not amazing but very happy. I am so fortunate to have this life. There is nothing that pleases me more than to be right here, doing what I'm doing."

"That's precisely the way I feel! Steph, too. And all because of a certain very special man."

"*Exactement!*" she agreed.

Sunday, August 4

Note of the day:

> *In love are we made visible*
> *As in a magic bath are unpeeled*
> *to the sharp pit so long concealed*
> —May Swenson
> from *Love Made Visible*

Marie and Steph and I were dining on leftovers on Sunday night when I realized it was 8:00 p.m. and time for Richard's wake-up call. I excused myself, and after making them promise they'd save some flan for me, I retired to the comfy couch in the library and grabbed my iPad.

"Your lark calling. Time to greet the day," I said softly when he answered my FaceTime call. He looked sleepy.

"Ummmmm…" he mumbled.

"Another late night, my Prince?"

"Yup. Do you think I'm getting too old for this?"

I laughed out loud. "Hardly! I think you're just grumpy because I'm here and you're there and you feel sorry for yourself."

That made him laugh. "You certainly have a high opinion of yourself."

"Only because you have a high opinion of me."

"That's true. I do," he agreed. "And for many good reasons. What are you doing?"

"Marie and Steph and I have just finished a great dinner of Southwestern leftovers. And they've both sworn to save me some flan for when I've finished with you."

"So it's become a chore, has it?"

"Hardly."

"I'd hate to keep you from that flan," he teased.

"Well, I was hoping for something creamy, but if you have nothing to offer…"

"How about this?" he asked as his very hard penis filled my screen along with his hand stroking it.

"That's very nice. Looks delicious. And the cream part?" I asked innocently.

"Open your mouth. You may have to suck it out…" His breathing shifted. "Or maybe not…"

I focused his view on my mouth, licking my lips and teasing with my tongue. Meanwhile, he was showing me his face and his beautiful smile. (Probably didn't want to mess up his phone!)

"More than a drop, please," I whispered.

"Here…" he groaned. His eyes closed as he came.

I backed the camera off and put two fingers in my mouth, sucking and licking them with a little extra audio for his benefit. And a smile.

"Oh, yes," I whispered, along with some heavy breathing between sucks. "Exactly what I wanted! One of my favorite desserts!"

Richard cracked up. A few moments later he said, "I know I've mentioned this before, but you really need to think about an acting career."

"Silly man. Show me," I said and he gave me another look at his cock. He was still stroking himself slowly.

"You are so beautiful," I sighed.

"I am so lucky you think so."

"I may not be a Trained Professional, but I know beauty when I see it!"

"Well, let's not argue aesthetics this morning. How did your focus party go?"

"It was great and I have so much to tell you. I even took some photos but let's save that for Wednesday. The results of the survey were really interesting and I'd also like to discuss them in detail, if you're up for it."

"Can't wait. You should get a little treat from me tomorrow in payment for the bet I lost."

I frowned. *What is he talking about?*

"How quickly they forget," he sighed. "Your 'suit,' remember?"

"Of course. And here I assumed you'd forgotten"

"Uh…please allow me to point out that it seems to be you who's forgotten."

"It had better be small," I warned.

"It is. And it came from Verona. I thought my Juliet should have something from her namesake's home town."

"Richard! How wonderful!" *That* was exciting.

"I also took the time to go to Juliet's house and leave a note on the wall."

"Like in the movie? What did the note say?"

"If I told you it would spoil the magic, wouldn't it?"

"Maybe." What a guy! "That was so thoughtful."

"Least I could do."

"Well, you have a surprise or two coming your way, as well. Not quite sure when they'll catch up with you, but sometime this week, I hope."

"I'll look forward to that. Meanwhile, I need to get moving. I'll leave you to your creamy dessert in the real world."

"You do know which one I prefer, don't you?" I teased.

"I do. And that's just one of the reasons I love you so much."

"Have a lovely day, Handsome, and remember who loves you."

Monday August 5

Note of the day:

> *The fingertips of love discover*
> *more than the body's smoothness.*
> *They uncover a hidden conduit*

STILL LUCKY

for the transfusion of empathies
that circumvent the mind's intrusion.
—May Swenson
from *Love Made Visible*

On Monday morning Richard's payment for losing that Birthday Suit bet arrived. It was a lightweight gold link bracelet, with a (yes, small) citrine and diamond (or yellow glass and CZs? How would I know?) heart charm that was removable. Very sweet, and most important to me, from Verona.

When he called from Marseilles to say goodnight, I was prepared to show my appreciation and greeted him with a picture of my wrist wrapped with the bracelet, as I stroked a well-lubed Zoor.

"Hmmm….wanting something tonight, are you?" he asked.

"Just to show my appreciation for your amazing gift."

"I'm just about to go down to breakfast. Glad you didn't catch me on the stairs with that view."

"Where have I caught you?" I was giving him a very hot, breathy conversation. It wasn't acting. I'd gotten myself pretty well aroused in anticipation of him being ready to get back on the road. I wanted to be quick for him, but I was anxious to slide onto my rubbery substitute.

"Well…" he said and I could hear him doing something. "In my room and now with my pants around my ankles."

"Really?"

He gave me a view of his feet and then his hand massaging his penis, which was transforming into business-mode.

"Oh…good, because I'm needing a little *La La, La La, La La.*" (I sang that bit.)

"Good. I just happen to have what I think you want. What shall I do with it?"

I caressed Zoor's head slowly, around and around, giving Richard a good look. Then I set my iPad in the spot I'd pre-tested for the view, and positioned myself above Zoor. I bent forward, my breasts close to the camera. I squeezed them and then ran my hands down my body as I sat up straight.

"Are you ready?" I asked.

"Let me in, Sweetheart."

I spread myself with both hands so he'd have a good view and then slowly lowered myself onto Zoor. The inevitable gasp followed, echoed by Richard's groan.

"Fuck me, Richard," I whispered as I began to slowly slide up and down on my new best friend.

"Like this?"

"Exactly. Now a little faster....please..." I lost myself in the sensations and closed my eyes, imagining Richard was really there with me.

"You feel wonderful, Cress."

"So do you. I can't get enough of you. Go deeper. I want to feel your balls against my ass." I increased my speed and took Zoor deep. I could feel my orgasm building.

Richard groaned again and I could tell his hand action was mimicking my strokes.

"Just fuck me," I breathed. I urged my body to that climax and slowed momentarily as it broke. My thighs were trembling and I hoped he could see it.

"Can you come again?" he whispered.

As usual, I responded with, "Yes, please..."

"Feel me, I know you can," he said by way of encouragement as I began to move faster.

"Come with me. Please ..." I rose up off Zoor just enough to grab him and stroke my clit with his sweet smooth head. Back and forth. And then I slid him down and back inside me as I came again.

Richard joined me, at the same time whispering, "I love you."

"I love you more, Magic Man."

12
Memories of Nights Past

Wednesday August 7

Note of the day:

Sleep well: for I can follow you, to bless
And lull your distant beauty where you roam
And with wild songs of hoarded loveliness
Recall you to these arms that were your home.
— Siegfried Sassoon

I was really looking forward to our afternoon together on Wednesday. I spent the morning finishing the next set of quotes for him (complete with a picture every third day!) and putting the finishing touches on my work for Ben and Jerry. Then I added the survey results data to my PowerPoint so Richard and I could look at it together. I intended to share it with the Ice Cream Boys because I had been pretty close on my logic menu choices. I also made a file of the pictures from the party to show him and even had a bunch of videos with everyone saying "hi," of our buffet table, people eating and laughing—I wanted him to know for sure that I was OK, working hard and having fun.

I missed him, but as I'd told Marie, he was so good at keeping in touch that I felt like we were doing OK. Still, the thought of his arms around me…it always created a mini-aftershock. And I admit I did spend a certain amount of time imagining what it was going be like when we were finally together again.

I set up the flat screen at the end of the couch in the library and made sure all the tech components were ready to run, then went upstairs to put on something that might please him. My choices were pretty limited since I still hadn't done much shopping. I finally decided on one of those shirred elastic top dresses. And it was a new one that he hadn't seen. It was a green shade of turquoise, ombré with white flecks in the pattern. It reminded me of the ocean. And I thought he'd appreciate the fact that I was going commando for his benefit. A little trip down memory lane!

I put on my diamond earrings for fun, my new bracelet, and pulled my hair up into a ponytail. I saw myself as looking summery to fit the season. Before I went back downstairs I turned down the bed, tucked Zoor under the pillows along with Bob (just in case) and a couple of towels.

As I passed through the entry on the way to the kitchen I saw there was a small FedEx box from Richard on the table. I picked it up and started to open it, but written in large letters it said, DO NOT OPEN UNTIL WE TALK. *Hmmm...interesting.*

"Smells wonderful," I said when I arrived in the kitchen. "What's on the lunch menu today?"

"Croissants stuffed with ham and cheese, and apple, raisin and walnut salad," Marie said as she pulled a cookie sheet from the oven and slid two croissants onto a plate beside the salad waiting on my tray. "I know you will be talking to Monsieur Richard, but I think this is simple to eat, *non?*"

"*Ouais.* And I may eat it before he calls, not sure how long I can resist!"

Marie laughed. I know she enjoyed my enthusiastic responses to her cooking, all of which were completely sincere and well deserved. I picked up my tray and headed to the library.

"Remember, I'll be taking a nap after lunch," I tossed back over my shoulder (with a wink) as I left.

I'd actually finished one of the croissants before Richard arrived on the flat screen. At least my mouth wasn't full this time.

"*Hey, Good Lookin',*" I sang out when he appeared.

"Hey, yourself. Pretty dress. What's for lunch today?"

"Yummy ham and cheese croissants and a salad."

"Aren't those stuffed croissants great? Marie makes a bunch of different fillings for them. Has she made you her *vol au vent* yet?"

"Nope. Something else to look forward to. As you must know, Steph and I continue to be well fed and we're keeping our hand in by cooking for Marie on Tuesday nights. It's Girls Movie Night now."

"Are you destroying the perfect order of my home life?"

"I hope so. We're having a lot of fun."

"Good. So tell me about the weekend. How did you like having a house party?"

"First let me say I know Mark also suggested it—with your prompting—but it was so much fun! I think everyone enjoyed it as much as I did. I even talked Marie and Antonio into participating in the survey. I think they were pleased to be included."

"So, you're finding the one percenters' lifestyle not all that hard to adapt to?"

"Nope. Steph and I think of it as practice for being the rich girls we're destined to become."

"It couldn't happen to two more deserving women," he assured me.

"I'm positive that's not true, but we're making the most of this amazing gift. Don't think we don't appreciate your generosity. Are you ready for the visuals?"

"I am. Looking forward to it. And I have some for you as well."

And so I showed him photos and my videos from the party with the attendees hamming it up in their greetings to him. We laughed and talked about everyone while I assured him I was enjoying the population of his universe.

"They are such great people. Thanks for sharing your subjects, my Prince. You must really enjoy entertaining a house full of wonderful friends."

"I'm looking forward to doing more of that in the future. It will make a huge difference for me to have you there."

"Aw, guess you still love me, huh?"

"Je t'aime plus qu'hier, moins que demain," he reminded me.

"Good. Because I need to know how you feel about me cutting my hair."

He laughed. "Your hair?"

"Yup. I'm tired of dealing with washing it twice a day and spending time drying it. I'm jealous of Steph and her short do. I'm ready to get rid of it. Any thoughts?"

He laughed. "I think it's your hair and you can do anything you want with it. Feel free to go all Ann Hathaway/Fantine on me. It's funny to me that you'd ask."

"Not taking any chances on chilling your ardor. I'd be crushed if I cut it all off and you didn't want me until it grew out. I couldn't bear to wait that long for you to love me again."

"Somehow, I think you'd be enterprising enough to get yourself a wig if that were the case. And it's hard to imagine anything that would make me stop loving you."

"Really? Anything? What about if I ran off with Ji?"

"I'd miss you and my heart would be broken, but I'd still love you and I'd be happy for you because Ji is a wonderful man."

He sounded perfectly serious and I suddenly burst into tears.

"Cress…"

My turn to laugh. "Sorry. That came out of the blue. I guess knowing that you really mean it hit me in a very tender spot. How can I be so lucky?" I said before blotting my tears and blowing my nose.

"You and Leda," he reminded me, lightheartedly. "By the way, did you get the package?"

I'd totally forgotten, though it was tucked right beside me on the couch.

"Yup. Can I open it now?"

"Please. It's your anniversary gift."

"What anniversary?" I asked as I zipped open the envelope and removed a thick square blue jewelry box. Not one of Giano's.

"Hey! I thought you girls were supposed to be the romantic half of the equation."

"I don't think I hold a candle to you, there."

"Hmmm…you're wrong. That was a pretty hot photo you sent with today's note."

It was the fedora picture with a line from *Romeo & Juliet*: *Tresspass sweetly urged*.

"I'm so happy you liked it. Just a reminder of my own Full Monty I shared with you."

"One glance and the whole night comes back in an instant," he said with a smile. "It's one of my fondest memories. The things you said to me that night meant a lot. Thank you."

"Just trying to keep you from forgetting me."

Richard laughed. "As if… So are you going to open that?"

"First, tell me what anniversary."

"Beautiful girl, it's been two months since the night we met."

I just looked at him. "How is that possible?"

"Well," he began with exaggerated patience. "It's August seventh and we met on June seventh…"

"Richard, I feel like we've been together forever, how can it only be two months? So much has happened…"

"Time is an illusion, Cress. You know that. I think we're just living our 'nows' to the fullest, one right after the other. It's the way we should live life, don't you think?"

He could see me welling up again.

"Sweetheart, what is it going to take to keep you from crying when I give you jewelry? You need to tell me, because I love jewelry and I will be giving you a lot of it, so you're just going to have to find a way to deal with it. Help me figure out what that is."

That made me laugh. "It's the gobsmack factor, I guess. I'm going to work hard at getting over it. Maybe if you just warn me ahead of time…"

"I'll remember that. Open the box. I saw it in a window while I was in Rome and thought it was perfect."

I opened the box and there was a heavy gold curb link bracelet with a rectangular inset of Leda and the swan! It looked like a casting from an ancient coin or a depiction of a Greek statue. *How on earth had he found something so perfect?* Leda images weren't exactly ubiquitous! (Words, remember?)

I'm sure he could see how delighted I was. I took it out and when I undid the clasp so I could put it on, I noticed it had *Lucky Girl* engraved on the back of the image. I wrapped it around my right wrist, next to the "bet" bracelet. I couldn't stop admiring it.

"It's hard to believe that this actually exists, and that it found its way to you and now to me."

"Welcome to my world. I hope you decide to make it your permanent home."

"I never want to be anywhere else, but I have to say I like it best when you're physically closer."

"I know. But we're approaching the halfway mark in my absence. Well on our way to being together again."

"Sweet, sweet man, I live for the moment when I can feel your arms around me."

"Soon. Meanwhile, show me how your survey went."

We spent a while on that. Richard was impressed by how close I'd come to what my focus group chose.

"Now it's your turn," I said. "I want to see where your travels have taken you."

"First, tell me if you've talked to Giano."

"Actually, I have. I called him to thank him for the beautiful ad and he's taking me to lunch tomorrow."

"Good. It makes me happy that you're so fond of him. He can't say enough good things about you."

"He's just another, albeit very important, exceptional human being in your realm. One of these days you're going to have to explain to me exactly how you created this world."

He laughed. "Until then, in the lower cabinets there, next to the closet, are all my self improvement materials. You might enjoy that focus meditation. I still use it quite a bit."

"Have you been holding out on me?" We'd talked about some of those CDs, but I'd forgotten to ask where they were before he left. I'd been so busy I hadn't thought about them.

"Nope. I guess I imagined you'd come across them. I keep forgetting you're not snoopy."

"Is it a bad thing?"

"Not at all," he assured me. "Kinda refreshing, actually. I'm that way myself, and as a kid my friends thought it was quite strange."

"You may be strange, but I love you anyway."

"A fact that gives me comfort every day. Now, let me show you some things."

Richard led me through his PowerPoint and pictures of where he'd been on his drive from Rome to Monaco. I was looking forward to seeing it all with him next year. It was such a treat to have him tell me the stories, to see that he was having a good time and I marveled at the way he approached his travels: open, ready to enjoy whatever and whoever he interacted with. It was that magic energy in action, the thing (beyond his beauty!) that drew us all to him.

When we came to the end of that series I asked about the art he'd mentioned a few days before.

"There's a folder in 2J for you. MAGNIET."

I opened it and slowly went through the slide show.

"How big are these?" I asked.

The paintings were done in bold strokes of vibrant colors and the subjects were common things shown from odd angles. I was particularly taken with an open window that looked out on blue water and blue sky. It was all blue and white and sunlight. It really struck me because it "felt" like I imagined Mykonos to be. I could almost smell the ocean. And the image was three quarters white wall with the upper right hand section being the lower corner of the open window and its sill, with the sky and water beyond in bold slashes of color. It was still very abstract but, to me, quite obviously a window on the sea. I realize it may be hard to picture from my description, but it was an image that seemed non-objective and at the same time was representational.

"I really love that window!"

"Great minds. That was my favorite, as well. It's about sixty inches by eighty inches wide. I love the juxtaposition between the subject matter and the unconventional angle of presentation."

"Wow! Talk about having words."

"TP."

"Say what?"

He laughed. "Trained Professional, remember?"

"Sorry, TP has only one connotation for me. We'll have to find another shorthand."

"OK. But what do you think? It would be somewhat of a departure from what we usually show, but I'd kind of like to give her a shot. I was curious to hear your reaction."

"Well, you know the only work I associate with the gallery is the strings and suitcases, so I don't know anything about other artists you show beyond the ones you have here in the house. I did notice that the paintings in your gallery office were easy for me to like."

"I'm a little surprised you noticed."

I laughed. "Well, I was focused on something else at the time, but after you went back into the gallery, I took time to look at them more closely. Not snooping. They were, after all, hanging there on display."

I was still looking at that window painting. "What's the price of that piece? Can I afford that window?" I wondered where that came from. *Me, buying art?* But, wow, that one really made an impression. It was like Richard's designation of Buyer Number One when he'd described the types of people who buy art on the night we met. I was definitely having a visceral reaction to that painting.

"The window she has priced at 6,000EU."

"Oh. Well, so much for that plan. Maybe when I'm a mogul I can shop for art. But then where would I put it? It will be nearly impossible for you to pry me out of your house now, and your empty wall space is somewhat limited."

Richard laughed. "Maybe when you're a zillionaire you'll want to build yourself a mansion somewhere."

"I can't imagine being anywhere besides here with you. But I suppose I could buy us a little hideaway for us for private vacations somewhere and I could buy art for that."

"Something to start imagining."

"Meanwhile, I vote for you having her work. I think it's great and it should appeal to a broad range of buyers."

"I'm so looking forward to next summer and you interviewing artists with me," he said. "It will be wonderful to have your take on the work because you're coming from a completely different place."

"Can you really say that, knowing I would never have favored strings and suitcases?"

"Sure. The odd things are easy. It's some of the very different but more conventional work I need a second opinion on."

"Well, I can promise I'll always have an opinion."

"Good. What's your opinion of this?" he asked as he unzipped his pants and exposed his flaccid penis.

"It looks like it needs some loving and I'm just the girl to do it."

"You certainly are. How about a quick one now and then we'll take our time upstairs?"

"Sounds good to me, but what brought that on?"

"I suddenly realized you're probably commando under that dress. At least that's been your habit in the past when you wear that style. Will you show me?"

"Hmmm…" I said looking down at the top of my dress.

STILL LUCKY

I rolled down the top edge very slowly and continued to pull it down, watching as the elasticized fabric rolled over my nipples (hard now!) until my breasts were exposed. I studied them and looked up at him expectantly.

He was smiling as he stroked himself with one hand and fondled his testicles with the other. He was almost completely erect.

"What about down below?" He was trying to keep his voice even.

I smiled as I slowly began to raise my skirt, as if I, too, were curious or maybe just couldn't remember if I was wearing panties or not. I cocked my knees then spread them wide, which made the skirt fall between, keeping me covered.

Richard gave a little groan.

"What?" I asked innocently.

"Show me, Cress."

"What do you want to see?"

"That hot wet place where I wish I could put my mouth right now."

"Your mouth?" I teased, acting like I had no idea what he was talking about.

"I want my tongue inside you, I want to taste you. I want to suck your clit and listen to you come."

I heard his breathing shift, a telltale sign he was close to coming, himself.

"What would you do with that, then?"

"Exactly what I am doing."

I pulled my skirt up and gave him a pouty lip as I fingered myself. (Dripping!)

"But I wanted you to put it here. I wanted you to fuck me." I did my best to sound disappointed, even knowing a close encounter with Zoor was in my immediate future.

"Oh, I'll fuck you, but right now there's only one thing I can do."

"What's that?"

He got closer to his camera and caught his cum in one hand while he sort of milked himself with the other. He groaned as he slid the handful down over himself, stroking the sticky mess of it. It was very exciting to me and I gave myself a quick rub and came right behind him.

"It feels so good, my beautiful girl."

"It looks so good, my Prince. I wish I could taste you."

"Close your eyes. Maybe you can."

He was right. I knew the taste of him, the feel of his semen in my mouth, the texture of his penis. I came again. Wow! Memories, eh?

13
A Crown for My Prince

Wednesday, August 7

Note of the day:

> *How do I know you good?*
> *Because, dear love,*
> *In needing you,*
> *My inmost soul most urgently desires*
> *Great goodness too;*
> *Pure skies alone can win a turbid sea*
> *To perfect blue.*
> — Louisa Sarah Bevington

No sooner had Richard disconnected our FaceTime than my cell rang out with *Magic Man*. I answered to hear an iGram of *Afternoon Delight*. Funny boy!

He "met" me again upstairs about fifteen minutes later. He wanted to clean up before we settled in for his bedtime and my "afternoon delight." (Delightful for both of us!) He showed me the view of his face in the mirror over the sink. He'd just gotten out of the shower.

"How are you feeling about the facial hair?" he asked as he offered several views.

"Actually, I think it's hot. The only thing I don't like is where it grows down your neck."

"Here?" He pointed to the upper part of his throat.

"Would it look weird if you trimmed that off? You'd still have the beard on the underside of your jaw, just not down your neck where it sort of runs amuck."

"*Amuck*, is it?"

"I don't know. For some reason the scruffy stubbly beard doesn't look unkempt to me, but the throat hair does. Maybe it's because you don't have a bunch of chest hair growing up onto your neck."

He cracked up. "I'm afraid I can't do anything about the absence of chest hair."

"I wouldn't want you to. I love that hard bare rippling part of your anatomy....along with a number of other parts."

"Care to elaborate?"

"Really? I thought I gave you a detailed accounting of how I felt about all of your parts."

"Indeed you did. Still, I never tire of hearing how much you adore me."

"Gees...glad to hear you're not having trouble keeping your ego in check." I had to laugh. "Seriously, look around at guys who have those beards and see if they trim their throats. I'd hate to have you do it and then look odd."

"It might be a relief to look odd, me being so handsome and all." He could hardly keep his face straight.

"Got a full length mirror there, mister?" I asked. I needed to see all of him.

"Yup." He went into the bedroom of his elegant hotel room and faced a wall of mirrors for me.

"You're right. You *are* so handsome." I sighed. (I realize you may be tired of hearing how beautiful he is, but I never tire of looking at him and I suspect you'd feel the same way if you saw him.) "Show me those buns, big boy."

He cracked up but turned around, holding his iPad over his shoulder. He flexed his ass and gave it a smack. My turn to laugh.

"What do you think? Will you let me in bed with you?" he asked.

"Even if you do seem to be little full of yourself at the moment, I feel a need for some afternoon delight and you seem to be the most convenient purveyor of such things."

"Interesting, since I'm halfway around the planet."

"Exactly. You're the closest member of the opposite sex I have any interest in spending the afternoon with in bed. Besides, I'd like to be full of you, myself. Will you join me?" I asked as I held the camera in one hand and reached out to him with the other.

I settled into bed with my surrogate squeeze (wearing his Tshirt) and my warmed Zoor in his anatomically correct location in relation to the pillow. Where Richard's head would be, I propped my iPad.

"How may I please you, my love?" Richard asked softly. The teasing had dissipated as we lay down.

"I want us to lie here in each other's arms for a few minutes. I want to imagine you and the length of you against me."

"Where's Zoor?"

"In his proper location, pressed against my belly as I hold you close."

"Then close your eyes, Sweetheart and listen."

I did as he instructed and cuddled my pillow. I inhaled the smell of him.

"You smell so good," I said with a sigh.

"I'm smelling your perfume. It seems such a perfect scent for you. I can't smell that without thinking of you. I told you, I take one of your notes to bed with me each night so I can fall asleep imagining we're together."

As his words continued to bring my lover to life, I pressed myself more tightly against his alter-penis and felt those balls shift against me.

"You feel so good, Cress. Running my hands over your body only reminds me how beautiful you are."

"It's making you hard, too, if what I'm feeling between us is any indication."

"I love you. It's the natural result. I want to share myself with you"

For a full minute I just savored the feel of him.

I wanted us to take our time so to slow the inevitable I asked, "What are you doing tomorrow?"

"I ran into some friends at Monte Carlo and they invited me to sail over to Corsica with them."

"Ooooh, Mister Fancy Pants, sailing off to Corsica, probably with a Grimaldi or two on board."

"Uh…actually…"

"No!"

"Well, a royal cousin. My family, their family, wine connections in Monaco…"

"The world of the one percent," I giggled.

"Aren't you the woman who just told me how much she was enjoying that lifestyle?"

"Yahbutt…"

"*Yahbutt* what?"

"Yahbutt…*I* wanna sail off to Corsica with you!" I said all pouty.

"Next year we'll add that to our itinerary. I'd love to take you to Corsica. Maybe it's the place for that little hideaway you were thinking about buying art for."

"Hmmm…Meanwhile, think you can distract me from my jealous thoughts?"

"Probably. Throw that beautiful leg up over my hip. Let me see if you're ready for me."

I hooked my leg up over the pillow and angled Zoor against myself. I wasn't quite prepared to accommodate him, so I let my hips move against him as he pressed for entry.

"Not quite," I breathed.

"Let me touch your breast, Sweetheart."

My hand took the place of his as I caressed myself, tugging gently at my nipple, imagining his mouth on me. Moments later the thrust of my hips opened me and Richard heard my gasp. It was followed by his own soft groan.

"Oh…" (I've mentioned how good he felt to me many times so let's just say "ditto" and leave it at that!)

"Cress…"

I let Zoor stroke me on Richard's behalf. I wanted to prolong the sensations and just kept moving slowly.

"Are you going to come for me, Sweetheart?"

"I'm resisting."

"Why?" He sounded puzzled.

"Because you feel so good, I don't want it to end."

"It won't end until you're ready, until you ask me to come with you."

"Promise?"

"I do. I'm with you for as long as you need me."

"As long as I *want* you," I corrected. (Even in the throes of passion I maintained my feminist perspective! *Go Girls!*)

Richard chuckled. "You don't need me?"

"Nope. I have Zoor." (This said as I continued moving, picturing Richard moving in and out of me as we both watched!)

My stating of the obvious was greeted with silence.

"Whatsa matter, Handsome? Your ego take a hit?" I whispered.

"Nope. But I've got many things Zoor doesn't have."

"Like?" I tried to sound normal but my orgasm was just about to explode.

"Like the heart that drives that cock you're so full of at the moment," he growled.

I tried to laugh and squeal at the same time. The result was a strangled sort of squeak as I came.

"Yeah, that one. And I'm not done."

"Good," I said between breaths. I shifted my angle just a little and came again.

"More? There's more here for you, Cress."

I came again.

"You may not need this but it seems like you want it." His voice was husky.

"Yes!" I laughed as I came again. Richard going all macho on me was hot and my body and I were having a great time.

"I'm not done with you," he reminded me.

"Good. Don't you dare stop 'til I'm GTF."

"Don't worry. I'm not stopping 'til you beg me to."

"I'm liking this, so don't hold your breath."

"Let's see if I can make you hold yours." He said that, sounding for all the world like he was fucking me hard and it certainly felt like it. Zoor was getting a workout and I was loving every minute of it.

"Open your mouth," he said.

I did, moving closer to the camera, not knowing if he was looking at his screen or not. I didn't care, I was in the midst of another orgasm.

Richard groaned loudly. I watched his eyes close, a sweet and ecstatic expression on his face. I gave him a minute.

"Uh....I don't recall begging you to stop..."

He laughed. "My bad. Good thing Zoor is indefatigable, eh? Can you come again for me?"

"Yup!" and I did. And then I was ready to quit, even if Zoor wasn't.

For a minute neither of us said anything.

"Uh, what happened there, exactly?" I asked. "Here I was planning a tender session rocking you to sleep and if you'd been here in person for that we might be making Harry Potter references by now.

Richard cracked up. "We might, indeed. No clue where that came from. I wasn't expecting it either. Are you feeling GTF?"

"Lord, yes. How 'bout you?"

"Well, I think I should sleep pretty well. And good thing. I need to get up early and get ready to sail."

"La-dee-fuckin'-dah, my love!"

Thursday, August 8

Note of the day:

> *"All that I ask," says Love,*
> *"is just to stand and gaze, unchided,*
> *deep in thy dear eyes;*
> *For in their depths lies largest Paradise.*
>   – Ella Wheeler Wilcox

After my meeting with the Ice Cream Boys in the morning, I met Giano for lunch at Chez Mimi in Pacific Palisades. The hostess showed me to his table on the patio and as usual, he stood and greeted me with open arms and double kisses.

"Cressibella! It is so good to see your beautiful face."

"I'm happy my face pleases you. The ad was absolutely beautiful. Thank you for choosing me, though I confess it was quite a shock."

"Why a shock?" he asked with concern as he pulled out my chair for me.

"I guess I never expected you'd use the photos in international advertising."

"But you are not displeased?"

I reached across the table for his hand.

"No! Of course not. I am unbelievably flattered! It's an exquisite photo and I look almost as good as that incredible necklace!"

"It is you that makes the picture, *Bella*, not the necklace. Do you not see it is a photograph that captures *Amore* itself?"

I laughed. "That's what my friend Steph said."

"Of course. The love in your eyes is obvious. It is something people need to see, something they must be reminded of. Of course it does not come from a necklace, but we hope they don't notice that part!" he said with a wink.

"Well, you have certainly allowed me to see myself in a different light. In that picture I can actually admit I look beautiful."

"You are beautiful, *Cara*. Surely you know this?" He sounded sincerely puzzled.

"I know people find me attractive, but I can honestly say I never really felt truly beautiful until I met Richard. He almost has me convinced."

"You need only look in a mirror. Your love shines out from your soul. Nothing makes a woman more beautiful."

"Giano, your skills in flirting and flattery are unmatched."

"Bah," he said with a wave of his hand. "I speak the truth. Nothing more."

Time for a change of subject.

"So tell me about this restaurant. How did you find it way out here?" I was curious. There were certainly plenty of great restaurants within a mile of his store.

"I have known Mimi for many years. She used to be on Robertson and when she moved here, I could not abandon such wonderful food. You must tell me what you think of her cuisine when we have eaten."

I let Giano order for me and when our food arrived I could see why he had followed Mimi to Pacific Palisades. I also developed a passion for aioli! Good grief, I couldn't imagine how I'd never come across that before. And Mimi's bread was as good as Marie's, so I was anxious to ask Marie to add aioli to our menu. Steph was a garlic lover, too, and I was pretty sure she'd share my new obsession.

I had a perfect quiche and Mimi's fabulous *frites* (that I dipped in aioli!) Oh, dear! I wasn't sure it fit in with my new fitness regimen but I couldn't have cared less.

Giano's conversation was a delight. He told me about his other stores—the ones I saw listed in the ad—about traveling between them, shows with some of his own pieces that were circulating in museums around the world.

While we waited for dessert, he reached into his pocket and pulled out a distinctive yellow ring box and handed it to me.

"It is Riccardo's ring. Tell me what you think."

I opened the box. There, nestled in his signature taupey-grey velvet was exactly what I had envisioned when I explained to Giano what I wanted him to make for me. I took it out and slipped it onto my pointer finger to admire. My eyes began to fill.

"This does not please you?"

I had to laugh. "Just yesterday Richard told me we had to find a solution to my reaction to jewelry. It usually brings me to tears. Apparently, even when it isn't for me."

I couldn't take my eyes off the ring. It was just what I'd asked for and yet Giano's artistic skill had made the proportions exquisite yet still masculine. It was a narrow band on the bottom, topped by the same posey band and words as my ring—*vous et nul autre*. Atop that was a crown in relief, and finished with another narrow band. In the center point of the crown was a small diamond and very tiny ones in the other points all the way around.

"Giano, I see diamonds." I was accusing him of going beyond my budget.

"Yes. Only very small ones. I thought it a better match for your own ring."

"And how much did those add to my bill?" I was teasing him. I fully expected he'd lie to me.

"Only $211. They were such a nice addition that I resolved to follow my artistic inclination and include them. If you don't like them, they can be removed. I will also be happy to assume the expense since I went ahead without consulting you."

I smiled. "Giano, I love the ring, diamonds and all. It is far more than I'd imagined. Your impeccable work has created another masterpiece, and even though I suspect you haven't been truthful with me about the cost, I appreciate it and I know Richard will, too."

I looked inside and saw the words I'd asked be engraved there: *To my Prince with love from your Juliet.*

"When will you give it to him?" Giano asked.

"I haven't decided. I'll find the perfect moment, preferably when he's home again, but something could happen that would make me want to send it to him."

Giano looked at me. He was smiling.

"Riccardo is a very lucky man, and one who is deserving of the gift of your love."

"I strive to be deserving of his."

14

Trade Agreement

Sunday, August 11

Note of the day:

And in Life's noisiest hour,
There whispers still the ceaseless
Love of Thee,
The heart's Self-solace and soliloquy.
— Samuel Taylor Coleridge

I arrived at Seiji's studio at 8:00 a.m. on Sunday morning. We had talked on Friday and decided on a "bed" set up. He'd asked me to bring two flat sheets and a couple of pillows, so between those and the gym bag I'd packed with a few things, I looked like I was leaving the house and heading for a slumber party!

Seiji had built a platform about two feet off the floor and put a double-size futon on it. He'd already set up lights and on two sides had hanging white background paper.

"Are you up for this?" he asked as he showed me the set.

"Yup. Wanna help me with the sheets?"

He did and we spread them over the futon and tossed the pillows in the middle before he showed me to the dressing room.

"I didn't intend to put on any more make-up than I'm wearing, unless you think I need it. Since my face won't really be showing and the set is 'bed' it didn't seem necessary."

"I think you're good to go. I'll be ready when you are."

I was only wearing one of my shirred top dresses and a thong, so I think I surprised him when I quickly reappeared in just a little short cotton wrap robe and holding Zoor casually by his shaft. I handed Seiji the digital card I'd brought for the camera.

Seiji smiled, but I saw his surprise when he spotted Zoor.

"Isn't he beautiful?" I asked as I proudly balanced him on the palm of my hand, business end up.

Seiji came out from behind the camera for a closer look. He was polite enough not to handle my friend.

"I'm stunned. I have to say that's the most beautiful dildo I've ever seen. Where did you get it?"

I could hardly tell him it was a cast of my lover's penis—talk about TMI!—so I simply said, "It was a gift. Obviously pretty personal but much appreciated!"

I had to laugh. Sort of an odd discussion to be having with someone other than Richard! I'd never even shown Zoor to Steph.

Then I demonstrated the realistic scrotum and pinched it so he could see the shape of the Neuticles inside. I could tell he was really impressed.

"If there's any way you can find out where it came from, I'd sure be interested in knowing. THAT is a beautiful penis. Seriously, it's a work of art."

"I agree. I've become very attached to him." I added a wink.

Before I shed my clothes, I'd given him my sketches for the three shots I was thinking of: A close up of Zoor penetrating me, Zoor between my breasts and me tonguing him, and one of him in my mouth. I assured him if he had any other ideas I'd be happy to hear them.

"If you're ready, why don't you take off your robe and let me look at you with an eye to seeing you as a model. That way, if I think you suit my ideas, we'll have more options on the shots I do for you."

I removed my robe and waited for his assessment.

"You're lovely, CJ," he said as he moved around me, studying my body. He squatted down several times, looking at me from different angles.

"Do you want me in a different position so you can get a closer look or in a particular pose?"

"Why don't you climb up on the bed and lie on your back."

I kicked off my sandals and lay down and he continued to move around me. Surprisingly, I felt no embarrassment. I just felt like an artist's model. There wasn't any sexual vibe, although he was focused on me. I was surprised I couldn't read him, but I was hoping we could make the trade. I'd begun to think it might be nice to have some additional shots for Richard that did show my face.

"Can you turn on your side, and sort of balance, keeping your legs together? Now move your arm forward so I can see the line of your side and hip."

He continued circling me, studying me from different heights.

"Now, if you'd lie on your stomach with your legs together"

Next he asked me to do a yoga cobra position, then on my hands and knees, and then with my chest down and my bottom still in the air, knees apart, offering a pretty clear view of my nether region.

"That's fine," he said.

He was smiling when I sat up.

"You're perfect. If you're sure you don't have any reservations about my project, I'd be really happy to have you as my model."

"Great! I'm excited for the opportunity. And can't wait to see what other ideas you have for my shots. I've actually been thinking I might like some sexy but not explicit poses that could show my face. I think Richard might appreciate some that other people could see."

"I'd love a chance to try to capture that expression you had in the jewelry ad."

"Then you saw it?"

"I did. It's beautiful. One of my friends at the agency that books for that company forwarded the shot to me before it went into the magazines. He was over the moon about it."

"Magazines…as in more than one? So far I've only seen the Italian *Vogue*."

"I think the buy was for several. You can ask the jewelry people."

"Giano's a friend. I'll have to see where else I can expect to turn up!"

"It was a spectacular shot, especially for a candid photo. To capture that moment so perfectly… What were you looking at?"

"Everyone asks that. Richard had just come back to our table."

"Well, let's try for a few more of those 'love' shots for you."

STILL LUCKY

We spent the rest of the morning on the poses I mentioned and then Seiji took a number of less explicit shots of me. Some wrapped in the sheets—suggestive but not really showing anything. I mussed up my hair to look GTF and we did a few of those. Then he had me hold my hair up on top of my head and he got some of the side of my face, neck and shoulder. I was anxious to see them.

A little before noon Seiji shut the lights down.

"We've managed to get some really good ones. I think you'll be pleased. But I'd like you to consider something."

I looked at him as I put my robe back on.

"I'd really like to have a whole day of your time. I can pay you or we can trade another half day. I sort of think we've exhausted this series but maybe you have some other ideas? I can also pay you if you prefer. That would be about $2,000."

Wow! Suddenly I'm a model worth $500 an hour?

"I'm so flattered, Seiji! I would love to trade. Would you consider taking some shots of Richard when he gets back? I'm not really thinking portraits and I'm not thinking anything explicit either, but he is incredibly beautiful and I wouldn't mind some of him or of us together."

"That's a great idea. It would give me a chance to meet him and maybe get a foot in the door. If he's interested I could show him some of my pieces."

"Just remember not to show him anything where he can recognize me as the model. At least until we see his reactions. I don't think he'll mind me modeling—he's very open—but as I told you before, I don't want to do anything that might cause a problem for him with his businesses."

"Of course. Why don't you get dressed and we can compare calendars and find a day when you're free."

We decided on the following Saturday. Steph would be with Michael and I was free. Richard was driving to Paris and not expecting me to be available.

He helped me fold the sheets and put them in my bag, then carried my pillows out to the car for me.

"Seiji, I can't thank you enough. Can I give you a hug?"

"Of course." He laughed and gave me a squeeze.

"Thanks again. I'm looking forward to a successful run as your mystery model!"

So how did the shoot go?" Steph asked when we sat down to dinner.

"Seiji is really easy to work with and it turns out I'm suddenly worth five hundred dollars an hour to him, so we're doing a trade. I'm going to model for him and in exchange I got some extra shots. Plus he owes me a few more and I'm hoping I can get Richard to be photographed when he gets home."

"Are you going to force poor Seiji to take porn shots of you and Richard?"

She was obviously appalled and I cracked up.

"Hardly, but you have to admit Richard is beautiful and I'd love a glamour shot or two of him, or maybe the two of us together. All G-rated for friends and family. Seiji also took a few of me that are model-y, naked but covered. I'll look at them after dinner."

Steph was excited about a new idea for a painting that had come to her over the weekend.

"Those Michael injections, maybe?" I suggested as I stuffed another piece of Marie's bread into my mouth that had been dipped in the aioli she now made for us. (Steph was equally enthusiastic about it and if the two of us were constantly reeking of garlic, Marie had been too polite to mention it!)

She laughed. "Maybe. Or maybe just being really happy leads to more ideas."

"It certainly works for me. So when can I see what you've done?"

"I'm not ready to show you yet. I want it to be a surprise, but you'll be the first to see, I promise."

"Has Michael seem them?"

"Nope. Maybe we'll have a little celebration with the three of us when I'm ready."

"Well, you can count on me to be there. I'm so happy for you."

"So where are you with the Ice Cream Boys?" she asked.

"They're almost ready to start sending out a few discrete feelers to see who might be interested. We're putting together a promotional PowerPoint. I should have the rough version ready for this week's meeting, but do you think I could get a consult with Michael first?"

Steph picked up her phone and punched up Michael.

"It's me. CJ has a question for you." She handed me the phone.

"Hey, Michael. Is there any chance you'd have time for a consult between now and Wednesday night?"

We decided he'd come for dinner the next day. I offered Steph's charms by way of enticement and he laughed as he agreed to take me up on it. I handed the phone back to her so she could say goodbye.

"I'm so excited. I know he'll be able to tweak it for me. I promise to share the wealth when it comes rolling in!"

"You go girl. No matter how well I do with my paintings, I'll never be in the tax bracket you're likely to end up in."

I laughed. "I think we both know now that the number of figures in the bank balance isn't what counts as long as there's enough. Nothing compares with working hard at something you love, right?"

"I'll drink to that," Steph said as she lifted her glass. "And a hot hunk on the side never hurts, either!"

"Ditto!"

Steph went upstairs to catch up her emails so I headed for the library to take a look at the photos and start on Richard's notes for the week. I'd missed our wake-up and good night calls since he left on the boat for Corsica. He had phoned when the times coordinated and they were on shore, but those calls had been brief and not appropriate for more intimate conversations. Zoor was good company but not the same as when he was paired with my lover's voice and visuals, and certainly not the same as having Richard there in the flesh! Still, there was plenty to keep me busy and I had put in a little extra training. Ji was going to help me with the salmon ladder on Friday. I was feeling pretty strong and hoping I could surprise him.

Well, I was blown away by the pictures Seiji had taken. It is so interesting to see yourself through someone else's eyes. Like the shots of me in the necklace from the gala, it was difficult to get my head around the fact that the woman in the photos was me. The graphic porn-y ones gave me a hint of what Richard found so exciting about the visual aspects of the two of us together. Steph's photos of me were more playful, tease-y things where the shots Seiji had taken were… well…beautiful. He had suggested I look at them first in grayscale, rather than color, and sure enough, it transformed them into serious art photography. Even the ones of me and Zoor looked as though they could hold their own on a museum wall.

The "bare but covered" poses were exquisite and things I wouldn't be embarrassed to show my folks. I emailed my three favorites upstairs to Steph. The house phone buzzed a couple of minutes later.

"All I can say is wow! I guess you really *are* a model. You have to show these to Michael, though I suspect there are a few others in that batch that neither you nor I would want you to share!"

I cracked up. "You're right, of course. Can hardly wait to see what Seiji does with Richard as a model. I'd love a shot of Richard and me just looking at each other."

"It might melt the camera! I swear you're picking up his energy stuff. Sometimes I can feel it rolling off of you."

"I can only hope. Not sure exactly what it would be good for unless I can figure out how to share it with the people I care about."

"Use it on the art buyers at my first show."

"I doubt any extraordinary efforts will be required for those little red dots to start surrounding you work."

"One of these days we'll find out, but for the time being, save some of your newly acquired power for me, will ya?"

"Absolutely. Meanwhile, I need to get Richard's notes done for this week.

"He's a lucky man."

"I'm a lucky girl."

15
At A Loss For Words

Tuesday, August 13

Note of the day:

> *Is there anything sweeter than this hour?*
> *for I am with you, and you lift up my heart—*
> *for is there not embracing and fondling*
> *when you visit me*
> *and we give ourselves up to delights?*
> *If you wish to caress my thigh,*
> *then I will offer you my breast also…*
> >   —Ancient Egyptian

A little before lunch on Tuesday Richard called.

"Ahoy, matey. Are you finally back on solid ground?" I asked.

"I am and have settled myself into a guest suite at our partner winery at Fontvielle, where I found several of your notes waiting." He sounded tired.

"I hope you didn't open them all at once."

"Nope. I'll space them out with the incoming and treat myself to two a day until I catch up. Thanks for putting numbers on the envelopes. I've noticed you have little themes running through them—mini-series, if you will."

"My, aren't you the observant one."

"Need I remind you, *yet again*, that I am a Trained Professional?" he said with a snooty offended tone.

I cracked up. "I only wish you were here to show me just how well trained you are. So which note have you opened today? "

"Number 27."

"Do you like it?"

"I'm really enjoying the Egyptian things. How do you find them?"

"Research to while away the lonely hours until you return," I told him with a sigh.

"Somehow, I have the feeling you're keeping busy."

I laughed. "No pulling the wool over those beautiful eyes. I'm not lonely either, but I do miss you."

"Ditto. So what are you doing?"

"Writing notes to my lover."

"Hmmm…should I be jealous?"

"Nope."

"OK. Would you like to share part of your day with me tomorrow?" he asked. "I got a little off schedule with that impromptu excursion to Corsica."

"Can hardly wait to hear all about your trip. I've missed you, my Prince."

"I've missed you, Sweetheart. But I'm a little frayed tonight and can't do you justice. Can we save it for tomorrow?"

"Only if you promise I can have my favorite dessert with my lunch. And I need some serious *La La La La La La*, too," I sang.

He laughed. "I've got some *Ooh La La La La La La* I've been saving for you," he assured me, emphasizing the *Ooh*! "We'll have your whole afternoon tomorrow and then you can tuck me in. I have to hit the road again on Thursday."

"I'm counting the hours."

"I'll FaceTime you at 11:00. Meanwhile, remember I love you."

"You can refresh my memory, tomorrow."

He was laughing when he hung up.

STILL LUCKY

Wednesday, August 14

> *Sometimes he is slightly smiling,*
> *but mostly he just gazes at me gazing,*
> *his entire face lit.*
> —Sharon Olds, *The Knowing*

At 10:45 I got a text from Richard:

Apologies. Delayed. Will connect at 11:30. Promise. Remember ILYM.

I was disappointed but found I had butterflies in my stomach as I set up the flat screen and tucked Zoor and Bob between the cushions. It was almost like first date nerves, which was silly, of course, but it seemed like forever since we'd had any intimate time. I'd dressed for the occasion in a little bronze lacy bustier (Yes, I'd paid Victoria a visit last week in my restless longing for my lover!) and matching pair of split crotch panties. I removed the panties. Split or not, I wanted to be sure he had a clear view. I'd even gotten a pair of sheer but sort of iridescent bronze stockings that looked great with a cheap pair of chase-me-fuck-me slides that matched.

I was wearing a sleeveless maxi dress over it all so as not to embarrass myself or Marie when I went to get my lunch. The shoes, however, were a dead giveaway that something was *afoot.* (Ha! Couldn't resist!) Marie was quite capable of guessing what it was!

"You tell Monsieur Richard that I say he is a very lucky man," she told me with a wink.

"I hope he hasn't forgotten, but I intend to give him a very pointed reminder! And remember, I'll be taking a nap this afternoon."

"I've already turned down the bed for you."

I hugged her. "Marie, what would we do without you? I'm so happy to know you."

"Enjoy yourself, my friend. It is I who am happy you have come into our lives."

I swear, I was so emotional I could have burst into tears. So much for sexual tension—or was it sexual frustration? Maybe it was just love. And the funny part was that it hadn't hit me hard until that morning. The anticipation, I supposed.

I'd opted for a smoothie so I was finished before Richard came on. I'd also decided to get right to it. He'd kept me waiting long enough! So I removed my maxi and sat on the couch, facing the camera and the flat screen, with my knees up and my legs crossed. The view was my head, shoulders and legs from the knees down. Shoes and stockings were visible, but not any portion of the center of me or what—if anything—I was wearing.

"Whoa!" Richard said in surprise when he saw me.

"*Life is uncertain. Eat dessert first.* It's my new motto and I'm taking it to heart. I hope you're somewhere where you can serve my treat properly."

"I'm in my room. I excused myself and said I had some work I needed to catch up on."

"Work is it? And after so long?" I displayed a pouty lip.

"It seemed a more polite excuse than announcing that the woman I love was almost as anxious as I am for some long distance sex."

"I see. So what do you have for me?"

"Well…"

He pointed the camera away as he crossed the room and stepped out onto a balcony and panned the view. It was spectacualr but I wanted to see something else.

"Excuse me, but who are you and what have you done with the man I love? You know, the one who insists the mere thought of my charms instantly triggers his transformation into a love machine? The one who used to tell me he wanted to kiss me all over."

"This one?" he asked as he pulled the camera close until his beautiful eyes filled the screen.

Aftershock!

"Yes! That's him! Charming, I thought I'd lost you! Are you safe, my love?"

"Safe and missing you. And I have the dessert you requested. It will be ready in a minute," he assured me. "Why don't you show me what you're wearing?"

Very slowly, I straightened my legs. Now he could see the bustier, but because the couch was squashy and my bottom sank into it, he couldn't tell that I'd skipped the panties. (OK, he could probably *guess*, but it wasn't obvious!)

"Very pretty, Cress."

When he didn't say anything else—he was just looking at me, sort of amazed and grateful at the same time (my interpretation!)—I slowly raised my leg and hooked it over the back of the couch as I slid down a little, displaying something that I assumed might interest him.

Apparently, it did because he groaned.

"Where's my dessert?" I asked pointedly.

"Right where it always is."

"Show me," I said as I started to slowly finger myself. I pulled the camera closer.

He turned toward his fly, slowly unzipped it and with a little difficulty released his penis, which was more than ready for me.

"Hmmmmmm....looks delicious. Standing or sitting?" I whispered.

"Sitting," he said as he dropped his pants. He gave me a good closeup of him fondling his testicles before he settled into a chair.

I shifted my iPad for a good shot as I moved Zoor up to the back of the couch, surreptitiously slipping Bob into me as I began tonguing my Richard substitute. His view only showed Zoor and my mouth and part of my face. I licked and sucked, Richard groaned. Same old, same old, but it was nice to have him digitally nearby.

"I've missed the taste of you," I whispered.

"I've missed your mouth."

"I want more than a drop..."

"Don't worry..." His breathing shifted.

I heard him come and took Zoor deep, imagining the pulsing, imagining the taste of him, imagining...while I moved on Bob. As I came, I continued to run my tongue over Zoor's head, hoping my lover was mimicking my moves as he recovered.

"Thank you, Handsome. That is exactly what I needed," I said with a wink.

"Me too, but I wasn't expecting your dessert to be served before we shared the week."

"I trust you're not complaining?"

"Do I sound like I'm complaining?" he asked.

"Noooo..."

"I just have a lot I'm anxious to talk to you about, so it surprised me."

"Good. I enjoy surprising you."

"You're very, very good at it," he assured me.

"I can't say I'm a Trained Professional *like some people*, but I do what I can."

"And you do it very well."

I stood up and started to pull the maxi over my head.

"Wait. Give me one long look first."

I did some cheesy modeling for him, even with the bend-over-and-look-back move. Then I stood waiting, hands on hips .

"You're probably getting tired of hearing this," he said, "But you *are* beautiful."

"Honestly, between your comments and Giano's advertising, I'm starting to believe it. He told me love makes me beautiful."

"Well, I thought you were beautiful the first time I saw you, but the love has added energy to what you project of yourself."

"Flattery will get you everywhere, but can I cover up now? If I don't I'm afraid your attention may wander."

"I can't argue with that, but Cress, you know the way I feel about you has nothing to do with what you're wearing. And speaking of appearances, did you change your mind about the haircut?"

"Nope, just haven't had time. I'll get to it."

"Give yourself a break, Sweetheart. All work and no play…"

"I know. I've just been trying to get this PowerPoint together for tomorrow. I had Michael come over on Monday and tweak it for me. I'm really happy with it but I want to know what you think. There's a copy in your 4R folder."

We watched it together.

Richard pronounced it excellent. "Just enough info to make someone curious but not enough to give them anything to steal. I bet Ben and Jerry will be really impressed."

"Michael was a huge help. There's not much arty about me."

"Don't sell yourself short. You just haven't had time to think about much beyond your project."

"And you," I reminded him. "I think about you quite a bit."

Richard laughed. "Yes, and me. I haven't felt neglected, not even a little bit. Thank you for that."

"Well, it's difficult, but a girl's gotta do what a girl's gotta do."

"I'm grateful every day that what you do is me."

"Good, because I need some help with language."

"You? The woman who knows words?" he said.

"Yup. I'm looking to expand my vocabulary and need some synonyms. I've searched the web and the Thesaurus Rex on your shelf and haven't found anything."

"I'm not sure I'm your best bet, but I'll give it a shot."

"OK. Other words for *love* and *beautiful*."

Richard just stared at me.

"I'm serious. I keep telling you how much I 'love' you, but I can't figure out how else to say it. I'm the word girl; I should be able to express myself with a little more variety. And ditto with 'beautiful.' When I tell you you're beautiful I don't mean you're pretty or exquisite or lovely. I mean you're *beautiful*—your physical self but also the person you are—your soul, all of you. To me the word 'beautiful', like the word 'love', is sort of a mega-concept that means many things, but both words seem diminished by anything that replaces them. Am I making any sense?"

I saw and felt Richard's focus shift, but I couldn't identify his new target.

"I find it fascinating that this is something you've invested some time in."

"Are you being a smart ass?"

"No! Not at all," he assured me. "I'm serious. That you would devote that complicated brain of yours to this question is really very interesting."

"Interesting, how? Like it might look good on commitment papers or something?" I know I was frowning. I had spent time thinking about it because I was constantly using the words with him. I just wanted to change it up and say the same thing in different ways, but somehow I couldn't solve it. It was annoying!

Richard laughed softly. "Cress, it is interesting to me when I try to discover how your mind works. And maybe more to the point, I have a feeling it's a conundrum you've conveniently passed off to me. I may have trouble NOT thinking about this!"

"Ha! That'll teach you not to mock me!"

"I sincerely hope you never have reason to think I'd mock you. I'm just constantly surprised by the things you do and say. It's a good thing, Sweetheart. I can't imagine I'll ever find you predictable."

16
Shop 'Til You Drop

Still Wednesday

"Well, before we descend into the labyrinth of *that* discussion," I said by way of changing the subject, "tell me about sailing to Corsica with the royals."

I opened his file and followed along as he described the photos. There were even a few short video clips of his friends saying "Hi" to me and toasting me, telling me they were looking forward to meeting me next year, congratulating me for capturing "the Hunter."

His friends seemed nice, like fun people—typical of his kingdom. There were three couples—one of the women was really beautiful—plus Richard and an older woman. He led me through the names and backgrounds.

Corsica looked incredible. I hoped we really would be able to go there together. I was fascinated by Bonifacio at the southern tip of the island. It seemed to be precariously perched more than two hundred feet above the water on a long narrow finger of limestone that had been deeply undercut by the sea.

"Is the water really that color?" I asked. It was a beautiful shade of turquoise.

"It is. I just love that little town. Can't wait to show it to you. There are shops and little hotels along the water—the *marine*—and two ways to get up to the *Haute Ville*—a steep staircase at the far end of the harbor or you can walk up a broad street lined with businesses that ends at a saddle overlooking the sea on the east side of the island. From there you can turn left for a nice walk up a narrow cobbled path and along the ridge, or go right and make your way up and into the high part of town over a drawbridge and under a defensive portcullis. The city was pretty impregnable in the twelfth century."

"I can't wait to see all the ancient buildings on that side of the Atlantic. What we think of as old here is no comparison."

Richard laughed. "I'm planning next summer will be mostly just for us traveling with a few minor stops as we go through wine country. And what we don't get a chance to do next year we can schedule for the one after."

"It's hard to imagine. There's so much I want you to show me."

"I intend to be an amazing tour guide."

"A tour guide with benefits?"

"Absolutely!" he whispered seductively.

"I expect nothing less."

He continued the description of his travels and ended with the winery in Fontvielle, a small town near Arles in the south of France. It was an old estate and he had many images of the grounds. There was a manicured garden in front of the warm colored stone building that had a pretty double staircase. He took pictures of the chapel and the olive grove. The chateau was being restored and the estate specialized in wine and organic olive oil. I mentally put it on my "must visit" list!

"There is something about this region that seems so familiar to me, and this place in particular." He hesitated for just a moment. "I don't really know why, but I just feel very comfortable here."

"It's beautiful."

"It's more than that. You'll have to see how you feel when you see it in person. I've always loved Provençe. My family used to spend the summers down here. This is Van Gogh country. I'm sure you'll find some of the landscapes familiar."

"I hope you know how lucky you are."

"Every time I look at you, Sweetheart."

I smiled. "You silver tongued devil. I mean, to be able to travel to such wonderful places and to do it with such ease."

"The money helps."

"I'm sure it does, but I was referring to the way you open yourself up to all those experiences. The people and places are amazing, but from my perspective, what you get out of it seems to be a great deal more."

He just looked at me.

"Am I wrong?" I asked.

"No. That's exactly the way I try to approach everything I do. Opening myself to whatever life brings results in so many unexpected rewards. Like you, for example."

"I'm happy to be the grand prize. I hope you'll always feel that way."

"Can you imagine any reason I wouldn't?"

Actually, I couldn't. "Uh…no…"

"Good, because neither can I. And we can't create what we can't imagine."

We talked until 3:00 p.m.—midnight for Richard and past his bedtime—so I suggested it might be about time for me to rock him to sleep.

"There's one more thing. I need you to do something for me." He sounded very serious.

"Name it."

"I suspect you'll resist but I'm afraid I'm going to hold you to your frequent declaration that you'll do anything for me."

"Hmmmm…intriguing," I said. "Well, name it and it's yours."

"I want you to go shopping."

I frowned. "For what?"

"Clothes, shoes, accessories. The ladies in the office have mentioned you haven't put a dent in that Amex card."

I laughed. "I have everything I need, Charming."

"You are on the verge of some serious fortune creation and should dress the part. You'll be meeting with prospective investors. Make them think you don't really need them all that much and that you have others to choose from."

"And this is done sartorially?"

Richard cracked up. "Good one. But, yes. So promise me. You will spend $5,000 on things to wear in the next week."

"FIVE THOUSAND DOLLARS?" *Seriously?* I couldn't imagine how much I would have to buy to run up that tab.

"And no fair spending it with Giano," he insisted. "You can go over and above with him, of course, but $5,000 on clothes, shoes, and bags."

"At least that would be easy with Giano. Richard, what am I going to do with all those clothes? I mean seriously…"

"When you start shopping the upper tiers and spending three hundred to five hundred dollars on a pair of slacks, it will add up fast. I'd be surprised if you knew you could spend $600 on a pair of jeans. A nice leather jacket can run you into four figures."

"Good lord, where do you shop? The day will never come when I spend $600 on jeans, no matter how much I love you. That is ridiculous! Somebody is yanking your chain."

Richard shook his head, apparently conceding, but I have to say not very graciously.

"What are you doing tomorrow?" he asked.

"Ben and Jerry at 10:00 a.m. and that's probably an hour to an hour and a half. Nothing else lined up yet."

"Good. Go to the gallery afterward and take Mark to lunch. He'll take you shopping again."

"I am a grown woman. I can certainly buy myself clothes," I said indignantly.

"I know you can, but I doubt you've ever been to the stores Mark will introduce you to."

"Is this a snob thing?" I was suspicious. I crossed my arms and gave him a very defiant and penetrating look.

Richard shook his head and laughed. "You know how I feel about sharing the wealth. And I think you'll be surprised how nice it is to have really good clothes. You appreciate my cashmere hoodie, don't you?"

I couldn't help smiling. I adored his cashmere hoodie.

"You know I love your hoodie. But maybe it's just because it's yours."

"Maybe it's because the cashmere feels so good on your bare skin?" He wiggled an eyebrow at me.

I smiled. The photo of me in that hoodie should be arriving for him in the next few days. I sighed.

"Is that a begrudging 'yes'?"

"Yes. I'll call Mark this afternoon and plan on shopping with him tomorrow. But no $600 jeans. No matter how you beg."

"OK, I grant you that on the jeans. I swear convincing you to enjoy the finer things in life is like pulling teeth. I'm hoping it will get easier."

"I already have the finest thing this life has to offer. What more could a girl want?"

"Now who's doing the sweet talking?"

"There's more where that came from," I hinted.

"I'm counting on it. Give me fifteen minutes for a quick shower and I'll call you back. Can't wait to pull you into my arms and remind you how much I love you."

"I'll meet you in bed," I promised.

"I'll be there shortly."

I went upstairs and put Zoor in hot water in the bathroom sink. No chilly willies for me—unless they're attached to Richard and quickly transformed! Zoor retained heat but wasn't much fun when he wasn't thoroughly warmed. I closed the bedroom drapes and turned on the lamps. I thought it would make it seem a little more like bedtime for Richard.

When Zoor was up to temperature, I dried him and got into bed with him and my Richard's-Tshirt pillow. While I waited, I sent a quick text:

Got a mirror? I need a nice long look at your 'word-for-beautiful' *body!*

When he appeared on my iPad just a few minutes later he was all there, pointing the camera at his reflection in a full length mirror that seemed to be on the back of the bathroom door.

"Thanks, I needed that. I admit I love to look at you. You're so…fill-in-the-blank-with-a-word-that-means-beautiful!"

Richard cracked up. "How about devastatingly handsome? Remarkably good-looking? Unbelievably attractive? Sizzling hot?"

That raised my eyebrows! "Well, it's pretty obvious 'modest' won't be in there anywhere!"

"I'm just grateful you like the way I look. What would I have done if you'd never given me a second glance?"

"More importantly what would I have missed?"

"I don't know. What *would* you have missed?"

"A life I could never have imagined in my wildest dreams," I admitted with a sigh. "And a man I'm still not sure is real."

"I'm real, Sweetheart, and I promise to prove it to you when we're finally together again. Meanwhile, believe, and enjoy the things we can share at a distance."

"Have I mentioned how much I pick-a-word-that-means-love you?"

"Love is the right word and you know I feel the same. Have you seen enough?" he asked.

"Never enough, but come to bed with me, Handsome, and wrap those beautiful arms around me."

I kept our connection until Richard was asleep and then got up, tidied up, slipped into my bathing suit and one of the elastic top dresses and returned to my computer. I called Mark.

"CJ, how are you?"

"Not completely pleased with you and your boss ganging up on me."

"Come on, you know you love having me as your personal stylist. Look how the gown I picked propelled you to international supermodel stardom."

I had to smile. He was right, of course.

"OK, I'll give you that one."

"That was only the beginning, I assure you. Let me help you pick your wardrobe and the sky's the limit. You'll have stories of success and good fortune and even some about fending off creeps like Malcolm."

"Uncle!" I laughed. "I'll see you tomorrow when my meeting's over. And I'll have a new batch of notes for Richard. He goofed up the flow of my correspondence by sailing off with the royals."

"You can't blame him, can you?"

"Nope. I'm just jealous, but he's promised to take me next

summer, so I guess I have to forgive him. And before I forget, do you know Richard's friend Chris, who works at Universal?

"Sure, Chris Stanton.

"Do you have a phone number? I have a SPFX question for her."

"Let me check the boss's contacts."

He found the number and repeated it to me.

"Thanks. I'll come to the gallery after my meeting. Maybe you can talk me into some fashion over lunch."

When I finished with Mark, I called Chris. I got her voice mail, introduced myself as Richard's friend and asked her to call. She rang back about ten minutes later.

"Hi, CJ, it's Chris. What can I do for you?" Seems she was nothing if not direct.

"Hi, Chris. Thanks for calling back. I think you've already done something pretty special for me."

She laughed. "Well, it's actually not the strangest project I've ever tackled, but it was certainly interesting. I have to say Hunter was really great about it. The process is no picnic."

"So it seems. I saw the *Spartacus* bonus features."

"A person's head is one thing, something as changeable as a penis is a different thing, entirely."

"Well, you did a remarkable job of it and I wanted to say I'm grateful. And I have a question for you: Would you consider making another one?"

"Have you had a problem with it or do you just want a spare?"

"Neither. I have a photographer friend who asked me where I got it. He thought it was beautiful and was wondering if he could get one."

"Hmmm…I'm not sure I should ask how a photographer happened to see such a personal item," she said with a laugh.

It was my turn to crack up. "I was having some photos taken for Richard—it's a long story, but one I'd be happy to share with you when we finally have a chance to meet in person. Meanwhile, are you interested? It's such a magnificent thing that I'm sure you could charge a premium."

"Does he want Hunter's cock instead of a duplicate of his own?" she asked.

(As I said, direct!)

"That was my impression. He has no idea whose cock it is or even that it's a casting rather than a sculpture, and I assume Richard would want to remain anonymous. The photographer is hoping to have a chance to show with Richard's gallery, so I didn't want to involve Richard in the process. They haven't met yet. And soooo... I called you.

"If you're interested," I went on, "I can give him your number and you can make any arrangement with Richard that's necessary. I'd just prefer that I'm out of the loop on this, at least while Richard's still out of town. I was hoping it might be an opportunity for you to make some money. The photographer's quite successful with his commercial business but hoping to branch out into fine art. He's also a great guy."

"Well, have him call me. I'll find out what he wants. Then, if I need to, I can talk to Hunter to see how he feels about it."

"Thanks, Chris. I hope we get to meet one of these days. You're certainly an artist and I think you must be my kind of girl since Richard told me you appreciated the perfection of his asset."

Chris cracked up. "He probably told you I'm into women, but that cock of his is a work of art all on its own! You're a very lucky woman."

"I am, indeed, and thankful every day. I'll have Seiji call you. I suspect you'll be hearing from him sooner rather than later."

I decided that if I was going to be trying on clothes the next day, I'd better get my hair cut first. I called the salon and got Skye (yes, really!) who had been cutting my hair and Steph's for the last couple of years. I told her I needed it cut and she said she could take me at 11:30. I said I'd be there and then called Jerry and moved our meeting to 9:00 a.m. An hour should be enough with the Ice Cream Boys since, basically, we were just going to watch and go over the new presentation.

I called Mark back. He was with a client so I asked Lynda to tell him I had to push our lunch back to 1:00 or 1:30. I said I'd call with an update as soon as I knew. *Gees, is this what moguls have to deal with?* When the money came rolling in I was thinking my first hire would be a personal assistant! And I had to smile because I was proud of myself for handling it all so efficiently. Maybe Richard's focus CD's were starting to work!

17
Bonjour Fantine!

Thursday, August 15

Note of the day:

> *Even*
> *After*
> *All this time*
> *The Sun never says*
> *To the Earth.*
> *"You owe me."*
> *Look*
> *What happens*
> *With a love like that.*
> *It lights the*
> *Whole Sky.*
> —Hafiz

You Light up my life! XXOOJ

As predicted by my lover—a Trained Professional, if you recall—Ben and Jerry were impressed with the presentation. After all our time together they were finally accepting me as a business woman (!) who knows her way around her project and is able to explain it coherently. I'm sure the potential profit factor had urged them along in that direction. The possibilities were huge and now it was time to find the money to support my dream.

Then on to the beginning of the new me. Well, not really

the beginning—that started back when Steph and I set up our new fitness regimen. And I'd also been diligent with both the language programs and the focus training. It was amazing to me how I seemed to have left my slug-like existence behind. And, OK, relaxing on a warm towel by the pool still felt really good in the afternoon, but all the extra physical pursuits had raised my energy level, despite the continuing hours spent at the computer. It surprised me, but I was enjoying my new lifestyle. Now, it was time for the next step: the haircut!

I got to the salon about twenty minutes early and Skye was able to take me. Her earlier appointment had cancelled.

"Hey, CJ, great to see you. You look fantastic! Are you in love or something?"

"Actually…" I began as I followed her toward the shampoo chair.

"Really? Then Stephanie wasn't kidding when she said you were head over heels?"

"That's the pot commenting on the color of the kettle!"

Skye laughed. "And is Michael as hot as she says he is?"

The warm water felt great along with those massaging fingers. I closed my eyes.

"Oh, yes! No matter what she said about him, be assured she wasn't exaggerating. He's gorgeous and a great guy, to boot. He treats her like the princess she is."

Skye sighed. "Sure aren't enough of those kind of guys to go around. So tell me about yours."

I tried to give her a very measured, general overview. No names and vague about his businesses. I did tell her he was in Europe for the summer and that Steph and I were housesitting.

"From Stephanie's description, it sounds like a really sweet deal. She's so excited about having the summer to do nothing but paint. Have you seen any of her work?"

"I think she's waiting to have some pieces finished, but I'm anxious to see what she's done." I was so excited for her.

"So," Skye said, as she raised me in the chair at her station, "What are we doing today?"

"Cut it off, all of it."

She looked at my reflection in the mirror. "Are you sure?"

"Yup. I'm swimming twice a day now and I'm tired of messing

with it. I want it short enough that I don't even have to use my dryer. Ann Hathaway in *Les Miserable*."

"Really? You have such pretty healthy hair."

"It will still be healthy if it's short and if I don't like it, I'll grow it out again."

She took a long hard look at my face to be sure there was no indecision behind my words. Apparently seeing none, she combed it up into a loose ponytail.

"I assume you want to donate it to Locks of Love?"

"Absolutely!" I'd be free of it and someone would benefit. A win/win.

She took one last look at me as her scissors were poised between the rubber band and my head.

"Go for it," I said, confidently.

And she did. She was still watching me. I know going from long to short can be traumatic for some women, but I was so incredibly happy—and so sure I wouldn't be causing any problems with my Prince—that I was relieved and anxious to see what the new me would look like!

Skye started combing and snipping. It surprised me that there was so much time invested in a short cut, but I was really excited to watch it take shape…what there was of it. When she was satisfied, she kind of scrambled what was left with her fingers and reached for the clippers to shave my neck.

"Wait just a second," I said as I reached for my cell. "How long do you think?"

She shook her head. "It's a whole new program. Maybe five minutes, seven max."

I checked my watch and gave the gallery a quick call to let Mark know when to expect me.

Skye did blow my hair but it literally took less than a minute. She gave me a sample of some waxy stuff so I could spike it if the mood struck me and then, with a flick of my AMEX card, I was out the door.

Wow, it felt great! I was tempted to visit Giano and pick up some earrings now that they could be on full display. *Hmmm…might have to do just that. It will please you-know-who!* With my neck uncovered I was feeling quite swan-like. And then I had to laugh as I thought of that other lucky girl, Leda. I was even thinking of taking Mitzi the Mercedes for a spin so I could feel the wind in my hair. Amazing what a trip to the salon can do for a girl!

Lynda, Christina, and Mark were all excited about my new look. I'd resigned myself to the shopping trip and, honestly, I was feeling so good about my hair that I know I surprised Mark by not whining through our lunch. I even managed to be interested in the clothes he suggested at our first stop. By the third store I was bordering on enthusiastic! And I hate to admit it, but Mark and Richard were right: the high-end clothes, just like those high end shoes I tried on when we were shopping for the gala dresses, did feel terrific.

Who knew? Well, the one percent have probably always been privy to this information, but it was news to me that there was such a huge difference besides the plethora (yup, word girl, remember?) of digits on the price tags. And you know what? The fancy-schmancy stores do custom alterations, serve champagne, and basically make parting with your money seem painless. I guess for me it *was* painless because a certain good looking guy I knew was picking up the tab. I managed to relax into the process and stopped looking at the numbers. Maybe it was the champagne.

We finished off at two different shoe boutiques. Oh, my! By then I was willing to let Mark choose whatever he liked and I tried them all on, admiring my reflection in the mirrors conveniently located at floor level and masking the rest of a customer's body. There was a full-length mirror as well, but it was kind of fun watching that "other" pair of feet match mine, step-for-step, as I walked around the store.

"I'm really proud of you, CJ," Mark said we drove back to the gallery. "You have exceeded the boss's minimum requirements for today and it doesn't seem like you found it too painful."

I laughed. "I hate to admit it, but I had a great time. And that's thanks to you, of course. I'm on the verge of giving up the fight on the money-spending thing. If I can't beat him, I might as well join him. Did he tell you I drew the line at $600 jeans?"

"He did, and honestly, I can't blame you on that one. I wear Levi's 501s, myself. If the pants fit, wear 'em."

I gave him a high five.

"So, how's the long distance love going?" Mark asked.

"I miss him, as you can imagine. We spend time together every day and usually manage one whole afternoon a week. He's been great about taking lots of pictures and providing me with a travelogue. I can't wait for him to show me all of it in person next summer. And I've been busy with my project, as well as the time required to create the new me. I'll have a few surprises for him when he gets home."

"How do you think he'll like you hair?"

"I did ask him if he cared if I cut it and that struck him funny— you know, that I was asking permission. He did promise me he'd still love me, even if I went skinhead."

Mark laughed. "That's the boss in a nutshell. I hope I can be like him when I grow up."

"Me, too!"

Friday, August 16

Note of the day:

> *That is the great distinction between the sexes. Men see objects, women see the relationships between objects. Whether the objects need each other, love each other, match each other.*
> —John Fowles, *The Magus*

> *We match! I see it! XXOOJ*

At 10:00 a.m. Friday I was enjoying a second mug of Marie's coffee and feeling all full of myself. I had managed (with admitted difficulty!) two rungs on the salmon ladder that morning. Ji was impressed and I was determined to improve my technique before I tried for three. I wanted to look good when I showed off for my hunk!

My cell rang out *Magic Man*.

"*Wherefore art thou, Romeo?* And yes, I know that's not the correct usage of *wherefore!*"

He laughed. "Sweet Juliet, Princess of Proper Usage. Have I mentioned I love you?"

"Not today."

"Well, I do."

"I'm depending on that," I reminded him.

"For what?"

"Oh, I don't know...life, breath, existence?"

"Gee...who knew?"

"I think if you ask a certain Trained Professional I'm acquainted with..."

"I yield. The match is yours."

"Is there a trophy involved, perchance?" I hinted.

"Hmmm...a trophy or some sort of prize. We'll have to see about that. Now, to your question..."

"What question?" I was distracted by my body's reaction to the sound of his voice. *Was there a question?*

"I believe you asked, albeit improperly, where I'm calling from."

I glanced at my watch. A little after 6:00 p.m., his time.

"Can you FaceTime me back on your laptop?"

"Is everything OK?" I could hear the concern in his voice.

"Yes, I have a surprise for you that requires visuals," I explained with an air of mystery.

"At this hour of the morning?"

"Well, you *are* falling behind in your duties as my lover, but not *that* kind of surprise. Nevertheless, it's something I think you'll enjoy."

"*D'accord. Un moment,*" he said slipping into French.

Richard hung up and about three minutes later appeared on my FaceTime and was treated to a view of the new me.

"Wow! Beautiful! Are you happy with it?"

"I love it. For some reason it's very freeing. I'm even thinking of taking one of your pretty little convertibles for a spin so I can feel the wind in my lips and my hair at the same time."

Richard laughed. "Do it. Take Steph, drive up or down the coast and take yourselves out for a fancy dinner. Just don't forget who loves you. Meanwhile, I want to tell you how proud I am that you're beginning to drop your resistance to spending money. Mark said you found some great clothes and ran up a respectable tab. He also said there wasn't even a hint of whining. It sounds like you got some really nice things."

"I have surrendered—mostly—and I hate to admit it, especially to you, but I actually enjoyed it. It has something to do with the haircut, but I can't quite put my finger on it yet."

"Maybe it's a Samson thing. Your resistance was in your hair."

My turn to laugh. "Maybe. When I left the salon I was entertaining thoughts of a visit to Giano for some earrings to accentuate my swan-like neck that's now on view fulltime." I ran my hands slowly down the sides of my neck, turning my head one way and then the other. I tilted my head back and closed my eyes as my hands slipped down to cup my breasts.

"Hey!"

"What?" I said, batting my eyes innocently.

"Don't tease me."

"You deserve what you get. No rocking me to sleep last night and no wake-up call this morning. And me all alone in my hot and sexy new hairdo."

"Who are you kidding? You've always been hot and sexy. As I said in my text, I drove late last night so I could get to Tours today. I wanted to be here to take some pictures of the flower market tomorrow for you."

"Really? All that to take pictures for me?" I was suspicious.

"I do have some wine business here, but I thought you'd enjoy seeing the flowers. Can't wait to show you."

"Can't wait to see it all with you. Can't wait to see all *of* you."

"Well, I think I can promise you a wake-up call tomorrow wherein I can give you the attention you deserve. What time do you prefer, Milady? I am at your service."

"Five will be fine. I have things to do tomorrow."

"What things?" he asked. I know he was surprised I was getting up so early on the weekend.

"Mogul things. Besides, now that I've taken over your schedule, sleeping in isn't as easy as it used to be!"

Saturday, August 17

Quote for the day:

> *Where we love is home –*
> *home that our feet may leave,*
> *but not our hearts.*
> —Oliver Wendell Holmes

There's no place like home! XXOOJ

My wake up call was all my Prince had promised and I arrived at Seiji's studio promptly at 8:00 a.m. on Saturday. (Probably with "cheeks like the blush of a pink rose" as Giano had described being GTF!) Seiji gave me a hug when he opened the door for me.

"Hey, CJ. Great to see you." He studied my hair. "I like it. Are you ready for your close-ups?"

"Ready, willing, and anxious to see what you come up with."

He took me into the office and gave me the release to read and sign. It had a non-disclosure agreement that protected my identity. It was a short document, and to the point and I signed it without hesitation.

"So how do you want to start?" I asked.

"Do you have some sort of cover-up that won't leave any marks on your skin, you know like waistbands or elastic?"

"I've got my short robe and one of those strapless cotton dresses with the shirred top. It's not tight on me, and doesn't leave marks. And I'm comfortable in the buff if that's what you prefer."

STILL LUCKY

He smiled. "Try the dress for a start. It might make it easier for you to be partially covered. You may be surprised but a lot of the areas I want to focus on are pretty innocuous."

It was interesting to watch Seiji work. He was able to see things that I never would have been able to notice or focus on. One of the most astonishing images to me was my toes. This is hard to describe but I'll take a shot. Cross your leg across your knee, then push your big toe down and sort of lift your other toes. He got a shot—from the inside edge of my foot—of that odd shaped space between my big toe and the next toe, the sort of u-shaped negative space that I would defy anyone to identify. (OK, maybe a podiatrist would recognize it!)

He also did the wrinkly part of my elbow, the outside edge of my hand from little fingertip to wrist and made it look like a horizon. There were a few genital shots, but most of what he was interested in were curves as edges, like where my breast connects with my body. Honestly it was fascinating to see the things he came up with. And the lighting was a big part of it, emphasizing shapes and planes. To me, a whole new way of seeing.

When we broke for lunch, I shared Chris's number with him. "She's a special effects artist at Universal Studios and I guess she's the one who made it. I have no idea if she has more, but you're welcome to talk to her."

"Thanks. I'm interested in the photographic possibilities, though the practical applications are intriguing," he said with a wink.

I had to laugh and hoped I wasn't blushing. "It's a piece of art for sure," was all I said. "There's something else I wanted to ask you. Have you ever considered shooting a black man for the same type of series as this one? My trainer is African and very dark with a totally sculpted body. I know he does modeling for artists and I thought you might want to shoot some of the same shots you've already done again—as opposites, you know, positives and negatives?"

Seiji just looked at me.

Suddenly, I realized I might be offending him. "I'm sorry, is that some sort of artistic *faux pas*? Telling you what to do with your vision? Forgive me and remember I'm a computer geek!" I laughed.

"No, actually, it's an interesting thought. A very dark skinned guy might make a great contrast."

"He's incredibly beautiful and a truly nice man. I can give you his number if you want to meet him and see what you think." I added Ji's contact info to the sheet I'd brought with Chris's number.

"You're just full of surprises, aren't you?" he said with a little amused smile.

"Hmmm…you're not the first person to say that."

I parked in front of the house. Steph pulled in behind me as I was getting out of Connie with my gym bag and pillows in hand. Michael had flown north again earlier that morning and wasn't going to be back until Monday afternoon.

"Wow! Great hair! How does it feel?"

"Terrific!"

"Once you go short, you never go back," she assured me.

I laughed. "It easy to see why. I really like it so far."

"Where have you been?" She nodded toward my armload.

"My first professional modeling booking," I said with my nose in the air.

"Well, lah-dee-fuckin'-dah. Suddenly, she doesn't mind being so beautiful," Steph said sarcastically.

I pony-stepped my way to the front door, swinging my hips dramatically. "When you've got it, flaunt it," I added.

Steph cracked up. "Are you sure you don't want to take another look at a career on the stage?" She took the pillows from me as we went in.

"Funny, Richard says the same thing…and he insists he's not just referring to porn!"

"Well, if Internet mogul doesn't turn out to be your thing, you can try flaunting what you've got. If my art career ends up in the toilet, I'll come looking for a job as your choreographer, as you previously suggested."

I hooked my arm through hers. "Then I guess no matter what happens, we'll be OK, eh?"

"No doubt about it. But can we hang on to our hot lovers a little while longer?"

"Lord, I hope so! I don't mind a change of career, but I'm pretty happy with my current hunk, even if he's halfway around the planet."

"Where exactly is he these days?"

"Due to arrive in Paris sometime tomorrow afternoon."

"*Ooh-la-la!*"

"Exactly. Want anything from Paris?"

"Nope, but sure would love to get to the museums there one of these days!"

"I'll put that at the top of my mogul list: *Take best friend to Paris*."

"Can I bring Michael?"

"Yup. While we're waiting to see which direction our lives will be taking, how about a swim before dinner?"

At eight that evening I retired to the library and gave Richard his wake-up call.

"*What light from yonder window breaks?*" I asked when he picked up.

"None. I have the drapes closed."

He didn't sound his usual playful, early-morning self.

"My Prince, art thou unwell?"

He chuckled. "No, just tired. Late night and a long day on the road with no beautiful girl to love me to sleep."

"What? No beautiful girls where you are?"

"Actually, quite a few and a couple might have volunteered, but none of them had what I needed."

"And what would that be?"

"You, Sweetheart."

"Awww…Do you want me to give you a few more hours?"

"Yes. Can you call back in three? I'd like a nice leisurely wake-up call, but I'm not up to it at the moment."

"Rest well, Handsome. Talk to you soon. Just remember who loves you."

18
When I Say You Suck…

Sunday, August 18

Note of the day:

> *The only real meaning in life*
> *can be found in a good man.*
> *And maybe in Paris.*
> *Preferably the two together.*
> —Marilyn vos Savant

And preferably the two of *us* there
together next year!   *XXOOJ*

     Steph and I were at the breakfast table Sunday morning when my cell sang out.

     "I'm hoping you'll tell me you've safely arrived in gay Paris (I used the accent and said *Pare-ree!*) and are ensconced in the bosom of your family."

     "Well, I'm in Paris, in the townhouse and in my room, but there's no family to be seen. My mother should be home by six, so I'm going to unpack and get cleaned up."

     "Can we FaceTime in about an hour? We're just now starting our breakfast."

     "Perfect, I'll call back then."

STILL LUCKY

"ILYM—and that M's for most!"
Richard laughed and hung up.
Steph was shaking her head.

Later, when I opened the FaceTime connection I was treated to a full-length view of my lover in what must have been his closet. He was slowly stroking his erect penis with one hand and fondling his balls with the other.

"Hell-o Handsome! Is someone holding the camera for you?"

"Yvette, my little French maid."

I must have looked surprised.

"Kid-ding! Honestly, have you ever tried looking 'gullible' up in the dictionary? It's not in there."

"Oh, no you don't. I've heard that one before!"

Richard laughed. "I had to give it a shot."

"So where do you intend to shoot *that*?" No doubt about to what I was referencing.

"I know where I'd like to shoot it, but you're so far away."

"Sad, isn't it?" I tried to look sympathetic, despite the fact I was getting turned on. *God I miss him!*

"Very. But I thought you'd help me forget there are so many miles between us."

"Nothing would please me more. What can I do for you?"

"I'd like a close up of that sweet little cunt of yours."

"Happy to oblige, but you'll have to call me back so I can take it on the iPhone. It's sorta hard to wrap my thighs around the desktop."

Richard cracked up as the FaceTime closed. Moments later my cell rang. This time the image was the tip of his penis, dripping a little.

"Gees, give a girl a minute, will ya?" I propped the cell on my chair and slowly slipped my shorts down.

"Panties? Really?" is what I heard, though the image didn't change. The urge to wrap my lips around that beautiful cock was surprisingly strong. *Aftershock!*

"When you're not here to keep me in a constant state of anticipation, I fall back on the rules of decency."

"Decency doesn't interest me at the moment. I'm looking for something hot and wet."

I slipped my panties down very slowly. Richard groaned. I picked up the phone and gave him a long, leisurely view of my landing strip as I turned and sat down in my chair. I put both my feet up on the desk and spread my knees By then I was dripping, myself.

"Is this what you had in mind?" I asked as I slipped first one finger, then two into my vagina and stroked slowly. I ran my hand over myself, spreading my folds, teasing my clit and then opening myself as wide as I could with my fingers.

"Exactly..." he said breathlessly as I heard him come.

While he recovered I treated myself to a quickie. Where was Zoor (or even Bob) when I needed him?

"Care to tell me what that was all about?" I asked as I pulled my panties and shorts back on.

"I was in the shower and started think about you with the inevitable result. I just needed a little more connection. I'm grateful that you're so accommodating."

"Anything for you, my Prince, but I'm thinking I may need to keep an extra Bob handy down here."

"Sorry about that. I should have warned you."

"No problem. I'm perfectly capable of taking care of things without the aid of appliances."

"I'm sure you are, but I wish I could offer you the real thing right now. Believe me when I say I miss you every bit as much as you miss me." He did give me a close-up of those beautiful eyes along with enough of a jolt to create an aftershock.

"Oh, you Magic Man, your mojo is still working and it's as strong as ever." I couldn't help sighing. "The practical part of me thinks we have one month behind us and only two more to go, but it seems like a really long time."

"I know, Sweetheart. I do. What can I do to make it easier?"

"You're already doing more than I imagined possible. For now that will have to suffice."

"Well, how about you take an early lunch tomorrow and we'll spend some time together? Wednesday won't work for me this week, my mother has made dinner plans that are likely to run late."

"Perfect! I'm waiting for pictures of that flower market."

"I've got 'em. And speaking of pictures, let me tell you again how much I'm enjoying the ones you're sending. You, my beautiful girl, are the most amazing woman I've ever known. I remain in a state of perpetual gratitude, and I mean that literally."

"Awww…you sure know how to keep a woman happy. And by the way, I'm really liking your beard. How are you feeling about it?"

"It's interesting. And look, I trimmed those neck hairs you didn't like. Apparently it's a style called 'cutthroat.' Who knew? What do you think?" He lifted his chin to show me. "The response has been positive, so far. Now I await *Maman's* approval, which, to be honest, is unlikely to be forthcoming. She has never had anything good to say about facial hair, even moustaches."

"You might be surprised. She'll probably think it's really sexy. Women like that look."

He laughed. "I don't think my mother would ever find me sexy in any way. At least I hope not."

"I meant it as an observation. You'll have to let me know what she has to say about it. It's perfect to me. I feel a very strong urge to run my tongue along your jaw and take a taste."

"You are so oral, my love."

"Surely that's not a complaint?"

He laughed loudly then. "Hardly. I can't imagine anything sexier than your mouth on me, whenever and wherever. It's hard not to think about it, and if I do, *I'm* hard. Cress, I love you. Am I being redundant?"

"Here's a quote for you: *My love is made out of three things: the dawn, the sunrise, and redundancy.*"

"And you just pulled that one out of thin air?"

"Nope. It's from Jarod Kintz. Found it when I was looking for those synonyms for *love* and *beautiful*. Just waiting for a chance to toss it your way." I said that with a very superior tone.

"At the risk of being redundant, *again*, you never cease to surprise me."

"*Déjà vu all over again?*" I suggested.

"Now who's redundant?"

"I think we may have to agree to redundancy when it comes to how we feel about each other. It's just part of the package until language affords us more options."

179

"I need to get dressed. Not a good idea to keep *Maman* waiting."

"I bet you've got her wrapped around your little finger. Are you going to tell her about me?" I was curious because I'd been pretty reluctant to share too much of Richard with my own folks.

"One look at me and she'll know I'm in love. Of course she'll want to know the details."

"For heaven's sake, show some restraint there!" I was laughing and so was he.

"Good idea. Until tomorrow, Sweetheart."

Monday, August 19

Note of the day:

> *So he thoroughly taught her*
> *that one cannot take pleasure without*
> *giving pleasure,*
> *and that every gesture, every caress,*
> *every touch, every glance,*
> *every last bit of the body*
> *has its secret, which brings happiness*
> *to the person who knows*
> *how to wake it.*
> — Hermann Hesse, *Siddhartha*
>
> *OK, I swapped a couple of pronouns*
> *but you catch my drift?*   XXOOJ

At a 10:30 on Monday morning I was finishing my set up for Richard's call when Marie arrived with a rather sizable box sporting an iridescent lime green bow. The logo said, *Déclarations~Bordeaux.*

I looked at Marie but she said it had only just been delivered. She was as curious as I was as I set it on the coffee table and untied the ribbon. Amidst all the layers of tissue paper my fingers touched something very soft. I kept digging and found not one, not two, but THREE cashmere hoodies! One in sage green, one in yellow, and one in soft heather grey, the color of Richard's. Leave it to Magic Man to find something so special for me and then deliver it in triplicate. I slipped one on. It fit perfectly!

"Confess, Marie! You have been leaking size information to your boss."

She shrugged and tried to look innocent, but she was smiling.

"Let me take those upstairs for you. Your lunch will be ready in a few minutes." She collected the box and the sweaters and disappeared.

I was smiling, ear-to-ear. What a guy! I was hoping he'd received the quote intended for today.

"How fares my remarkable lover today?" I asked when Richard appeared on my screen. "And before you answer I want to thank you for those yummy hoodies. They just arrived this morning."

"Thought you'd enjoy those. How about the colors? How'd I do?"

"Perfect! Probably because you're a Trained Professional and all. But on to other things. I see you still have your beard so I trust your mother wasn't too displeased?"

He laughed. "No, she granted me a reprieve and informed me she has to think about it. There was some teasing last night at dinner, though. She had a few friends over along with Henri, the man she's currently seeing."

"Is Henri new or has this been a long term thing?"

"Very long term. They've been together for about seven years. He wants to get married, she doesn't. He's actually a great guy and treats her very well."

"I'm happy for her. We all need a great guy in our life, husband or not."

"Should I read anything into that?" he asked.

"Like what?"

"Are you thinking about marriage?"

I had to laugh out loud. "Nervous, are you? Now that you've

committed yourself to abiding by my matrimonial whims, are you getting cold feet?"

"Not at all. Just curious. Say the word and I'll be on the next flight home to accompany you to the justice of the peace."

"I want you here in the flesh so badly it's a temptation, for sure, but for the time being I'll let it ride."

"Dang!" he said, with a snap of his fingers.

It surprised me. "Are you disappointed? Are you wanting to marry me all of a sudden?"

"I told you when I gave you the ring it was your call. If that's not what you want, I'm still yours."

"Good thing! All I want is you. I don't need to become Mrs. Hunter."

"You could keep your name, you know," he offered.

"Richard, what brought this on? Seriously…" I was concerned. Despite his playful tone, this was the first time he'd mentioned marriage since that night he promised me he'd marry me if and when I wanted him for my husband.

"Nothing. When they were pumping me for information about you last night, there was talk of a wedding. I insisted that it was too soon for that, but I guess I was thinking about it after I went to bed."

"And what, exactly were you thinking about it?"

"Only how much I love you and how happy I am."

"Sounds to me like you've gotten over your fear of proposals."

He laughed. "At least I can honestly say that I'm no longer concerned that this separation will damage our relationship or cool this remarkable passion we share. I'm convinced you'll still love me when your millions come rolling in."

"Thanks for that, Captain Obvious! If I recall, I assured you of that before you left and many times since."

"As usual, you were spot on."

"Gonna have to trust me, I suppose."

"With my life, Sweetheart."

"Good. Now, show me what you got."

"I'm still at the table, Cress. Can we save that for later?"

He whispered the last rather loudly and sort of tongue-in-cheek and I saw someone's hand remove his plate and set a salad in its place. I laughed.

"I was referring to the travelogue you promised!" I whispered.
"It's in your folder."

We went through his PowerPoint while he finished his meal. He had more pictures of Corsica, of the winery near Fontveille, and other towns and vineyards he'd visited on the drive to Paris. He'd also interviewed eleven more artists, only three of whom I was really enthusiastic about.

By 2:00 a.m. Paris time Richard was ready to call it a night and I was ready for him. I warmed Zoor up while he took a quick shower. I was in bed and had an idea when he called back. I'd suggested we use our cells for the visuals.

"Hi, Beautiful. Fancy some company?"

"Some fancy company?"

"If you like. What's your fancy?"

I punched up *I Want to Kiss You All Over* on my iTunes and adjusted the volume so it made a nice background theme for us.

"I think we can pull this off if we use our imaginations. Here's my plan. Tell me what you think. It's sort of a you-show-me-yours-and-I'll-show-you-mine kind of thing—not that that's anything new. But if we start with the cheek, which is where I would give you my first kiss..." The camera moved from my mouth to my cheek. "Now you put your camera on your cheek. If you just follow my locations I think we can pretend we are kissing each other all over."

"Works for me. Just be sure to linger where you can."

"Ditto. Now let's start with our eyes." I could tell he was smiling by the crinkles in the corners of his. I zapped him with a jolt of energy and was rewarded when his picture wavered. *Yes!*

He laughed. "Really?" And zapped me back. Hard!

"Oooh...if you were closer..."

"Yes?"

"You'll have to wait until you *are* closer to find out. Now, back to my plan for a long slow one. And yes, I know you have a long one, I'm counting on that."

Richard chuckled then moved his camera to his mouth. He licked his lips slowly then shifted to his cheek. I did the same. I closed my eyes and imagined a slow tender kiss.

Next our mouths. Then I moved the camera behind and just below my ear. His image had that scruffy beard.

"I love the way that feels. It's softer than I imagined." In my mind I ran my tongue over the stubble (and couldn't wait to do it in person!) I slid the camera down the side of my neck, very slowly.

"You smell so good," he whispered.

I followed my collarbone across to the little dip at the base of my throat where that diamond star was nestled, while I imagined my own tongue lapping at that spot on him. I inhaled his scent from my Tshirted surrogate.

"So do you. I can't help myself. I have to press myself against you so I can reach around and cup that delicious ass of yours." In my mind I held him tight and squeezed.

"My hands are holding you on both side of your breasts, but I'm not touching them yet," he told me.

I held the camera in front of one of my breasts, then moved in for a close up of my nipple, hard already and I hadn't even touched myself yet! (The mind is an amazing thing.)

"A beautiful little pearl. Let me spend a little time here."

"Yes, please," I said while I teased my other breast, imagining his mouth. "Can you feel my tongue? I like sucking yours, too."

"And you do it so well. When I say 'you suck, Sweetheart,' consider it a compliment."

We both laughed, but I was so turned on it didn't dampen the mood.

"I want your cock so badly but I'm going to wait. I need to run my mouth all over your belly. I want to feel your abs against my lips."

He gave me a view of his whole abdomen and then moved closer, slowly panning from one side to the other. I reciprocated with the undersides of my breasts (I loved it when he kissed me there!) as I moved down.

"Put your tongue here," I said as I slowly massaged my belly button.

"Follow that line of hair below mine and see where it leads you," he suggested. He moved his hard cock to the side and followed that little trail down with the camera.

"Show me those balls. I want to suck them into my mouth and massage them with my tongue."

He obliged and gave me a view of his scrotum. I spread myself open for him.

"Is this where you want to be?" I asked.

"I want to taste you. I want to tease your clit and listen to your breathing change. I want you to tell me how my beard feels against your cunt. I want you to like it."

"I do...oh, I do." I still had the camera there, now propped against a boudoir pillow as I massaged myself with both hands, rubbing and spreading for his benefit (and my own!)

"I want you Richard, I want your cock. Please!" I said that as I got Zoor in one hand and moved the camera higher while I very slowly slipped my sweet substitute into me. As I gasped, Richard groaned.

"You watch this, let me watch you."

He kept the camera on his penis as he stroked himself and I tried to match his movements with Zoor. When he realized that's what I was doing, he added a little variety in the moves.

"I want to stroke your clit," he said.

I worked Zoor in the up-and-then-back-in move. I took a double rub and came.

"I love you, Cress."

"I love you more," I insisted breathlessly.

"Again?"

"Yes, please."

I was still matching his moves on my phone to Zoor, and even long distance, my magnificent lover could still bring me to climax as perfectly as he did in person. Of course it wasn't the same, but we were both totally into it.

He sped up a little and I came again.

"Come with me next time," I urged.

"One more for you and then I want your mouth, Sweetheart."

I squealed softly through that next orgasm and then brought the camera first to my smile and then my mouth.

"I want everything you've got. More than a drop…and I want to see," I told him.

I watched him ejaculate as I continued to suck Zoor. I performed some tongue magic for him, sucked Zoor's tip and tongued it before taking him back in my mouth, attempting to mimic his own strokes.

Finally, I gave Zoor a lick and a kiss.

"Thanks, Charming. You never fail to please," I said softly.

"I would have to say the same about you. You are nothing, if not creative."

"That's what I've always said about you. I can hardly claim that attribute."

"No? Are you sure?" His voice was gentle.

We were both enjoying the afterglow.

"I thought you were the one who came up with the blind date idea," he continued. "And it wasn't me dancing around to *You Can Leave Your Hat On*. I also think you're the one who found such a unique way for us to share what we love about each other's bodies. And never mind your brilliance with your Internet."

"Oh…"

"Should I also mention that you can be very, very creative when you make love with me?" he said in a very logical tone.

"Hmmm…I guess since you're a Trained Professional, I'll have to take your word for it."

"Yes, Sweetheart, you will."

19
My World Wobbles

Wednesday, August 21

Note of the day:

Amazing sex stays with you.
It soaks into your skin.
It floats through your dreams
and has you silently smoldering
with delicious remembrances
for hours after.— Roberto Hogue

Where there's smoke... XXOOJ

I was just coming in the door from yoga on Wednesday when my cell rang. It was my mom.

"Hi, Mom, what's up in Walla Walla?"

"I've got some bad news, CJ. Your father had a heart attack."

Her words hit me like a hammer. "Is Daddy OK?"

"I'm at the hospital now. I'm waiting to meet with the doctor, but he may need surgery."

"Let me see what I can do. I'll call you back as soon as I can figure out how to get there. Hang in there, Mom."

"I will, Honey. Send your Dad some good energy."

"Lots of love, Mom, commin' your way."

I hung up, frantically wondering which way to jump. I could drive. It was about twenty hours if I drove straight through…probably not a good idea since I'd already been up for twelve hours.

I thought of calling Richard, but my watch reminded me it was the middle of the night for him and there was little he could do from halfway around the world. I realized I just wanted the comfort of the sound of his voice.

I punched Mark's number in but got his voice mail. I left him a message to give me a call as soon as he could. Maybe he'd know some air freight company or something that could get me there faster than a regular airline.

I went to the computer to check flights. There were no seats available until tomorrow afternoon. I racked my brain and decided to call Giano.

"Cressibella! You have brightened my afternoon."

"Giano, I need your help."

He must have sensed my desperation because he was immediately serious.

"How may I be of service?"

"My mother just called. My father had a heart attack and is in the hospital. I can't get a flight until late tomorrow. I'm thinking of driving, but it's about twenty hours if I try to drive straight through, I'm not sure I can. It's the middle of the night for Richard so I don't want to wake him. I was hoping maybe you'd have an idea. Can you point me toward a charter or something? I'm sure Richard won't mind the expense, but I have no idea where to start."

"How soon can you be ready to leave?"

"I don't know. An hour? Less if necessary."

"Let me call you back. Do not worry, we will get you to your family."

Giano was reassuring. He would have a solution for me. I unplugged my laptop, grabbed it, my iPad and the chargers, and the week's worth of notes for Richard that I'd intended to deliver to the gallery the next day, and headed upstairs to pack some things.

A few minutes later Giano called back.

"I have a ride for you Bella. Can you be ready to leave the house by 6:30?"

"Yes."

"Good. I will call Antonio and give him the information."

"Giano, I can't thank you enough!"

"I am pleased to be able to help, and now I must go."

"Of course. Thank you!"

I hung up and the phone rang again. It was Mark. I told him what had happened and that Giano had found a ride for me.

"You're in good hands, CJ. Keep us posted, we'll all be thinking of you."

I called Steph. She was still at the studio.

"If I don't get home before you leave, call me later and catch me up. Promise me," she said sternly.

"I will. Keep the home fires burning. I'll talk to you tonight. As soon as I know what's going on."

I called my mom, told her I was on my way and would call her when I landed. The doctors were still monitoring Daddy.

I was ready to go. I changed my clothes and went down to tell Marie.

Antonio was waiting out front with Miyuki Miata. He was wearing jeans and a V-neck tee with a hoodie. He smiled at me reassuringly as he opened the door for me and then put my bag in the trunk.

"Thank you so much for doing this, Antonio."

He laughed. "It is my job, you know. But I am happy to help. Please know your father will be OK. Remember how broad Hunter's influence is," he said with his soft accent.

I looked at him. "I'm not sure he can affect my father's health from the other side of the world."

Antonio gave me a knowing smile as he pulled out of the drive and onto the street. "Well, I think it's a very good possibility. You know how Hunter's world works."

I had to smile. I had faith in my Prince where Steph and I were concerned, but I guess I hadn't thought about his amazing alternate world extending to my family.

"I know I'll feel better after I talk to Richard. He doesn't know yet. It seemed pointless to wake him."

"Calling Signore Barsanti was a good alternative. He, too, is a very influential man."

"A very kind man, I think. I am so happy I've had the chance to know him."

"Do you know he is my uncle?"

This surprised me. Antonio told me how he'd come from Italy and became a driver for his uncle until the job with Richard happened. He'd never mentioned Giano before.

"It's what I've always dreamed of, this living with the most wonderful cars. I've learned how to work on them, I get to drive them and my home is in a most beautiful place."

"You live here?" This surprised me as well, though I suppose if I'd thought about it, how else could Antonio be available at a moment's notice?

"Yes. I have a sweet little apartment above the garage. It is so beautiful!" Antonio made that kiss-your-fingers-and-toss-the-kiss-away gesture that Italians do so well. "You must come and see."

I made a point to remind myself I simply had to visit Richard's garage! I'd never gotten around to it.

Antonio continued to distract me with conversation, some of it in Italian, which kept my anxiety level from rising.

I was curious about what sort of transport Giano had arranged as we pulled into the private hangar section of the Santa Monica airport. We drove down the road between the buildings and at the end turned left toward the open area where the runways were. There was a little white plane waiting and beside it Giano was talking to a man in a uniform. He came to greet us.

"Cressibella!" he said as he opened his arms to me.

"Giano, I can't thank you enough," I said as I hugged him.

"It is the least I can do. Come, let me introduce you to our pilot," he said, taking my hand and leading me toward the plane. "This is Capitano Santorelli."

I shook the captain's hand as he smiled and tipped his hat to me. Antonio arrived with my bag and ran it up the stairway and into the plane. When he returned he gave his uncle a big hug.

"Have a safe trip, Signorina. We will be praying for your father," Antonio said and then he was gone.

"So…" Giano gestured toward the stairway. "Are you ready?"

"I am. But do I need to pay someone or...?"

Giano laughed. "You are my guest," he said. "I shall accompany you to Walla Walla and then go on to Vancouver to conduct some business."

Gobsmacked, me. When would I learn to expect this sort of miracle? I teared up.

"Bella, Bella, do not cry. We will take you to your papa and the sight of your beautiful face will make him well again. This is a promise."

In for a penny, in for a pound, I thought as I climbed the stairs into the little white jet.

Giano's plane was amazing and it was actually his. I had no idea that jets came in such small sizes. He told me this one was built for 12 passengers but he had re-designed the interior to accommodate six (if it was full) so everyone would be more comfortable. It was beautiful, and quite a wild ride taking off so fast in such a small vehicle. (Well, it seemed small compared to the jumbo jets I'd flown on commercially! What did I know about private jets? La-dee-dah!)

Like his nephew, Giano did an admirable job of distracting me on the flight. We talked about Richard and he told me some amusing stories about his son Max (Massimiliano) and Richard, and the trouble the two young men used to get into. We talked about my family and what it was like growing up in Walla Walla. He also asked about my project, which I updated him on.

I kept an eye on the clock and at 8:00 p.m. I excused myself and moved farther back in the plane to call Richard.

"I wake this morning to the voice of an angel," he said softly when he answered.

"Unfortunately the tidings I bear this morning are not of joy, my sweet Prince." I was having trouble disguising the catch in my voice as I started to tear up. He must have heard it because his tone changed immediately.

"Cress, what's wrong?"

"It's my dad. He's had a heart attack."

"Is he all right?"

"I don't know. My mom called from the hospital and I'm on my way there."

"Where are you?"

"In Giano's jet. He's flying me to Walla Walla. I called him to help me find a charter and instead he's giving me a ride."

"You're in good hands. Hold on a minute."

When Richard came back he said, "It's going to take me awhile to figure out how to get back there, but I'll let you know."

"No, Richard. No. Much as I'd love the comfort of your arms, there's no reason for you to come back. Wait until I know more. I'll call as soon as I have new information. Don't change your plans right now. There's nothing you can do."

"Promise me something." He was dead serious.

"Of course."

"If your father needs anything—transfer to another hospital, mediflight, special surgeons, anything—DO NOT hesitate to put it on your AMEX. It's what the card is for. Get him the very best of whatever he needs. Don't let cost govern any decision you make."

"I won't. I promise. I may hesitate when it's for myself, but I would do anything for my folks."

"Good. And call me the minute you have any news."

"I will. Richard. I love you. Please don't worry about me. I'll FaceTime you when we land."

"I'll be waiting. And your father will be fine. Believe, Sweetheart. Keep a picture in your mind of him fully recovered."

"Work you magic, Magic Man."

By the time we landed, Giano had arranged a rental car for me and it was waiting where we stopped. He carried my bag and briefcase to the car himself and put them in the trunk.

"Cressibella, I will be waiting to hear from you. I will make arrangements for your ride home when you're ready. Just say the word."

"Giano, thank you so much. This means the world to me. I'll be in touch." I threw my arms around his neck and he gave me a big hug and a kiss on the cheek.

I watched him return to the plane and board, waved to him

and then got into the fancy little Mercedes. I pulled out my phone and called my mom.

"I'm here, Mom," I said when she answered.

"Here? Where?" she asked.

"We just landed at the airport. I've got a rental car and I'm coming your way. How's Daddy?"

"They've just taken him in for bypass surgery."

"I'll be there as soon as I can." I hung up and started the car.

I parked in the hospital visitors lot and took a minute to connect with Richard. It was a relief to see his face. I swear I could feel the energy the minute he appeared.

"Any news, Sweetheart?"

"I just parked at the hospital. Mom says Daddy went into surgery. I wanted to let you know I'd arrived safely…and, honestly I just needed to see your sweet face."

"Cress…"

"I know."

"I can be there by tomorrow night."

"No. You'd be a comfort to me, but there's really nothing you can do at this point."

"I can give you someone to lean on who loves you," he reminded me.

"I would never argue that. But until we know the outcome of the surgery, what recovery's going to require…all those things…it's not worth disrupting your plans. If I need you I'll ask you to come."

"Promise me?"

"I promise. Now just work some of that magic of yours for my dad."

"I'm already on it," he assured me. "Stay in touch. I don't care what time of day or night. All right?"

"Yes."

"Now look into my eyes," he said as he offered a close-up. "I love you, Sweetheart."

I smiled. "I love you more," I assured him as I disconnected.

Still Wednesday

"Mom?" I said when I spotted her on the other side of the waiting room.

She stood up and gave me a fierce hug. "I'm glad you're here, Honey." She ran her hands over my short hair. "I like it. Very Fantine."

"Exactly! Any news?"

"The doctor said it would be five or six hours." She glanced at her watch. "They took him in forty-five minutes ago."

"Have you eaten?"

"No, I was waiting for you. Let's go down to the cafeteria and get something and you can tell me how you got here so quickly."

I told the nurse at the desk where we'd be, and arm in arm, we went to find some food.

It was my turn to do some distracting and I elaborated on my swift arrival and Giano's generosity. I could hear the little warning bells going off in my mother's head. How was her daughter suddenly moving in the circles of the uber-rich who owned their own jets?

"And now you need to tell me about the ring," Mom said, nodding toward my left hand.

I could feel my cheeks coloring. "Richard gave it to me before he left."

Mom just looked at me. It was difficult to read her.

"Mom, it's not an engagement ring," I said hastily when I realized what she must be thinking."

"No?"

"Don't you think I'd tell you if I was planning to get married?"

"I'd certainly hope so. But then you haven't really said much about him. You told us he was spending the summer in Europe and that you and Stephanie were going to housesit. You said it was a beautiful house, that Richard was very generous and 'special'. Not much to go on. Now that I see the ring, I think you may have a lot more to tell me."

I looked at her. I had tried to temper my talk about Richard and focus more on the project and the progress I was making whenever I talked to my folks. Everything between me and my Magic Man had happened so fast and was so profound. I knew that if I tried to share that, my folks would be worried, concerned I wasn't being cautious enough. After all, I'd never even had a steady boyfriend. To try to explain Richard and his incredible universe would have made me sound like I'd lost my mind—nothing like the practical and studious daughter they'd raised.

We finished our meal, such as it was—neither of us was very hungry—and Mom headed back to the waiting room while I went to the car to get my iPad. I had some of the pictures from the party on it and some I'd taken of the house. There was even one of Marie! I also had those pictures Giano had given me from the gala. I knew my mom would love them, but I had delayed sending them to her because showing her images of me at such an upscale event would only have led to more questions. I was still determined to hide the depth of my feelings for Richard a little bit longer, but this would give me a chance to ease her into our relationship. I didn't want to worry her, and at the same time I was hoping she'd have a chance to meet him before the end of the year.

And so I spent the next two hours distracting Mom—well, both of us, really—by talking about Richard. I started with the house. That alone was a shock to her. I'd told her it was a really nice house in the Hollywood hills, and that there was a pool. I'd downplayed it and hadn't emailed pictures (though she'd asked for some!) because the house made Richard's financial situation obvious.

"The house is really beautiful. You're a lucky girl. But why have you been afraid to tell us how wealthy Richard obviously is?"

I sighed. "It all happened so fast, since the moment we met… it…" What could I say? "I was afraid you'd worry about me."

She smiled at me and gave me a big, long hug.

"Honey, I've suspected you were in love since you first mentioned him. Now that I see you, I know it's true. So let's start at the beginning, shall we? Tell me everything."

Relief washed over me. It had been hard not to share Richard with my family. To be so full of love and not let the people closest to me share my joy…well, I was pleased that the cat was finally out of the bag.

As time ticked along I told her quite a bit—the story of how we met and even about the *Some Enchanted Evening* accompaniment, which made her laugh. I skipped over the fact that I'd gone home with him but told her he took me to Santa Barbara the next day. I told her about our double "date" with Mark and Steph.

She was thrilled about Richard's choice of graduation presents (*Les Miz*, not my necklace—which I didn't mention.) The fact that Richard was a fan impressed her, maybe even more than his amazing house!

I told her how he'd helped with the move and the cleaning. (The cleaning crew thing really made an impression. Like daughter, like mother!)

She loved the pictures from the graduation party and took a minute to study the one of Richard watching me dance, the one that had made me burst into tears that day in his office.

"He's incredibly handsome, CJ, but more important, it's obvious how much he loves you."

"Really?" This surprised me. Of course I could see it in his eyes when he was with me, but I never thought other people would notice. I took the iPad from her and looked at it again. My eyes started to fill.

"Honey, what is it?" she asked, filled with concern.

I laughed as I wiped my eyes. "I don't know. It's the same reaction I had when I first saw that picture. He's just so beautiful!"

"I think you're reacting to the obvious emotion—it shows. And yes, I agree. He is beautiful!"

She put her arm around me and I leaned in and rested my head on her shoulder.

"Mom, I'm so happy. I never knew this was possible."

"If anyone deserves it, it's you CJ. There aren't very many men out there who I'd think were good enough for you, but it seems like maybe you've found one who is."

"You have no idea," I said softly.

"You might be surprised!"

I sat up and looked at her. Before she could say anything more, the nurse came over from the desk to say that the doctor had asked her to let us know the surgery was going very well.

I glanced at my watch. It was almost 11:00 p.m., nearly 8:00 in the morning for Richard.

"Wanna meet him?" I asked.

She just stared at me.

"I promised I'd call him when we had news."

"I guess this is good a time as any, though I wish I looked more presentable."

"Don't worry, Richard sees people from the inside out," I said as I punched him up.

He answered the call right away and his beautiful face filled the screen.

"Cress? What news?"

"We just heard from the doctor. Daddy's still in surgery but everything is going well."

"Good."

"My mom wants to meet you." I handed the iPad to my mom.

"Mrs. Bailey. I'm sorry we have to meet long distance and under such difficult circumstances."

"I'm just happy to make the connection. I've been hearing quite a lot about you over the last couple of hours. And call me Bea, please."

"I hope CJ's told you that she has the means to handle any financial concerns that might come up. Please use it to get anything your husband needs."

Mom was gobsmacked but recovered quickly. "Thank you. That's very generous."

"Allow me to help. CJ can explain how I feel about the money thing. It is no consideration on my end and I hope you'll take advantage of it. Anything to hasten his recovery, please don't hesitate."

I was surprised when Mom sort of wobbled in her chair. I took the iPad back from her.

"Your mojo's still workin', Handsome."

"Good. I have to get on the road but call whenever you have more news."

"I will."

"LY, Sweetheart."

"ILYM," I replied.

"What was that?" Mom asked in surprise. She'd obviously gotten a jolt of the magic.

"I don't know, but women—and even some men—wobble in his wake. It's an energy thing. I'm just surprised it works from halfway around the world."

"Easy to understand why you're in love."

She didn't even try to hide her surprise and I could see she was having a little trouble assimilating her first exposure to my Magic Man

20
The Boys in the Bed

Thursday, August 22

Note of the day:

> *I am so lucky that I can know him.*
> *This is the only way to know him.*
> *I am the only one who knows him.*
> —Sharon Olds, *The Knowing*

At long last the surgeon came out to talk to us. We both felt a huge wave of relief when we saw he was smiling. He explained to us that Daddy had a triple by-pass and was in recovery. He said he should be coming around shortly and that we could go in and wait.

Daddy woke up a few minutes later, with both of us holding his hands. When he saw me, he smiled.

"Hey, Daddy. Are you trying to scare me?" I asked.

"Looks like maybe I succeeded." His words were slow and a little slurred.

"Yup. But I win. The doc says you're going to be fine." It was so good to see him. I could just tell he was going to be OK.

He glanced at my mom. "Thanks, Bea."

"I'll accept complete recovery as fair compensation. Nothing less." She bent and kissed his cheek.

He squeezed my hand weakly and his eyes closed. But he was smiling.

We sat with him for another two hours until they came to move him to the ICU.

"CJ, take my keys and go to the house. The cats need to be fed and you should get some sleep. Then you can come relieve me in the morning. OK?"

I was exhausted and now that it looked like Daddy was out of the woods, I was happy to take her up on the offer.

When I got to the house, the cats, Bennie and Jetz (Don't blame me, talk to my mom. And they were wild and wonderful as kittens!) greeted me loudly. I wasn't fooled. They were more interested in their late dinner than the fact that I'd come for a visit. I fed them and called Richard.

"Hi, Cress. How's your father?"

What a relief to see his face.

"He came through the surgery with flying colors. Mom and I were there when he woke up and stayed with him 'til they came to move him to ICU. Mom sent me to the house. I'm gonna shower and sleep for a few hours, then go back to the hospital so she can come home and rest a little."

"Sweetheart, I'm so sorry. But I'm confident your father's going to recover."

"Do your best, Magic Man, I'm counting on you."

"You know I will. Do you want me to come, Cress? There is nothing more important to me than to be there if you need me."

"You sweet man. As I said before, I'd love to feel your arms around me, but so far, so good, here. We'll see how things go the next couple of days. Mom and I will meet with the doctors tomorrow afternoon—oops, guess that's *this* afternoon—and find out what the road to recovery looks like. Then I can make some decisions. Right now I want to sleep. Tomorrow I'll take a look at my calendar and see what needs to be done. I need to let Ben and Jerry know I won't be there for the meeting."

"I'm so sorry you have to go through this alone."

"I'm not alone. As you said before, you're here in every way that matters but one. I know that."

"Get some sleep. Do you want me to wake you?"

"That would be wonderful." I glanced at my watch. It was 3:10 a.m. "Can you call at nine my time?"

"Rest easy. I promise everything will be OK."

"I love you, Richard."

"I love you more," he reminded me as he hung up.

I woke with the two cats piled on top of me, purring loudly—again, probably more from concern for their morning meal than affection. But it was pure love on Richard's face when I answered.

"Looks like you're not alone in that bed," he said.

I turned the phone toward them as I introduced them.

"These are the two boys I used to sleep with. They're handy for warmth but not much else. They don't hold a candle to you, my love."

"Good. Meanwhile, I know you want to get back to your father so I'll let you go. Call when you have an update."

"I will. I love you."

"I love you more, and you know it!" he laughed, but hung up before I could respond.

As I showered I took a few minutes to think about how remarkable Richard's response to this crisis had been. Despite the distance between us he was one hundred percent there for me, even to the point that he was willing to come back to help me through it. Though I'd nixed that option for the time being, he was still doing enough to make me feel that I had his complete support. And I realized everything else between us—our customary teasing, texting and even our regular long distance sex—was no longer on the table. Richard was offering nothing but love and allowing me to focus on my dad with no worries about neglecting him. It was pretty impressive.

Before I left the house I called Ben and Jerry to let them know I was in Washington. I also called Mark and updated him. I reminded him that Antonio would be bringing my week's worth of notes for Richard (which I had fortunately finished before I left.)

"He was just here, I have them in my hand," Mark told me.

"I don't want to miss any if I can help it, and I don't know when I'm coming back. Can I FedEx you the next batch if I need to?"

"Of course. Send them on Tuesday, overnight, just in case. Then email and let us know to expect them. I'll email you the gallery FedEx account number."

"Mark, thanks so much. Don't know what I'd do without you."

"Just take care of your dad and keep us in the loop. We're all rooting for him!"

On the drive to the hospital I heard a great song (*Next to Me* by Emeli Sande.) Exactly the way I was feeling. Even halfway around the world Richard was next to me—as he'd said, "in every way that matters but one." I parked the car and iGramed him that one (and downloaded it for myself!) before I went in.

It was a little before 10:00 a.m. when I knocked lightly on the door to my father's room and heard, *"Somebody's knockin', should I let him in?"* sung in response. I opened the door and there was my grandmother.

I threw my arms around her. "Gran! When did you get here?"

"A couple of hours ago. If your father insists on creating all this drama, the least I can do is come and support my girls." Just as my mother had, she ran her hand over my new haircut. "I like it, it suits you."

Daddy laughed softly, clutching a pillow to his chest. I looked questioningly at Mom.

"They gave him the pillow so he doesn't strain the incision if he laughs or coughs," she explained.

"Incision is one way of putting it," he said. "They spread me open like a pig ready for the spit!"

I leaned over and gave him a kiss. "You're not going to be a bad patient, are you?"

"Probably," he said. "When did you cut your hair?"

"Just last week. Like it?"

"Maybe."

"Well, ponder my new look and just forget about being

difficult. You'll do as you're told and get back on your feet as soon as possible."

"I'll have you know they've already walked me twice," he said defensively. "See what you missed?"

Actually he looked pretty good, considering what he'd been through and the tubes and beeping monitors he was connected to. His sense of humor reassured me, despite the weakness of his voice.

As I looked around the room I noticed there were quite a lot of flowers and several GET WELL balloons.

"Looks like an awful lot of people are thinking about you!"

"Well one of them is from Richard Hunter." He squeezed my hand. "Your mother says you have some pictures to show me of your new beau. She's a sucker for a pretty face so I want to make a rational assessment."

"Rational? You're full of drugs. Whadda you know?" I said skeptically.

"Let's see him," he insisted.

First, I got my mom pointed toward home. She would be back in time to meet with the doctor at 4:30 p.m. When she was on her way, I sat down to share the photos of the man I loved with Dad and Gran.

As I had with Mom, I started with the pictures of the house.

"Good grief, CJ, looks like you and Steph are living in the lap of luxury. This is far beyond what you described in your emails," my grandmother said with just a hint of accusation.

"I know. I confess I was afraid of what you guys might think. Obviously, Richard's bank account is pretty impressive, but it's nothing compared to who he is."

"I'm just grateful you found someone who can treat you the way I think you should be treated," my father said.

"Daddy, the important thing is that he loves me the way you want me to be loved." I think I blushed a little.

Gran gave me a squeeze. "You've waited long enough for that! And from the look of you, he was worth the wait!"

"Yeah, yeah," my dad said. "I want to see this guy. If he's older than I am, I'm not letting you go back!"

I cracked up. "He's thirty-two, Daddy."

I continued through the pictures, showing them the ones from the party and ending with the one of Richard watching me dance.

"Good grief!" Gran said. "He is flat out gorgeous! And he obviously feels the same way about you that you feel about him."

"Damn," my father said.

"What, Daddy?"

"That guy stole my little girl's heart and from the look of him, he's got no intention of giving it back."

I gave him a kiss on his cheek. "You've still got a pretty hefty chunk of it. Funny how there's always room for more love, eh?"

I looked at my watch. It was almost 9:00 p.m. for Richard.

"Wanna meet him?" I asked them.

"Bring it," my dad said. "I'm hoping he's a jerk in person."

"You are not, and you know it," I scolded.

I sat down and FaceTimed Richard. He was sitting at a table outside with some other people.

"Hi, Sweetheart. Any news?"

"All of it good, so far. My gran is here and my dad is fiercely guarding my virtue, despite the fact he's flat on his back. Physical limitations aside, he wants to meet you. He insists Mom and I are just suckers for a pretty face."

Richard laughed. "Let me go into the house so we can have some privacy." He excused himself and walked inside and sat down in a chair with a lamp beside it. "How's that? Do I look harmless but handsome?"

"Don't know about the harmless thing, but you're your beautiful self."

"Don't let your father hear you say that. He'll know you're in love."

"Cat's outta the bag. Time to explain to him how much you love me."

"Uh...I don't want to tire the poor man, Cress."

Gran and Dad were hearing all this and they were smiling.

"Sorry, you're on your own."

I held the iPad so both my father and Gran could see.

"Mr. Bailey, as I told your wife, I'm sorry we have to meet long distance and under such circumstances. I'd hoped it would be in person later this year. And Cress, you need to introduce your grandmother."

Of course! He didn't know her name!

"My bad. Richard this is my mother's mom, Katherina Rosaline Freeborn, better known as Kate. Gran, Richard Hunter."

"Mrs. Freeborn, nice to meet you, too. I have to thank you for sharing some of your passion for music with your granddaughter. You'd be surprised how many of those oldies we both know and love."

My sneaky lover zapped Gran and she had to grab for the edge of the bed. She looked startled.

"Don't you do that to my dad," I warned.

Richard cracked up. Then he got serious.

"Mr. Bailey, how are you feeling? You look pretty good considering what you've been through."

"Call me Matt, and you see the lengths I have to go to get my little girl away from you?"

"Well, there're close to six thousand miles between us at the moment, so I'm not sure you can blame her absence on me. Actually, she's been working really hard on her project. I think she's going to be hugely successful and very soon."

"When you're back in the country, I'll be expecting to meet you in person."

"I promise you that will happen. In the meantime, you'd better get yourself back in shape as fast as you can, in case we have to wrestle over her."

"Just you wait," my dad teased, trying to look fierce, "I might surprise you!"

"I'm counting on it."

When Richard disconnected my dad asked, "No razors in Europe?" Like Richard's mother, he wasn't a fan of facial hair.

"He grew that for me. I wanted to see how it looked."

"I think it's hot," Gran said with a wink. "It's the style these days. Look how many actors are wearing that five-o'clock-shadow thing." She gave Daddy an appraising glance. "Looks pretty good on you, too."

"Well, I'll let you keep him for the time being," he said, running a hand over his own stubbly cheek and frowning. "I'll reserve judgment until I can shake his hand."

Just then two nurses came in. It was time for Daddy to walk again, so Gran and I headed for the cafeteria to see what we could do about lunch.

"So what was that, exactly?" she asked as we made our way down the hall.

"What?"

"You know very well what I mean. Good thing I had something to grab onto!"

I laughed. "As near as I can tell it's a jolt of energy. He seems to have pretty good control of it, but even when it's not focused on someone, people tend to stagger a bit. Mostly women, but some of the men, too. The night we met, I nearly fell over when he said hello and I was standing still at the time. He thought maybe I'd had too much to drink!"

And so over lunch I told her about our meeting and what followed—the G-rated version I'd shared with Mom. And about the ring.

"And the sex?" she asked.

"Gran!" I know I blushed then!

"Well?"

I paused. "He's the most engaged, considerate and skilled lover I could imagine. And he's got one hell of a set of tools!"

Gran cracked up. "Glad to hear it. And particularly glad you haven't settled for anything less. The sex is important, as you've apparently noticed. I'm so happy for you. How's the long distance thing working for the two of you?"

I laughed out loud. "I forgot to mention that he's also quite inventive and doing an amazing job of keeping us connected."

I told her about the quotes I was sending him and how much he appreciated them. And about the music and iGrams and my shower surprises. I also mentioned the photos—only that Steph took some "sexy" ones of me that I was adding to some of the daily notes. I didn't give her the details of the poses or mention Seiji.

"Do you have any concerns about those pictures finding a broader audience?"

I could see that worried her.

"Nope. No heads or faces on them. Just the occasional smile."

"I've always said you were the sharpest tool in the family box, honey."

And then we talked about my project and how well it was going. She was really impressed that Richard had introduced me to the Ice Cream Boys. I could just feel Richard's sphere of influence expanding to include my family and it felt great. I could hardly wait for them to meet him. I knew they'd love him as much as I did.

At 4:30 that afternoon my mom and I met with the doctor and went over Daddy's prognosis. The doctor was really pleased with his recovery so far and discussed the coming days with us. He expected Daddy to move to the rehab center in another four or five days. Depending on his progress, he should be able to go home in a couple of weeks.

We went back to the room and shared the news with my father and Gran. We had a group hug. Daddy had to settle for kisses.

21
Stay But a Little...
—(Juliet on the balcony)

Friday, August 23

Note of the day:

> *The fingertips of love discover*
> *more than the body's smoothness*
> *They uncover a hidden conduit*
> *for the transfusion*
> *of empathies that circumvent*
> *the mind's intrusion*
> —May Swenson, *Love Made Visible*

I took off at 5:30 p.m. with the intention of picking up some things for myself and making a run to the grocery store. Mom and Gran would stay and sit with Daddy while he ate a little and then meet me at the house. I was going to make dinner for all of us so we could kick back and relax.

First, I hit the craft store and bought some notepaper. I didn't want to have a lapse in Richard's 'dailies', if I could help it. I stopped at the patisserie for some baguettes (yes, Marie had spoiled me!) and also got croissants (plain and chocolate) for breakfast. Then the grocery store for the things I needed to make Marie's curried chicken salad, including a rotisserie chicken, some cheese, wine and odds and ends I hadn't found at the house that morning.

Off to the Walla Walla Roasterie for some serious coffee— yes, also Marie's influence. And last (but in no way least) a quick stop at Walgreens for a discreet vibrator. I was hoping to talk Charming into a wake up call tomorrow! Now that Daddy was on the mend, I was ready to revert to my previous schedule of long distance love!

After I had Bennie and Jetz fed, the salad made and chilling in the fridge along with the wine, and the table set outside on the patio, I sat down and called Steph with an update.

"How's your dad?" were the first words out of her mouth when she answered.

"He's doing great. On the mend. And he still has his sense of humor so that's a sure sign he's on the road to recovery."

"I'm so happy to hear it. How are you holding up?"

"I'm fine. Just finished getting some dinner put together for my mother and grandmother. They stayed at the hospital to sit with Daddy while he had what passes for a meal and then they'll come home and let me feed them. We can plan strategy for his rehab and relax a little."

"How's Richard dealing with all this, long distance?"

"He's a prince among men, but then you already knew that. He keeps offering to come back, but there's really no reason. We talk several times a day and I confess I'm surprised at how supportive he can be from so far away."

"You're a very lucky girl," she reminded me.

"That's an understatement. How's your love life?"

"Just as great as you may be imagining—and then some. I'm still crazy in love, but you didn't expect that to change in the last two days, did you?"

I laughed. "Nope. I'm counting on the two of you being as happy as Richard and I are. How's the painting?"

"Well, wish you were here. I've kinda hit a crisis…maybe. I'm not sure. I got a sudden inspiration and tried something totally new. I'm really liking it, but I don't know if I should continue with the first series or move to this new one."

"Can you do both?"

"Maybe."

"Well you know the level of my expertise in art so I'm not sure my advice has any value, but maybe you should just go with the flow and see where it takes you."

"I'm leaning that way but wavering. When do you think you'll be coming home?"

"I'll probably fly home on Wednesday so I can meet with Ben and Jerry on Thursday and then come back up here on Sunday or Monday. It will depend on what we can arrange for rehab and home care and all that. We're going to talk about it tonight."

I gave her the doctor's estimates on how and when Daddy was most likely to move through the stages of rehab. At least, for the time being, I was feeling really good about his prognosis.

"Well, maybe while you're here you can come take a look at what I have so far."

"I'd love to see it, but, as I said, what I know about art may not align with your potential market. Maybe you should ask Mark for an opinion."

"I thought about that but what if he doesn't like any of it? I'd hate for him to share anything negative with Richard in advance."

"You're not falling back into the what-if-he-doesn't-like-it place, are you? I thought the good Dr. Hunter disabused you of that line of thinking. And besides, you know Mark is pulling for you and I'm sure he'll give you an honest opinion."

"Damn, " she said, laughing. "I think you're picking up some of Richard's mad clarity skills. Thanks for the reminder. But maybe Mark can tell me if one or the other series seems more promising."

"Let's plan to get together with Michael and Mark when I get back and we can all boost your ego and tell you how brilliant you are."

"Only if it's true. Blue sky is the last thing I need!"

"Agreed. You put a plan together and I'll be there. Thursday through Sunday. As soon as I book my flights, I'll let you know."

"Want me to pick you up at the airport?"

"I'll see if Antonio can. He loves an excuse to drive Richard's pretty little cars."

"Well, lah-dee-dah, listen to Miss Thing with a chauffeur!" Steph laughed.

"I just don't want to do anything to distract your from your creative pursuits."

"Uh, yeah. Well, give my love to your family and keep me posted."

"Will do. And tell Marie I made her curried chicken salad for our dinner tonight."

Mom and Gran got home about ten after seven. Gran was complaining about what they were feeding Daddy.

"Babyfood-like stuff along with intravenous something-or-other?" I guessed.

"At this point, yes, but there's no reason that what they serve couldn't be fresh organic stuff they pureed. I just can't fathom why hospitals don't serve healing meals. Think how much better it would be for the patients."

"Well, you can take over as soon as we get him home. I'm happy to appoint you head dietician," Mom assured her.

"Don't think I won't!" Gran threatened.

We had a long leisurely meal, talked about plans for my dad and also about Richard. He'd made a big impression, which, of course, was no surprise to me!

"What about you?" Mom asked. "How long can you stay?"

"I was thinking I'd fly out next Wednesday so I can have my Thursday meeting, then return on Sunday."

"Does that require pick-up by private jet?" Gran teased.

I laughed. "Nope. I'll buy a round-trip ticket for this run and continue to do that while I'm back and forth. When I'm sure you guys are settled into a routine and it's going well, then I'll worry about the one way. And that's only if everything is moving along for Daddy. Do we need to do some exploring in the home health care and rehab realms?"

"We were discussing that on the way home, and it's on the agenda for tomorrow."

Before I went to bed I called Richard.

"I need some *La La La La La La La*," I sang in a sexy voice.

"I take that as a sure sign that your father's doing well?"

"Yes, my love, and no doubt a good bit of thanks belongs to you."

"I'm not sure I can take credit, but I'm happy to hear that news."

I told him we intended to research the care situations tomorrow and I hoped I'd be able to fly home (listen to me!) on Wednesday and then return to Walla Walla on Sunday night.

"I've got some *Ooh La La* for you, but I'm just getting ready to catch the train to Chantilly for a meeting, then dinner with Robert and his wife. How about a wake-up call tomorrow?"

"Five a.m. my time? Does that work for you?"

"Dream of me and I promise to wake you and show you how much I love you."

"I love you most," I reminded him.

Saturday, August 24

Minutes before the phone rang the next morning, I'd woken enough to smile and roll over to put my arms around my big pillow and whisper into imagined Richard's imaginary ear, "Methinks I hear the lark."

I nuzzled the pillowcase, sensing his warm skin and showered him with kisses. He got the message and my phone softly sang out his ringtone.

"Did my whispered kisses remind you to call, my Prince?"

"Your kisses and the desire they engender," he said softly.

"And what desire might that be?" I asked as I slipped my little finger vibe on.

"I think you know."

I imagined my fingers were his as they slipped between my legs, gently caressing my folds and poking slowly, testing, seeking entrance.

"Hmmmmm…can you feel how wet I am? I love it when you probe me so gently, teasing me, making me want you all the more."

"I can feel the moisture. It feels so good, Sweetheart. Do you know how much I want to taste you?"

"Will you give me your mouth?" I asked as I stroked my clit.

"Do you have to ask? I want my tongue inside you and then I want to move up and lap at your little penis, and feel how hard it gets."

"It may be little but it loves being sucked, just like yours does." I sped up my vibe just a bit and my orgasm exploded. I imagined Richard's tongue continuing to lap at my clit. *"Stay but a little. I will come again..."* I said, breathlessly quoting my namesake.

Richard chuckled then quoted some of the next lines as I heard him come.

"All this is but a dream, too flattering sweet to be substantial."

When I caught my breath, I cracked up.

"Aren't we the literary lovers? And by the way, it feels substantial to me!"

"Me, too. Let's concentrate on the sweet part."

"It's all sweet with you, my love."

BTW Ladies, I recommend an orgasm as the perfect start to the day so you can align yourself with all the good the universe has to offer. Hmmmm...maybe I should write a book...

22
I May Not Know Art,
But I Know What I Like

Wednesday, August 28

Note of the day:

> *Sleep well:*
> *for I can follow you, to bless*
> *And lull your distant beauty*
> *where you roam*
> *And with wild songs*
> *of hoarded loveliness*
> *Recall you to these arms*
> *that were your home*
> — Siegfried Sassoon, *Lovers*

On Wednesday morning I drove to the airport and found a spot in the long term parking for the little Mercedes Giano had rented for me—he'd told me I had it for a month and that if I needed to extend that, he would take care of it. Ah, Richard's universe...was there no end to the kindness and generosity of its inhabitants?

The flight back to L.A. was without either incident or annoyance—how often can you say that about air travel these days?—and Antonio was there at baggage claim to meet me.

"Signorina, welcome home! We have missed you!"

"Good to be back," I assured him, as I gave him a hug. (It's okay to hug staff, isn't it? Especially if they feel like family?)

Marie was waiting for me in front of the house with a fierce hug of her own.

"You have been missed, but I'm so glad your papa is doing well and that you will be here for a few days."

"I'm so happy to be back. I hope you can have dinner with me tonight. I'll catch you up."

"Stephanie and Monsieur Michael will also be here."

"Wonderful! But promise you'll join us."

Marie was smiling broadly as she nodded her assent.

Richard had warned me to expect some surprises when I got home. He'd sent things before I left town that had arrived in my absence and he didn't want me to have one of my peculiar reactions to what was waiting for me. He was doing as I'd previously suggested and giving me a little heads-up with the hope of softening my resistance to his generosity.

Well, I have to admit we may have found the key, because when I went into the closet to start unpacking I was delighted rather than appalled by what I found waiting for me! Laid out on the island were six bra and bikini panty sets in the prettiest colors and most amazingly delicate laces, appliques and embroidery that I'd ever seen. Honestly, they bordered on too-pretty-to-actually-wear. The black set had lace so fine it was as insubstantial as smoke. I had no idea that lingerie of that quality even existed. I know my Prince had enjoyed my Victoria pieces when I'd worn them, but these were in an entirely different category! (And I had to wonder how many times they could actually be worn without disintegrating!) I decided to unpack later and instead go down to my desk and FaceTime my thanks.

It seemed that undies were just a taste of Richard's never ending generosity because when I walked into the library I was stunned to find there'd been a change in décor. On the east wall, in the space surrounded on four sides by bookshelves where a quartet of small paintings had previously hung, was the window painting we'd both liked so much by the artist he'd discovered in Avignon. It was the painting I'd wondered if I could buy. And there it was, having found itself wall space where I thought none existed!

I spontaneously burst into tears. (So much for believing I'd conquered my adverse reactions to his gifts!)

I FaceTimed my sweetie and he answered on his iPhone. My tears must have alarmed him.

"Sweetheart, what is it? Is your father OK?"

I laughed as I blew my nose. "Daddy's doing great. I just came into the library and saw the painting."

He smiled. "And do you still feel the same way about it, now that you see it in person?"

"I absolutely do. I love it even more! Buyer Number One, for sure. To be honest, I'm flat-out stunned. Of course it may mean I won't get any work done in the next few days. I have a feeling I'll have to just sit and stare at it for a while."

"Good. I feel exactly the same way. And it's the first piece we've chosen together. The beginning of a new collection!"

"Seems you've started me on another collection, as well. Are you hinting I should start wearing underwear?"

Richard laughed. "I hope you'll still feel an inclination to go commando when I'm around, but for the times you're feeling a little more conservative or proper, I thought you'd enjoy those."

"They're almost too pretty to wear."

"I know, but I can only imagine how wonderful they'll look on you and how exciting it will be to divest you of them."

"*Divest*, is it?"

"I have words, too." He sounded quite proud of himself.

"You have so much more than words, my love. I'll be happy to remind you of your other attributes when I get the chance, but I'm afraid it will have to wait. Michael and Steph are having dinner here tonight and Marie has promised to join us so I can update them on Daddy's progress."

"I'll wake you tomorrow morning."

"I can't tell you how much I look forward to sleeping in our bed tonight. Wish you were here."

"Me, too."

I was so excited to show the painting to Steph and Michael. They both really liked it. I still couldn't get over how it had suddenly appeared in my office. It was more than Richard's generosity, it was the fact that not long ago I had seen the photo and talked about it with him and *presto!* there it was on the wall.

At dinner I gave a detailed account of my trip. Everyone was relieved to hear Daddy was doing so well and exceeding the doctor's expectations. I was aware it was early days yet in his recovery, but it seemed like the team we had on his case—Mom and Gran, the medical folks and Richard's subjects—were all doing everything they could to ensure his road back to health was a smooth one.

Steph planned for us—including Mark and Michael—to meet at her studio the next day to take a look at the work and see if we could help her decide which direction to pursue. She was ready to share what she'd done and also prepared to hear what we thought of it!

As I looked around the table, I realized how very good it felt to be home and how grateful I was to have such wonderful friends. Of course I couldn't help but wish that a certain devastatingly handsome and incredibly thoughtful man was there with us.

Ben and Jerry were glad to see me the next morning. They asked about my father and were pleased to hear he was doing well. We discussed the possibility of going beyond their solicitations for funding and putting out a few feelers for a possible sale of my project as it was. We talked about the pros and cons of developing the project or selling it off before it was up and running. They weren't sure that anyone would be interested, but they wanted to know my thoughts before they moved forward on that track.

It was something I'd never considered and I told them I wanted to have a chance to mull it over. I'd always assumed that the next step after funding was to set up the corporate structure, make some hires and become the executive who managed the team that would implement the whole thing and prepare to integrate it into the Internet. I asked for a week to ponder the pros and cons and promised we would discuss it next time we met.

Mark and I both pulled up at Steph's studio at the same time. He had a big hug for me.

"Welcome home. You look beautiful, but then you can't help it, can you?"

"You sound suspiciously like a man who wants to go shopping with me again."

He laughed. "We had a good time last time, didn't we?"

"Absolutely. Now that I'm moving up in the world, I promise you the job as my personal stylist."

"I accept."

The door was open and Mark and I went right in.

"Steph?"

"Come in," she called from the kitchenette and appeared with a bottle of Champagne (Chasseur, of course!) to give Mark a hug. "I know it's early, but I thought we had to celebrate, for better or for worse."

She led us deeper into the studio and I turned toward an amazing array of vibrant colors splashed across a number of large canvasses. They were sitting on the counter and leaning against the south wall, all along the remaining length of the studio.

I was gobsmacked! I didn't know what to say, even though I knew Steph was anxiously awaiting my reaction. Mark beat me to it.

"Wow!" was all he said as he stopped to stare at the work before moving in to take a closer look.

Steph watched him, waiting.

I turned and gave her a big hug. "I am SO happy for you! I had no idea you'd already done so much. These are amazing!"

"Well, that's a relief!"

"Surely, you're pleased?" I couldn't take my eyes off the images and went to stand beside Mark.

Steph set the Champagne on the counter and joined us.

"Steph?" Michael called from the door.

She went to meet him, took his hand and brought him in for a first look. I turned to smile at him in time to see a huge grin spread across his face before he turned back to her and took her in his arms and kissed her.

"I don't know about you," I said to Mark, "but I'm blown out of the water. I've only seen her smaller pieces and these are so much more—more color, more exuberance and it looks like she's gone far beyond her previous imagery."

"I agree completely, and I see you're picking up some of the language. I'm not sure I could have said it better, myself." He turned back to Steph. "Are these in the order that you painted them?"

"Yup, first ones on the left."

"It's a really interesting transition as you move from the more traditional flower shapes into images that feel more sexual."

Steph blushed.

Michael cracked up. "Sounds like a strong selling point, to me."

"Provocative language always helps with sales, especially when the work stands firmly behind it." To Steph he said, "You told me you'd started something new. Are you referring to the way you've moved a little more to the abstract?"

"Nope, this came to me out of the blue and I had to take a shot." She went to the row of paintings and slid the sections of the center diptych apart to reveal two much smaller canvasses.

She stepped back and told Mark, "I think of these as monthly calendar pages with the events indicated by the graphic expressions in the area that would be the space for the particular day. Obviously, the good days tend to spread into those nearby."

For those of you who are interested, let me take a minute to describe what we were looking at. First, Steph's previous subjects— the ones that I was familiar with—had most often been flowers and plants. Botanical, if you will. In the two years I'd known her, she'd upped her canvas size and become somewhat more impressionistic, maybe more abstract but still clearly identifiable. The flower paintings we were looking at now were images so beyond what I'd seen before… well, as I said, I was blown away.

The "calendar" pieces were much smaller, maybe 18" x 24". The paint was very thick, a white background with the "date boxes" scored through the paint. Some boxes were carefully filled with one or two colors, some with balls of color exploding into other boxes. They were very abstract, interesting, and surprising to me—both because of how much I liked them and how different it was from the other work.

I stepped up to the smaller pieces and looked more closely.

"May and June?" I said.

"My turn to say wow!" Steph laughed in surprise. We exchanged a high five.

"How could you possibly know that?" Mark asked in surprise.

I started on May, pointing to the various boxes, counting across, naming the dates.

"This looks like stress and confusion to me, so that would be finals. Here on the twelfth where the colors begin to brighten—that's the night we went to dinner together, the night we met you, Mark. And Michael—here, what could be interpreted as a heart with all the hot colors—that's obviously you. I could go on..."

All three of them just stared at me.

"So, I'm not even close?" Their reactions confused me. I was so completely sure I was right.

"Nope, you're spot on. And thanks for not going into more detail!" Steph gave me a hug and then we all turned to Mark, waiting.

Mark was still studying the paintings. I couldn't read him.

Steph jumped in. "Well? Should I drop the calendars, drop the flowers, do both...what do you think?"

"What do you feel like doing?"

"Honestly? I'm feeling pretty committed to both. I'd like to complete a year of the calendar pieces before I show them and I still feel like I have a lot more to explore with the botanical images. And I know they're getting more sexual, so if that's not a good direction, best stop me now...or at least offer your opinion. Not sure I'm ready to quit, regardless of advice to the contrary."

Mark broke out in a broad smile. "Exactly what I was hoping to hear!" He gave her a big hug. "I think you're doing the right thing by continuing with both. I see the transition clearly in the flower images and I'm sure over the next couple of months it will continue to evolve. And I'm in love with the whole calendar concept. The paintings have a very graphic feel to them and I think people will react without trying to figure out exactly which date is which. An installation of twelve of them, all on one wall could be spectacular."

"What do you think about the size? Too big? Too small?"

"I think this size is perfect. They would be so impressive hung in one block. You could always go back and go larger on a single month and see what happens."

STILL LUCKY

Steph was beaming and I suggested we break out the Champagne. With glasses high we toasted the beginning of what was sure to be a brilliant and successful artistic career.

I took everyone to lunch at Sur (Thanks Handsome!) and when the men left us to go back to work, Steph and I lingered, sharing a sinful dessert. (Their *Old Fashioned Chocolate Cake*...oh my!)

"So how are you feeling about this preliminary showing? It's obvious that Mark is excited about the work."

Steph was ecstatic. "I couldn't have asked for a better reaction...from any of you. And collectively, I'm bordering on overwhelmed. I have to say that the freedom of having the space and the time to work with no restrictions—not to mention staying with you at the house and having Michael's support—well, I'm excited, inspired and incredibly happy. I owe it all to Richard, and to you, really, for introducing me to him and somehow engineering this opportunity."

"Whoa! I promise this whole thing was Richard's idea. He may have been afraid I'd be lonely without you, but I'm sure he only gave you the studio because he recognized your talent from the photos he saw of your work." I reached over to hug her. "Believe me, I know exactly how you're feeling. I think we both must be equally grateful for this new life we sort of wandered into. I can't imagine how it could be any better, unless Richard was here with us."

"You must miss him."

"Of course, but we're so close—even at this distance—and as you so wisely predicted, I'm so busy that I can honestly say I'm not suffering too much. So now, I want to take you to Giano's and celebrate. You can pick out a fabulous treat, my gift to you to commemorate this day. You can paint it into one of the calendars!"

When we got home there was a copy of Paris *Vogue* waiting for me from Giano, with that same double page spread!

23
Brothers

Friday, August 30

Note of the day

> *...in me nothing is extinguished or forgotten,*
> *my love feeds on your love, beloved,*
> *and as long as you live it will be in your arms*
> *without leaving mine*
> > *—If You Forget Me*, Neruda

On Friday afternoon Marie, Steph and I were lingering over an espresso and some chocolate dipped strawberries—a treat following our late lunch. Michael was in San Francisco again and we were all enjoying a day with no pressing chores. Even Marie was caught up with her work and able to kick back a little. At any rate, we were all together when my phone sang out with Richard's ringtone.

It was an incoming iGram and I put it on speaker, curious about what he might be sending at his bedtime (and assuming it would be G-rated!) Willie Nelson started singing *When I Dream* and by the time he hit the first chorus I burst into tears! I looked at Marie, whose cheeks were also wet and even Steph was tearing up! I replayed it and then punched up Richard.

"Oh, my love..." he answered.

"I thought you promised not to make me cry," I accused in a teary voice. "And not only me, but you've reduced both Steph and Marie to tears, as well."

I put Richard on speaker as he cracked up.

"On s'amuse?" Marie said indignantly.

"Not funny, Mister Wonderful," Steph added.

"Ladies, it sounds like you may be suffering from estrogen poisoning. Need a little testosterone in the house to balance things out?"

"Careful, my Prince. I warn you the ground you tread is dangerously unstable."

"Yeah, sexist, but actually, it's a great idea," Steph said. "Let's take a drive in one of those fancy cars of his and see if we can find anything worth bringing home. Or maybe Antonio would deign to spend the afternoon with us. Is that in his job description?"

Richard was still chuckling. "Perhaps I missed with the musical message, Sweetheart. I only intended to remind you I'd be dreaming of you tonight as I do every night."

"Better. So I shouldn't be concerned about someone taking you to the moon?" I tried to sound skeptical. It was so much fun to tease him.

"The only lunar excursions I intend to make will be with you."

"Good one," Steph assured him.

"Should I believe him, Marie?" I asked.

She gave me a bored French shrug. "Maybe yes, maybe no."

"Hey," Richard objected. "You're supposed to be working for me. How about some loyalty?"

"Respect must be earned," she pronounced (as she winked at me!)

"She's right. You have shattered my illusions. Now you must regain my trust," I added.

"Go upstairs and call me back with visuals. I'd love the opportunity to do just that."

I was laughing as I left the table.

Far be it from me to prevent my Prince from indulging in pretend make-up sex! I headed up to our room and quickly removed what little I was wearing in the way of clothes. I FaceTimed him standing in front of the mirror in the closet, smiling as I captured a head to toe view of myself.

"There's my beautiful astronaut. Ready for a trip to the moon?"

"*Fly me to the moon...*" I sang.

"I'm less interested in life on Jupiter and Mars than a reminder of how it feels to hold you in my arms."

"Think you can remember?"

"It's something I'll never forget, though I'm longing to experience it up close and personal again," he said in a sexy voice.

"Me, too. Come to bed with me?"

"My pleasure…and yours, too. I promise."

As I started back to the bed he said, "Before I forget, my brother Robert is going to arrive there tomorrow. He always spends some time in L.A. each summer. I missed him in Paris by a day, so he didn't know about you. He only told me his plans this afternoon."

"Great! Is he as hot and sexy as you are?" I teased. "It might raise the testosterone level you were concerned about."

"That's for you to decide. He usually brings a friend or two, so you may have some additional choices."

"Sounds interesting. Do I need to do anything, make any plans for him?"

"Marie will handle the details, and Antonio will pick them up at the airport. Time to take Reggie out for a spin. I told you Robert loves that car. At any rate, you don't need to change any of your plans. I don't think he'll disturb you, but sometimes he invites guests for dinner or whatever. Marie will know what he's doing. I'm sorry I couldn't have given you more warning."

"Can't wait to meet him. How long will he be here?"

"Probably only a week but his plans are usually pretty fluid. He has meetings to attend and business to take care of so I don't think you'll find it too disruptive."

"I'm going back to my folks on Sunday so I'll be out of his way. And Steph can probably stay with Michael or at the studio if she feels awkward about it."

"For both of you, do whatever feels comfortable. It's your house now, after all."

"Hmmm…*my* house is it? Then I suggest you come to bed and let me express my gratitude for letting me know I'm suddenly a home owner!"

"My sweet Juliet, all that I have is yours."

"It is only your love that I seek," I said as I climbed into bed.

"That you have, and more to come."

"Then give it me!" I said gleefully, throwing my free arm wide.

After dinner I was in the library when my cell rang. The ID said "private number."

"CJ, it's Robert Hunter, Richard's brother. I thought I should call and introduce myself rather than just turning up on your doorstep tomorrow afternoon."

Hmmm…quite thoughtful of him to consider this doorstep mine!

"Richard called this afternoon to let me know you were coming," I told him.

"Well, I'm glad he shared *that* news. He seems to have neglected to mention you to me. I got the information first from our mother."

I laughed. "Well, we can get acquainted tomorrow. I'm curious to know exactly what your mother had to say. I'm not quite clear on how much Richard has been sharing!"

"Can you and Stephanie join us for dinner?" I could hear the smile in his voice. "I'd very much enjoy a chance to get to know you."

"Thanks. I'll talk to Steph, but I'm pretty sure she's available."

"I'll see you tomorrow."

And with that, he was gone. *Hmmm…interesting.* I texted Steph. She was upstairs doing her mail.

R's bro invites us to dinner tomorrow.

Great! Can't wait to meet him. Fancy dress?

MayB since he loves the Rolls. Will know tomorrow.

C.J. BAILEY

Saturday, August 31

Note of the day:

> *"All that I ask," says Love, "is just to stand*
> *And gaze, unchided, deep in thy dear eyes;*
> *For in their depths lies largest Paradise."*
> —Ella Wheeler Wilcox, *All That Love Asks*

Robert arrived about 2:00 p.m. Marie had let me know the Rolls was coming up the driveway, so we were all at the door to greet him. (It felt sort of like Downton Abbey.) Antonio was driving Reggie, but he was in a black suit and tie rather than the full chauffer's uniform he'd worn that night for my "bind date" with Richard. Antonio winked as he came around to open the door.

Robert—I recognized him immediately, the resemblance was quite strong—got out and was followed by a nice looking man who was carrying a briefcase. Both of them were dressed casually. I stepped up to introduce myself.

"Hi, Robert, I'm CJ."

He took my hand and gave me kisses on both cheeks.

"*Enchanté*! This is my assistant Denis Grisel."

(For the non-French speakers among you, that's pronounced De'nee Greezel!)

I shook Denis's hand and was introducing them both to Stephanie when I saw a third man get out of the other side of the car. He was good-looking, dark haired, maybe in his twenties and slim, about six feet tall.

"This is Nico Nizzola," Robert said. "His father owns one of our partner wineries in Campania and we're meeting with his uncle next week, which is where he's headed."

"Nice place," Nico said, looking around. He seemed more interested in the house than he was in us. Without even glancing at Antonio he said, "Get my computer. It's on the seat."

That was enough to make me wary. Nothing annoys me more

than people with money, a lack of manners and a sense of entitlement—actually any people with a sense of entitlement, money or not! Nico wasn't making a very good first impression.

Robert didn't seem to notice as he went to Marie and gave her a big hug. She was beaming as they exchanged some rapid French.

We all went into the house, down the stairs and out onto the terrace. Marie followed and served us fruit and wine as we sat down under the covered portion. Nico went wandering around the pool and beyond, looking at everything as if taking inventory. Robert was focused on me.

"Alright, CJ, time to fill in the story of you and my brother. How have you managed to snag a man who has been determined to avoid entanglements for his entire life?"

I laughed. "Are you sure about that?" I asked. "Perhaps he's simply been determined to keep his previous relationships out of the family spotlight."

Robert gave me a skeptical look. "Not possible. We're very close and I can read him like a book."

"Did you skip the CJ chapter, then?"

Steph cracked up and I could see that Denis was enjoying my response. Perhaps people didn't contradict his boss very often. Robert smiled, but I could sense he was taking my measure.

'"Nooo…we just haven't had a chance to catch up in the last few months."

"Why don't you tell me what your mother had to say?" I suggested.

"Hmmmm…it seems perhaps my little brother has met his match." He took another sip of his wine. "*Maman* was astonished to find her child prodigy in love. She didn't know what to make of it but said she was convinced there will be a wedding in the next year."

I burst out laughing. Robert looked surprised.

"I suspect that if there was a wedding in my future, your brother would have probably mentioned it to me."

"So that's not an engagement ring?" he asked, nodding toward my left hand.

"Nope. Sorry to burst your bubble."

"I hope this doesn't mean you don't have feelings for Richard."

I heard the concern in his voice.

"On the contrary. I love him. Truly, madly, deeply. It's just that there are no wedding plans."

"I'm relieved. He's waited a long time to make a commitment and I wouldn't want to see him hurt."

"I can promise you that won't happen on my account."

"Good. So why don't you tell us how you met?"

Having no clue how much Richard had revealed, I kept my version vague.

"We met at an opening at his gallery. It was very odd work, but I was intrigued. We hit it off and when he learned about my Internet project, he offered me the house for the summer while he's gone."

"Pretty sweet deal for you, no?" Nico said with a wink as he returned to pour himself another glass of wine. "You must be very good."

Though I knew that he wasn't referring to my work, I said, "It was a very generous offer, to be sure."

My displeasure with his lack of manners was lost on Nico. He seemed a little edgy and I sure didn't like his vibe. He came off as sleazy and I couldn't have said exactly why I felt that way. Maybe it was just the way he looked at me.

"Richard also introduced me to some people who could help me line things out so that I can start looking for capital funding to get it up and running."

"And you, Stephanie?" Robert said, obviously trying to deflect any further remarks from Nico.

"CJ and I were housemates. After graduation I was heading back to Montana, but your brother liked my paintings and offered me the gallery's studio space for the summer. Honestly, I think he wanted CJ to have the company, but it has been terrific for me. I'm doing some exciting work and looking forward to showing it to Richard when he comes back."

"Smooth, eh? Your brother has two beautiful women just waiting for him to return!" Nico laughed, but he sounded sarcastic rather than amused.

Steph doesn't suffer fools gladly.

"Who's waiting for you, Nico?" she said before Robert could, once again, attempt to rescue the conversation.

"Oh…there are always girls," he said dismissively.

"Nico, you said you wanted to swim. Let Marie show you your room and you can change into your suit," Denis suggested.

"Great…yes!" He got up and went to find Marie.

When he was out of earshot, Robert immediately apologized to both of us.

"I'm sorry. Nico's not really a bad kid, just full of himself. We're sort of keeping an eye on him as a favor to his father. We'll be shed of him on Tuesday. Please try to ignore his lack of manners."

I smiled. "I'm flying back to Washington tomorrow, so maybe that will alleviate some of the problem."

"Richard said your father has been ill?"

"Heart attack and bypass surgery. Totally unexpected, but his recovery is going very well."

"I'm glad to hear it. What does your father do?" Robert asked.

"Both my parents teach at Whitman College in Walla Walla. My mother is in Theater Arts and Daddy's in the Music department with a lot of focus on performance."

"Did Richard tell you he was a child prodigy on the piano?"

"He did." (It was the night he told me about Maryse. I'd never mentioned it to Steph. I considered it private.)

"Hey, wait…" Steph said. "Why didn't I know this?"

"He doesn't play anymore," I said, intending to put a damper on her curiosity.

"He quit quite suddenly when he was eighteen and moved to the U.S. to live with our father and go to school," Robert continued. "None of us ever knew what caused him to drop his very promising career so suddenly."

Close, are you? And then my heart felt a little twinge. Poor Richard had been so deeply hurt that he couldn't even share it with his big brother.

"I know Richard went to Harvard. Did you go to school there, as well?" I asked.

"I went to Harvard, then did graduate work in France—international business, finance and so forth. I'm five years older, so we weren't at Harvard together. By the time he started, I'd gone back to France."

"Are you married?"

"Yes. My wife Danielle and I married nine years ago. We have two children. Louis is six and Gabrielle is four. We live about an hour from Paris at Chantilly."

"And the rest of your siblings?" I think Robert noticed that now I was the one asking the questions.

For a moment he just looked at me. "Richard hasn't told you this?"

"I know you have a sister, Cybelle, and the youngest is Grégoire. Richard has a photo in his office of you all together."

"Those two got the artistic genes," he explained, "if you discount Richard's musical talent. Cybelle is an interior designer. Her husband is an architect and they have a home in in Brazil but travel a great deal with their work. Grégoire does all the art and advertising connected with the wine business. He lives in Paris."

I turned the bottle on the table to look at the label. It was beautifully designed.

"The wine labels, too?"

"Yes. His work."

"I've admired the labels since before I realized that Chasseur was your brand," I said. "Very nice work. I hope to meet the rest of your family one of these days."

"There's usually an opportunity at least once a year—a wedding, a party, some sort of holiday celebration—any excuse for *Maman* to throw a reunion. She does love to orchestrate events. And I'm hoping my brother will be willing to share you soon."

"I'd enjoy that. I'm an only child so I find family dynamics can be fascinating."

Robert laughed. "Well, they can be confusing and sometimes frustrating, but also rewarding. It's wonderful to have the support of a large number of people who feel a blood obligation. Our mother's family is a large one, so when you're finally presented to the clan, I suggest you prepare yourself!"

Marie came out and asked if she could speak to me, so I excused myself and followed her back inside.

"I wanted to tell you that I have activated the locks on your closet, Monsieur Richard's office and on the library. I do not trust this Nico."

"I know what you mean," I said as she showed me how to deactivate the locks with the house cell when I needed access. It was reassuring to know I wasn't the only one uncomfortable with Nico.

STILL LUCKY

Robert took all of us to Spago for dinner. We were seated in one of the smaller private rooms so we could hear each other talk (And take selfies for Richard!) The restaurant was busy, of course, and the noise level rather high, but the food was outstanding. The sommelier, Chris Miller, came out to greet us and offered us several wines to sample with the various courses, including some of the Chasseur high-end selections that I hadn't tried.

We had a lovely time. Nico behaved, more or less, though he continued making inappropriate remarks that we all just ignored. He did excuse himself several times and I found myself wondering if he was doing a little coke. When Steph and I went to the Ladies, she told me she was getting the same impression. I suggested she might think about locking her room that night as I planned to do.

It was annoying to have Nico spoiling our enjoyment of Robert and Denis, who had been intent on showing us a nice evening.

24
Little Nico

Later that evening

When we got home—and by the way, we were traveling in Reggie with Antonio at the wheel (the pretense still bothered me, but Robert seemed to consider it simply good fun, not privilege) we collectively decided to go for a swim among the stars. I was going to turn on the lasers, too. We were all feeling the wine and I was more convinced than ever that Nico was bumping along on the white stuff, but Steph and I were enjoying Robert and Denis and confident that they could control Nico. I was secretly hoping dancing might happen!

I hurried to change and put on my most modest bikini while wishing I had a one piece to deter unwanted attention. When I came back out onto the landing, I found Nico trying the locked door to Richard's office.

"Can I help you, Nico?" I asked, my tone putting a fine point on it.

He turned and instead of looking embarrassed at being caught doing something he had no business doing, he grinned at me.

"I was looking for you, *Bella*. I have something I thought you might want."

Such a difference between Nico calling me "Bella" and Giano using that word!

"Really? And what would that be?"

He grabbed his crotch and jiggled the bulge in his speedo. He took a step toward me. I took a step back.

"Believe me, I have no interest in your penis." (I've found

specific language often deters unwanted attention. Egos easily deflate in the face of clear speech as with Malcolm that night at the gala.

"No? Are you sure, *Bella*? It is a very nice one and I think maybe you have not been fucked for a long time." He pulled down the front of his suit and began stroking himself.

I gave his penis a dismissive glance and said, "I'm quite sure. You have nothing I want."

"I'm sorry for that because you have something I want. Little Nico wants a nice wet place…"

Have I mentioned how weird I think it is that men name their penises? I've never heard Richard call his anything but his cock. I mean, do we girls name our breasts? But I digress…

"Then take little Nico and give him a nice cold shower," I suggested.

I turned toward the stairs, but he caught my shoulder and spun me around hard, grabbing for my breast with his other hand.

"Stop playing games, *Figa*!" he snarled. "I can only imagine what you had to do to end up spending the summer here. I'm going to do you a favor and remind you what it is to have a man inside you."

I was incensed that he'd dared to touch me. "TAKE YOUR HANDS OFF ME!" I shouted.

Then everything happened at once. He reached for my other breast and tore that side of my top down. I kneed him in his exposed balls, giving his erection a good slam in the process, but it only made him angrier. Either the alcohol or the coke (or both) seemed to have rendered him oblivious to the pain.

He slapped me hard and jerked the center of my top and I felt the ties let go. I'd hesitated to do it, but now I was the one who was mad. *How dare he?!* I grabbed his hand, intending to flip him, but his arm hit the steel railing around the stairs and I heard a sickening snap.

By then both Robert and Denis had hold of him and the pain had finally gotten his attention. Steph grabbed my hand and pulled me toward my room as I heard someone's fist connect with what must have been Nico's jaw, because he was suddenly quiet.

She closed the door behind us and just looked at me.

"I'm fine, but they need to get Nico to the ER. His arm is broken. I heard it crack on the banister."

There was a light knock on the door. Steph grabbed a towel

from the bathroom and tossed it to me so I could cover myself before she opened it.

"CJ, are you OK? Did he hurt you?" Robert was concerned and in that moment he reminded me very much of Richard.

"I'm OK, but you need to get him to the hospital. I broke his arm. It was an accident."

"A shame it wasn't his neck!" he said softly, but I detected a hint of the same rage I'd seen in Richard that night at the gala when he confronted Malcolm.

Unfortunately, Nico had been a much bigger challenge than Malcolm, and I didn't feel I'd handled it as well as I should have.

"I saw what happened. I just wasn't fast enough. I'm so sorry," Robert said. "Do you need anything? What can I do for you?"

"Nothing. Really. Just get him out of here."

Robert seemed torn between staying with me and going to deal with Nico. In the end, he went back to help Denis take Nico to his room so they could put some clothes on him.

"Let's go to the studio tonight," I said to Steph. "And then… Can you drive me to the airport tomorrow?"

"Sure. Can you get packed? I'll see about getting Sue Sue Subaru. Maybe Antonio can bring her up before he gets a car for them."

When we got to the studio, I punched up Richard.

"Sweetheart. Are you OK?"

Robert must have called him.

"I'm fine. But Richard, I'm afraid I may have opened you up to a lawsuit or something. Breaking his arm was an accident, it hit the banister and…"

Richard laughed.

"Honestly, I don't think this is funny." I was annoyed. *Why is he laughing?*

"Of course it's not. I just want to be sure he didn't hurt you."

"I'm fine."

Then he asked me to tell him what happened and I went over it in detail. All I could think of was scandal and lawsuits and I couldn't bear to cause him any difficulties. I wasn't paying attention to the fact that he might be having a very different reaction, but I heard it when he asked the next question.

He was carefully controlling his voice when he said, "Do you have any bruises?"

I turned to Steph and lifted my Tshirt. "Bruises?"

She nodded. "Not yet but looks like you'll be pretty colorful by tomorrow."

I could see from her expression that it must be worse than it felt.

"Apparently there will be," I told him.

"Have Steph snap some pictures, just in case. Will you do that for me?"

"Yes. Of course." I was thinking t was a good idea to have evidence in case the situation escalated.

"Now, let me call Robert again and I'll get back to you in a bit. Are you truly all right, Sweetheart?"

"I'm fine. I'm just worried that this will cause trouble for you. I'm so sorry."

"Don't ever wonder why I love you. Now, let me talk to Steph for a minute."

Steph assured him that I was truly OK and then he hung up.

"Gees, here you are doing nude modeling again," she said as she took me into the bathroom where the light was good. "We'll take some more tomorrow morning."

I stopped and stared at my reflection. There was a sizable red mark on my cheek and along my jaw where he'd hit me, more from his fingers on my shoulder and upper arm, and on one of my breasts, and some scratches where he'd grabbed the front of my top.

To be honest, it surprised me. I was a little shaky, probably from the adrenalin, even though I'd never, even for a minute, felt that I wouldn't be able to handle him. I'd felt rage when he put his hands on me, but I hadn't been afraid of him. I was only scolding myself for the problems I may have caused Richard.

I handed her my phone. "Take the pictures, Steph, but I have no intention of showing them to Richard unless there's a real need for him to have them. I'm afraid that if he sees these, he'll charter a jet and come back here and strangle Nico himself."

She looked at me. I could see she was still trying to figure out how upset I was.

"I'm OK," I told her again. "Really, I am. Ji has taught us well and I was never afraid of Nico. I just didn't want to hurt him. He obviously couldn't do much damage with that little penis of his."

Stephanie burst out laughing and then I knew she believed me. We continued exchanging disparaging remarks about Nico's delusions of grandeur as we got ready for bed. It was almost 2:00 a.m.

Richard called just after I pulled on my sleepshirt.

"Are you ready for bed?" Richard asked.

"I am. And Steph is going to take me to the airport tomorrow, so I'm all set."

"I don't want you to worry about any repercussions from this. I've talked to Nico's father. He knows what a problem is son is, which is why he sent him to the U.S. His uncle there should be able to straighten him out. And Robert explained to Nico that he could go along with the story that he tripped and fell on the stairs or face prosecution and jail for attempted rape, so he's behaving. There are no problems for me, Sweetheart. My only concern is for you."

Sunday September 1

> *It frightened him to think*
> *what must have gone*
> *to the making of her eyes.*
> —Edith Wharton
> *The Age of Innocence*

Scared? XXOOJ

Steph was right. The bruises were obvious in the morning and she took more pictures for me. I intended to transfer them to my hard drive later, though I hoped Richard would never need them.

I managed to mostly cover the marks on my face with make-up and then Steph dropped me off at the airport. You can imagine my surprise when I found Robert waiting for me at the gate.

"Are you leaving today, too?" I asked as I glanced around for some sign of Denis.

Robert smiled and took me gently by the shoulders for a double kiss.

"I got a gate pass. I didn't want to miss the chance to apologize in person."

"That's not necessary."

"It most certainly is. My decision to invite Nico put you in danger and drove you out of your home. I am so sorry, CJ."

What a sweet man. Then he looked a little closer and noticed the bruise along my jaw and on my cheek. It still showed a little.

"Richard said he asked Steph to take some pictures. I need you to give them to me."

I studied him for a moment.

"Just in case Nico needs reminding," he added.

"Will you promise me you won't show them to Richard? He would be furious if he saw them. Despite what he thinks, I really can take care of myself."

"You certainly proved that last night, but I regret not being there in time to prevent you from having to defend yourself."

I smiled.

"The photos?"

I sent them to his phone and when he looked at them his anger was as transparent as Richard's had been that night with Malcolm. I put my hand on his and he turned off the screen.

"Robert, I'm fine. Really, I am. I regret that I wasn't able to handle it better. I should have been able to stop Nico without doing so much damage, and I'm sorry he got hurt. My main concern was that I might have created a problem for Richard, but you've solved that. Neither of us have to think about it anymore."

Robert smiled. "You might have had more trouble stopping him than you think. His blood alcohol level was very high and he tested positive for cocaine. He was certainly more trouble than any of us bargained for."

"Well, I can only warn you never to underestimate me. I still have a few tricks up my sleeve."

Robert laughed. "You're full of surprises, aren't you?"

"You know, your brother says the same thing."

"He's a very lucky man. I'm so happy he found you."

"I'm a very lucky girl."

Robert stayed with me for another hour until I boarded. I really enjoyed talking to him, even though I could tell he was still trying to assure himself that I was OK. It was funny to me that both Richard and Robert had hinted that their mother was a formidable woman. For some reason the impression I had of her was that she was not warm and loving, and yet she had raised at least two very thoughtful and caring men. I was looking forward to meeting her and Richard's other siblings next year when we were in France!

When I got back to Walla Walla, I got into the rented Mercedes and called Mom to see where everyone was.

"We're just about to leave the rehab center. Your dad's getting ready for another physical therapy session, so your gran and I are going to do some grocery shopping and then head home. Why don't you meet us at the house?" Mom suggested.

I got there first and got unpacked, set up my laptop to transfer the pictures and called Richard.

"Are you back on the ground?" he asked.

"I am. Just got to the house and am waiting for Mom and Gran to get home. Are you ready for bed?"

"Just about. A little bit more with the computer and I can get in the shower."

"Robert surprised me at the gate before my flight left. I think he wanted to be sure I was recovered. You're brother seems to be as thoughtful as you are."

"He's over the moon about you and he feels terrible about what happened. He never would have brought Nico to the house if he'd realized what a jerk he is. We both knew he had some problems, but neither of us suspected they were as serious as they apparently are. His father downplayed them when he asked for Robert's help."

"Well, everything is fine now. And on a much brighter note, I don't know if Mark has said anything, but Steph is going to have some pretty wonderful things to show you when you get home."

"Mark only said he was very impressed."

"Good. We all want you to be surprised."

"I'm looking forward to seeing what she's done. Most of all I'm looking forward to seeing you."

"Me, too. I miss you, Handsome. I wish I could rock you to sleep, but Mom and Gran should be here any minute. Might be hard to explain what I was doing in bed in the middle of the afternoon."

"Fortunately, I have a vivid imagination."

"Part of your Professional training?" I asked.

"Absolutely. Can't wait to have you review my skills in person. I suspect you may have forgotten some of my more subtle accomplishments."

"Hmmm…a review would certainly be in order. Meanwhile, can you manage a wake up call for me?"

"Your wish is my command."

"Then 5:00 a.m. please."

"Still so early?" I heard the surprise in his voice.

"Yup. Don't want to lose the momentum. My folks have a treadmill, but I may just go for a run tomorrow. And I want to get signed up for some yoga that I can do while I'm here. I still intend to surprise you with the new me when you finally come home."

"I'll take you in any form you come in. I love you, CJ."

"Funny, I love you, too! How great is that?"

"The greatest!"

25
Possibilities

Monday, September 2

Note of the day:

> *Music is the way our memories sing*
> *to us across time. The loveliest quality*
> *of music involves its modulation upon*
> *the theme of time. Songs, playing in*
> *the mind become the subtlest shuttles*
> *across years.* —Lance Morrow

And across distance! XXOOJ

I was half awake, probably in anticipation, when Richard's call came.

"I was just thinking of you, my love," I answered. I kept my eyes closed, enjoying that favorite place of mine between asleep and awake.

"And what were you thinking?"

"That you were lying here with me, spooning me. My big pillow is against my back and it's warm. Wish I'd brought one of your shirts to put on it."

"How shall I help you greet the day, Sweetheart?"

I opened my eyes then and clicked my phone to see his beautiful face. I kissed the screen. Couldn't help myself.

"Good morning, my Prince," I said as I stretched. "I think I'd like your mouth since I still haven't worked up the nerve to try to get Zoor through airport security."

Richard laughed. "I thought you said you bought yourself a little helper last trip."

"I did. But it's just one of those kind that slips on your finger. Nothing like you...or any part of you, sad to say. I may have to order something sent here. Just to keep on standby."

"We could always get you a Zoor's twin brother."

I cracked up. "I'm not sure I want to leave a replica of your penis here, unattended."

"Would your mother be scandalized if she found it?"

"A normal vibrator no, but Zoor is something else altogether. It might make it a bit awkward when you two finally meet."

His turn to laugh. "I can see your point. Maybe you'd best order one of Bob's brothers. Would that scandalize her?"

"I doubt it. We've always been pretty frank when we talk about sex."

"Does that mean you've discussed the two of us?"

I cracked up. He sounded so serious and maybe just the tiniest bit concerned.

"Hardly! I'm sure they all realize we're having sex...or had it before you left, anyway. Not sure any of them imagine what's going on in our long distance relationship. Except maybe Gran. It was Gran who asked me point blank how the sex was."

"Really? And what did you say?"

I could tell he was surprised.

"Only good things, of course. After all, nobody does it better."

"Let's see what I can do for you right now. Close those beautiful eyes and let me touch you."

I had a nice run in the cool morning air and after breakfast I went to the rehab center to see Daddy. Mom was in meetings at school and Gran was going to start interviewing physical therapists willing to make house calls, to find someone who would work with Daddy after he came home.

When I knocked lightly on his door he sang the expected response, "*Somebody's knockin'....,*" which immediately let me know he was feeling stronger.

"Hey, beautiful! Come back to check on your old man?"

"It's a dirty job, but somebody's got to do it," I said as I gave him a hug and a kiss.

"Well, fortunately the women of my family seem to feel I'm worth preserving."

"Yup, we've decided we'll keep you around."

"Tore yourself away from that boyfriend of yours, did you?"

"You know Richard's still in Paris," I reminded him.

"London, actually."

"What?"

"He FaceTimed me when he arrived in London last night," my father said smugly.

Hmmm...Richard is in touch with my father? He hadn't said anything to me.

"You're talking to Richard?"

Daddy frowned. "Of course. I want to see who this guy is. I'm not going to allow you to make the wrong choice, you know."

"And so?"

He gave me a calculating look. "Well, I hate to admit it, but he seems pretty great."

"Ha! Told ya!" I said smugly.

"Yeah, well...I still want to meet him in person and he's promised to come up for a visit when he gets back."

"Good. I guarantee you won't be disappointed. So, now what about school?"

"I'm going to telecom the Friday department meeting. Then my TA will take over the orientation and basics for the classes next week. After that, I'm going to see what I can do remotely until I can get back in the classroom."

This surprised me. I assumed he'd be taking the semester off.

"You're not taking on too much, are you?"

He could see I was concerned.

"Nope. I talked to the doc and I've handed off two of my classes to Mosher. That leaves me with two classes and three graduate performance students. I should be fine."

"Well, at least I can set up your telecom system for you. Put me in touch with your TA and I'll find out what you need." I took a good long look at him. "Promise me you'll pace yourself. We want a full recovery with no glitches. Understood?"

He laughed softly. "Understood."

When I got back to the house, Gran was on her way out.

"Where are you off to?" I asked.

"I'm going to the college, your mother needs my help. The situation with your father has sort of put her behind the eight ball. We're going to work through lunch, then stop by to see your dad on the way home this afternoon."

"Let me take us out to dinner. It's on Richard."

"Done. Make us some reservations somewhere for 7-7:30 p.m. I'll call if we're running late."

She gave me a squeeze and got into her car.

I looked at my watch. It was almost 11:00 and I was planning to call Richard between 11:30 and noon. I went in and phoned Saffron for a dinner res. Then I called Brad Nichols, Daddy's TA, and left him a message. I wanted to see if he could come by sometime the next day. I had a few ideas about setting up a video link from the house and I wanted to find out exactly what was needed.

With that taken care of, I made myself a smoothie and settled down with my laptop to FaceTime Richard. Jetz immediately jumped into my lap to investigate my choice of food. Benny opened one eye briefly to regard me from Daddy's recliner, but decided I had nothing he was interested in and promptly went back to sleep. Jetz came to the same conclusion and jumped down.

"So you got to London last night?" I said when Richard's beautiful face filled my screen.

"Yup. Back to old Blighty."

"Old Blighty?"

"Originally a World War I reference."

"Guess I missed that one. I'm not a fan of war movies," I said, assuming that was the only place I might have come across it. "I'm not interested in books about war, either."

"Neither am I, but you hear it over here occasionally."

Out of the blue I said, "So when were you going to tell me you've been spending time with my father?" I gave him a stern look and he laughed.

"Did he rat me out?"

"He did. What are you up to?" I said suspiciously.

"Just trying to do some preliminary groundwork so he'll be well disposed to like me when we finally meet. I'm not above sucking up when necessary. If you ever decide to marry me, I'll have to ask his permission and I wouldn't want him to say 'no'."

"I'm hardly chattel he's allowed to dispose of, but putting archaic misogynistic practices aside, what sort of conversations are you having?"

"Actually, we've been talking about music and his teaching. I'm really looking forward to spending some time with him when we get together."

"Did you tell him you were a child prodigy?"

Richard hesitated. "No. And I'd be grateful if you don't mention it. I'm not sure I want to revisit that situation just yet."

I could see it bothered him.

"He won't hear it from me," I assured him. "But I thought you were beyond that. Is it still painful?"

"No. Not really. It's just that I'm still processing the fact that I voluntarily gave up the piano. It was such a huge part of my life before I left France, and then in my attempt to understand my feelings for Maryse, I totally abandoned it. Your father asked if I played and I just said it had been many years and let it go at that."

"Robert did ask if I knew you'd had a promising career and said that the family never understood why you stopped. It surprised Steph, so I just said you don't play anymore and changed the subject."

"Thank you for that. When we're back together again we can talk about it. I should have it sorted out by then."

"I'll follow your lead. My father is amazing on the piano and works with the masters students on performance. You two have a lot in common."

"I want to hear him play. Your father loves you as much as I do, Sweetheart."

"You just remember that if you ever think about doing me

wrong, Daddy would come after you!" I said, hoping to lighten the mood.

"I promise to keep that in mind. In the meantime, I'm enjoying getting to know him better. I intend to find a way into your mother's heart, as well."

"You're already there. You two can talk musical theater."

"I'll have to ring her up one of these nights."

"Do it. She'd love the surprise. But time for you to focus on me! Don't make me jealous that my parents may be getting more of your attention than I am."

He laughed. "I thought you weren't the jealous type."

"Yahbutt…" I said, all whiney.

"Not to worry. You'll see how much you've been on my mind when you get home. Surprises will be awaiting your perusal. And that's fair warning, so you don't burst into tears."

"Well, they *are* tears of gratitude, after all."

"Good. I don't want you forgetting how very much I love you. Now, are you ready for a PowerPoint?"

"I am," I said as I pulled up his file.

OMG! I couldn't hide my surprise when he got to the pictures of his mother's house in Paris. It looked like something straight out of *Dangerous Liaisons* and I said so. That made him laugh.

"Well, not quite, but I admit it's pretty palatial. Mother's family has nobility scattered throughout and she never let us forget it when we were growing up, despite the fact that it was abolished in the name of *égalité*."

"I hope that doesn't mean she tried to make you believe you were above the masses." Knowing Richard I couldn't imagine that.

"No. Not at all. Rather it was a way of reminding us that we had an obligation to behave properly at all times and concern ourselves with the needs of others."

"Well, I have to say that stuck on you and also seems to be part of Robert's makeup."

"We're all still pretty well behaved."

"I'm looking forward to meeting your mother. I hope she won't be disappointed in your choice of lovers."

"I think she's still processing the fact that I even *have* a lover."

"I'll try to do you proud when the time comes," I promised.

We spent the next hour looking at his photos and a couple of videos, one he made at the winery in Fontvieille and another of some work by an artist I didn't care for.

"Not for me," I told him, "but take that for what it's worth. Even you couldn't have sold me on the stringy pieces."

"Bet I could have," he suggested seductively.

I had to laugh. He was right, of course. "If you did, I would suffer buyer's remorse as soon as you were out of sight. Give me a gorgeous window painting any day." Even as I said it, I realized how much I missed that painting! I told him that surprised me.

"It happens. I feel that way about a number of pieces in my collection. Fortunately, I can usually just close my eyes and recall them pretty accurately."

I tried it, and sure enough, there was my window. "Wow! Who knew it was so simple?"

We talked for a while, just chitchat as people do. It was so nice to get back into that comfortable place that felt almost as good as actually having him share the library couch with me. Of course, as I've said so many times, what I missed the most was having his arms around me.

There was something else I wanted his input on.

"Can you switch to business focus for a minute?" I asked.

"What do you need?"

"Ben and Jerry are considering putting out feelers for a sale of my project as it is, while they wait for responses on the funding. I don't know how to feel about that."

"It's really encouraging that they think it's a possibility, however remote, at this stage. Why not go for it? You don't have to take an offer, even if there is one."

"But if someone does want to buy it, I don't know how I would know if the price they offered was the right one."

Richard laughed. "You'll know, believe me."

"Because you're a Trained Professional?"

"Exactly. You can trust your instincts when it comes to a big decision like that. If the deal is right, you won't have any reservations. If there are too many concerns, then pass on it."

"You make it sound so simple."

"It's not simple, in that you have to be sure you understand all the aspects of a proposal, but when you do, then the decision you make can be based on both knowledge and how you feel on a gut level. I'm happy to help you analyze any plans moving forward if it will help. At this point, your best interests are in the hands of your Ice Cream Boys."

"No wonder I love you," I said. I was in total awe of his ability to change gears and go into pragmatic business mode.

"And all this time I thought you were just responding to how much I love you. Who knew it was my brain you were after?"

"That and a few other body parts," I reminded him.

"Care to elaborate?"

"Maaybee...are you ready for bed?"

"No. I had an early dinner and have been doing some reading, but I find myself craving dessert. I was wondering if maybe I could interest you in a little soft serve?"

"Yes, please." I said, thinking to myself, *if only*! "Are you ready?"

"Give me a minute, I need a towel."

"What are you wearing?" I said in a sexy voice.

He laughed. "My 501s and a tee."

"Want me to talk you through this?"

"Can you talk with your mouth full?"

"Noooo...but I can still create some interesting sound effects for you and since your hands will have to double for me, I can toss in some commentary. But if you have something else in mind..."

"You had me at 'interesting sound effects'," he assured me.

"Don't you dare tell me you started without me!" I was all outraged disappointment.

"Wouldn't think of it."

"I'm sort of imagining this as a purely aural experience..." I suggested.

"Uh, yes...soft serve has always been oral, hasn't it?" He sounded a bit confused.

"That would be aural with an 'A', Mister Trained Professional."

Richard chuckled. "Snap. Guess the anticipation has fogged my brain, blood moving south and all that."

"I can only hope. So where do you want to be?"

"You tell me."

"Just stand there for a minute, and turn off your camera."

My screen when dark even as I flipped off my own camera. I let a few moments pass before I said, "Take off your tee."

"Yes, ma'am."

"That's better. You know how I love to look at you. Are you wearing underwear?"

"Actually, no. I just got out of the shower."

"Mmmmm….good. I love the taste of you with a hint of soap. Now leave the top button on your fly closed and open the next two. I want your cock, but not your balls."

"Like this?

"Exactly. Your cock is so lovely. Hard or soft it is incredibly tempting. Let me just have a few licks of the tip. Mmmmm…"

"Too much of that and there won't be any soft serve." he warned me.

"Then I'm going to fill my mouth with you until you're so hard I can't contain you." I put my mouth close to my mic and made sloppy wet sounds, hoping he had a lot of warm lube on his hands.

"Mmmmm…as always you're delicious. Do you like it when I press my mouth tight against your jeans?"

"I do."

"How about this? When I slip my tongue in just below your cock to tickle your balls?"

"My beautiful girl…."

"You're too big now. But I still want to explore all of you with my tongue. Not your balls, though. Not yet."

Richard groaned.

"Oh, my Prince, you are so magnificent. Even with one hand around you, I still can't get all of you in my mouth. I'll have to settle for running by tongue slowly over that smooth tip and just sucking and licking. I'm worshiping you Richard, I hope you know that."

"I do. Let me drop my pants. I want you to touch my balls."

"Not yet. I need to feel your nipples first. They're as hard as your cock. Can you feel my tongue and my teeth on them? Don't worry, I won't hurt you, but I know you like my mouth on your nipples as much as I like yours on mine." I gave him a soft laugh. "I think your cock gets even harder when I do that."

I could hear Richard's breathing shift.

"Don't come yet. I'm not finished tasting you. I need to run my tongue down your belly, over those ripped abs, so I can dip into your belly button. "Mmmmm…" More noises for my Prince.

"Now you can drop those pants. And step out of them. I'm going down on my knees, Richard. I've still got one hand on your cock, stroking you slowly, but now I need your balls. Oooh… they're so tight. You must want to come."

"I do."

"Not yet. I want to lick those balls, first one, then the other. Yummm…I have to press so close to get one in my mouth. Does it feel good?"

"Wonderful," Richard said breathlessly.

"Shall I suck the other one?"

"Yes, please," he said, stealing my usual response.

"You are such a polite boy. I like that. I like your beautiful cock even more. Do you want to come in my mouth?"

"Only if you want me to."

"You know I do. Fuck me, Richard."

Moments later I heard him come. I continued to make wet sounds until I could tell he was done.

"My Prince, you honor me with your beautiful body. Thank you."

"I love you, Cress. You never cease to surprise me."

"As is my intention," I assured him.

26
Muguet des Bois

Sunday, September 8

Note of the day:

> *The supreme happiness of life is the*
> *conviction that we are loved.*
> — Victor Hugo

> I was "convicted" the first moment I
> looked into your beautiful eyes!
> XXOOJ

At just after noon on Sunday I was through security and waiting at the gate for my flight to L.A. I had turned in Giano's little Mercedes a week early and would be driving my father's car when I returned. I found a seat facing the window and gave Richard a call, hoping he hadn't already gone to bed.

"Hey, Beautiful," he said when he answered.

"I'm at the airport, waiting for my flight to board. I was hoping I could catch you before they called it."

"I'm just sitting here reading."

"Anything interesting?"

"Your recommendation. *Sparrow*."

"I love that book," I said, fondly recalling how amazed I was by the completely unique story and all the unexpected turns.

"So you said. I've only just started. I'm looking forward to discussing it."

"Our own little book group?"

"I suspect our discussions might be very stimulating," he suggested, tongue firmly in cheek.

I laughed out loud. "And what makes you think so?"

"Well, great minds…unusual subject matter…a combination that could easily lead to interesting conclusions."

"Conclusions as in 'intellectual clarification of thought' or meaning what happens at the end of the discussion?"

"I suspect we'll just have to wait and see," he teased.

"I guess we will. Can't wait to be curled up on the couch with you and find out."

"Me, too. So, when you get home remember your anniversary present is waiting for you and a new piece of art I hope you'll enjoy. I think you'll immediately see why it appealed to me."

"Hmmmm…that sounds interesting." I was still amazed he insisted on celebrating our monthly anniversaries.

"I'm sorry these things seem to be coming all at once. At the time I arranged the shipping on some of them, your father's heart attack wasn't a factor."

"It's fine. Nothing like surprises stacking up in my absence!"

"Does this mean you're getting over your aversion to my offerings?"

"A little bit. You always manage to find such meaningful gifts, it's pretty easy to appreciate your thoughtfulness." And I meant it. It wasn't like he was just showering me with odds and ends. Everything he'd given me had been carefully selected in an effort to please me in some special way. Even Zoor!

"I just get a kick out of finding things I think you'll enjoy. For me, it's the sharing that makes it fun. I hope you'll get comfortable with it one of these days."

"Be careful, Handsome, you may be creating a monster," I warned.

"I'm not worried, are you?"

"Maybe, a little. If you could toss in a few things with smaller price tags, it might make it a little easier."

"Well, Sweetheart, the neighborhoods I find myself in are

generally pretty pricey. But if you'd been in Tours with me, I would have bought you an armload of fresh flowers."

"Next year."

"Next, year," he promised.

"They're calling my flight."

"I'll give you a wake up call in the morning. Have a good trip."

"I love you most!" I said gleefully.

"Damn! You beat me to it!"

"You've got to be quick," I pronounced smugly.

"I thought you preferred I take my time?"

"Say goodnight, Richard," I laughed.

"Goodnight, Richard," he repeated.

Steph was just walking up to the front door when we pulled in and Antonio got out to open the car door for me.

"Hey, stranger," Steph said. "How's your dad?"

"Just great. He should be ready to come home from the rehab center in another week or so. How's Michael?"

"Perfect-er and perfect-er. I'm still not clear on how things just get better and better, but you've convinced me to stop asking questions and just enjoy."

I laughed. "Glad you've decided to follow my advice," I gave her a hug. "I still say we're the luckiest girls on the planet."

"How's your hunk?"

"Same old, same old—as in 'still amazing.' I found out he's been Skyping with my dad."

"Really?" She was as surprised as I'd been when I found out.

"Yup. My dad let the cat out of the bag. But he had to admit Richard seemed pretty great."

Steph gave me a high five as we started up the stairs.

"How 'bout a quick swim before dinner?"

"I was thinking the same thing," she said. "Meet you in the pool in five."

As I headed for the closet to change, I noticed Richard's addition to "our" art collection standing on the tansu chest. She was beautiful! It was bronze sculpture about eighteen inches tall of a nymph or fairy—she had little double wings—and looked to me to be very art deco. She was standing on her tiptoes, bending down and looking back over her shoulder with a finger to her lips, urging the viewer to keep her secret. She was nude and had short hair, like mine. Of course the reason Richard had fallen in love with her was obvious. From the rear, the angle in which she was posed gave a tantalizing view of her very ripe little cunt—one of his favorite views. I had to admit that seeing that 3-D example made me appreciate his enjoyment of that particular sight. I turned her so the view was straight-on, from the rear.

I patted her little bottom and went to change. On the island another gift was waiting, the anniversary present no doubt, and from the size and shape of the box I suspected more jewelry. There was a card with it, and tempted though I was, I decided to wait and open it at dinner.

Steph and I both admired my anniversary present when I opened it at the table. Richard had found a beautiful lily of the valley bracelet with enameled leaves, and pearls for the blossoms.

"Because of your perfume?" Steph asked.

Muguet des Bois, (lily of the valley) my perfume, was my favorite and Richard had given me a very fancy—and much more expensive—bottle of that scent not long after we met.

"That would be my guess, though it may be just the fact that it's beautiful."

"How long do you think he'll keep celebrating your monthly anniversaries?"

"No telling. He's a hopeless romantic. I have suggested that he might want to find some less extravagant ways to commemorate us meeting." I laughed, shaking my head as I slipped the bracelet on and held up my wrist to admire it. "We'll see if he can adapt."

When Marie brought our food, she noticed the bracelet.

"Such a good man to remind you that he thinks of you, even if you are so far apart," she said.

"He *is* good. The very best!" I winked at Steph. "I still can't imagine how I got so lucky."

"Obviously, it was your turn to be loved by someone who has so much to give," Marie offered with conviction.

I smiled and found myself blinking back a tear. "I'll do everything I can to deserve him."

Marie patted my shoulder. "You're doing just fine," she assured me as she turned back to the kitchen.

"As I've told you many times, you two are so obviously perfect for each other that none of us who know you can imagine anything else. Enjoy!" Steph said as she lifted her wine glass in a toast.

"So enough about me and my fabulous life. Tell me what's happening in yours."

"I've been painting like a mad woman. I finished three more pieces this week."

"Wow! Sounds like inspiration." I was impressed.

"Exactly. I spent two nights at the studio because I couldn't put my brushes down. It is such an exciting place to be: consumed by creative energy."

"Have you been doing calendars or flowers?" I asked.

"Both. I'm backing up on the calendars with the intention of doing all of this year. So I managed January and February and then did a pretty sizable botanical piece. Michael wasn't too happy that I didn't spend Wednesday night with him, but he understands. He's hugely supportive, which is exactly what I need from him when I'm on a roll."

"It's pretty amazing the way our men open up so many possibilities for us, isn't it?"

"Here's to Richard's amazing world and all its inhabitants," Steph said, offering another toast. "And the new reality we find ourselves living."

"May we continue to be contributing citizens with all the implied obligations and obvious benefits!" I added as our glasses clinked in a toast.

STILL LUCKY

Tuesday, Sept 10

Note of the day:

> *The wisdom of the earth in a kiss*
> *and everything else in your eyes.*
> —Ancient Egyptian

Some things never change! XXOOJ

On Tuesday evening, Marie and I were just leaving the dinner table when Richard called on my cell.

"My Prince!"

Before I could say anything else he said, "How soon can you be ready to leave?"

"Where am I going?"

"I thought you might consider spending a few days with me in New York."

"Really?" I wasn't sure if I should believe him or not. "It's not nice to tease the woman you profess to love," I warned.

"Wouldn't think of it. Just found out I have an opportunity to attend an event and it wouldn't be the same without you."

"What do I need to bring?"

"Just pack a carry-on. We'll get whatever you need when you get there."

"One of my fancy gowns?"

"No, it's a black and white event so we'll need to find you something new. Prepare yourself for shopping, Miss Hot Pants. No time for meltdowns this trip. Meanwhile, just toss a couple of outfits in a bag and be ready to leave by 9:00 p.m. Can you manage it?"

I glanced at my watch. It was already 7:40!

"Anything for you, Handsome. Where are you?"

"I'm in London. I'll be a few hours behind you. I'll call you back on your way to the airport with details. Get a move on, Beautiful!"

He was gone before I could even say goodbye! I just stood there staring at the blank screen on my cell.

"*Qu'est-ce qu'il y a?*" Marie asked.

"It was Richard. He wants me to meet him in New York, but I have to be ready to leave by nine."

Marie turned to look at the clock.

"How can I help?" she asked.

"I think you'd better help me pack!"

Soon we were in the closet, trying to make some decisions. I'd checked the weather on my way upstairs and it was warm in New York—80s and 90s. I chose a pair of white Bermudas, some linen trousers, a new summery halter dress from that shopping trip with Mark, a light silk shirt and a raw silk blazer. Marie hung them on the hooks along the wall so I could see what I was taking. Then I had her gather up the fancy new bras and panties Richard had sent (I tucked in a pair of splits when she wasn't looking!) along with my fancy white set, and she also suggested a pair of my good black jeans, a pair of white capris and a couple of Tshirts. I asked her to add the sage cashmere hoodie.

I changed into a pair of distressed jeans, a white V-neck tee and took a sweatshirt hoodie that matched the jeans. Comfort on the plane was a priority. I put on my loafers—easy to slip out of for getting through security. I pulled out the new yellowy purse Richard sent from Italy, told Marie which shoes to pack and went to the bathroom to collect my cosmetics and the "liquid" travel bag I was using to go back and forth to Walla Walla.

Suddenly, I realized Richard hadn't said how long we'd be together in New York. I was scheduled to fly back to Washington on Friday. I punched a reminder into my calendar to change my reservation as soon as he could tell me what our plans were.

When I went back to the closet Marie had my suitcase ready to go and we selected some of my jewelry, which she put in a pouch for me to carry in my purse. I grabbed the yellow leather box with Richard's ring, sure I would find the perfect time to give it to him.

Good grief! A wax job was in order—something I had sort of neglected in Richard's absence. Marie must have seen the look of panic on my face.

"*Qu'est-que c'est?*" she asked.

I know I blushed as I said, " I need a wax and a manicure is probably in order if we're attending some fancy event. Can you recommend someone in New York? I don't even know where we're staying!"

"You will be at Monsieur Louis' house. That is where the family always stays—where I used to work. I will make an appointment for you and Mee-Cha will come to you. Is Monsieur Richard there yet?"

"No. He said he'd be a few hours behind me. Do you think she could come early tomorrow?"

"I'll text you, but I know she will be happy to accommodate you. She always attends family and guests at the house."

I gave her a hug. "Marie, I couldn't live this life without you. Truly!"

She laughed. "Just love up that special man of ours."

"No worries there. I'm so excited, I can hardly breathe! The thought that we'll be together by tomorrow…"

"Let me finish here. You go down and get the things you need from your office."

"I need to call Steph…"

"Do that on the way to the airport. If he told you to be ready at nine, he doesn't expect you to be late. Sometimes he schedules things very precisely and it is best to take him at his word."

She winked at me playfully, but I could tell it was a warning that being late could throw Richard's plans off. No problem, I thought, as I headed for the library.

I was at the door at five minutes to nine. Antonio was just opening Miyuki's trunk and in moments had my suitcase and briefcase stowed and me settled in the front seat. When he got in he handed me an envelope with my tickets, confirmation, seat assignment and itinerary.

"Wow! You two run this place like a well oiled machine," I said with no small amount of admiration.

Antonio laughed. "This is our job—to make things work for Hunter. It is a very good job."

"And both you and Marie perform it perfectly. Thank you so much, Antonio. There is no way I could manage this lifestyle without you and Marie. I wouldn't have a clue where to start."

"Both you and Signorina Sheperd are doing just fine. It is a pleasure to serve you. And it is very nice to have you here while Hunter is away."

My cell rang out *Magic Man*.

"My Captain, oh, My Captain…" I began.

"Has that ship sailed?"

"Ensign Bailey reporting, Sir," said as I saluted the screen. "Miyuki Maru underway to…" I glanced at my ticket. "…LAX and five minutes ahead of schedule. First Mate Padalino at the helm." I turned the phone to prove my point.

Antonio chuckled and I gave him a wink.

Richard laughed. "I was sort of hoping you thought of me as your first mate."

"First and only," I assured him. He sounded more relaxed than the last time we talked. "So do you have time to give me some details now?"

"I do. And I apologize for the rush. It's been kind of a cluster fuck trying to pull this together, but I think we're on track now."

"So what's the plan?"

"You'll get in early in the morning and Alain will meet you at the baggage claim. He'll have a sign with your name."

"Lah-dee-dah! People really do that? I've only seen it in the movies."

Richard snorted. "People really do that. He'll take you to the house and his wife Elise will help you get settled. I should be there by 3:30-4:00 tomorrow afternoon."

"Hard to imagine I'll see you in just a few hours."

"I'm counting the minutes."

"So how long will I be there? I have a flight Friday to Washington that I need to reschedule."

"We'll both be leaving Tuesday afternoon. I'll talk to your father and take the blame for delaying your visit."

"Oh, you will, will you? What if he doesn't agree with your change of plans?"

"I'm afraid we'll just have to agree to disagree about who will be spending the weekend with you."

My turn to laugh. "And so, my Prince, what is the ball you're whisking me off to?"

"A Black and White fundraiser at MOMA Saturday night. I ran into Peter Norton yesterday and he asked me to come. He wants me to meet with him about another project and the man is hard to catch up with, so I thought I'd better take advantage of his invitation."

"Not Peter Norton the software designer?" It was a common name, but I had to ask.

"Yes. He's on the MOMA board. Do you know him?"

"Hardly. But I've heard him speak a couple of times. It will be exciting to have a chance to meet him."

"I have a few more exciting experiences in mind for you," he said seductively.

"Such as?"

"As previously mentioned, there will be shopping. I have Mark doing some recon for us to leave more time for…other things."

"And those other things would be?" I asked innocently.

"Anything else the Big Apple has to offer that might be of interest you."

"We might need a month to cover those bases." I had a long mental list of New York sightseeing I hoped to have the chance to work through someday. "I'm afraid my list is longer than the time allotted. Besides, there is something at the very top of the list that will require quite a chunk of our time together."

"And that is?"

"Revisiting a few of my favorite places."

"Didn't you tell me you'd never been to New York?" he asked.

"I did and I haven't. The sight I most want to see is still in London at the moment."

"You're a girl after my own heart."

"What?" I feigned confusion. "I thought I had it?"

"My heart and all the rest of me. Always."

"Thank Heavens! I count on that, as I've told you many times."

"So, let us set aside the distraction of our passion for a few minutes…" he began as he went on with the more practical instructions of how to find the VIP lounge at LAX, instructing me to sleep on the plane if I could, and to be sure to ask Alain and Elise for anything I might need. "You can have almost anything delivered pretty quickly in New York, so don't hesitate."

"Just deliver yourself."

"As soon as I can. Text me when you land. I should be in the air, but I'll get it when I hit the ground. And I'll give you a call then."

"Travel safe, my Prince."

"And you, sweet Juliet."

Well, what can I say about my first experience of paid-for first class travel? I think I already mentioned that I'd been moved up to those coveted seats by chance a couple of times in my life, but to have the whole experience from the time I hit the VIP lounge to landing in New York…I can only say that it was instantly something that I very deeply appreciated about Richard's money. And in case you haven't enjoyed a first class seat, I'm here to say how easy it is to fall asleep in comfort. I popped in my ear buds, selected my thunderstorm track (my preferred method of sleep inducement when you-know-who wasn't next to me!) and managed to sleep a few hours.

27
Someday My Prince Will Come

Wednesday, September 11

> *Your love*
> *has gone all through my body*
> *like honey in water...*
> —*Ancient Egyptian*

And like honey, sometimes sticky!
XXOOJ

Sure enough, there was man waiting for me at baggage claim who was holding a sign that said BAILEY. He smiled when he saw me and came to take my bag, greeting me with, "*Bienvenue,* Mademoiselle, I am Alain."

He was probably in his late forties, not too tall, with sandy hair and wearing a dark suit and tie. He had a charming smile and I greeted him as I would any inhabitant of Richard's universe.

"Thank you, Alain. It's so good of you to come pick me up at this hour." The digital display in the center of the nearest carousel said it was 6:15 in the morning. "How did you know it was me?"

"My pleasure," he assured me. "Monsieur Richard texted a photo. I must say it didn't do you justice."

I laughed. Leave it to my man to make things as easy as possible for all concerned.

"We are so happy that you and Monsieur Richard will be

visiting," he said as he made a call on his cell instructing someone to pick us up.

I followed him through the airport and out. Moments later a town car pulled up at the curb. Alain opened the door for me, then put my bag in the front seat. He introduced me to our driver, Akhil Rao, who looked to be Indian and had a smile that was as broad and genuine as his greeting of "*Suprabhaat*, Madam. That is 'good morning' in Hindi. Welcome to the great city of New York."

In minutes we were moving into the flow of early morning traffic. Alain carried on a lively conversation, asking about my flight, if I'd ever been to New York and so forth.

"Marie told me we're staying at Richard's father's house," I said.

"*Oui*. The building was originally purchased by Monsieur Richard's grandfather, René, in 1921. It was being built as a small deluxe hotel in the area where the wealthiest families had built homes. The man who began the project, a lumber baron, intended it would be a place the visiting elite would choose for extended stays. Unfortunately, he died suddenly, before the building was completed. Monsieur René was a friend of the family and took over the project."

"And he was able to turn it into a home?" I was getting the impression it must be a really large house!

"Because it was unfinished, he was able to redesign the interior somewhat and split the building into his own family residence while committing the other half to luxury apartments. Monsieur Richard's father, Monsieur Louis, upgraded various parts of the building over the years. After his death in 2007, Mademoiselle Cybelle and her husband did a complete remodel of the family residence. It is very modern now."

"I'm eager to see it. There's so much I want to see here in the city, but I'm afraid this trip will be a short one."

"I am sure you will visit us many times," Alain said with a smile.

As we crawled along, Alain provided a great overview of the city, the neighborhoods, and his own history with the house until at last the car pulled up in front of a beautiful stone building that faced Central Park and looked to me like a French château. *Wow!*

A uniformed doorman came to open the car door and Alain helped me out, then retrieved my bag from the front seat. I leaned down to thank Akhil, who assured me he would see me again.

"Geoffery, this is Miss Bailey," Alain said by way of introduction as the doorman smiled broadly and tipped his hat. "She will be staying with us for a few days."

"Welcome, Miss. Just let me know if there's anything I can do for you."

"Thanks, Goeffery," I said as he held the wide glass door for us.

The foyer was a nice space, sort of a mini-hotel lobby. The floor and walls were polished stone, there was some comfortable furniture to the right, in front of the large arched window— 2 taupe leather couches and four chairs covered in a colorful but tasteful fabric that included the colors in the hydrangea arrangement that sat in the center of the low square glass table. Beyond that was a desk. The woman behind it rose as we came through the door to greet us with a smile.

"Alain," she said, nodding, "And this must be Miss Bailey."

I extended my hand which she clasped warmly as Alain introduced her.

"This is Elayna. She is our head concierge and can help you with anything at all."

"Please don't hesitate to ask," she said.

"I'm not sure how to deal with so much attention, but I'm very grateful," I laughed. To be honest, it all seemed a bit much.

Alain gestured to the elevators beyond the desk. There were two to the left and one to the right, which is where he guided me. He slipped a plastic card into the slot and the door opened. He gestured me in, pushed the button for the first floor and we silently rose, then stopped smoothly. The doors slid open.

"*Bienvenue*," said the smiling woman who was waiting for us in the entry.

"This is my wife, Elise. She will assist you while I take your bag up to your room." With a smile the doors closed on him again.

"I'm so happy to meet you," Elise said. "Marie has told me so much about you."

"I don't know what I'd do without Marie. This lifestyle is a bit out of my frame of reference, so please don't hesitate to help me along. I'm happy for any guidance you can offer."

Elise smiled broadly. "Would you like something to eat?"

"Yes, please. And I could really use a good cup of coffee."

"I started a pot just a few minutes ago, so come with me and we'll see what appeals to you for breakfast."

I followed her beyond the foyer and took a turn to the left with only a glimpse of the massive stone stairway to the right and the huge living room beyond. The kitchen was large and almost two kitchens side by side. Two six burner stoves, two massive refrigerators and a smaller one, a floor to ceiling wine storage unit, three dishwashers, three sinks and the sizable island with two smaller prep sinks of its own.

"This is quite a kitchen," I said in awe.

Elise laughed as she went to pour my coffee into the mug was already waiting on a tray beside the coffeemaker.

"That end we only use when the family is entertaining," she said gesturing toward the section with the multiple appliances. "It doesn't happen very often but when it does, it's nice to have the convenience."

She came to me with the tray and my coffee. "Where would you like me to serve you?"

I had a feeling that the dining room was of a scale that matched the little of the house that I'd seen. I couldn't see myself sitting at a table alone that was probably intended for some sort of state dinner.

"Would you mind if I just sat here, if I won't be interrupting your work?"

"Of course," she said as she set the tray in front of me on the island. "What can I fix for you?"

I pulled a stool out and sat down, adding cream and sugar to my coffee.

"I would love some eggs if it's not too much trouble." I took a sip of the coffee and closed my eyes in shear bliss. Marie had completely spoiled me and I was pleased that Elise shared her coffee making skills. "Perfect! You French women certainly understand the concept of coffee."

Elise smiled and gave a satisfied nod. "So eggs with bacon and toast or would you like an omelet?"

"Omelet would be great."

"Mee-Cha will be here at nine, if that suits you," she said as she deftly put a pan on the stove and pulled the ingredients for my breakfast from the fridge.

STILL LUCKY

The clock said seven-thirty.

"Perfect. That will give me time to shower and get settled."

When I finished, Elise took me up to Richard's room...and I use that term loosely. A luxury suite was more like it! It dwarfed Richard's room at Giancarlo's home in Santa Barbara and consisted of the bedroom, a sitting room big enough for a family, a private office with three computers, a closet even larger than the one at home and a bathroom that included a spectacular tub along with a sizable shower. Elise showed me where the house phone was—the same system we used at home—and mentioned there was something from Richard for me on the coffee table in the sitting room, then left me to get ready for Mee-Cha.

The bouquet was beautiful, lavender and soft pink roses, just like the Paul Simon song. The card read *You're Where I Belong, XXOOR*. Am I the luckiest girl on the planet, or what? And that wasn't all. Next to that day's New York Times and several current magazines there was a pristine flat white box with a lavish bow out of that beautiful ribbon that is sort of an iridescent lavender that shifts to pinks depending on the light. It matched the flowers perfectly.

I sat down on the couch and sank in deeper than I'd expected. It made me laugh as I took the box and untied the bow. In the center of the layers of tissue paper was a beautiful long nightgown of the sheerest silk. I stood again to hold it up so I could marvel at the incredible garment.

Now stick with me on the description and try to picture what an amazing bit of artistry this was. The theme was calla lilies—our old friend Leonard Cohen and his "cave at the tip of the lily" reference was no doubt what Richard had in mind—and they were worked in a shiny satiny thread for the leaves and stems. The actual flowers were more matte, the spadix (yup, I looked it up!) in the center in some sort of iridescent thread and just slightly raised. The rest of the gown was pretty transparent.

The design started in the back with multiple leaves taking up most of the area from the center of the hem to what I expected would hit me just around my bottom. From there, the stems split with two going up over one shoulder, and three over the other. It was just a straight sheath, a simple slip design, and the stems followed either side of the scooped back and became straps, blending back into the fabric in the front.

Now on the front, the two lilies from one shoulder spread to where the flowers would probably cover my breasts, and the other three went farther down, curving for some coverage in the crotch area. I couldn't wait to try it on before I got in the shower! But first I wanted to text Richard my gratitude so he would have it as soon as he landed. I'd texted him when I was waiting to get off the plane, so I guessed this would be the second thing he had from me when he could access his phone. That done, I went into the closet to unpack.

Moments later my phone sang out Richard's ringtone.

"My Prince, have you arrived already?" I was frantically thinking of Mee-Cha and wanting to be perfect and sexy for him when we saw each other.

"If only," he said, sounding cranky. "I'm still sitting at Heathrow waiting for the fog to lift."

"Oh, I'm so sorry!" I tried to mask my disappointment, but had the feeling I failed.

"I'm the one who's sorry, Sweetheart. I wanted this to be so special for you."

I had to laugh. "It's pretty special already. The only thing that's missing is you. And thank you so much for the beautiful flowers and that exquisite gown. I can't wait to wear it for you."

"I'm still hoping I'll be there for dinner with you. I just hate the thought of us losing any time together. I miss you more than you can imagine."

"Maybe exactly as much as I miss you?"

"Just a little more," he assured me.

"Mee-Cha is coming to do my nails in an hour and I need to get in the shower. Can I FaceTime you when I get out?"

"Of course. Meanwhile, I'll keep trying to shift this cursed fog!"

"If anyone can do that, you can, Magic Man!"

I got undressed in the closet and slipped on the incredible nightgown. It was absolutely perfect. All the blossoms and leaves demurely covered my nipples and my landing strip and only left a hint of the cheeks of my ass showing. If I didn't know better I would have thought it had been custom made for me. I could hardly wait for Richard to see me in it. I hung it up on one of the fancy hangers where space had been cleared for me.

No surprise that the shower was a smaller WATTOR model, and no surprise the man I loved had programmed *That's Where I Belong* for me. I needed to find the perfect music to welcome him back into my arms. I pondered that and by the time I was drying myself, I decided to see if Gran had a suggestion. I sent her a quick text. I followed that by iGraming Richard *Unchained Melody*, the LeAnn Rimes version, just to remind him I hungered for his touch!

I put on the short white seersucker robe I found in the closet (and assumed was for me) and checked the clock. It was 8:25, so I went back to the squashy couch with my iPad and FaceTimed Richard. He looked tired.

"There's my beautiful girl," he said with a sigh.

"Your brow is wrinkled, my Prince. How can I ease your spirit?"

Richard cracked up. I could see the relief flood across his face.

"The thing that would do the most good is not something I can participate in at the moment."

"Alas. You must save that energy for when we're together," I cautioned him.

"You don't need to worry about the level of my energy, sweet Juliet. That I can promise."

"I would never doubt you. So have you been sitting in the airport since yesterday?"

"Lots of pacing between the sitting. Lots of fruitless attempts to find a way out of here. A little bit of meditation on accepting 'what is,' eventually followed by more attempts to change reality."

"Have you considered the fact that it is not change which is painful, only the resistance to change?" I asked.

Richard laughed again, my favorite sound.

"That's not actually something Buddha said, you know," he reminded me.

I attempted a wise guru accent. "Does it matter who said it, if it's true, Grasshopper?"

"Ah, Mistress. You school me in the things I know well but so often forget."

"I'm looking forward to schooling you in a few other things, though somehow I doubt you've forgotten them."

He was still chuckling, but to my surprise he zapped me with a bolt of energy that nearly made me drop my iPad.

I laughed. "There's one thing you haven't forgotten."

"More where that came from," he promised.

"Mee-Cha is due any minute. May I leave you with something to ponder, my love?"

"Of course."

I flipped open my robe and let my breasts fill the screen, saying,"Byeeeee…" as I signed off. That would give him something to think about!

Moments later there was a knock at the bedroom door. I hopped up to answer and found a diminutive Korean woman with a smile as wide and solid as she was.

"Mee-Cha?" I said, though of course it was. Who else would be knocking on Richard's door at precisely nine o'clock, dressed in a set of pink scrubs with *Most Beautiful You* embroidered in dark pink script?

"Missy Bailey. I come to make you beautiful," she said enthusiastically, "I see this will be no problem."

I laughed and followed her to the "lift." We went up one floor and then down the hall. She opened a door and I found myself in a mini-spa. Three massage tables, three high shampoo sinks with what looked like roll-away pedicure stations and three regular manicure tables. There were two candles burning and a misting fountain. Soft pan flute music played in the background. Mee-Cha had obviously been there ahead of us, preparing the space.

"This is wonderful! A private spa for the family?"

"For the family, yes, and friends who come. I make everyone most beautiful so they may enjoy their visit." She smiled up at me.

"I've heard nothing but good things about you from Marie."

"Marie is great friend. I miss her, but she is most happy in her job with Mister Richard."

She directed me to one of the tables and I lay down. Mee-Cha looked at my legs and then spread my robe open.

"We will do your legs. Do you wish to keep current design?" she asked, referring to my pubic hair. "We can make nice surprise for Mr. Richard if you wish."

I was curious. "What are you thinking?"

"I can make here nice heart shape at top, smaller as it goes down. Will not require much change, but maybe will please him?"

I liked the idea and Mee-Cha went about her business with astonishing speed and a very gentle touch. I was really happy with the results.

I had to ask. "I'm curious, do the French women in the family also wax? I'm just wondering if the European style is different."

"Everyone wax today. Men, also." She smiled at me. "This is why I know you very lucky girl." She winked, but her cheeks colored just a bit as she giggled.

"I am the luckiest girl in the world, and I know it."

"Mister Richard is very nice man. Very good man."

"He is indeed. I met Robert a few weeks ago and he also seems very special."

"Yes. Also good man. Very serious about business, but also very loving to wife and daughters."

"I can't wait to meet the rest of the family. I only hope his mother approves of me. She sounds like a very formidable woman."

Mee-Cha laughed softly. "Madame very interesting. People don't know, think she is tiger lady, but she know who she is. Very direct. Some cannot see this."

"That means we already have something else in common. So tell me about the rest of the family." Suddenly I realized I might be crossing some privacy line. "Only what you think you can share, of course. I hope to meet Cybelle and Grégoire sometime in the next year."

"Miss Cybelle is much fun. You will enjoy. She very kind, like her brothers. Has much humor. She spend a great deal of time here while they redoing this house. Also her husband. Umberto. He is architect. They redoing another apartment next year. You will meet them."

"They live in Brazil?"

Robert had mentioned they traveled quite a bit with both his work and hers.

"They have house in Brazil, but also stay with Madame in Paris. Also here. His work is very busy. Hers, also. They have two girls, Christella and Arabella. Very sweet. Thoughtful. Well behaved."

"Well, that's a bit unusual these days!" I said, thinking of the unruly children that seemed to be everywhere. I often found reasons to wonder what had become of the concepts of manners and discipline.

"Yes. Perhaps Miss Cybelle recalls way she raised so follows Madame's example? Is excellent family. Mister Robert's children also kind and well behaved. Miss Danielle, his wife, is very beautiful. Sweet. You will like her much, I think. She bring friends sometimes to go shopping and enjoy city."

"I so look forward to meeting everyone."

I returned to Richard's room feeling like a new woman. Massaged, waxed and buffed with a soft pale pink polish on toes and nails, my hair with some extra shine and my skin glowing. Mee-Cha was flat out amazing. Was I surprised? No. I had yet to find anything in Richard's world that didn't somehow add to the energy that surrounded him. Apparently his family must share that skill. Maybe it's genetic?

There was no text awaiting me so I decided to call him again.

"Are you beautiful?" he asked when he answered.

"Uh…you always tell me I'm beautiful, but I think Mee-Cha's magic has made me completely amazing."

Richard laughed. "You know I always find you completely amazing, and I'm anxious to carefully study what she's done."

"I bet you are. I want to be sure you can examine the results of her efforts and give me a Trained Professional's opinion. When do you think you might do that?"

Richard let out a long sigh. "Well, it's pretty obvious I'm not going to be there to have dinner with you. They're predicting it will be clear enough to fly in another hour or two. Of course flights are backed up, so who knows how long it will be until my plane will go? I'm trying to find a charter. When I have an ETA I'll call you."

"I'll be here whenever you arrive."

"I know. I just hate missing any time we could be spending together. Let Elise know what you'd like for dinner. And Alain will be happy to take you anywhere you'd like to go for the afternoon. There's a big city out there, Cress. Plenty to do."

"I know, but I'd rather be doing it with you. Plus I have some work to take care of. I did leave rather abruptly and I'd prefer to get it out of the way so I can give you my full attention when you get here."

"There is no way to explain to you how much I look forward to that."

"I think I can guess," I laughed.

"I bet you can."

28
Castles of Stone

Still Wednesday

I asked Elise to give me a tour of the house after lunch. As you can imagine it was so over the top of my frame of reference that I half expected velvet ropes at the entrance to the rooms. Silly, I know, but his father's house was as far beyond Richard's magnificent home as Richard's L.A. house was above the rental Steph and I had shared.

Despite the scale of the place, Cybelle and Umberto had managed to maintain the beauty of the original architectural details—feature them, even—while mixing modern furniture and art with the antiques and period pieces Elise told me had been in the family for a long time.

The art was everywhere, perfectly complemented by what surrounded it. I was looking forward to a more detailed tour with my Trained Professional. I did notice that the huge music room—to me it was a ballroom!—contained a grand piano. I couldn't help wondering if it bothered Richard.

"Does anyone in the family play?" I asked Elise.

"Madame Danielle plays a little and her girls are learning. The other children —Cybelle's three—are learning instruments, but they are too young to be serious about it yet. They sometimes talk about Monsieur Richard playing when he was a boy, but apparently he gave it up."

And so we continued through the floors, from the swimming pool on the lowest level all the way to the roof where there was sort of a solarium with window walls that opened onto the rest of the roof. It had to be a stunning place for entertaining, but I couldn't help wondering out loud how often it was used since none of the siblings actually lived there.

"It is true that much of the house is only used occasionally. All of the young people are very active in philanthropic organizations and they host fundraisers from time to time. It is very special when the house is decorated for a party and filled with people," Elise assured me with a smile.

"I can't imagine how much work it must be for you," I told her. "Even day to day upkeep is beyond my imagination."

She laughed out loud. "I do not do this alone. I have a great deal of help. Like Marie, I manage this house and the people who handle the maintenance and cleaning, arrange things when family comes or when they entertain. It takes many people to keep this house running."

"Marie has plenty to do with Richard's house and this is so much more. You ladies are amazing."

"*Merci*," she said with a smile. "Like Marie, I love this job. It is an honor to be here." And then with a wink she added, "It is also a very nice place to live!"

When I returned to our room, I sank into the couch and called the gallery.

Lynda answered and when she found out it was me said, "So how's the Big Apple?"

"Pretty amazing from what I've seen of it. I'm still waiting for Richard to arrive."

"I know. Poor man. He's pretty upset by the delays. I hope he gets there soon, for both your sakes."

"I can't wait. It's been far too long!"

Lynda laughed. "Just be sure to take advantage of this surprise break from your separation."

"Don't worry about that. I won't miss a minute of it! Is Mark available, by any chance?"

"I think so, hang on."

"Hey, CJ, I'm doing everything I can to get the boss to this continent," he assured me when he picked up.

"I'm sure you are. But that's not why I called. I'm trying to figure out what to do about the daily notes."

"Well, with him spending time in New York with you, you've got a break. You're back in L.A. Tuesday night, right?"

"That's the plan. And then I'll fly back to Washington Thursday afternoon."

"Can you get some notes to me before you leave again?"

"I can, and I may see what I can do this afternoon. I was just concerned that you wouldn't have anything from me before Friday."

"No problem. Do whatever works for you. Just touch base with me again before you leave to see your folks."

"Will do. And thanks for the long distance fashion work. Richard said you've picked out a few things for us to look at."

"I have and I think you'll enjoy them."

"What would I do without you, Mark? I'd look like a gutter snipe if I didn't have you to counsel me."

"You'd look like nothing but your beautiful self. Still, I really enjoy helping you. You make everything you put on look good."

"Save it for the art buyers, Mr. Salesman!" I laughed.

Mark pretended to be offended. "I assure you I am completely sincere, Madame."

"Yeah, yeah. Bye, Mark, I'll be in touch. Just get your boss here as fast as you can!"

"I'm on it," he told me as he hung up.

I set my laptop up at one of Richard's desks in the attached office. The windows looked out across the terrace to Central Park. What a beautiful view! I was determined to become enough of a mogul that I could visit New York at least a couple of times a year. I assumed Richard would have to be here for business sometimes and I would find ways to convince him that I needed to accompany him. (I didn't imagine it would be too difficult!)

Just after I finished re-booking my flight for Washington, my phone buzzed with a text from Gran and three suggestions for shower music for Richard's return. I popped all three up on YouTube and chose Doris Day singing *It's Been A Long Long Time*. Perfect! Good ole Gran, I so loved her vast knowledge of the music of her era and I had to admit I tended to embrace her favorites. Maybe it was just that I'd been around it all my life. I liked that music. It seemed to have more complex stories than most of what I heard today.

And there was SO much music out there now, I honestly didn't know where to start to catch up to the latest and greatest. Sometimes, I heard something new by sheer chance, like that Emeli Sande piece I sent to Richard. Richard shared my taste for some of the older things, but he was much more on top of what was going on in the music world. And yet, from his iTunes playlist, it was obvious that he had a very broad interest in classical works as well, no doubt because of his piano career. I found myself thinking what a shame it was that he'd abandoned something that had been so much a part of his life, and all because of a broken heart.

And then I thought, not for the first time, how lucky I was that my own heart had never been broken. I'd never been in love before Richard came along. Somehow I had avoided that frantic, angst-ridden, desperate teenage love thing. I watched my friends go though it and while I was sympathetic to their highs and lows, I never really understood what they were feeling.

I'd had lots of friends who were boys, but no real boyfriends in those days. In high school they treated me more like one of the guys, and I was more tomboy than girlie-girl. That, in itself, may have been my first serious act of rebellion against the assumption that I was too pretty to be smart. And I knew the boys found me attractive, but I could see their interest dissolve into confusion when they couldn't participate in a conversation. Unlike most of my friends, I didn't feel desperate enough for their attention to play dumb. (That I can thank my folks for!) But really, in high school aren't the girls always way ahead of the boys? The boys seem to be trapped by their hormones while the girls are desperate for that emotional connection.

And for some reason I just wasn't attracted to the boys my age. Now my biology teacher, he was a different story. I did have a crush on him, but when I got to know him a little better I realized the attraction I felt for him was purely physical. Well, I've told that story before.

I also think that both Mom and Gran had really prepared me to at least be aware of the effects of raging hormones, both my own and those of the opposite sex. Mom had told me a few years ago that more than once she'd wondered if they had made me too wary of boys. I know she was a little concerned that even by the time I was in college, there didn't seem to be a steady guy in my life, or even regular dating. (Of course I never told her about my frequent, if short-lived, encounters off campus!) More than once I'd had to assure her that I was just waiting for the right guy to come along. After all, my parents had the kind of relationship I wanted for myself. The kind I had with Richard. It had certainly been worth the wait!

So, I did the quotes for the week, though the break Richard was taking from his travels would certainly put a hitch in the daily deliveries. I was so grateful Mark was taking care of it for me. Richard had mentioned many times how much he enjoyed and appreciated what I sent. They were nothing, of course, compared to the things he sent to me, but he seemed to treasure my missives. That convinced me to do a couple of extras for the coming days together. I assumed I could leave them in unexpected places right there for him to find. The first one I made for him:

> *It is through kisses that a knowledge of*
> *life and happiness first comes to us.*
> — Kristoffer Nyrop
> *The Kiss and Its History*

I thought it would go with the shower song. I would leave it in the bathroom so he could find it when he took his first shower.

The office closet was full of supplies and I pulled a Fed Ex envelope, popped the notes in and filled out the form for the gallery. I called Elise to see how to arrange a pick up and about four minutes later Alain was there to take it for me. Wow! I wasn't sure mogulhood was something I'd be able to manage. Such service assumes you have much more important things to do, and at that moment I didn't. The important thing I wanted to do was stuck in London!

I wandered out onto the terrace, wondering when Richard might finally arrive. His room was technically on the third floor (if you counted the ground floor, which apparently they didn't) but the ceiling height in the building's entry was probably in the range of twenty feet, so it was more like being four floors above the street. (Is that confusing? They didn't count the ground floor, so the bedrooms were on the second floor, third floor to me. It's a French thing.)

Anyway, in contrast to the green expanse of the park across the street, the cars and folks on the sidewalks below seemed a bit frantic. The energy everyone spoke of as being unique to the city was obvious. It was fun to watch.

When I went back inside Richard called.

"My poor weary traveler," I answered.

"Weary, yes, but it looks like I'll be in the air before midnight London time."

I tried to do the calculation in my head. My watch read 4:55.

"Damn, I never set the chrono for London. Have mercy and tell me when you'll be here?"

"If we actually leave as scheduled, somewhere between three and four in the morning. Mark hooked me up with some other folks and we're going to share a charter, so I'm a little vague on exact departure and arrival."

He sounded tired.

"I will be here waiting, whenever you arrive."

"I know that. But don't wait up for me. You know I'll wake you."

"I'm so excited I'm not sure I can sleep, but for your sake, I'll give it a try. Do you think you'll be able to sleep on the plane?"

"I'm pretty sure I could sleep standing up at this point. I trust my fellow passengers are equally exhausted and there may well be more snoring than chatting."

For a minute I didn't say anything.

"Cress? Are you alright?"

I was tearing up, which surprised me. I laughed. "Guess the anticipation is getting to me. *Come, gentle night; come, loving, black-browed night; Give me my Romeo,*" I quoted as I gazed out at the late afternoon sun.

Richard laughed. "I just realize I've never asked: Do you know the whole play?"

"Nope, just a lot of Juliet's lines. That one just popped into my head out of the blue. I miss you, my Prince."

"And I, you. Only hours separate us now. I have to find my ride to the gate for our plane. Soon, Sweetheart."

"Soon," I echoed as he hung up.

29
Welcome Home

Thursday, September 12

I was sleeping, but woke when I realized Richard was in the bathroom. Maybe it was my body sensing that the energy had changed in the room…or…OK, maybe it was just the sound of the shower running. I glanced at the clock. It read 3:45. Just then, I heard the water shut off. Silly as it seemed, my heart began to pound. The excitement of seeing him again was, of course, a factor, but I wasn't sure how it would be when we were face to face. *Only one way to find out!* I took a deep breath, turned back the covers and got up.

I shifted my beautiful gown around so it hung properly. (I hadn't tried to sleep in a long nightie for years and had forgotten how they tend to go all twisty!) Then I quickly ran my hands over my hair. As short as it was, there wasn't much to go askew. The only place that occasionally insisted on sticking up was "where the cow licked me," as Gran used to say. I smiled to myself, knowing the last thing that Richard would be focused on was the state of my coiffure.

I was halfway between the bed and the bathroom when the door opened and he turned to shut off the lights. There was ambient light from the lamp in the sitting room that illuminated his gorgeous naked self. My heart stopped and for a fraction of a second I was overwhelmed by the realization that the man I loved was standing there, in the flesh, just a few feet away.

I knew he could see me, so I walked toward him slowly, intending to take my cue from him. I remember being vaguely surprised (and a little disappointed!) that I felt no aftershock. I stopped about four feet away and quoted my namesake.

"Where is my lord? I do remember well where I should be and there I am. Where is my Romeo?"

He smiled and I felt his energy then. I'd half expected a tsunami that might knock me over, but this was more like being engulfed in an unimaginably warm and tender cocoon of…well…love. Corny? Maybe to you, but for me it confirmed everything about our feelings for each other. They were wider, deeper and stronger than ever.

He came to stand in front of me and looked into my eyes. *Then* the wobble kicked in. Talk about being knocked off your feet!

"My beautiful girl," he said softly as he very slowly pulled me to him and wrapped his arms around me, keeping me upright.

I let myself melt into his embrace. No need for hands on each other's hearts this time. I felt the strong steady beat of his and the fluttering of my own as it gradually slowed to match it. The sensation of his arms around me at last, his body against mine… It was such a relief that time seemed to stop. He simply held me, not moving, not saying anything at all. He didn't need to, I could feel his emotions curling around my own.

I began to notice the heat rising in my body. A sense of need began to build as I became aware that only a thin layer of silk separated us and I slid my hands down to cup that beautiful ass of his and press him closer.

He leaned back a little and touched my cheek. He smiled.

"Do you mind if this first one is mine?" he whispered.

"How could I?" I answered as I—yes, with a little twinge of regret!—moved my hands back up to his waist. "Just *kiss me once, then kiss me twice…*" I sang softly, mimicking the shower song I'd left him.

I got the three kisses the song requested, each deeper and more intense than the one that preceded it. On another level I became aware of his new beard and was surprised by how soft it was.

I admit I'm at a loss for words to describe what I was feeling just then—and that's me, the girl who brags about having a good supply of them! It was simply overwhelming in the most delightful and exciting way. I was torn between the anticipation of what was about to happen and the excitement of all the sensations

I was experiencing in each successive moment. And on another level I was amazed by the fact that Richard was doing no more than holding me against him and kissing me. Don't ever let anyone tell you that there is nothing to all the talk of the interactions of energies between people.

He released me slowly, led me back to the bed and turned me to face him where the glow from the sitting room shed the most light on me. He studied that beautiful gown for a long time before slowly easing the lily-stem straps from my shoulders. The gossamer silk slithered to my feet and I stepped out of it.

Richard's eyes moved over me slowly, from head to toe and I easily read a number of emotions in his gaze—wonder, appreciation, gratitude and, most of all, love. He took both my hands and kissed them.

"Lie down, Sweetheart," he urged.

As I settled myself in bed, he turned the covers all the way down and then back over the far side of the bed. When he moved onto the bed beside me, he propped himself up on one elbow to look at me. He gave me a brief kiss and then let his eyes follow his fingers as he slowly mapped the curves of my body. My very wet thighs were already trembling, though I had the feeling Richard fully intended to stretch the joy of our reunion to the limits by proceeding with excruciating slowness. I wasn't at all opposed to his intentions, but oh, how I wanted him! I didn't need to remind myself that my Prince had never once disappointed me, so if patience was what he required, then the least I could do was embrace the experience.

When his fingers finally reached my freshly groomed landing strip, they followed the new curves at the top. He stroked it gently, as if recalling the texture of my pubic hair even as he admired Mee Cha's artwork. He bent to kiss the tip of the heart there, then gave my clit just the lightest tease with his tongue.

I couldn't help myself, my hips tilted in encouragement. If I had to wait for his beautiful cock, I wanted his mouth, his fingers— anything to ease the need I was feeling, the desire that begged for the joining of our bodies.

He leaned closer and whispered in my ear. "Patience, Cress."

He kissed my cheek and smiled, then gave me a deep kiss as he cupped me in his palm and slowly massaged my pubic bone with his thumb and the heel of his hand. I was desperate for his fingers if he wasn't ready to share the rest of himself! I reached for his cock but he caught my hand.

I snorted in frustration.

Richard chuckled softly. "Relax, Sweetheart. I'm here. I can promise you'll have everything you want. We have time."

He slid his hand up my belly at a snail's pace until he reached my breasts, where he lingered, running his fingers lightly along the underside of first one and then the other, the place he knew I was the most sensitive. He moved on to my nipples, brushing their hard little tips with maddening tenderness, then bent his mouth to one of them, and massaged me with his tongue while he cupped the other. He nuzzled me and sucked and all at once my orgasm exploded! This was a complete surprise to me, my first time that way, and I rode the sensation as he continued nursing me slowly, alternating with licks and teasing me with his teeth.

Finally, he urged me over onto my stomach, and straddled me across my thighs. I could feel his cock, hard and heavy, resting against the crack of my ass. I crossed my arms and rested my head on them, trying to slow my body down, but it was useless. The tenderness with which his fingers moved over me only made me anxious for more. I squirmed beneath him, mindlessly begging for connection.

He stroked either side of my neck, he touched my hair, then followed my cheekbone lovingly with the tip of his finger and leaned forward to kiss me there as his cock slid up my back. He sat back and his hands began to caress me lightly, spread so that his fingers moved back and forth down to my shoulders, electrifying every inch of my skin as they went. He teased the sides of my breasts then ran a single finger slowly down my spine before gently beginning to massage my buttocks. He worked his hands in opposite directions, gently squeezing and kneading, each circle spreading me open just a little more.

I was panting for him, and on the verge of abandoning my somewhat passive role when he rose up on his knees, taking hold of my hips and lifted me, urging me up. I started to raise my head and shoulders to get all the way up onto my knees, but he laid a gentle hand on my back, letting me know I should stay down. Rather awkward, I was thinking, as he spread my knees a little farther apart. He held my hips and then used his thumbs to open me. I knew how much he loved what he was seeing, but I wanted him, I needed him and I was just about to break my silence and beg him to fuck me.

And then I felt his tongue. I was already so hot I think he could have just blown on my skin and I would have come, but he ran that clever tongue of his up to my clit and then back and forth down my folds and deep into my vagina. I cried out. It was exquisite! He stroked me a couple times, then lapped at me slowly, licked and sucked at my cunt until I wasn't sure I could take any more.

He must have sensed exactly where I was, because he backed away and shifted to move beside me, easing his rigid penis down to slip along under my belly and rest there, reminding me that there was much more he intended to share. I squirmed, rubbing against his cock as he moved one hand lazily up and down my back, while the other alternately stroked my clit and slipped fingers in and out of me as the moisture dripped down my thighs.

I could see his beautiful cock from where my cheek pressed against the mattress and feel the length of him hard against my stomach. That was what I wanted—all of him deep inside me, hard and demanding. I was beyond ready to take what he obviously had for me. I couldn't wait a moment longer.

I rolled away from him and onto my back, looking up at him, still on his knees, penis throbbing in time with his heartbeat.

"Richard Hunter, if you don't fuck me right now, I'm not sure I'll be able to forgive you." I said it softly. I could barely breathe.

He just looked at me. Then he smiled and moved between my legs. Still, he hesitated.

"Richard!" It was more of a sob than the encouragement I'd intended it to be.

He touched my cheek and whispered, "I love you," as he slid into me.

I cried out in relief when I came and I clung to him, my hips jerking as I kept moving. He held me tightly as I bucked against him and when I finally slowed to catch my breath, I realized the movement had been all mine. I looked up at him and he was smiling, proud of himself, no doubt, for managing to exercise such restraint, but so overflowing with love that all I could say was, "Welcome home."

He kissed me, and then finally began to move. He stroked me deep and slow and I could feel the next orgasm rising, back to that rolling wave thing I hadn't been able to accomplish on my own.

"Come again for me, Sweetheart?" he whispered.

"Yes, please," I breathed against his ear. I added a little tongue and that time when I came, I begged him to fuck me hard while I was at the height of my orgasm. He obliged. It went on and on, his balls banging against my ass, his cock driving deep inside me, binding us together on such a profound level that it left me breathless.

"Come...for...me...please..." I begged, as each word was punctuated by a thrust.

He rose up then and cried out softly as I felt him rigid and pulsing inside me. After a few moments, he wrapped his arms around me and continued to stroke me gently as his mouth found mine.

It's hard to describe my feelings then, held tight in his arms, the two of us wrapped in and around each other—tongues, cock and cunt, and most important, hearts pressed close and beating together. I was so filled with love, so relieved to feel the depth of our connection again after such a long time, and boundlessly grateful. Our long distance lovemaking had been as much as we could possibly make it, but that physical coming together was not only over the top with the down-to-earth reality of the experience, but the breadth of our emotional connection—and if you will "spiritual" connection—felt truly and unfathomably sacred to me.

That surprised me a little—that I would suddenly find myself thinking of the word "sacred" to describe what I was feeling. I loved Richard, of course, and I certainly knew how special our relationship was and how incredibly fortunate I was that he loved me as much as I loved him. But for some reason, this reunion after our long separation made it obvious to me that there was something very spiritual about what we shared. I thought of the line from *Les Miz: To love another person is to see the face of god.*

And then I felt the tears beginning to fill my eyes. When he looked at me, I saw his were wet, too.

"Joy?" we both whispered at the same time.

We laughed softly and hugged each other tight.

Richard rose up on his elbows, still moving very slowly inside me as his erection faded.

"It's so good to be home," he said, and followed those words with a kiss, keeping that promise he'd made so long ago.

STILL LUCKY

We fell asleep in each other's arms and later, when I first felt that formerly familiar nudge, it took a split second to realize it wasn't Zoor and that the warmth against my back was Richard and not my pillow. I physically felt a surge of gratitude in my heart as I rearranged myself to accommodate him, guiding him gently into my body. He reached over me, his hand covering mine as we moved together to share a gentle orgasm. Almost immediately after, he was asleep again, evidenced by his soft snore. I was enjoying the sensation of him still inside me as I glanced at the clock. It was ten minutes to eight and though the curtains were closed in the bedroom, the light from the sitting room promised a sunny day.

I dozed, waiting for him to wake and hoping he wasn't sleeping through any plans he'd made for us. He had to be exhausted, he'd been trying to get to New York since Tuesday night and here it was Thursday!

Some time later I felt his lips against the back of my neck, followed by a whispered, "Good Morning, Beautiful."

I rolled over to face him and placed my hands on his fuzzy cheeks.

"My Prince, is it you? Truly?"

"Indeed," he assured me, pulling me tight against him as proof.

"*It's been a long, long, time...*" I sang softly.

"Have I kissed you enough?" he asked, nuzzling my ear with a bit of tongue thrown in for good measure.

I laughed. "Not by a long shot!"

"Good. I was sort of thinking I might want to do some more of that." He ground his hips against me for emphasis.

"I think I'd like that."

"I'll do everything I can to make sure you do," he promised, as he slipped his hand suggestively over my ass and pressed the tip of his finger into me.

I laughed but angled my hips so he could get more penetration, albeit maybe only an additional inch. I was wet and sticky from our previous lovemaking and the sensation was delightful! I was tempted to abandon myself to another round of sensual pleasures, but I wanted to be sure we weren't supposed to be somewhere.

"Before you go distracting me with your vast array of sexual enticements, tell me what our schedule is, and remember you lost a day."

Richard rolled onto his back and yawned, momentarily abandoning his prurient thoughts along with that teasing finger (though his penis was showing some signs of life!)

"OK," he said with a sigh of resignation, "Tomorrow is Friday, so prepare yourself. There will be shopping—shoes, gown and jewels. Mark has made some pre-selections for us so it won't be too tedious."

I couldn't help laughing.

"What?" he asked. "I know you don't like shopping, so I thought you'd appreciate a direct approach. Am I wrong?"

"Nope. But maybe Mark forgot to tell you that I actually enjoyed that last foray into the establishments that cater to the one percenters. The only caveat is on the jeans thing," I reminded him.

"Understood. And if we manage to get the shopping out of the way, we can spend the rest of the day any way you like. Museums, Central Park, galleries, a cruise around the city with me as your guide…"

"Is that a carrot and stick thing?" I asked.

"Absolutely."

"Is this the carrot?" I asked as I reached for his tumescent cock.

"Might be the stick. Not clear on that yet. Time will tell."

I leaned over him for a quick kiss as I stroked his penis. He was doing a pretty good job acting as though my ministrations were having no effect on him, but his body made it evident that wasn't the case.

"So Saturday," he went on, "we have the day to ourselves and then the gala is Saturday night, the Black & White Ball at MOMA. I'll be meeting with Peter Norton at some point, probably for three hours or so, but I won't know when that's happening until I talk to him today. I was also thinking you might be interested in catching a Broadway show."

At that point I squealed as I released him to clap my hands in delight. Richard laughed.

"It would be a shame to drag you to the Big Apple and not

take you to a musical."

"Unconscionable," I agreed solemnly, as I returned to slowly stroking his cock. "Especially since I was *so* reluctant to come here and spend time with you."

Richard smirked and turned to give me a quick kiss on the cheek. "Thanks for taking the time out to come." He laughed.

"I expect to come again."

"Trust me when I tell you you will." He said it matter-of-factly as he clasped his hands over his belly and stared at the ceiling as if no double entendre were intended.

I poked him in the ribs and he pretended not to feel it.

"Tuesday you're back to L.A. and I'm on my way back to Paris, hopefully with no glitches."

"Poor sweet man, I'm so sorry you had so much trouble getting here. Do you think it was worth the trip?"

He rolled toward me and pulled me close. "Hmmm…let me think about that."

I pushed back against his chest.

"Hey wait a minute. What about today?"

"What about it?"

I could see he was confused.

"No plans for today?"

He pulled me close again and teased me with his hard cock against my belly.

"I'll leave it up to you. I'm yours to command."

"Good. Let's get in the shower!" I rolled away from him and got out of bed.

He was right behind me.

We hurriedly brushed our teeth with lots of jostling and teasing at the bathroom sinks, followed by plenty of kissing, before we got in the shower. Under the pulsing water, we did more of it, with John Denver singing *Back Home Again*.

I eased him back out of the overhead spray of water so he could sit down on the marble bench, and so I could kneel between his legs.

"I've been waiting for a taste of you for far too long," I reminded him, as I wrapped my hand around his cock and began to stroke him very lightly with the tips of my fingers. I cupped his balls in my other hand and stretched them up and then pressed them against his shaft and slid them back down as I'd seen him do when I'd watched him masturbate.

Richard groaned. I smiled.

"Does it feel good to have my real hands on you?" I asked, head tilted as though I were merely curious.

"Far better than the imaginary ones," he assured me.

I slid my hand up and tightened my grip, then gave the head of his cock a long slow lick. I rubbed him around on my tongue.

"And that…which is better, me or your imagination?" I looked up innocently as I gave him another slow caress with my tongue followed by a couple of quick flicks.

Richard caught his breath and twitched as he watched me. He didn't answer.

I gave him a good quick suck and this time his groan was louder.

"I'm waiting. Me or your imagination?" I was trying to look stern but I was dying to take him in my mouth. I could see he was anxious for me to do it, too, but nevertheless, he managed a really sweet smile.

"You. Always you." He ran his fingers lightly over my cheek.

"*Moi et nul autre?*" I asked, repeating the words on my ring.

"*Ouais,*" he answered. "*Toi, seulement, mon amour.*"

I held his cock out of the way and sucked his balls, first one and then the other, tenderly taking them into my mouth and rolling them around, sucking gently and enjoying the sounds he was making. I held the head of his cock lightly between two fingers and wrapped my lips around the underside of his shaft and slowly slid my mouth down, pressing my tongue deep into the top of his scrotum and rubbing him there slowly, back and forth.

My hand followed my mouth down and I moved my face away to press the heel of my hand against him. He strained, pressing back as I studied his beautiful penis.

"Will you come for me?" I asked.

"Try me," he dared.

Then I fell on him, both hands around him lightly, working him quickly even as I gloried in the feel of him in my mouth again. I pulled back, stopped, and very slowly wrapped my lips around just the head of his cock, giving him a strong suck before taking him as deep as I was able. Richard cried out as he exploded, pulsing into my throat while I continued to stroke him. I gave him a good suck, then held onto him as I rose and turned my back, easing myself down onto him.

He immediately put his hands on my shoulders and pressed me against him and stroked me hard. He cried out again and wrapped his arms around me, one across my hips, the other cupping my breast as he pressed his cheek against my back.

John Denver sang, *"Oh, the time that I can lay this tired old body down, feel your fingers feather-soft upon me. The kisses that I live for, the love that lights my way, the happiness that living with you brings me."*

"Exactly, " Richard said as he planted a kiss gently between my shoulder blades.

30
Painless Cartier

Still Thursday

We soaped each other playfully and danced, slipping and sliding against each other and couldn't stop kissing. When we finally shut off Baby Z (as I was calling that less elaborate version), we dried each other, marveling that we were actually together again.

"So what does a girl have to do to get breakfast around here?" I asked as we headed for the closet.

Richard picked up a house cell from the edge of the table as we passed and I glanced at the time.

"First she'd have to get up earlier. It's ten-forty."

"All right, brunch then."

"*Bonjour*, Elise," Richard said, and then proceeded to carry on a brief conversation in French.

I heard an apology for getting Alain out of bed in the middle of the night and a request for an early lunch. He told her we'd be down in about fifteen minutes.

In the closet, he pulled on a pair of jeans and a Vneck tee. No underwear, I noticed. *Hmmm…*

"Can I get away with this?" I asked, holding up that turquoise shirred top dress.

"Sure," he said as he came over to me and reached around to grab my ass and pull me against him. "It will make it a little difficult to focus on my meal knowing what you're wearing under it."

He gave me a quick kiss and released me so I could step into the dress.

We took the stairs down to the kitchen rather than using the "lift" (still an elevator to me) where we found Elise preparing our meal.

"*Bonjour*, Monsieur, Mademoiselle," she greeted us. "What would you like to drink with your meal?"

"Coffee, please," I said.

She looked to Richard.

"*Moi, aussi.*"

"And where shall I serve you?"

"On the patio," he answered as he took my hand and led me around the corner, beyond the kitchen to what they called the "patio."

It was a large space—an atrium, really—open all the way up through the other floors and roofed in glass. On the two long sides were glass window-walls opening to a wide hallway and to one of the living rooms. The end walls were faced in stone. It was light and bright, edged with planters and pots of flowering plants. There were even two small orange trees in massive terra cotta pots on one end, two lemon trees on the other. There was a glass-topped table and six chairs in the center, but there was room enough for a banquet. I imagined when the family gathered they could all comfortably share a meal in the space.

"I need to call Peter, Sweetheart. Do you mind?" Richard said after he pulled out a chair for me. "The rest of our plans sort of hinge on when I can meet with him."

"Just save a little time for me as your calendar firms up."

He smiled and kissed my cheek as he sat down, then took my hand again and placed it on the part of his anatomy most likely to change.

"Things can firm up quite quickly," he reminded me with a wink as he thumbed his iPhone.

"I know all about that, including how to make it happen."

He gave me another quick kiss and then Peter answered as Elise delivered our coffee.

The call turned into brunch plans with Peter and his wife Gwen on Sunday. Meanwhile, they'd see us at the gala. Richard hung up and asked me what I'd like to do with the rest of the day. I just smiled and he laughed. He knew what I was thinking.

"Me, too. But maybe you'd like to go for a walk with me around the neighborhood? I can show you a few things, we can get a little exercise and then we'll probably want to take a nap before dinner." An eyebrow wiggle accompanied the word "nap."

He gave my hand a squeeze. And much as I couldn't stop thinking about the vast number of aspects of his beautiful self I was anxious to re-explore, we were both off our exercise routines and a walk was actually a much more interesting solution than time on the treadmill in the gym that Elise had told me I was welcome to use.

It was a beautiful day. I changed into my white capris and a silk tee, deterred from going out in just that shirred top dress by visions of Marilyn's dress blowing up. (Uh…also deterred by a basic sense of decency! I may be a free spirit but there *are* basic guidelines…)

It was quite warm without being too hot and we walked for a couple of hours, exploring a few blocks in the immediate neighborhood and then came back, skirting the edge of the Park facing Fifth Avenue. My mind boggled at how much there was to see, basically right on Richard's doorstep. I could only imagine that it would literally take years for me to see everything in the immediate area, never mind the rest of the city!

Then something caught Richard's eye. I followed his gaze to the Cartier store across the street.

"Would you like to get the jewelry part of the shopping out of the way today? It will give us more time tomorrow."

"Sure. Whatever works for you." Surprisingly, I didn't feel any trepidation. I did wonder if I was getting accustomed to the high life and decided I could ponder my slip into decadence later. I wanted to focus on Richard.

He pulled out his phone, punched up a number and swiftly inquired if Jean Claude was available. Apparently he was, because Richard took my hand and stepped into the street as the light turned.

"The necklace won't arrive until tomorrow," he told me, "But they know the color match of the pearls, so you'll have some choices."

"You know it doesn't matter to me," I told him. "I'm happy to be a model for any beautiful creations they want to hang on me."

"These will be keepers. I want you to choose something you like," he said as we stepped onto the sidewalk.

I stopped and he turned back to me.

"Why are these keepers?" I was confused.

Richard laughed. "What, you have too many pearls?"

"No. But do I need pearls?"

He kissed me quickly and with a very serious expression said, "Cress, every woman needs pearls. You're moving into a different level of business. You should be able to enjoy dressing the part."

If you can't fight it, enjoy it—that was the motto I was trying to embrace. I smiled and followed him into the Cartier store. About forty minutes later I emerged with a pair of dynamite earrings. They were platinum pavé diamond disks with dangling strands of small pearls. They weren't too long, but looked outstanding (if I do say so myself!) with my new short hair. I also got a simple three strand pearl bracelet with a pavé diamond clasp. (Did I actually say "simple"?) Richard assured me that wearing only two bangles was unlucky... *hmmmm* (and I did notice Jean Claude repress a smirk when Richard told me that!) so THREE platinum bangles in varying widths that had random small diamonds scattered and inset all the way around.

I managed to draw the line at rings, though Richard insisted I needed something in white metal to match the as-yet-unseen necklace. I told him he'd have to cut off my finger if he expected me to remove the ring he'd given me. (That earned me a quick kiss!) For my right hand I assured him I'd brought something of the CZ variety that would be just fine for an evening out. Seeing I was determined, he acquiesced, no doubt counting himself lucky that I had participated in the experience with a reasonable amount of enthusiasm! (There's no way to express the relief I felt never seeing the price tags on those items we left the store with!)

Elayna stood to greet us when we returned to the building. (And by the way, what should I call it? The apartment? The house? The mansion? Mansion fits the bill in my book. I made a mental note to ask Richard what he called it!)

"Did you enjoy your walk?" she asked with a smile. I could see her reacting to Richard's presence, though her words were addressed to me. She was apparently practiced at controlling the wobble.

"There's so much to see, I hope I'll be able to visit many more times."

Richard assured me I would with a squeeze of my hand.

"Can you get us tickets to *Lion King* for tomorrow night, please?" he asked her as we headed for the lift.

"Yes!" I dropped his hand and gave him a fist bump to the chest.

Richard laughed. "Good choice?"

"Perfect, as usual." I gave him as kiss as soon as the elevator doors closed.

He returned it and upped the ante. "Ready for a nap?" he whispered, against my ear. His tongue teased my ear lobe and one of the diamond hearts I was wearing.

"I am. But this time it's my turn."

"Can't wait. But in the meantime I'd like to take you out to dinner tonight. I have a favorite little place I think you'll like."

"Fancy?" I asked. I hadn't brought my little black dress and wasn't in the mood for any more shopping, at least not until tomorrow.

"Nope. Casual with great food."

"Perfect." I added a quick kiss with just a hint of tongue.

Then the lift door opened on the bedroom floor. As we entered the room I could feel the energy between us starting to rev up. Great to feel that again.

In the closet Richard kicked off his shoes while he called and let Elise know that we were going to take a nap and that we'd be going out for dinner. He asked her to have Akhil pick us up at seven-thirty.

While Richard made our dinner reservations, I picked up my cell and noticed the Ice Cream Boys had called four times. I'd left the phone and my purse behind when we went for our walk, assuming there was no need to take anything. I'd talked to my folks the night before and everything was going well on the Walla Walla front. I frowned as I called Ben.

"CJ, where are you? We were expecting you at ten."

I heard the irritation in his voice. I put him on speaker in case I needed some input from Richard. I wasn't used to Ben talking to me that way.

"Pardon? Didn't you get my email?" I asked.

"No. Is your father alright?"

"My father is fine. But I sent an email on Tuesday telling you I wouldn't be in today. Last week you told me we were on hold until we knew if there was any response to the contacts you've made. I assumed there was no reason for me to come today and something else came up."

Ben sighed. "Some people flew in to meet you today. Important people. Frankly, they're not too impressed by the fact that you didn't show up."

Boy, did that hit me the wrong way! I went into my don't-fuck-with-me mode.

"Listen Ben, I'm sorry you didn't get the email, but if you go arranging important meetings for me, I suggest you make me aware of them by phone if you expect me to be there. And please be sure to tell those people that the mistake was yours. If you don't, I will, if I have the opportunity I meet them in the future."

Richard was just watching me. I could see a little amusement in his eyes, but he kept his expression neutral.

Ben paused as if deciding what tack to take. "Fine. Let's move on. Can you be here by two? They've gone to lunch."

"No, I can't be there. I'm not in Los Angeles," I said firmly.

There was a long pause before he asked, "Will you be available next Thursday?"

"I can be. If you want me to come in, please be sure someone actually speaks to me. I'll be back in town Tuesday evening and then I'm flying to Washington Thursday afternoon. If I need to change that flight, I will, but please let me know by Monday morning."

"OK. I'll be in touch."

With that he was gone. I looked at Richard.

"Nicely played," he said with a smile. "Mogulhood suits you."

"I'm not a mogul yet, not by a long shot. But if they're planning on making millions off of me, the least they can do it behave a little more professionally!" I was still irritated. "That's no way to treat a meal ticket!"

Richard's cell rang and he looked at it, then showed me the

caller ID. It was Ben's office. Richard winked and put it on speaker when he answered.

"Hi, Ben. Is everything OK?"

"Yes and no. I'm sorry to bother you. I hope it's not too late."

Ben was assuming Richard was in Europe. I thought he must be calling to tattle on me, which annoyed me even more.

"No, I'm up. What's going on?"

"I had a really important meeting set up today and CJ didn't show up."

"That doesn't sound like CJ. Are you sure she knew about it?"

"She says she emailed me and told me she wouldn't be in this week."

"And?"

Apparently the realization finally hit Ben that he might not find an ally in Richard.

"Do you know where she is? She said she's out of town."

"She's in New York."

"New York?" Ben sounded confused.

Richard winked at me again. "She said something about meeting with Peter Norton."

"What? Are you sure?"

"Pretty sure. I don't know any details. His name was mentioned and something about brunch. I leave CJ to her own business concerns unless she asks for my help."

"I can't believe she's seeking funding on her own," Ben said, obviously dismayed.

"I don't know that she is," Richard said. "If that's what she's up to, I'm sure she'll let you know if Norton has any interest. I doubt she would negotiate anything on her own."

There was a pause. "Well, if you talk to her, you might suggest she try to stay on top of this. We're at a crucial juncture and..."

Richard immediately interrupted him. "Ben, are you suggesting CJ isn't holding up her end of the project?" I could detect a slight threat in his tone. His expression had changed and I could see he was irritated.

Ben picked up the cue immediately.

"No, not at all. She's been exemplary in all our work together. Her project has huge potential."

Before he could go on Richard said, "Then I suggest you remember that and treat her with the respect she's earned. She may be young but I'm sure you've noticed there is an outstanding intelligence behind that beautiful face. You might want to keep that in mind when you're dealing with her."

"I understand," Ben said respectfully. He no doubt did not want to get on the wrong side of my Trained Professional, who I'm sure supported a respectable portion of his company's billing.

"Good," Richard said. "Is there anything else?"

"No. Thanks. I appreciate your perspective. I'll see you when you get back to L.A."

"Talk to you then," Richard said and hung up. He shut off the phone and set it on the island.

31
Chance Encounter

Still Thursday

"Wow," I said with admiration. "Impressive, throwing in the Peter Norton thing."

"These guys get too complacent sometimes. It helps keep them on their toes when you remind them they're not the only game in town. Besides he was accusing the woman I love of misbehaving." He smiled with that.

I moved closer and ran my hand over his fuzzy cheek. "I assure you the only person I have any intention of misbehaving with is you." I kissed him. Then I pushed his Tshirt up. "And speaking of misbehaving, you need to take this shirt off."

He smiled. "What about the jeans?" he asked innocently.

"Leave the top button done but just let me see your penis. Remember when we did this long distance?" I'd enjoyed it and wanted to try it up close and personal.

"I do. It will be much nicer in person." Richard pulled out his cock, re-buttoned that top button, then clasped his hands behind his back, waiting.

I slowly slid my capris down and stepped out of them. I was wearing the pale yellow bra and panty set he had sent.

"Pretty," he said.

"I have a man who picks out my lingerie for me," I said nonchalantly.

"Sort of a personal service, isn't it?"

"It is, but he's very good at personal services," I said, as I pulled my top over my head. "What do you think?" I modeled the bra for him.

"He has good taste."

"He tastes good, too," I said as I quickly dropped to my knees and took his barely tumescent cock in my mouth.

He brought his hands to my head but I said, "Don't touch me until I say you can."

He snorted with a smile, but put his hands behind him again.

I stood up very slowly, rubbing my breasts and their lacy covering back and forth against his cock while I licked at his navel and ran my fingers over the contours of his magnificent abs. I undid my bra and slipped it off, then slid myself up very slowly so I could suck his nipples as I pressed my own against him.

Richard groaned softly and I ran my hands up around his neck and kissed him. He started to put his arms round me but I said, "Unh uh. Not yet."

He kissed me more deeply but I pulled away.

"Get down on your knees and taste me through the silk."

Richard smirked but lowered himself saying, "Yes, Mistress," with a wink.

I laughed. "You don't like being told what to do?" I said. "Funny, your cock seems to be into it."

"I'm into you. Can I have a taste?" he asked, looking up at me with a smile.

"Please," I said as I rubbed myself lightly against his face. I could feel the prickle of his beard through the panties as he began to lick the fabric.

"You are delicious, Sweetheart," he whispered as his tongue continued to perform magic in my nether region.

I didn't stop him when his hands wrapped around my calves, massaging them gently. I wanted more, so I hooked the toes of one foot through the handle of the bottom drawer in the island and pulled it out enough that I could brace my foot on the edge, offering Richard's tongue a broader canvas.

First he licked some of the moisture from my thighs, very slowly, and then teased me a little more before he slipped his tongue beyond the elastic to slither in and out of me.

"Enough," I said breathlessly.

"Really?" he asked, all innocence.

"For the moment. Stand up. I want to study this," I said as I dropped to my knees again.

I lifted his penis out of the way and ran my tongue into his pants, stroking his scrotum—just as I'd told him I was doing when we'd tried it long distance. He was making some rather interesting sounds.

"You're going to make me think you like that," I warned.

"I do like that," he confirmed. "I'd like you to do it more."

"What are you thinking while I do that?"

"I'm thinking how much I love you. How much I love the things you do to me, the things I do to you, and what we do together. I'm interested to see if you will want me to beg you to let me fuck you, or if you just want to experiment. I want to see where you're taking us and wherever it is, I'm anxious to go there with you. I'm thinking of how you're going to draw this out."

"Anything like what you did to me last night?" I asked with a smirk.

"Exactly. But last night you made me believe that you didn't mind in the end."

"I didn't mind. You know I love being with you any way we're together. But now I just want to remember your body—all of you. One part at a time."

"What part do you want to reexamine next?"

"Your balls. Take off your jeans."

Richard laughed but dropped his pants and stepped out of them. I shook my head as I admired all of him.

"Something wrong?" he asked.

"Nope. Even more beautiful than I remember. Come here."

When he stepped closer, I reached around and pulled him against my face, inhaling the musky smell of his pubic hair. I licked the tops of his thighs then ran my tongue between his balls and his leg on one side and then the other. His cock jerked with each lick as I massaged the twin globes of his ass. *God, I could get lost in this man!*

I got to my feet and put my hands on his shoulders, looking him in the eye. He looked back questioningly.

"I love you, Richard Hunter."

"I love you more," he said softly.

"Good. Then you won't mind proving it," I said as I took his hand and led him into the bedroom. When we got to the bed he reached for me, but I shook my head.

"Not yet. Help me turn down the bed." When the covers were out of the way, I said, "Do you want to fuck me?"

"Do you want me to?"

"I do. Very much. But I want you to do as I tell you. Can you do that?"

"I can try."

"Do or do not, there is no try," I said in my best impression of Yoda. (Lame, by the way, but he got it!)

Richard laughed out loud. "But what if I fail?" he asked.

I shook my head in dismay, struggling to keep a serious expression on my face.

"Then you'll just have to do it again and again until you get it right."

"Uhmmm…I'm not sure you should have said that."

I suppressed a giggle. "Yup, probably not much of a deterrent. Nonetheless, I want you to stroke me slow and deep but don't come yet." And I bent over the bed, wide open to him.

Being the amazing man he is, Richard stroked my clit gently with the head of his cock a couple of times and then pressed into me, deep, tight against me. He stayed there, unmoving for a few breathless (on my part!) seconds before he very slowly eased back, and then repeated the stroke. After the fourth time, he pulled out completely and bent down and put his mouth on me, holding my hips tightly. I didn't bother to tell him "hands off" because I started coming and wouldn't have stopped him for the world.

When he finally slowed he said, "I have something I think you might like."

I could barely breathe but I turned around and faced him. "Show me."

He sat on the edge of the bed. "Have a seat," he suggested.

"On that?" I asked staring at his cock. "Let me see," I said as I bent down and took him in my mouth and gave him a good suck. He grunted and before he could say anything, I straddled him and quickly came down on him.

We moved against each other hard and fast. I leaned forward, pushing him onto his back, my hands on either side of his face, my knees spread wide so he could stroke at whatever speed pleased him while I rode that orgasmic wave as it crested over and over again. He sucked my breast as he came and I could feel him explode inside me. He continued to stroke me until I finally sat back on him.

I stared at him, reveling in that love energy that was pouring out of him. Richard ran his hands down the front of my body, caressing my breasts gently, then coming to rest on my hips.

"Well, I tried and failed. Guess I'll have to take another shot," he said with a look of complete failure.

I laughed so hard I lost him and I fell over on the bed beside him.

"Sorry!" I giggled.

More kissing.

Dinner was exceptional. The restaurant was a hole in the wall Italian place with maybe only a dozen tables. Both the owner and the chef knew Richard (of course) and were delighted to see us. We were treated to a variety of small special dishes, giving me the opportunity to try a lot of different things, all amazing, and all accompanied by several Chasseur wines.

"I'm surprised to see your wines here," I said. "I'd think a small restaurant like this wouldn't be on the corporate radar."

"Off the corporate radar, but all of us have a number of small business favorites we support."

"All of you?" I asked.

"The Hunter siblings. We're all involved with the business one way or another and we all have our favorite places around the world that we service personally."

Of course. That was just like him.

"So it's genetic?" It was hard for me to imagine, though I had noticed many of Richard's traits in Robert.

Richard laughed. "Well, I confess it was my idea, but everyone else jumped on the wagon immediately. It's worked out well for all of us and all of the businesses at the same time."

"Mutual good, it's the way your world works, and just one of so many reasons why I adore you." I raised my glass in a toast.

"Care to elaborate on the others?" he asked with a wiggle of that animated eyebrow of his.

I sighed and shrugged as if I were bored. "Maybe later. We'll see."

A tall thin man with brown hair and startling blue eyes approached our table.

"Hunter? Is that you?"

"Jeff!" Richard said as he got to his feet and embraced the man.

"What are you doing in town?" Jeff asked. "I thought you were in Europe."

"I ran into Norton in London and he convinced me I needed to attend the Black and White. CJ, let me introduce you," he said turning back to me. "This is Jeff Koons. Jeff, CJ Bailey."

Jeff shook my hand warmly.

"How's the show prep going?" Richard asked.

"Chaos, of course. It's a lot to pull together. Are you free tomorrow? I'd love to show you what we're doing."

"We have an appointment in the morning. Can I give you a call after that and see where we are? I'd appreciate a look."

"Perfect.

"Nice to meet you, CJ," he said with a smile. "Hope to see you again. Enjoy your evening." He gave Richard a pat on the back as he turned away. "Talk to you tomorrow."

Richard sat down. "Well, that was a surprise. Do you know Jeff's work?"

I shook my head. "There's a faint artist bell ringing, but beyond that nothing."

"Well, you can check him out online. I bet you'll recognize some of his work. He's taking over the Whitney Museum for a retrospective as the last show before they move to their new location."

"The whole museum?" I didn't know how big it was, but I certainly knew the museum by name. I assumed it must be pretty large.

"I think they're reserving the fifth floor for the permanent collection, but he has all the rest. Something approaching thirty thousand square feet, I think."

"Good grief! I'd better study up if we're going to see him tomorrow. I don't want him to think you're hanging out with me just because you like the way I look!"

Richard laughed and reached across the table to take my

hand. "We don't have to do that, Sweetheart. Norton wants to discuss curating a show with me scheduled for three years out and it would be helpful if I could see how Jeff is approaching his project, but Jeff's show doesn't open until next June, so I can meet with him later. I want you to have the chance to do the things you're interested in while we're here."

"The thing I'm most interested in is the man holding my hand. New York is going to be here for awhile and I'm thinking I'll find a way to convince you to invite me back."

He got up and leaned over to kiss my cheek. "You're welcome at the house any time, with or without me. Meanwhile, let's see how the dress shopping goes and how we're feeling tomorrow before we decide about Jeff."

32

The Emperor's New Clothes

Friday, September 13

Note slipped into the pocket of his jeans:

> *To the clear day with thy much*
> *clearer light…*
> —Shakespeare, Sonnet 43

> Nothing like spending the day in
> your light!   XXOOJ

We got up early for a run in Central Park, which was delightful. I think we were both missing our exercise routines, (never thought I'd find myself coming to a conclusion like that!) but the weather was just too glorious to stay inside.

A little sex in the shower with musical accompaniment (*Hot Stuff,* Donna Summer), a perfect omelet and delicious coffee, and then Akhil drove us to Bergdorf's where Mark had made an 9:00 a.m. appointment for us in the formalwear department. Just like when we had gone to Neiman Marcus in Santa Monica to start the hunt for my other gowns, Bergdorfs could offer us multiple designers to choose from.

"This isn't a hint or a nudge, is it?" I asked as we entered the formalwear department that was, of course, right beside the wedding dresses.

"Noooo…" Richard said, "but if you'd like to try some of those as well…"

"No way, José. We're here to find something for the party. Nothing more."

Before he could respond, an older woman approached us and asked if she could help. It turned out she was the person our appointment was with. Dorya ushered me into the dressing room where the gowns were waiting, leaving Richard sitting in a fancy chair to await my transformation.

Mark had picked five dresses. I noticed they were all strapless, I assumed to accommodate the necklace I had yet to see. Two of the dresses I didn't care for, one was too bridal (it made me wonder if Mark was colluding with his boss!) and the other was lacy and formfitting, something I wanted to avoid this time because of the toileting difficulties. The other three I was anxious to try.

The first dress was plain but pretty and fit me perfectly. The only decorative thing in its favor was that the fabric looked like a pique but was a sort of dull satin. Plain top, full skirt.

I walked out to show Richard. He shrugged.

"Do you like it?" he asked.

"The fabric is interesting but it doesn't strike me one way or the other. If the necklace is showy, then maybe plain is best?"

"The necklace isn't that showy. Nothing like what you wore in San Diego."

"Back to the drawing board, " I said as I returned to the dressing room.

"This one is a Monique Lhuillier," Dorya said as she helped me into the next dress.

"Really? I have one of hers and I'm very fond of it. It even ended up in a magazine ad."

"Really? Are you a model?"

"It was a candid shot of me at a fundraiser wearing an exquisite necklace."

"Perhaps that's why you look familiar." She zipped me up.

I turned to look in the mirror. The dress was beautiful. It had a sort of crisscross band of the same chiffon twisted into roses going along the top on one side, then crossing down the middle and following the empire waistline to the side seam. From there it was just several layers of chiffon to the floor. Plain and really beautiful. And it even had a matching stole of multiple layers of chiffon trimmed in those same chiffon roses.

I was smiling when I went out to show Richard. I did a little spin for him.

"Very goddess-y," he said.

"Good for the necklace?"

"I think it would be perfect. Do you like it?"

"I do," I said. "But there's one more I want to try."

"Go for it."

The third dress was also chiffon but the bodice—again empire—and underskirt were sort of a dull satin with a very fine silver thread running through it making a large diamond pattern. From just under the bust it had an additional layer of chiffon to the floor.

"And you see," Dorya said as she unhooked something in back, "It is two dresses in one." She demonstrated by completely removing the chiffon layers attached to a band that split in the front, showing just a little of the underskirt. That left me in a sort of A-line shape, with a little more fabric in back, all in the bodice fabric. I liked that. I had her put the chiffon overskirt back on and went out to show my Trained Professional.

"I like this," he said. "Turn around for me." Then he said, "That silver thread might be a nice accent for the necklace."

I did the turn and then said, "But wait." And Dorya removed the chiffon layer. "*Voilà*! Two for the price of one!"

Richard laughed. "It's nice. Is there anything else to try?"

"There are two more I don't care for. I'll try them for you if you want me to, but one has that access issue and the other is too bridal for me."

That remark elicited a smirk. "I like both of these last two. You choose. Whatever you feel more comfortable in. Does either of them need to be altered?"

"Nope. And I can wear a low pair of heels and spend the evening without crippling myself. I want to warn you, I'm going to take a stand on the shoes. Mark keeps forcing me into stilettos, but I don't see the point when my feet are hidden under floor-length skirts."

"Sweetheart, you can go barefoot if you want, though I wouldn't recommend it. The sidewalks aren't very clean in this city."

Dorya slipped a satin wrap around my shoulders and went off to get me some shoes to try. I continued to admire myself in the large three-way mirror. Richard got up and came to stand behind me.

"I don't think I've told you how much I like your hair."

"So I don't need to look for a wig so you'll still find me attractive?"

"Nope. You're sexier than ever, Miss Hot Pants." He edged the wrap off my shoulders and put his hands there as he met my eyes in the mirror. "Surely you've noticed my ardor hasn't cooled?"

"Good thing, since I can't seem to get enough of you," I said. He shot me a jolt of energy and I wobbled. "Stop that!" I scolded.

"Really?" he whispered as he gave the side of my neck a quick kiss.

"Well, for the time being, anyway. Back off or I'll be dripping all over this dress."

He laughed and returned to his chair as Dorya arrived with shoes. Richard had no interest in footwear. He just wanted me to be comfortable, so I chose an amazing pair of dull silver kitten heels. They were open on the inside from the ball of my foot to where the back cupped my heel. On the outside they looked like a plain pump. Sexy! And I staggered with a little aftershock when I suddenly pictured Richard planting a kiss on my arch! (Dorya thought I'd tripped...)

Richard paid for the dress and shoes and arranged for them to be delivered, then glanced at his watch. I looked at mine. It was 10:15.

"See, I'm an easy shopper, especially with Mark's help."

"You did great and we have the rest of the day to ourselves. We have *Lion King* tonight, curtain is at eight. We can dine out or in, your call."

"Let's eat at home, if you don't mind. That will make for a less frantic night. And by the way, I may as well warn you that I'm likely to burst into tears."

"What?" Richard looked at me with a frown. "Why?"

"Mom and Gran have been talking about *Lion King* for years and I've seen some of the documentaries on Julie Taymor and her work across the board. She just blows me away and the animals she's created just for this...I don't know...I get so excited I just burst into tears because they're so flat-out amazing."

Richard totally cracked up.

"Be nice," I said with a pout. "I just wanted to give you fair warning so you wouldn't get crazy and call 911 when it happens."

By then we'd reached the door and on the sidewalk, he stopped and hugged me.

In an exaggerated soothing voice he said. "How 'bout I stick a couple of extra handkerchiefs in my pockets for you?"

"OK," I said brightly. "Now can we go see Jeff?" I was really curious after the *Vanity Fair* article Richard had found for me last night.

"Are you sure that's what you want to do?"

"I'm fascinated. I can't imagine what kind of man has himself photographed for a magazine article—and by Annie Leibovitz, no less—while exercising naked in front of a wall of mirrors. (I'd read the article online last night) "I think he should maybe be in the dictionary with the definition of narcissist." I looked at Richard just to be sure I wasn't offending him but he smirked.

"I have no clue why people like his work," I went on, "But I'm intrigued because obviously, I'm in the minority. I mean, the man made what? A few hundred million from the sale of his work just last year? Things that are so foreign to me…they interest me. And I'm curious about how such a huge exhibition comes together."

Richard punched up Jeff while we waited for the car and made arrangements to meet. Moments later Akhil was whisking us off to the Whitney.

"Well, what do you think?" Richard asked as we got back in the car just before 1:00 p.m.

"He's a really interesting guy. I'm not sure if he's eccentric, a genius or just a glorified carney." I looked at Richard, still hoping I wasn't going too far for him with that observation. He seemed interested in what I had to say, so I went on.

"Jeff talks a great line, but I can't tell for sure if he believes it or if he just likes to shock and surprise people. The same with his work. I mean some of it seems like he's just daring someone not to adore him for making something so wacky. It's kind of an Emperor's New Clothes thing—that's what Steph and I have taken to calling things that a group of people decide to admire while making anyone who disagrees feel too ignorant or unsophisticated to understand it."

Richard was just staring at me, unreadable.

"What? Are you unhappy with my take on it? It's just an observation, not a criticism."

"Not at all. You have just encapsulated what the art world's critics have been arguing about regarding Jeff and his work for years. How did you do that?"

I laughed. "Just callin' 'em as I see 'em. But seriously, you know my exposure to art has been very limited. I've taken some Art Appreciation in school, mostly to try and keep up with Steph. And I do appreciate some famous work, both old and new, but I'm afraid my taste is pretty pedestrian. Remember my observations on strings and suitcases?"

"I'm really interested in your perspective on these things," he assured me. "Look how you honed in on the window painting. We both love that piece and I would lay money on the fact that you could show it to twenty people and only one or two would appreciate it. It's back to that old Buyer Number One thing. The people who buy Jeff's work are in the third category for the most part. They don't love the work, they love being able to say they own it."

"That's a relief!" I said, really happy he wasn't disappointed with my impression of Jeff and his empire. "But I'm really glad we went to see him. I loved learning how a show like that comes together. It's more work than most people realize—certainly more than I could have imagined."

After a pause during which he just looked at me, he smiled and said, "How long has it been since I mentioned how much I love you?" he asked with a smile.

"Too long."

"CJ Bailey…" He took my face in his hands. "You are full of surprises and I couldn't love you more!"

He kissed me.

"Well, you could try," I suggested reasonably.

Richard cracked up.

33
Can You Feel the Love Tonight?

Still Friday

Like *Les Miz*, seeing *Lion King* with Richard was a completely magical experience. And before I go on, if you haven't seen it and ever get the chance, DO NOT miss it! (Didn't I say the same thing about *Les Miz*, you ask. Yes, I did. And don't miss that, either!)

As I'd warned Richard, I did burst into tears at the very beginning when those amazing animal puppets first came down the aisles. I don't know how to explain the weird reaction I had, but it was as if there was some sort of huge emotional response that suddenly built up inside me until it sort of exploded in tears. Very strange (and wonderful!) I probably don't need to tell you what a comfort it was to be there with a man who was completely accepting of me and my sometimes peculiar behavior—a man who had a fresh white handkerchief at the ready.

I managed to control my tears for most of the rest of the show, but I was completely carried away by the amazing production, costumes and masks, and puppets in particular. What an astonishing visual treat!

"I think we'd better make a point to include live theater as a regular part of our lives in the future," I said as we waited for the car.

"I'd like that. It's a great experience to share. I'm so glad you really enjoy it." He gave me a squeeze.

"For me, that's genetic," I assured him. "You'll see when you meet my folks." I gave him a quick kiss on the cheek. "Are you still planning on visiting them when you get home?"

"I am. And you know my birthday is next month. There's something I want you to give me."

I looked at him in surprise, unable to imagine what he might be thinking.

"Despite the generous salary you're paying me, you might find my budget a little tight when it comes to your expectations. And to suggest I charge up that Amex you pay for seems a tad disingenuous. Besides, on a very personal level, I think you've had pretty good exposure to what's available."

Richard laughed. "I was thinking more of your time."

"Well, that's not much in demand these days, if you discount the expectations of the Ice Cream Boys. So tell me, how may I serve you, my Prince?"

"I want a week of you, all to myself in the location or locations of your choice."

"Location of my choice? Like where?"

"I don't know. Where would you like to go? Anywhere in the world."

I just looked at him in confusion.

"Paris? Greenland? China? Tierra del Fuego? Australia? India? Morocco? Machu Picchu? I could go on... I want to a take you somewhere you really want to go, somewhere you want to go with me."

"This sounds more like a gift for me, not you." Intriguing as the possibility of such an escape might seem, it didn't make much sense to me.

"The gift is seeing something through your eyes and sharing the experience with you. There's nothing I would enjoy more. We've been apart too much this summer."

I could see my consternation amused him, but also that he was serious.

"Well, it's certainly something that will require a great deal of thought. You're sure about this?"

"I am," he assured me. "And you have until next Friday to decide where we'll go. I need to get our itinerary laid out."

When we got home, we did a little slow dancing on the terrace and then made love gently and sweetly, content just to be together.

STILL LUCKY

Saturday, September 14

Note placed in the pocket of his jacket:

> *I caught the happy virus last night*
> *When I was out singing beneath the stars.*
> *It is remarkably* contagious—
> *So kiss me.*   –Hafiz

*When he found it, he did!

On Saturday morning Richard took me to three galleries that Jeff Koons was associated with, just to show me some of the contemporary work currently on display. At Gagosian it was a De Waal show that consisted of various size frames with narrow shelves on which sat various porcelain cylindrical vessels in varying sizes, for the most part monochromatic in black, grey or white.

At David Zwirner we saw photos from Philip-Lorca diCorcia, the collection titled *Hustlers*, which struck me as mostly odd subject matter, none of which appealed. There was also an empty room with a three-screen video that didn't make any sense to me, either. And in another space they were showing Raymond Pettibon in something called *To Wit*. This consisted of clusters of odd drawings and paintings on paper—mostly amateurish and sometimes cartoonish (as in a twelve year old boy's work) and in most cases juvenile in subject matter, with a few statements on contemporary situations. These were all tacked to the walls loosely, in groupings with graffiti written on the walls around them (or in one case on a long stretch of paper towels?!) Again that one went right over my head.

At Sonabend Gallery they were showing Grazia Toderi's videos, strange somewhat ethereal lights and colors. Interesting to look at though, again, I suppose I was searching for a point, but couldn't find one.

As we passed through the exhibitions, I made my Trained Professional give me a rundown on the work, which he did with a level of serious, incredibly fluid high-tone jargon that had me in stitches. Finally, I had to ask him to stop.

"I have to say that suitcases and strings are looking better all the time," I told Richard as we left the gallery.

"Shame we sold them all," he said. "I might be able to convince the artist to do a commission for you." He was looking very serious, but I saw that twinkle in his eye that he never seemed to be able to mask.

"I think not," I said like a snooty customer, nose in the air. Then I moved closer to him and batted my eyelashes and said in a very breathy voice, "What you can do for me is take me to lunch and then I'm thinking of a nap before our big night out."

"Actually, I can think of quite a few things I can do to you… uh, I mean *for* you."

"Ditto!" I said as Akhil opened the car door for us.

We got back to the house at a 1:30. Richard put on a pair of sweatpants and a Tshirt while I slipped into the elastic top dress. It was warm outside and the French doors were open between this sitting room and the terrace. He went to his office to take care of some business stuff and I took my laptop and settled on the couch.

I had been thinking about that other dress, the goddess-y one, all day and decided I wanted it. Of course I hadn't seen the price tag, but if I could afford it (my money, not the Prince's) I decided I'd get it. I called Bergdorf's and was able to speak to Dorya. I was thrilled to find that the dress was still available and, best of all, was only $260! Piece of cake! I gave her my Visa number and asked her to send it and the matching wrap to California. I justified it by telling myself Richard would be taking me somewhere I could wear it. Did I have three gowns already hanging in our closet at home? Yes. Did I care? No. I loved the way I'd felt in that dress!

Then I called Steph, not sure where she was or if she'd pick up. She did.

"Hey Steph, what's going on out there on the left coast?"

"Michael's spending the weekend with me here at the house. He's in the pool and I'm doing the lounging lizard thing. How's the Big Apple treating you?'

"Great…but then that's the company I'm keeping. I have stories to tell you when I get home: art viewing, meeting Jeff Koons and a big do at MOMA tonight. Oh yeah, and there's this palace Magic Man calls home."

"Wow! Can't wait. When are you back?"

"I get in about 3:30 p.m. on Tuesday, but then I'm off again on Thursday afternoon to see my folks."

"You jetsetter, you. How's your dad?" Steph asked.

"I'm talking to him daily and he's doing great. Ahead of schedule on his recovery."

"Well, I'm hoping you'll be here a little more. Ji asked about you when he came yesterday."

"I miss those workouts. We've been running in Central Park in the morning, and there's a pool and a workout room here, but we haven't used them yet. And I need to get a move on and get things laid out for tonight."

"Take care. I'll make it a point to be home for dinner Tuesday so you can give me all the details. Tell Richard to behave."

"Now what fun would that be?" I laughed as I hung up.

I got up and after a glance in Richard's direction to be sure he was still busy, I went into the closet and tucked a note into the inside pocket of his tux.

Consider yourself warned:

I would always rather be happy
than dignified.
—Charlotte Brontë, *Jane Eyre*

XXOOJ

That was sure to make him smile. He might also wonder what I was up to! I settled back into the couch as Richard came out of the office.

"How about a glass of wine, Sweetheart?"

"Nice," I said by way of agreement.

"Preference?"

"You're the oenophile, you choose."

Richard smirked and shook his head as he picked up the house phone and told Elise what we wanted, then went down the hall to meet her at the lift. He returned a couple of minutes later with a tray, some cheese, sliced apples and grapes, crackers, two glasses and a bottle of Beaujolais that had already been opened.

He poured us each a glass, handed me mine and said, "Here's to a fancy night out with nothing to cause you to grab a strange man by the balls."

We often teased each other back and forth about that night in San Diego at the charity event and the way I chose to handle a very rude and very drunk patron.

He sat down beside me and we clicked glasses. The wine was amazing. I followed that first sip with a kiss.

"How about *your* balls?" I asked, just as he was about to take another sip.

He laughed. "Feel free. Anytime, anywhere."

"I'm thinking as soon as we finish our wine. I feel a nap coming on."

"Good idea. It may help us to behave while we're out in public."

I gave him a skeptical look. "I don't know, sometimes it just comes over me and…well, the new dress is a bit easier to slip under and…"

He stopped me with a quick kiss. "Do you have your phone?"

I pointed to where it lay on the coffee table. "Anxious to change the subject, are you?"

"Nope. Priorities. I want us to coordinate our calendars before my thoughts turn to what will be going on tonight underneath the skirt of that pretty new dress."

"Really?" I was a little surprised. Maybe he was anticipating our "nap" as much as I was. I know Richard was always willing, but he hadn't been very aggressive since that first coming back together.

"Really," he assured me as he reached for his phone. "Get up for a minute."

I realized that he wanted to swing his legs up so I could settle between them, like we used to do at home.

"This is one of the things I've missed the most since you left," I said as I scooched back to lean against his chest, adding a little wiggle against him. I was stunned to feel his hard cock.

"Richard!"

"What? This surprises you?"

"No…but…" I sputtered.

"But?"

"I can hardly concentrate knowing my favorite treat is ready and waiting."

"Try," he suggested rather pointedly.

"No. Put down your wine, and mine, and let's get this distraction out of the way."

With a sigh of surrender he set our glasses aside, and before he could say anything else I took his hand and slipped it between my legs, just to assure him that he wasn't the only one thinking about the two of us.

His fingers rubbed me gently and then one slipped into me, stroking me slowly as he turned down the top of my dress and began to caress my breast. It felt wonderful.

"I love you, Cress," he whispered against my ear as I leaned back against him.

"I love you more," I said breathlessly, as he continued to gently rub and tease me, massaging my clit and then slipping his finger inside me again. His other hand was squeezing my breast gently, working my nipple back and forth between his fingers.

"You are so beautiful, and you respond so perfectly to the things I do to try to please you," he whispered against my hair. "Everything you offer me, the way you invite me into your body— I don't understand how you can love me so much, but there is no way to tell you how grateful I am."

He pressed his tongue into my ear, just as I came. He continued to kiss my cheek and gently hold my breast until I quieted. Finally, I turned around on my knees and threw my arms around his neck.

"My beautiful man, if only you could see who you are when you look in the mirror, you'd know why I love you so."

With that I gave him a deep kiss filled with all the love I felt and he responded in kind. I paused a moment to look into his eyes, to put an exclamation point on everything I'd conveyed with that kiss before I pulled up his shirt and bent to tease and suck his nipples. He closed his eyes and laid his head back against the pillows as his hands gently caressed my shoulders.

I continued with the tongue and kisses down the center of his belly and paused to lick his navel in the same way he'd used his tongue on me. He groaned and thrust his hips forward, offering his cock, five or six inches of which had emerged from the front of his sweats. The tip glistened, held against his belly by the elastic waistband.

I smiled. He was so beautiful.

I bent to slowly lick the head of his penis, to run my tongue back and forth over the tip, even as I peeled his sweats down. I gently lifted his balls and let the elastic go back underneath them. I reached between my legs and then shared that moisture when I slid one hand down him slowly, gently fondling his balls with the other.

Lifting his scrotum, I pressed it down against his shaft, as I settled on my belly and took him in my mouth. I could taste us both as I slowly slipped him in and out. I let my saliva drip down to lubricate my hand, working him a little faster until I heard his breathing shift. Then I took him deep as he came, and he sat up, pushing his hands into the cushions as he pressed farther into my mouth. As his ejaculation slowed, I backed off and licked and sucked, savoring the delicious taste of him.

I moved up to lay my cheek against his chest as I continued to stroke him very tenderly. Richard slowly caressed my back as he held me. Finally, I slipped my arms around him and hugged him tightly.

After a few minutes he said, "Can we get back to work now?"

He was trying to look impatient but he wasn't fooling me. Of course I laughed as I got up to pull the top of my dress back up and shake the skirt back into place. I picked up our phones and returned to my place on the couch. Richard kissed the top of my head as we punched up our calendars.

"This will remain a little fluid for the next week," he said. "But at the moment I'm planning on coming home on October first. We could go to see your folks that Friday, the fourth, and stay up there until the ninth, if that works for them. We can then leave that next Thursday or Friday, the tenth or eleventh, for the birthday trip, depending on where we're going. We would be back on the nineteenth, more or less. Again, depends on destination, flights, and all that."

I was putting the dates into my calendar as he talked. He was watching my screen over my shoulder as he held his next to mine. He gave me a few changes as to where he'd be when he went back overseas, this New York trip having altered some of his plans.

"So we have brunch with Peter and Gwen tomorrow. I imagine that will last until two or so. Anything special you'd like to do tomorrow afternoon or night?" he asked.

"One thing I'd like to do while I'm here is walk the High Line. Is that a possibility?"

"Of course. What made you think of that?"

"I saw an amazing documentary on it awhile back on PBS. I'm really curious about what they've done."

"How about we see what comes up tomorrow afternoon and do the Highline on Monday? There's a lot more of Central Park to see. And I have a favorite little French restaurant I'd like to take you to tomorrow night. Do you want to do any shopping, look for a gift for Steph or something for your folks?"

"I wouldn't mind some shopping, but it will have to be somewhere down at my level. Is Chelsea or Soho a possibility? Or do you know someplace? I'm thinking boutiques, small fun places, places I can afford. And I don't mean your Amex card. I want something that fits my Visa."

"We don't have to have the money discussion again, do we?" he asked.

"No. I've been doing some shopping on your account, but for some things I just feel better if I pay for them myself."

"What are you going to do when you sell your project and you have more money than I do?" he asked, amused.

"If you're good I might give you an Amex card that *I* pay for! Of course when I consider the kind of money you spend…"

"If you end up with one of those multi-billion dollar deals, I doubt you'd notice anything I might spend."

"Good grief, let's hope that doesn't happen!" The thought of that kind of money made me really uncomfortable.

"Why?" Richard seemed surprised.

I could hear the concern in his voice, and turned to look at him.

"What on earth would I do with a billion dollars?" I honestly had no clue. And frankly, the idea seemed preposterous!

"Well, it's something you need to start thinking about. Even if you sell the project right now without further development, I'm sure it would bring multi-millions."

"Can I think about that when I have an offer?" I said, dismissing his concern. I thought it was funny, actually.

"You and Scarlett O'Hara?"

"Yup. Works for me."

34

One Swan A'Swimmin'

Still Saturday

After a light supper—salmon salad, fresh baguette, lovely brie—we took our wine upstairs to get ready. A quick shower with some teasing about what might happen when we came home, then I dried my hair and did my make-up while Richard went to the closet to get dressed. I put on my fancy white garter belt and some iridescent white stockings. No panties—that toileting thing. The skirts on the dress weren't too big but still, it's not easy to hold all that fabric out of the way. I was hoping I might make a bathroom buddy connection at the event, in case I needed help.

I put my short robe on before I went into the closet. I wanted to keep the underpinnings a surprise for when we came home, so I casually asked Richard if he would go and get my wine that I'd left in the bathroom. While he was gone I quickly jumped into the dress and got it zipped most of the way up before he returned. When I asked him to zip it the rest of the way, he obliged with a kiss to the back of my neck.

"You smell wonderful," he said.

I smiled at him in the mirror. "Same old, same old." It was the Muguet he'd given me. "Wanna put my earrings on for me?" I teased.

He opened the jewelry drawer where Elise had made room for me and arranged my things next to his. Like the closet at home, there were little divided sections lined with cloth. Richard picked up one of the earrings, and much to my surprise, gave my earlobe a quick suck before slowly pushing the post through. He groaned softly, the familiar tease. I laughed as he secured it. He repeated the action on my other ear after giving me a sincere long look and a little jab of energy.

"Funny boy. Want me to do your studs for you?" He had a set of pearls for both studs and cufflinks that I helped him with. He was wearing a plain gold Rolex with a black croco band. It was very sharp with his tux.

"Can I choose something else for you?" I asked.

"Of course."

It amused him when I decided he should wear a bracelet or a particular watch. But I closed that drawer and pulled out the one below it where my things were.

"Close your eyes," I said as I took the ring box out from under the cashmere hoodie and took out the ring. "OK, you can open them." I held it out to him.

For a moment he looked confused, but then he smiled.

"Really?" he said.

"Of course. My Prince deserves something special that wasn't charged to his credit card."

He opened the box, took out the ring and looked at it closely. I couldn't read his reaction.

"Don't worry, it's not an engagement ring. I just wanted you to have something like mine."

When he still didn't say anything I started to worry.

"Don't you like it?" I couldn't hide my disappointment.

"Cress, I don't know what to say…"

He noticed the inscription and read it with a smile. But he looked a little sad and I was beginning to wonder if maybe it wasn't something he'd enjoy wearing.

"You don't have to wear it if you don't want to. I just wanted you to have something with as much love as the one you gave me." Still he was silent. "Are the diamonds too much? Giano said he could remove them…"

"Cress," he said as he took me in his arms and held me tightly. After a moment he pulled back and looked at me and there was a hint of tears in his eyes. "Thank you, Sweetheart. Want to put it on for me?"

I ran my hand over his cheek before taking the ring and slipping it onto his left hand. It fit perfectly and looked great.

"Do you like it? And please, be honest."

He chuckled. "I do like it. It means the world to me. Thank you. I'll be happy to express the full extent of my gratitude when we get home."

I hugged him. Then asked him to do the clasp on my new pearl bracelet.

"Shall I wear the bangles or will it be too much?"

"Let's try the necklace and see what you think." He was smiling again as he reached up and pulled the red box from the shelf. It said *Cartier Paris*. "Your turn to close your eyes," he said as he positioned me closer to the mirror.

I felt the cool weight of the necklace as he gently laid it around my neck.

Then he put both hands on my shoulders and said, "Now."

Oh my god! The necklace was amazing! (Of course.) It was a torsade of multiple strands of small pearls, the same size as the ones in my earrings and bracelet, but in the center...in the center was a magnificent swan, all in pavé diamonds (I assumed). I was blown away.

"Good grief! Crown jewels indeed, my Prince. The swan...I can't believe it. I may not give this one back!"

"You don't have to, remember? It's yours. Like the rest of these, a keeper."

"Richard!" I turned to him, not knowing what to say. "I can't have million dollar necklaces...I simply...*can't*!"

He laughed. "Not to worry, the price tag was nowhere near a million dollars." He was smiling at me in the mirror. "I was walking in Paris and this was in the window at Cartier. I had to assume they'd made it just for you and it was my duty as the man who loves you to be sure it found its way around your beautiful neck."

It's hard to explain how conflicted I was. If the necklace had been exactly the same—maybe a copy of some famous piece—with fake pearls and a CZ swan (again, I was assuming these were real!)—and a price tag of five or six hundred dollars. I would have found a way to buy it. It was completely perfect. So was I being a snob about the money thing?

"The best part," Richard continued (no doubt reading my

thoughts as they flitted across my face) "is that the swan comes off the necklace and can be worn as a pin or a pendant. And you can put other things on the pearls or wear them alone. See, practical, really, like your dress—though in this case three in one."

He glanced at his watch. "We need to get going. See how you feel about the necklace as the night goes on."

I grabbed the pearly "Princess" purse he'd given me and we were off.

As I'd promised Richard, I grabbed no men by the balls at the event. In fact I had a wonderful time. I found I was getting a little better at remembering the names of people I was introduced to—Richard's focus CDs, I'm sure—and enough of those names were familiar in a way that assured me we were rubbing shoulders with New York's elite.

Peter Norton and his wife Gwen Adams shared a table with us. They were both delightful and when Peter found out I was a portal designer, he whisked me onto the dance floor to learn more about my project. In fact we kept dancing and talking shop until Richard finally tapped Peter's shoulder to cut in, insisting that he was entitled to a dance or two with me! At any rate, I was looking forward to having brunch with them the next day.

Gwen and I easily paired as bathroom buddies and she demonstrated that beaded dresses, while heavy, were easiest to sling over your arm, something I intended to keep in mind on my next shopping trip!

I really had a great time with her. She had a terrific sense of humor and there was a lot of laughter throughout the evening.

On the way home I was snuggled up against Richard, just enjoying going over the events of the evening in my mind.

"Penny?" Richard said as he planted a soft kiss on the top of my head.

"Just thinking about the gala and remembering what you told

me before we went to the one in San Diego. You made it sound like attendance was not much fun. And yet, I had a great time then and tonight. Do you really not enjoy them?"

"Well, I have to say, both then and now, I had a good time. Must be the company I'm keeping."

I sat up and looked at him. He did seem to be genuinely happy.

"I wonder if you'll decide that the price of my company is just a little too high?" I tweaked the lustrous necklace and gave a spokes-model flourish toward my dress. I even lifted one foot and gave it a wiggle.

"Hey, let me see that," he said, reaching for my pretty little shoe and the foot that was in it.

"Really?" I scooted back and put both feet in his lap with a giggle.

Richard lifted one of my feet and slowly ran a hand from my ankle down across the top of my foot.

"Are these the shoes you got when you got the dress?"

"Yup. Like 'em?"

"Can't believe I didn't notice. They're very sexy," he said with an eyebrow wiggle as he continued to caress my foot.

He slipped his hand under my heel and lifted my foot to press a kiss to my arch, just as I'd pictured when I was in the store. And the reality gave me an even bigger jolt than my imagination had the first time around. Richard's smile was a knowing one.

His hands slid slowly up my leg, caressing my calf and then I realized what he was up to. I tried to pull my leg back but he hung on for a moment before he released me.

"Oh, no you don't! That's for me to know and you to keep wondering," I said as I straightened my skirts, sitting up properly with my pearly purse in my lap and looking straight ahead. "At least for a little while." (That I added out of the side of my mouth.)

Richard laughed. "You know there is one thing you haven't done tonight."

I looked at him. "Only one?"

"Well, one I'd like you to do right now."

"Really? Right now?" I was pretty sure he wasn't suggesting actually having sex in the car. (I might have considered it with an anonymous driver but Akhil…well…)

"Scoot over here."

I moved back next to him and he carefully removed my wrap and folded it over his lap. I wasn't sure where he was going with that and didn't really think he was looking for a hand job with us in fancy dress. We were nearly home, why bother Lewinsky-ing our good clothes?

He leaned closer and whispered in my ear. "You haven't grabbed any balls tonight. Care to give me a more tender experience than the one you offered Malcolm?"

I smiled as I turned to him and kissed him. My hand slipped under the satin wrap and cupped my Prince's jewels. Such a tightly packed handful. I kept kissing him, teasing with my tongue while I fondled him through his pants. His cock was quickly rising in expectation, but I continued to focus my ministrations on his testicles.

"Your balls are fascinating, Charming. A perfect pair for that delicious cock of yours." I whispered as lightly ran my tongue around the curve of his ear. "What do I have to do to convince you to fuck me when we get home?"

"You'll think of something," he said as he turned to me, put both arms around me and kissed me deeply.

I wrapped my hand around his penis and gave him a squeeze just as the car pulled up in front of the building. Akhil got out and opened the doors for us. He was smiling—probably well aware of what we were up to—while maintaining a very professional demeanor.

Louise was on the door. (Does this make her a doorman, doorwoman or door person? It makes my lover an equal opportunity employer!) I had met her the other night when we came back from dinner. She was a tall woman, probably five-twelve in her stockinged feet. She was plain as far as her hair and make-up went—short blond hair, no noticeable make-up—and in her fancy uniform people might mistake her for a man at first glance, but she had a smile as bright as a searchlight and seemed to genuinely enjoy her job. Richard told me she was a retired New York policewoman and more than capable in the security department.

Louise tipped her hat to us as she opened the door. "Welcome home Mr. Hunter, Miss Bailey. I hope you enjoyed your evening."

"Thanks Louise. We had a wonderful time," I said, trying to

respond appropriately when all I could think of was what was waiting for me in Richard's fancy tuxedo pants.

Darnay, the night concierge, stood when we came in. He was a handsome black man, soft spoken with a lilting Jamaican accent and a head full of those great tight little dread twists that work with black hair. He, too, welcomed us home. Richard slipped his key card into the slot for the elevator. When the door closed behind us, I turned and kissed him, my other hand rubbing his erection.

When we finally reached our closet, I tossed my wrap and purse on the island and turned to Richard.

"Do you need help undressing, Handsome?"

"I'll take all the help I can get," he said as he pulled the ends of his tie.

I unbuttoned his jacket and lightly ran my fingers underneath the waistband of his pants, feeling the end of his hard cock beneath the fabric of his shirt. I started to remove the studs from the front of his shirt while he took off his jacket, then reached around me to remove his cufflinks. I set the studs on the island and ran my fingers up and down under his suspenders, giving his hard nipples extra attention before I eased his suspenders off his shoulders. Then I pulled his shirt out of his pants, undoing the rest of the buttons.

Richard was watching me, smiling.

"So will you fuck me?" I asked, not meeting his eyes as I helped him off with his shirt. I tried to sound both hesitant and pouty at the same time.

"I'd certainly like to."

"How exactly would you do it?" I asked as I tongued his nipples.

He couldn't help laughing. "Enthusiastically? Sincerely? With feeling?"

"With skill?"

"All the skill I have at my disposal," he promised, as he took off his shoes.

Fancy dress and all, I got down on my knees and slipped his socks off very slowly, caressing his feet and his calves as I did it, teasing him with light touches. Then I unzipped his fly and freed his cock. I just had to have a taste. Richard groaned and finally took me by the elbows and helped me to my feet. He gave me a long deep kiss.

He walked around behind me while I enjoyed the sight of his beautiful penis emerging from those black tuxedo pants, a view doubled in the mirror as he unzipped my dress and eased it down so I could step out of it. He was looking at my garter belt and lace topped stockings with appreciation.

"Question answered," he said. "And, I might add, very prettily."

He took my hand and lifted it over my head to turn me, as if we were dancing, so that I faced him.

"Do you need these pants?" I asked quite seriously as I reached to unbutton them.

"Not at the moment," he said, dropping both pants and underwear and kicking them aside.

"Black bikinis?" I said in surprise.

"Formal wear," he announced with a smile.

He put his arms around me and slowly pulled me close. His skin was warm and his hard cock between us made me even more conscious of my moist thighs. I pressed my breasts against him and reached around to grab his ass. So completely perfect!

Between kisses I said, "So when are you going to fuck me?"

Between kisses he answered, "I expect I'll get around to it pretty soon."

I laughed. "I certainly hope so!"

He lifted one of my legs and I wrapped it around him, fully expecting his cock, but instead he stroked the hood of my clit between his fingers. I caught my breath.

"Your little penis is as hard as mine," he whispered against my ear.

"Ummmm…" was all I could say. I could barely breathe.

Richard gently rubbed my clit with the tip of his thumb as two fingers slipped into me, spreading and stroking. I whimpered at the exquisite sensation and then I came as he stroked my G-spot, making me tremble all over. As it faded he massaged me gently, spreading my moisture all around that end of me. Finally, he brought his hand to his own mouth and licked his fingers.

"You are delicious," he assured me, and encouraged my agreement by offering his hand for me to taste, which I did, teasing his palm with my tongue as I would the head of his cock.

"So what are you going to do with this?" I whispered as I

caressed his penis with a light touch that I hoped would torment him… just a little.

"Any ideas?"

"Yup." I eased away from him, turned around and bent over, bracing myself on the seat of the chair with my head down. I wiggled my bottom in invitation.

I fully expected him to plow into me, but instead he squatted and put his mouth on me, spreading me as he licked and sucked. All that and with a wonderful view of his throbbing penis and those testicles!

I cried out when I came that time, and then he was inside me, moving slowly as he built my orgasm into the wave thing, at the same time gently squeezing my breasts.

And then his breath shifted and he drove into me hard and fast, upping the sensation for me even as his own orgasm exploded, rendering him rigid as his ejaculation pulsed inside me. When it subsided, he stroked me gently, slowly, his fingers moving lightly over my back and coming to rest on my hips. He pulled me tightly against him.

"Cress…have I mentioned I love you?"

"Now might be a good time," I suggested.

He pressed into me and gave me a good strong twitch.

"Well, in that case, I love you. But then you know that." He bent to kiss my back.

"I do," I said. "It shows."

35
Us

Still Saturday night or the wee hours of Sunday morning.

Finally, he released me with a kiss to my bottom before he unhooked my garters and removed my garter belt.

"Sit down," he said as he turned me around.

When I settled in the chair, Richard knelt down and gave me a long deep kiss. It was his promise, as always, fulfilled. Nice to have a man in your life who keeps his promises, even one as simple as that! He just looked at me for a long moment and then began to remove my stockings, slowly and with tender kisses starting at my thighs and moving down my legs, one at a time, as he slipped the stockings down.

"Any chance you might feel like visiting the spa downstairs?" I asked. "I'd enjoy a good soak. Thought you might, too."

"Perfect," Richard said. "No one I'd enjoy getting into hot water with more than you."

He gave me a quick kiss and then picked up the house phone from the island and punched some keys, turning on the spa, I assumed.

"We need to give it a few minutes to heat up."

Richard reached around my neck to unhook the clasp on the necklace. I put a hand to my throat, reluctant to feel it go. He smiled.

"Does this mean you've adjusted to the idea of seeing it in your jewelry drawer?"

I could feel my cheeks color. "I can't help myself. I love it and I love the thoughtfulness that's behind it. I have to warn you that I intend to wear it a lot!"

"It might be a little over the top for casual wear."

"Ah ha! A flaw in the façade of my Trained Professional's expertise!" I exclaimed with delight. "Costume jewelry with big stones and extravagant size is all the rage at the moment. I can wear it and if I'm casually dressed, everyone will assume it's fake."

"Well, enjoy it in any way that suits you. I'm so happy you're pleased with it."

"Me and Leda," I told him with a kiss. "Lucky girls."

"The swan's the lucky one," he assured me.

"My swan is Olympian in every way," I whispered as my hands reached around to cup his ass and pull him against me. "Every way," I repeated, easing back and sliding one hand down his limp cock for emphasis.

I reached up to remove my earrings and Richard's hands tenderly found their way to my breasts, his thumbs moving slowly over my nipples. We kissed for a minute before he handed me my short robe and put on his own.

"Do we need towels?" I asked.

"There are some down there."

"Let's walk down. I love drifting down those beautiful staircases. This house is so magnificent! I can't wait to meet Cybelle and Umberto and talk to them about what they've done here. Did you mind the remodel? Do you miss the way it was when you were growing up?"

"Not at all," he said as he took my hand. "I've always enjoyed the house, but it's just something that was a part of my life. I was here often as a kid until I moved into serious competition with the piano, then I was only in the city occasionally until I started college. After I graduated, I lived here full time while I was working in New York. Dad was always upgrading things and I just took the changes for granted. I never felt one way or the other about it."

"There is so much here, beautiful things and a lot of art which, by the way, I'd really like a guided tour of."

He squeezed my hand as we reached the landing overlooking the second floor.

"We can do that tomorrow morning, if you like."

The staircase narrowed only slightly as it descended. The first floor, which was at ground level, contained all the mechanicals for the

Hunter residence, the storage, laundry and so forth, as well as Elise and Alain's apartment.

When we reached the basement, Richard pulled the house phone from the pocket of his robe and punched on the main lights. The ceiling on the pool side of the room was barrel vaulted, supported by stone columns that made me think of an ancient Roman bath. The pool itself was covered in small tiles with images of fish and other sea creatures all over it. It reminded me of some of the mosaic work I'd seen in pictures of the Pompeii.

"Did Elise show you the lighting?" Richard asked.

"Just this. Is there more?"

He punched a few numbers and the lights dimmed with only the sconces along the walls lit, creating a more romantic mood as the bulbs flickered like flames.

"Nice." I smiled as I slipped an arm around him.

"Wait," he said and more numbers slowly changed the lights to daylight and the vault itself to clouds in a blue sky! I clapped my hands together in delight. It felt like we were outside. Richard chuckled. It was obvious that he enjoyed the Disney-esque effects as much as I did.

"It's amazing," I said, mesmerized as I realized the clouds were moving just a bit.

More keys changed the view to sunset, and then twilight and then he keyed the night sky.

"What's your pleasure, Madame?"

"I'll have stars, Magic Man."

"The moon and the stars for the woman I love," he said as a key punch added a full moon to the stars above us. Another turned off the pool lights and they were replaced by points of light—stars, just like at home.

He gave me a quick kiss then got us some towels. I followed him to the spa end of the pool where the hot water bubbled. The pool lights were still on there, and the mosaic design on the bottom was a sinuous line of marching lobsters with scattered shells and seaweed. I laughed.

"Cybelle's idea when she converted this end of the pool," he explained. Originally it was a shallow pool for the kids, so she made it deeper and added the heat and jets, but she wanted to stay with the style of the pool tiles—with a touch of humor. Funny, my sister. You'll get a kick out of her. And there are stars here, too," he said as the lobsters disappeared and the stars twinkled in the depths.

"I don't know what to say. I must show this place to my folks and Steph someday. It just so…so…" I paused, trying to come up with the proper adjectives.

"What? Did you actually run out of words?" He laughed. "I never thought I'd see the day."

I scrunched up my face, closed my eyes and took a deep breath. "I'm sorry to disappoint you but this is not the day," I assured him with a touch of my don't-fuck-with-me voice. "I believe what I meant to say was that the entire building—at least the residence side of it where you've so graciously accommodated me—is a marvelous example of the marriage of style and design in which contemporary sensibility melds perfectly with the original architecture. I can't help but admire the work of your sister and her husband and I look forward to discussing what they've done with them in the future. Need I go on?"

Richard had been staring at me and at that point he erupted in laughter that bounced off the hard surfaces of the space. I just looked at him, waiting for him to answer my question. My eyes narrowed when he kept laughing.

"Please get in," he said, attempting to stifle his mirth, but he kept chuckling.

I eased into the bubbling water, indeed feeling very much like a hapless lobster.

"Too hot?" he asked.

"Maybe a little. Can we go down a couple of degrees?"

Numbers clicked and I settled down on the deep seat along the edge. The water came up to my chin and it felt great as I adjusted to the shock of the temperature. I smiled at Richard as he slid over next to me. He looked at me for a minute and then kissed me.

"What was that for?"

"For being the most amazing woman I know."

"Oh, that…" I said dismissively.

"That," he said and kissed me again.

I relaxed against his shoulder, just watching the stars overhead.

"You're a very lucky man."

"I am. I don't think I ever realized how lucky until I met you." His arm slipped around my waist and gave me a squeeze.

I let my mind drift with the bubbles, the warmth of the water and the warmth of his body.

A few minutes later I said, "Why don't we ever fight?"

Richard snorted. "What?" He eased away so he could see my face. "Do you want to fight?"

"No. Not at all. But isn't a little strange? We never argue about anything. I mean $600 jeans, but that's not really an argument, it's more of a tease."

"Cress, what would we have to fight about?"

I couldn't come up with an answer.

"Think about it," Richard said. "We're in a very unique situation. We were only together a few weeks before I left for Europe. I think you'll agree fighting about anything was not something either of us was thinking about. While I've been gone our relationship has only grown stronger, rather than falling apart as happens with so many people. I think that's because we both realize how unique this thing is that we share."

"But doesn't it strike you as odd that we don't argue about anything?" I asked.

"We're both very independent people with work that consumes us yet somehow leaves us time for each other, right?"

"Yup," I confirmed with a kiss to his cheek.

"We love each other and neither of us is inclined to neglect the other. We enjoy the sharing of all sorts of things and are secure enough to say what we like and don't like, without feeling threatened by disagreeing about something."

It was obvious he'd thought about this, but I must not have looked convinced because he went on.

"Most people fight because they're insecure about their own feelings or their partner's. And some people treat a realtionship as a goal and once they feel like they've acquired it, they move on to the next thing. I don't think either of us is insecure and I don't think we see us coming together as something over and done."

"I certainly hope not!"

"And we don't have any of the stresses usually involved with living together." He continued. "First of all, I'm not even there."

He laughed. "I hope that isn't the major factor! But when I get home, I'm not likely to complain about money you spend, where you go or what you wear. You aren't concerned about where I am or what I'm doing, if I do the dishes or take out the trash. And I really I hope you don't ever feel like I'm not giving you enough attention, and if that happens I fully expect you to tell me."

"So how much of the lack of those stresses is because of your money?" I wondered.

"Most of it is our personalities, or at least I like to think so. But certainly some of it is financial. Money—and Marie—exclude arguments over trash and dishes, for sure," Richard smiled. "And general concerns about paying the bills. Despite my bank account, I do understand the difficulties most people face to try to make a living.

"And," he continued, "you may be surprised to learn I actually have some housekeeping skills of my own. I can even cook a little," he said with a degree of pride. "Max and I shared an apartment when we were in school and didn't have a problem with household responsibilities. If either of us thought the other wasn't pulling his weight, we discussed it."

"You must miss him," I said, thinking of Giano's handsome son in the picture on Richard's desk at home.

"I do," Richard said with a sigh. "He was really a wonderful person and my closest friend. The three of us would have had a great time—four of us, no doubt, because he would have had a terrific girlfriend, or maybe even a wife by now. He always seemed to hook up with great women."

"You don't have any close friends these days, do you?"

Richard was silent. I glanced at him and could see he was thinking about his answer.

"I have a lot of friends, and a number of people I would go to great lengths to help. I'm close to many of them on a somewhat superficial level—and I don't mean in a phony way. Superficial in the sense that our friendships remain more surface-focused. You're the only person who really knows my heart, Cress. I'm grateful that you've given me a chance to share it."

He gave me a squeeze and a kiss on the cheek for emphasis.

"I wonder if the level of those friendships is more gender specific," I said. "I don't have a lot of close friends, either. Steph, of course, but I've been so busy…and honestly, I have a problem with women friends—surface relationships. We don't share the same interests, and yes, I admit mine may be a little quirky. But it seems to me that men connect to each other on a less emotional level than women do—the exception might be soldiers in combat together or maybe some gay men. Girls spend a lot of time telling each other how they feel about things—about everything. Now, at this age, that turns toward gossip, which doesn't interest me. But I don't see that kind of emotional connection much between the men I've known. Of course, I haven't been there when they were alone together, so maybe I'm imagining it." I rested my head on his shoulder. "You seem very free sharing yourself with me."

He gave me a squeeze.

After a minute I said, "You know, I'm just thinking how unique my parents' relationship is. I've always admired them and how they behave toward each other, but since I've known you, I realize there are a lot of similarities. I can't help wondering how they were together when they first met."

"They say girls look for some of their father's traits in the men they marry," Richard said. "And speaking of your folks, I have to say I've really enjoyed getting to know them long distance."

"Them? Have you been talking to my mother, too?" It was the first I'd heard about it.

He laughed. "At your suggestion, if you recall. She's the one who recommended *Lion King* for you this weekend."

I turned to him in surprise then narrowed my eyes and poked him in the chest.

"You, sir, are sneaky!"

"I'm gathering allies."

"For what?" I asked. "You've probably assaulted almost everything I have. And, I might add, you did that all by yourself."

"I'm beginning to feel like I might want to do it again," he said, turning to tongue my ear.

I stood up and faced him, hands on my hips. "I don't think my folks can help you with that. I'm afraid you're on your own."

He flashed that smile that never failed to reduce me to jelly and threw a gentle zap of energy my way as he reached out and pulled me closer.

36
Remembrance of Things Past

Sunday, September 15

Tucked in his briefcase:

> *We can only learn to love by loving.*
> — Iris Murdoch

> I particularly enjoy the homework!
> XXOOJ

As we got out of the shower after our Sunday morning run, I asked Richard what he thought about me taking a flash drive to Peter with the PowerPoint presentation of my project.

"It's the promotional version the Ice Cream Boys sent out with the funding proposals, so the contact information leads back to them."

"Why not? From what you said, he seems very interested. He might be a great help in finding money for you."

Peter was, in fact, very happy to take my flash drive and spent quite a bit of time questioning me about my project over our meal. Apparently, he'd been thinking about it all night. I was flattered, certainly, but I knew Richard's trip to New York had been predicated on the chance to discuss an exhibition Peter wanted Richard to curate or co-curate. While I liked to believe Richard had come back just to see me, I knew business concerns were really his motivation. At least I was confident he was enjoying the perks (that would be me!) that went along with the possible job offer.

Finally I said, "I know you two have some business to discuss so maybe Gwen and I can give you some space," and with that we excused ourselves from the table and retired to the livingroom.

"Well, anything interesting for you with Peter's project?" I asked while Richard and I were outside waiting for the car. I could see he was deep in thought.

"I think so. I'm going to catch up with him again after our October trip. I'll tell you about it later, it's still coalescing. I want to ponder the possibilities a little more first. And speaking of October, any idea, yet, where you want to go?"

"Then you're serious?"

"Was there something about what I said that made you think I wasn't?"

I caught just a trace of irritation in his tone. I could see his focus was still in business mode: Peter's business proposal, the business of planning a trip for the two of us, the business of adjusting his calendar. I admit it was a bit of a shock—I had enjoyed his total attention (or what seemed like his total attention!) since he'd arrived. And he'd never spoken to me with that edge in his voice.

Rather than being hurt, I was a bit amused and wondered if he was even aware of it.

"No...I guess I haven't really thought any more about it. It does seem a bit fabtastical." The mixed up word came out of my mouth before I could stop it.

He missed a beat. "*Fabtastical*?" He frowned and looked a little confused.

Perfectly serious, I said, "Yes. It combines fantastic and fabulous. And though I admit I misspoke, I think I'll keep it."

He laughed out loud and I saw him relax as the multiple concepts he must have been trying to sort through shifted to the back burner. Perhaps "fabtastical" had been one thought too many to juggle.

STILL LUCKY

"*Fabtastical* or not, you have until Friday, so snap to. If we're going to pull it off, I need a couple of weeks to make the arrangements, especially if you have multiple destinations in mind."

He put his arms around me and hugged me as Akhil pulled up to the curb.

"Thanks," he said. "I'm sorry. I was just caught up in all the possibilities Peter's proposal holds. I confess it's a bit overwhelming, but really exciting. Can't wait to tell you about it. But first, shopping?"

We spent the rest of the day in SoHo. Richard didn't seem to mind the shopping and we had a lot of fun. I found treats for my family and for Steph and also little surprises for Marie and Antonio. I tried on a few clothes but didn't buy anything, despite Richard's encouragement. We had some ice cream in honor of the Ice Cream Boys (…or was it because I felt the need for chocolate?) and laughed a lot.

That night we ate dinner on the roof at the house and watched the lights of the city come on around us.

"I have to say I'm not really ready to go home," I sighed.

"Home to L.A. or home to Walla Walla?"

"Your home is my home now, Handsome. Dislodging me will be very difficult."

He chuckled. "I have no plans to dislodge you. I like you there." He leaned over and kissed my cheek. "I like you anywhere, actually, as long as we're together."

"You silver tongued devil, you. But I do need to get back and smooth the feathers of those Ice Cream Boys, and then go check on my folks."

"They seem to be doing great," he said. "I hope they're not just putting on a show for me."

"Nope. I really think Daddy's recovery is pretty remarkable, but Mom and Gran won't allow any slacking on his part. And he's really committed to working hard at his PT and following doctor's orders." I looked at him, thinking for the umpteenth time how lucky I was. "I can't wait for them to meet you in person."

"Hope they won't be disappointed."

"As if…" I snorted.

"You never know. Seeing us together might be hard on them."

"Nope. They'll see how perfect we are for each other and they'll be behind us all the way." I was quiet a moment and then said, "How do you think your mother's going to deal with it?"

"No clue. It should be quite an event. I expect her to be pleased. She's been hoping to marry me off for years. A girlfriend is a pretty serious step in that direction as far as she's concerned." He laughed softly. "And Robert his over the moon about you, which he's shared with her. It will be interesting, though. I hope it's not going to be too difficult for you."

"I'm not worried. If she doesn't adore me, it's her loss," I said nonchalantly, with my nose in the air and a flip of the hair I no longer had. Actually, I was a little intimidated, despite what Mee Cha had said about Madame Hunter.

"Good," Richard said, though his tone didn't sound like my bravado had convinced him.

Suddenly I had a thought. "Feel like dancing?"

He looked at me to see if I was serious.

"Here or in the music room?" he asked. "If we go downstairs we'll have a better selection to choose from and the sound system in there is pretty great."

"Music room it is," I agreed. "Stairs?" There's more than one way to get your exercise in the big city!

"Stairs," he echoed.

I followed him down one flight to the third floor, half of which was dedicated to private family space—spa, gym, additional guest rooms and a large family room that doubled as a playroom and informal living room. The other half was a large reception area and the "music" room which had access to the balcony on two sides.

The floor in the music room—and I have to say it was a ballroom as far as I was concerned—was inlaid with black and white marble, laid in a pattern of large and small squares and rectangles, some with black edges and a black center and some the opposite. It was a modern crazy pattern that was just amazing.

"Did Cybelle design the floor?" I asked.

Richard laughed. "Nope. It's a copy of the marble court at Versailles, circa 1670. My grandfather had grandiose ideas."

"Obviously! But it's fabtastic." (Had to start using my new word!) I would have thought it was the absolute epitome of modern design. "I imagine it would have looked *au courant* at any time, including today."

"They tell me—as a Trained Professional, mind you—that good design is timeless," he said with a wink as he took my hand and led me to the wall of bookshelves. He picked up an iPad and we discussed some musical choices. When we had a folder full, he punched two more buttons and music filled the room and the lighting dimmed.

"Good grief, that was fast! I don't suppose that was your computer friend who wrote your house programs."

"Yup. It's Cybelle and Umberto who sent him to Dubai on that project. I still plan to introduce you when he gets back to L.A." He led me to the center of the room and offered his hand. "May I have this dance?"

"Yes, please," I said as he pulled me close and Leonard Cohen began singing *I'm Your Man*. "That reminds me, "I said, "I need to get you that mask."

Richard laughed and spun me around that smooth floor, me wondering how it was possible to be so happy.

After we ran through a number of songs and reprised our routine to *The Time of My Life* with a lot of laughter, we collapsed onto one of the loveseats flanking the multiple pairs of French doors that opened onto the terrace.

"Would you like some wine?" he asked.

"I'm thinking something light. White and cold, maybe?"

"Your wish is my command," he assured me with a quick kiss before he headed down to the kitchen.

That left me to admire the magnificent room. There were three large chandeliers down the center of the ceiling. They were heavy with crystals, but rectangular and modern, Cybelle's selection, I was sure. And the fixtures were surrounded by moldings that echoed the patterns of the floor. It was brilliant!

At the far end was a grand piano, black and glistening in the muted light. I was still thinking about the piano when Richard came back with our wine.

He poured us each a glass and offered a toast.

"To the woman I love. May I always have what it takes to make you as happy as you are tonight."

We clicked glasses and drank.

"All you need is your wonderful self, my Prince. You are everything you need to be to make me happy." That got me a kiss. After a few minutes I decided to give it a shot, hoping I wouldn't destroy that perfect evening…for either of us.

"Remember when you said you'd do anything for me?" I asked.

"I recall saying that more than once," he reminded me.

"There is something I want," I said slowly. Immediately, I felt bad because I could detect just a faint hint that he might be thinking I was about to ask him to marry me. That hurt me. I couldn't understand why that seemed to be on his mind. I thought we'd understood each other. Though he'd assured me the ring wasn't an engagement ring when he gave it to me—explaining he was shy of proposing after the awful experience so many years ago—he did say that he would be happy to marry me if I ever decided that was what I wanted. But recently he'd teased me about it several times.

I put my hand on his chest. "My love, this isn't something you're going to like."

I felt his energy shift but his eyes held mine, open and willing.

"When I said 'anything', I meant it, Cress. What is it?"

"I want you to play the piano for me."

The light—the energy—whatever that emotional thing is that you can see in the eyes of someone you love—shifted in Richard's beautiful grey eyes. There was a hint of pain and an almost palpable resistance, but he didn't look away. He didn't say anything, either. He was studying me, no doubt wondering what had prompted my request. At the same time he seemed to be weighing his resistance and attempting to dissect it and decide if it was worth hanging onto.

I reached for his hand. He clasped my fingers but still didn't speak. I felt a moment of panic, wondering if I was asking too much, wondering what on earth I'd been thinking—to ask him to do something so obviously upsetting—and it was my turn to force myself not to look away.

Without a word, Richard lifted my hand to his lips and kissed my fingers. He stood up and released my hand before he turned away and walked to the other end of the room where the piano sat, its dark silhouette suddenly seeming a little sinister to me. I didn't move, just watched him as he regarded the instrument for a long moment before sitting down on the bench.

It was probably only two full minutes (that seemed like twenty) before he placed his hands on the keys and began slowly running scales. And then his speed and confidence increased and he played some rapid exercises I recognized. I had heard them from my father's performance students, things they played over and over to warm up their hands.

I listened, amazed that after so many years he could so easily fall back into the patterns his fingers had obviously never forgotten. *Muscle memory.*

I wanted to get up and move closer to him, but I stayed where I was. There was no problem with the acoustics, but I wanted to be near him, to see his face clearly, to feel the energy that accompanied the music flowing out through his fingers as if a dam had burst.

And then I heard the first notes of *Für Elise*, one of my favorites, a piece that had been on my iPod along with several other classic piano favorites I had grown up with, music that I'd worried might have bothered Richard when we'd traded playlists.

It was stunning to hear him play, to hear music I'd known all my life filling the room, amplified by the magnificent acoustics. I'd spent hours and hours listening to my father play when I was growing up. As a small girl I loved to lay under the piano, to feel the vibrations in my very bones while he played. I distinctly remembered my disappointment when, despite lessons and encouragement, we all had to admit I had no aptitude for it. And then my eyes filled as I recalled my father trying to comfort me with the promise he'd always be there to play for me.

Richard played on, going smoothly from one piece to the next with only an occasional missed note. Some of what he played must have been things he'd performed in competition. I was amazed he remembered so much of it, but I suppose when years of your life are devoted to the keyboard, the notes must stick with you. No wonder he had such an amazing ability to focus, coming from such early enforced discipline.

At one point I saw Elise standing near one of the doorways, watching in amazement. She listened for a few minutes, then smiled and blew me a kiss. Richard never noticed. He was totally absorbed in his music.

He played on and on, one piece after another, several more from my playlist—*Moonlight Sonata*, Rachmaninoff's *Rhapsody on a Theme of Paganini* (loved that movie!), some of the Andante from *Piano Concerto number 21*, which has always been "The Elvira Madigan theme" to me. (Love that movie, too, thanks to early exposure from Gran.) I was amazed that on that last one he had improvised some of the orchestral accompaniment. It was just flat out brilliant!

I couldn't hold back the tears as I listened, watching him totally give himself over to the music, unable to imagine what he was feeling, though it was obviously a very profound experience. My soul ached for Richard, a man of so many talents and such a profoundly beautiful spirit, a man who had waited so many years before allowing his broken heart to heal. The fact that he had chosen to love me only made me more determined than ever to never let him forget what an outstanding and amazing human being he was. He was a very good man.

Lucky girl, indeed.

37
Was I Wrong?

Still Sunday

Richard played for several hours. I couldn't say how long. I was in the music as I absorbed it and the energy of the man playing it. I *became* the music in a most extraordinary way—I was the music, conscious of nothing else. I'm sure the wine enhanced the experience, but I allowed myself to open to it completely. It was something I will never forget.

When at last the music stopped, it took me a moment to come back, and when I opened my eyes, Richard was just sitting at the piano, staring at the keyboard. I got up very slowly and walked soundlessly across that cold marble floor in my bare feet. He didn't look up as I approached, so I moved behind him and placed my hands lightly on his shoulders.

He reached up and covered my hands with his, though he didn't say anything.

"Was I wrong to ask?" I said softly.

He shook his head and cleared his throat before he said, "No."

"Are you ready to go to bed?"

With a sigh he stood up and turned to me. He'd been crying, too. I reached up and touched his cheek, wiping the tears with my thumb.

"I love you, Richard," I said. I couldn't tell exactly where he was emotionally.

"I love you most," he reminded me, his voice husky.

He led me back to the hallway and pressed the button for the lift. I don't think either of us felt up to the stairs. When the door closed, he pulled me into his arms and hugged me tightly.

He said nothing, but didn't release me until a few moments after the door opened again.

Richard maintained his silence and I kept my mouth shut. He had to be exhausted, both physically and emotionally. When we got to our room, I went in to brush my teeth and wash my puffy face, giving him a chance to undress alone. When I went to the closet, he was naked, but he headed for the door, touching my arm and kissing my cheek briefly as he passed.

"I need a shower. I'll be along in a few minutes."

I noted there was no invitation to join him. It was obvious he was still trying to deal with the last few hours and I wouldn't have interrupted that process for the world.

I got into bed and glanced at the clock. It was 2:20 a.m. Almost morning for us. I lay there waiting, hoping I'd be able to offer him comfort when he finally joined me. He was in the shower more than a few minutes and I couldn't help wondering what he was thinking. He hadn't touched a piano in more than fifteen years, not since the night Maryse had broken his heart. It was hard to imagine what he must be feeling, but I prayed that asking him to play for me had helped him resolve some of those emotions. Even if he didn't want to play again, I hoped he now knew that that momentous self-imposed sacrifice was no longer necessary.

My father played often, just for the sheer joy of making music. I'd always taken it for exactly that, long before I could see that he also spent his working hours with music, playing, or helping others play. He simply loved the piano, loved the music and loved his work. He'd always teased me with that familiar quote: *If you do what you love, you'll never work a day in your life.*

And that led me to think about how much my parents loved what they did—Gran, too—how it blended seamlessly with their time "off the clock," and for me, as well. I thought of my own project design as creative and absorbing, and I could relate it to the rest of my life because my thinking and the way I looked at things followed the same kind of code design logic. I could see it in Steph, and even though her process seemed chaotic to me, it gave her amazing results and suited her perfectly.

Richard's multi-tasking and compartmentalizing thought processes fascinated me and obviously had manifested his entire world of interesting and creative people, rippling out from his circle of associates into the wider world. Each to his own, I thought: *From each according to his ability, to each according to his need.* Exactly!

That's where I was in my own thought process when I finally heard the water shut off. It was a few more minutes before the bathroom door opened and Richard turned off the light. He came to the bed and I threw back the covers on his side. He stood there a moment just looking at me. The only illumination was the light from the sitting room and I couldn't see his eyes well enough to read him. On impulse, I opened my arms to him.

He smiled as he slid in next to me and pulled me against him. Slowly, I felt his body relax.

Finally, I whispered, "OK?" against his ear.

"Better than OK," he said, his lips brushing my cheek. "But I need some sleep."

"We both do," I said as I pulled back a little and then gave him a long tender kiss before turning away and offering him a chance to spoon me. Moving against my back he put his arm around me, his hand on my breast as he molded his body to mine. He planted a soft kiss on my shoulder and minutes later he was asleep.

I was sound asleep so it took several minutes to realize that the hard thing between my legs was not the seat of the bicycle I'd been riding in my dream, but rather my usual morning alarm. I couldn't help laughing softly as I glanced at the clock. Five a.m. on the button.

"Are you sure?" I said over my shoulder.

"Do I seem unsure to you?" he growled as he nipped at my neck, and stroked my thighs with a very hard, very hot (and very tempting!) portion of his body.

I turned over to face him, and smiled as I wrapped my hand around his cock.

"Nope, you seem committed. I have to say this is a lot more interesting than my dream." I grasped him firmly and ran my thumb in slow circles over the head of his penis.

He caught his breath but managed to ask, "Tell me about your dream?"

"The hard thing between my legs was the seat of the bike I was riding."

"Well, ride me, instead," he suggested as he fondled my breast."

"OK," I said brightly as I gave him a shove onto his back. Obviously, this wasn't going to be one of those slow introductions to a new day!

I straddled him just below his cock, took him in both hands, and just held him for a moment.

"Yup, I would never call this indecisive," I agreed.

When my hands remained still he raised his hips, pressing into them as his hands gripped my knees. I gave him a couple of quick strokes and stopped. Richard groaned.

"Tell me what you want. I'm still half asleep so I need direction," I tried to sound slow and relaxed but I was pretty sure he could feel my wetness on his thighs. I moved a little against his legs just to be sure he was aware of it. That would teach him to wake me from a deep sleep (and hopefully let him know how much I enjoyed it!)

"Put me somewhere hot and wet," he breathed, pressing himself harder against my hands.

I shifted one hand and started stroking his balls, still holding him tightly with the other.

"Oooh, I like the feel of those," I said. I slid my hand up and down his cock, slowly. "I like the feel of this, too."

"Let's see how it feels here," he said as he rolled up and grabbed my ass with one hand and pulled me up on my knees, positioning himself to slide into me.

"Where?" I asked innocently, as I moved in circles over just the head of his throbbing penis. "That's wet, isn't it? And it does feel good."

He grabbed my hips and forced me down on him. (OK, it didn't require much "force"—I didn't resist!) He groaned and I made that familiar little gasp, accompanied by a little, "Oh!"

"Was that an 'Oh, it feels good'?"

"It was an 'Oh, fuck me'!" I breathed as he began to move.

I leaned forward running my arms under his to grip his shoulders tightly as he pounded into me. My orgasm came quickly, and then again, but Richard showed no signs that he was ready to finish. He slowed for a minute and gave me a long, deep kiss before speeding up again.

"Come again, for me," he whispered and I happily complied. And complied again.

I was overwhelmed by the feeling of being so full of him and willingly abandoned myself to the illusion that he was pumping himself into my body, filling the space with all of himself, not just that beautiful cock. He was permeating my very soul, filling me with all the pure love he had to offer. It was an extraordinary sensation. And then I was aware that he was bombarding me with his energy, forcing everything he had into me until I felt like I might explode…and then I did, even as he did.

Richard let out a long shivering moan in sync with my own strangled cry of exquisite pleasure and joy, but most of all acceptance of what he had filled me with beyond the cum I could still feel pulsing into me. And then he started to stroke me slowly.

Without even thinking, I rose up off of him, turned around and took his still-hard cock in my mouth. I needed it, I wanted it, wanted to taste him, the two of us together. He caught his breath with a little moan, even as he pulled me to him and planted his mouth on me, licking, slipping his tongue into me and then sucking my clit until I cried out again.

Both of us were having trouble breathing and as his cock slowly lost its form I rubbed it against my cheek and took one of his balls into my mouth. He continued to press his face in the mess of me, nuzzling and licking me.

At last he said, "Come here, so I can kiss you."

I turned around again and folded myself down onto his chest as his arms slipped around me. He gave me a long, slow kiss, then framed my face with his hands and said, "You, Sweet Juliet, are a remarkable woman."

"It must be the influence of my Trained Professional." I kissed him again before saying, "And now to matters more practical: Washcloth or shower?" I touched his fuzzy cheeks and my hand came away quite sticky.

"Ah, you've been talking to snakes again." (An old joke between us involving a *Harry Potter* reference!) "Shower it is!"

Richard's chest bubbled with laughter before we both got up and headed for BabyZ.

Monday, September 16

Note slipped into his jacket pocket in the car:

> *Life seems to go on without effort*
> *when I am filled with music.*
> — George Eliot,
> *The Mill on the Floss*

We showered, went back to bed and didn't get up until 9:00 a.m. I sent Richard down to breakfast ahead of me so I could dress and surprise him. I put on the halter dress and the pair of split panties I'd brought, hoping to give him a sense of *déjà vu*. It was a little cooler that morning so I zipped up the cashmere hoodie, saving the surprise that the dress was, in fact a halter, for later. I was tempted to wear the swan necklace but decided instead to go with my star. I wore the Eros earrings Richard had gotten me, a few bracelets and my lime green loafers. We had walking to do and I had no intention of having sore feet! (Which reminded me that I'd left a pair of shoes in the music room last night!)

Richard was already at the table with a cup of coffee looking over the *Times*, when I went down. His eyes lit up when I came in and ever the gentleman, he stood up to pull out my chair for me.

"You have such lovely manners," I said. It had become kind of a tease between us, but he knew I really did appreciate it. It's not just a case of manners, but more a consideration for someone you care about.

He touched my shoulder as he kissed my cheek and gave that cashmere a little caress.

"And you're very soft and fuzzy this morning," he said.

"All the better to please you."

"And you know you do."

STILL LUCKY

To ease us away from the temptation I sensed was ready to blossom into something that would further delay our walk on the High Line I said, "Shall we be French or Italian today? I need to practice with my Trained Professional."

He responded in his very sexy Italian suggesting we could be Italian until after lunch and French until dinner, or vice versa if it suited me.

"*A lei la scelta, signorina,*" he said, offering me the choice.

"*Cominciamo in Italiano,*" I said choosing Italian.

And so we made our way though breakfast and down to the car, me able to keep up and only missing a few words, which Richard repeated. If I still didn't understand, he defined them for me in Italian. So much more fun than just working with the language programs. And of course he was being very considerate and speaking slower than he might in normal conversation, but I could see he was pleased with the work I'd done over the past couple of months.

38
Two Fingers

Still Monday

We had a delightful walk and covered the whole High Line. I was so excited! I hadn't really been aware of it until I happened to catch that documentary the year before, but I'd immediately added it to my list of things I was determined to see someday. Now, there I was, taking pictures with my phone for Steph and my folks.

The park was even more amazing in person. Despite the warm weather, some of the plants were leaning toward fall color. We stopped occasionally to listen to someone who was giving a tour, picking up additional information. I was particularly excited to see the Frank Gehry IAC building.

"I'm fascinated by his work," I told Richard. "The Guggenheim at Bilbao is on my must see list, too. I love Richard Serra's sculptures and I want to be *in* them."

"And you keep insisting you don't know much about art."

"An awful lot of what I know comes via PBS. Charlie Rose did a show on Gehry when he had that retrospective at MOMA. I wish I could have seen it, even though I didn't know who he was then. Steph showed me the video awhile back."

"Gehry's having a retrospective in Paris next month. Want to spend my birthday there?"

"Uh..." It was an exciting possibility and could include a trip to Bilbao, I imagined. But though I hadn't chosen a location, I was thinking of something more intimate. "I have a lot of ideas," I told him. "I'll put it in the hopper and let you know by Friday."

"I'm really interested to see what you choose. You always surprise me."

"It's part of my plan."

"And what plan is that?" he asked.

"The one that will make you love me forever," I said with a kiss to his cheek.

"It's a dirty job," he told me (still in Italian, mind you!) "But somebody's got to do it."

"Hey! That's my line. How dare you!"

"I am only stating a fact."

My phone buzzed in my purse. I stopped and retrieved it to find the Ice Cream Boys were calling.

"CJ? It's Ben."

"Hi, Ben. What can I do for you?"

"Can you come in Thursday morning? We have rescheduled that meeting and hope you can be here."

"I can. What time?"

"Nine? It will probably run a couple of hours. They're coming at 10:00 and we'd like to go over some things with you in advance."

"No problem. I'll be back in L.A. tomorrow evening, so if anything changes, please let me know."

"Will do. See you on Thursday."

Richard looked at me questioningly.

"Ben and Jerry. They have the people from the meeting I missed re-scheduled for Thursday. I guess they weren't as pissed off as the boys wanted me to believe."

"They may have told the interested parties that it was their error. Still, I'd mention it to whoever these people are when you meet them. If your Ice Cream Boys are still thinking of blaming you, it will let them know you're not inclined to let a thing like that slide."

I laughed and gave him a quick kiss. "My Trained Professional. What would I do without you?"

"I'm counting on you never wanting to find out."

We walked on, tried out the seating and views in various spots along the way, and took some time to study the expanse of the river. I think Richard was amused by the level of my enthusiasm. He told me he and Cybelle and Umberto had walked the High Line shortly after the final section was completed and they all shared my admiration for what so many amazing and creative people had made of a space that had nearly been torn down.

I told him how much I admired Diane Von Furstenberg and her part in the project. And it was exciting to get a view of her studio and buildings from that elevated location. I refused Richard's offer of a DVF shopping spree, insisting I wanted to save it for another trip. In the meantime, he suggested that I might want to become a Friend of the High Line.

"The memberships start at just forty dollars a year. We've been with them from the beginning of the project."

"We who?"

"We batch of Hunters. We have a lot of charity interests and some that overlap."

I had a startling thought. "Does that mean you actually know Diane Von Furstenberg?"

"I wouldn't say I *know* her but we've met and worked on a few things together."

"You are unbelievable," I said. I was flat out amazed and maybe a little jealous.

"You say that as though you're not pleased. Why not think how exciting it is that one of these days you may have a chance to tell her how much you admire her?"

I laughed. "Thanks for the attitude adjustment. I'll get the hang of it one of these days."

As we walked, Richard talked about the differences between New York and L.A., what moving to the Left Coast had meant to him and all the things he still loved about New York as well as the things he didn't miss about big city life—our conversation still in Italian. I was really pleased that I was able to mostly keep up and yes, he was still using relatively simple vocabulary for my benefit, but I felt as though my brain was adjusting to it.

Around 1:00 p.m. we went down to street level in Chelsea to look for lunch, and I had us switch back to English so my brain could rest. He let me pick the restaurant and the menu I read posted outside the third café looked interesting. We went in and were able to get a table after only a few minutes. And by the way, though Richard said he'd never eaten there, the staff had that wobble reaction, something I hadn't noticed with strangers for a while.

"Can you just turn that on at will?" I asked while we were waiting to be seated.

"What?"

I gave him a squinty-eyed silent reply. He knew very well what I meant.

"Oh…well yes, sort of. I just open myself to an exceptional experience with no judgment. The gratitude-in-advance thing. Seems to work," he said with a shrug of his shoulders.

"I demand you teach me that."

He laughed. "You're already picking it up. Haven't you noticed?"

"No one wobbles around me," I reminded him.

"It's different with men, I think." Then he leaned over and whispered, "You don't really know what might be going on in their pants, do you?" He quickly kissed my cheek.

"Richard!" I was scandalized. He didn't usually talk that way, unless he referred to what might be going on below his own belt. I cracked up.

"Just sayin'," he whispered, flashing an innocent smile at the hostess when she returned to take us to our table.

At a distance of about three feet, she wobbled. I could only shake my head and follow her.

The temperature had started to climb about an hour earlier, when the sun finally appeared and before I sat down at our table, Richard helped me out of my hoodie. I could see how surprised he was by my halter bodice.

"*Déjà vu?*" he said, with an admiring glance in the direction of my breasts.

"All over again," I laughed, pronouncing the expected rejoinder.

"So how far does this bit of nostalgia extend?" he asked suggestively as he placed the hoodie around my shoulders.

"Hmmm…" I avoided an answer as I smiled sweetly at him.

In return he hit me with a wave of energy. I had to laugh.

After lunch we strolled and window-shopped some of the galleries (closed on Mondays) discussing likes and dislikes in French. Richard still managed to use a little of his Trained Professional riffs on some of the work. In truth there were a few pieces that I would have liked to see more of but, like DVF Studios, I would save them for another trip.

Can you tell I was wangling a way to come back for another visit? And yes, he'd already told me I could return any time I wanted, with or without him, but I hadn't reached the point where I'd feel comfortable asking Alain and Elise to prepare to host me in his absence. I did want to come with Steph and with my folks one day. I was thinking I'd have to plan something special for my dad when he was fully recovered. And we could do a musicals marathon, too. Like so much else, all it takes is time and money! And then I remembered that Richard might be spending time in New York with Peter Norton's project. I asked him about that while we were waiting for Akhil to come and take us home.

"So can you talk about Peter's project yet?" I asked, lapsing back into English.

Richard smiled. "It's still percolating, but the basic idea is a show of contemporary artists that traces their influences back through the works of other artists." He paused a moment. "I'm trying to think of an example you'd be familiar with...OK, take Salvador Dali. There are any number of old masters he blatantly referenced in his works and then going forward, there are also a number of contemporary artists who show easily understandable connections to Dali. There are many possibilities, but the trick of the whole thing will be to make choices where the historical works, as well as the contemporary ones, are available to be loaned from their respective museums and private collections. Availability will be a more important factor than the choices of the contemporary work. As far as the public is concerned, viewing the historic pieces will probably be as much of a draw as the visible presentation of the connections."

"Wow!" I was blown away. "What a great idea! I would love it. I can't imagine how difficult it would be to arrange to collect all the work, much less to make the selections. It would be a sort of puzzle, I'd think."

Richard laughed. "Exactly. I'll have to combine a far larger number of possibilities and then let the availability dictate the final pieces. Fortunately, Peter has a lot of influence and he would handle that part."

I stopped a minute to think. "Does this mean Jeff Koons would be in the running? Some of his work looks like twisted rip-offs to me, though I understand they're intentional. Still, you'd have to listen to his dog and pony show about the origins."

"I think Jeff will have had his share of attention by then. I would be the official curator, so the overall designing of the show would be up to me. It will require a cohesive staff, of course…there are a lot of considerations. That's why I need to come back in October to spend some serious time with Peter working out all the requirements for defining the project." He studied me intently for a moment. "It would be very time consuming and I'd need to be sure I can handle the extra work and still cover my other bases. I'd also have to put a dependable team together to keep the ball rolling when I wasn't here."

"I hope you'll let me come with you on some of your New York trips. I promise not to distract you," I said, batting my eyelashes and looking hopeful.

"What makes you think I wouldn't want to be distracted?" He added an eyebrow wiggle, then leaned over and kissed my cheek and whispered, "You know I love it when you come with me."

I could feel myself blushing, but we were both laughing as Akhil pulled up to the curb.

In the elevator, Richard said, "I just want to be sure you understand something."

His tone was on the serious side and I must have been frowning when I looked at him. It made him chuckle.

"It's only that if you want to pick Paris as part of the birthday trip, it doesn't have to involve my family at all. We can stay in a hotel and do as we please. I won't even let them know we're there. You can save the audience with my mother for another day."

"Good to know," I said. "But I hadn't even thought about your family when you were dangling the temptation of French and Spanish art possibilities in front of me."

He gave me a squeeze.

As the elevator opened on the main floor I said, "I left my shoes in the music room last night. You go on, I'll be up in a minute." But Richard stayed with me. "And, by the way, I'm not afraid of meeting your mother."

"Really?" His tone was blatantly skeptical.

"Nope. I've decided you love me and that's all that matters. I'm convinced that even if she hates me, it won't change the way you feel about me."

He laughed. "She won't hate you. She doesn't hate anybody. She does tend to look down that Gallic nose of hers with what seems to be an air of superiority, but that's not really who she is. She's just sort of hyper-observant without being judgmental."

"Well, she won't be a factor in my destination decision. Are you really sure you don't want to choose? You could surprise me. You know I'd go anywhere with you, Handsome." I gave him a quick peck on the cheek.

He followed me over to the loveseat where we'd been last night. My shoes weren't there. I searched under the table and got down on my knees to look under the furniture. No shoes.

"Elise probably found them and took them upstairs for you," he suggested as I stood up.

I took a long hard look at him, trying to see if there were any residual emotions from last night floating around in those beautiful grey eyes of his.

"What?"

"I'm wondering how you felt about last night and your piano."

"It was profound and I'm trying to think of a way to let you know exactly what you did for me."

"I'd settle for a chance to hear you play again. I'm hoping that wasn't an singular command performance."

He laughed. "Hardly, though you might regret giving me back my music. Want to play with me?"

I pressed myself against him. "Yes, please."

Richard cracked up. "At this particular moment, I was referring to the piano, though I suspect we could both use a nap." He gave me a quick kiss.

"I hate to disappoint you my Prince, but none of the musical talent genes from my parents made it into my DNA. We tried for several years, but finally had to admit I had no skill."

"Chopsticks?" he said, taking my hand and leading me to the piano.

My brain shifted from Chinese cuisine to music.

"Er....yes, but..."

He sat down on the bench, scooted back and motioned for me to sit between his legs. My father had done that with me when I was little. Richard urged me up for a moment and pulled the bench closer so he could still reach the pedals. It was kind of a tight squeeze, but then I always enjoyed finding myself between Richard's thighs!

"I'm supposed to be able to concentrate?" I asked with a little squirm against him.

"Focus," he reminded me. "Go ahead, I'll accompany you."

I stared at the keys, looking for reference points, but it came back to me. I started, hesitantly at first and then with more confidence flowing through my two pointer fingers. Richard sat with his hands on his legs. I turned, wondering what he was waiting for.

"Go on," he urged. "Do you know the next part?"

I nodded, and went into that second section (four fingers!), amazed that I remembered. Even my unskilled digits apparently had some muscle memory of their own. As I struck the first note to repeat the beginning section, Richard joined in, his fingers confidently matching my notes on either side of my hands. My simple part-two he boldly embellished by chords and trills. At the end of that I put my hands in my lap and let him take over, pressing my shoulders together to give him as much access as possible.

I couldn't help giggling. He was amazing—OK, no surprise— and the best part was that it was very familiar. He played an over-the-top version, very theatrical. He went on for a couple of minutes and ended with a dramatic flourish and a kiss to the side of my neck.

I clapped enthusiastically. "Shall I get you a candelabra for you birthday? Liberace, right?"

"How can you know that? He was way before your time. Your grandmother again?"

"Not this time. Daddy used to play that for me to make me laugh. Works every time." I leaned my head back against his shoulder. "How is it possible to love you so much?"

"What do you mean? I'm irresistible," he laughed, as he wrapped his arms around me and gave me a squeeze.

We got up and headed for the door, only to find Elise waiting for us. She was smiling broadly.

"I was wondering if you had made any decisions about dinner," she said.

Richard looked at me. "Dine out, cuisine of your choice, or we can let Elise surprise us."

"It's our last night. Let's stay in." I looked to Elise. I could see she was pleased.

"*Bon.* Eight?"

We nodded and then headed for the stairs. Naptime!

39
Inflatibles

Still Monday

"There are two things I want from you now," I told Richard as we walked up the stairs.

"Has anyone ever suggested you take a hard look at your demanding nature?" he asked reasonably.

I looked at him, shocked. He sounded so serious! Then I saw that twinkle in his eye.

I shifted to innocence. "*Moi?*"

"*Ouais.*"

"Nope. Most people find me charming, considerate and I have even been described, on occasion, as doting."

He snickered. "Have you? Then I suppose you'd best tell me about those two things."

"First, more dancing tonight with the promise that someday, when I happen to have a fancy floor length big skirt on hand, you will waltz me around that amazing music room."

"Shades of *The King and I*?" he asked, as he opened the door to our room.

"How can you know that?"

"I suspect it's another example of your grandmother's influence."

I laughed. "Yup. You're gonna love her."

"Will she still be with your folks when we go? Can't wait to meet her."

"I think so. I'll know more by the end of the week."

"Do you mind if I ask you not to mention the piano thing to

your family yet? I need a little more time to adjust. I should have it worked out by the time I get home."

"Of course. That was number two."

He frowned. He'd obviously forgotten I had more than one demand. Imagine!

"The second thing I wanted from you..." When I saw he was on board, I said, "I was hoping you'd play again for me tonight, just a little."

Richard rolled his eyes as if I was exhausting him with my ridiculous requests. Then he laughed and kissed my cheek.

We were almost at the top of the stairs, me one step ahead of him, when I felt his fingers lightly skim the curve of my bottom, just as he had that very first night. The sensation, accompanied by a nudge of his energy wobbled me. I stopped and turned to him. He was smiling.

He shrugged. "I just thought since you'd chosen nostalgia for the theme of the day..."

"Funny boy," I said as I turned back up the stairs. I leaned forward and flipped up my skirt offering a view of those split panties he probably hadn't forgotten. "Remember these?"

He smiled as he stepped back down a step and kissed me on one side of my bottom, then stepped back up as he gently worked a finger through to give me a gentle rub.

"I do, do you?" he said as his finger slipped into me.

"Well," I answered, catching my breath, "I distinctly remember something so large and hard slipping in there that I had an instant orgasm."

"Hmm, let's see what we can do about that." He stepped up to the landing and took my hand, pulling me against him for a long kiss, while making it clear that he was still well equipped to satisfy that particular bit of nostalgia.

I followed him into his office, where he moved the laptop off one of the desks. When he turned back to me he looked at me for a moment and smiled. I could feel the energy he was directing my way and I was struck by that overwhelming need for him as it bubbled to the surface—something that hadn't happened in awhile when we were both dressed! (I always felt it when we were making love, but this was that old aftershock-inducing urge that used to catch me unawares when he wasn't even around.)

STILL LUCKY

"Nice," I murmured, as I slipped my arms around his neck.

We kissed and continued to kiss as I felt the heat in my body growing and expanding, even as my thighs tingled with damp desire. Richard cupped my breasts and ran his fingers tenderly over my nipples, which were already standing at attention in anxious anticipation. He took one of my hands and pressed it against his erection and I grasped him firmly, with gratitude and admiration. *What a guy!*

I unbuttoned his jeans and unzipped his fly and pushed his pants down just enough to free his cock and his balls, which I gently began to fondle. Richard pushed my halter to either side of my breasts and scooped them beyond the fabric. I kissed him again, my fingers still wrapped around his cock.

"Do you want me as badly as I want you?" I whispered.

In answer he reached under my skirt, grabbing my ass and pressing me against him. I could feel his penis throbbing against my belly. And then before I realized what he was doing, he lifted me and, as I locked my legs around his waist, he brought me down onto him, just as he had that very first time. I squealed with pleasure as I came and he lifted me onto the desk and began to stroke me slowly,

"Now that's what I call *déjà vu*," he whispered as he watched himself move slowly in and out of me.

"Even without the little ceiling spot for dramatic effect?" I asked breathlessly.

He smiled. "Even so. And just like that first time, I can feel you getting ready to come again. Mind if I join you?"

"I so wish you would," I said looking into his beautiful eyes.

He held me tightly as we came together, just as we had that first night in his office at the gallery.

As our breathing slowed, he said, "I won't ask you if you're GTF this time," he said, "because I haven't even started."

I laughed softly. "I like the sound of that."

"You're gonna like the feel of it, too. I promise."

He slipped out of me and eased me off the desk, leading me into the closet so we could undress. I got down on my knees, sliding his jeans down while I had him in my mouth, tonguing him as he subsided. I gave his balls some oral attention as well.

He helped me out of my dress and then, much to my surprise, lifted me up onto the island.

"Taste for you, taste for me," he said, urging me to lie back.

First he lapped at the slit in my panties and then slowly licked my now heart-topped landing strip (thanks, Mee-Cha!) as he eased my panties off. He pressed my legs apart and began stroking the hood of my clit between two fingers. I was quite sticky and it felt exquisite!

"Your little penis is getting hard," he said, looking from me to my clit, smiling.

"It wants to be sucked, just like yours does."

He bent to me and continued stroking both sides as his tongue caressed the tip. He was gentle but relentless, and I arched my back as the fingers of his other hand slipped into me. When I started to come he removed them and slipped his tongue inside. It felt like my entire body was going to explode and the wave of sensation just kept rolling as his tongue and fingers continued to work their magic.

Finally he slowed, and as I caught my breath, he slid me off the island and into his arms.

"I'm going to miss you, Sweetheart."

"I certainly hope so!" I laughed. "I'd hate to think you were sharing all this with the women of Europe."

"*Vous et nul autre*," he reminded me as he kissed me again.

We got into bed and did more talking than napping, reviewing all the things we'd done in our short time together in New York.

When it came to Jeff Koons's work and my impressions of the galleries Richard had taken me to, he did an entire gallery-owner riff on the cultural significance of Jeff's work, focusing on the inflatables and moving on to the giant lobster. I started laughing, totally in awe of his mastery of pointless jargon and when he refused to stop, I struggled to get away from him but he held me tightly and went on until tears of laughter were streaming down my face. I had to beg to get him to stop.

When he finally wound up his discourse, he relaxed his hold on me.

"Well, I'm hoping if you ever get mad at me, a repeat recitation on the Koons Inflatables will make you forget my transgressions."

"More likely it would make me wet my pants!" I laughed. "And then I'd be even madder."

"Can you be mad and laugh that hard at the same time?"

"Don't know. It's never come up. Besides, I thought you told me we had nothing to fight about." I gave him a kiss on the end of his nose. "So just what sort of transgressions are you planning on committing?"

He released me and rolled onto his back, his hands clasped across his stomach.

"Hmmm, haven't really thought much about it. There must be something I'm dying to do that you wouldn't approve of," he said reasonably.

"Like…?" I prompted.

His brows knit together into a frown. "Everything I'm dying to do at the moment involves you and things I think you'll enjoy, so we may have to wait awhile to test my theory for shifting your mood."

I reached down to caress his cock. "In that case, how 'bout I shift your mood?"

He looked at me as if he had no idea what I was referring to. "To what?"

"Oh, I don't know. Maybe to Impossibly Hot Lover?"

"*Moi?*" he said, innocently.

"*Toi,*" I assured him. He could play dumb if he wanted to, but his body was going my way. I intended to take it very slow this time around.

"It's been an amazing four days," I said. "Thank you, Magic Man." I kissed his cheek lightly. I released his cock for the moment but kept my hand on his thigh.

I was amazed by how much we'd managed to cram into the last four days without ever feeling like it had been a forced march. When we were together there was something about Time that seemed to stretch like pulled taffy—don't you love watching those machines?—and fold back on itself without any defined ending or beginning. Is that analogy too out there? When I come up with a better one, I'll mention it. Anyway, Richard had said it was because we managed to live in the moment, which kept us in the flow. It was something I wanted to spend serious time thinking about—and mastering, if I could.

He must have heard the cogs of my brain turning because in response to my lengthening silence, he rose up on one elbow to look at me.

"What?" he asked.

"Just thinking about how much we've done in such a short time, and how this trip seems to be much longer than it has been."

"The Time thing?"

"Yup. It's fascinating. I'm going to have to give it some serious thought one of these days."

Richard laughed. "I'm willing to bet you'll come to the same conclusion I have."

"Maybe…" I said, speculatively. "But it is strange that you've been gone more than two months and at this moment it doesn't really feel like we've been apart."

"It's part of my master plan."

"What master plan is that?"

"The one that will keep you with me for a very long time, and all the while you'll be thinking it is just the start of a pretty special relationship. That way you won't get tired of me."

"Hmmm…and what if you get tired of me?" I asked. I smiled into those beautiful eyes of his and hit him with an energy wave of my own that flat out dared him to even think he could get tired of me.

He smirked and zapped me back, and we both laughed.

"I have you wrapped around my finger, haven't you noticed?" he said. "Who could get tired of that?"

"Well, I admit you frequently have me wrapped around one part of your body or another." I slipped my hand around his cock again.

"Exactly where I want you."

40

Big and In Your Face

Tuesday, September 17

The next morning (after a very tender wake-up call) we went for a run in the Park, through yet another area I hadn't seen yet. I planned to do a lot of exploring on subsequent trips. It is hard to describe the magnitude of the transition from big city to rural paradise that could be achieved by just crossing the street in front of the house. That, by the way, is how Richard referred to the mansion: "The House." I couldn't quite comprehend how that worked, but I suppose if you'd grown up with it, it was the house, just has he referred to his mother's palace as her "house." Different strokes. Neither of them—and yes, I'd only seen bits of hers from his video—fit the idea of a "house" in my frame of reference!

And I have to say (yes, again) that Richard seemed to take his father's mansion and his own palatial domicile in L.A. with a grain of salt. He was perfectly aware how fabtastical (yep!) they were, but he didn't seem "attached" to them in a "look-what-I've-got" way. It may have been his general sense of self-possession. He knew who he was and managed his life deftly while providing some pretty amazing opportunities for others as he moved through it. Really, that alone made me love him, no matter how much I enjoyed those amazing bells and whistles that were included in the package. Yes, stars in my eyes, without a doubt, but as I said early on, I was totally in!

C.J. BAILEY

We made love in the shower accompanied by *Leavin' On A Jet Plane* from Peter, Paul and Mary. It made me wonder if the "I'll wear your wedding ring" line was a not-so-subtle hint.

As we set about packing, I left a few things to travel with my new acquisitions, which Richard said Elise would send along to California. The lighter my carry-on, the better! He asked if I wanted the swan necklace sent by courier and I laughed.

"I told you I intend to wear it. I was serious."

He smiled and shook his head. "And the other pieces?"

"Safe in my purse. I promise not to let them out of my sight."

That earned me a kiss, though I'm not sure why. At any rate, our flights were within forty minutes of each other with Richard leaving first. Since we were both flying on Delta from the same terminal I waited with him until he boarded.

"Remember, I need that destination from you by Friday," he said after he'd kissed me and given me a long hug.

I saluted. "Yes, sir! And call me when you land."

"Travel safe, Sweetheart, and remember you are loved beyond measure." He whispered against my ear.

I watched him hand the woman his ticket. She wobbled and had to grab for the machine. And then, with a wink at me, he was gone.

I went on to my gate and took a seat. My phone vibrated and I opened an email from my Prince:

> *I caught the sunlight pining through the sheers, traveling millions of dark miles simply to graze your skin as I did that first dawn I studied you sleeping beside me: Yes, I counted your eyelashes, read your dreams like butterflies flitting underneath your eyelids, ready to flutter into the room.*
>
> *Yes, I praised you like a majestic creature my god forgot to create, till that morning of you suddenly tamed in my arms, first for me to see, name you mine.*
>
> *Yes to the rise and fall of your body breathing, your every exhale a breath I took in as my own, wanting to keep even the air between us as one.*
> —*Freedom to Marry* by Richard Blanco

STILL LUCKY

I love you, Miss Hot Pants.
XXOOR

It brought tears to my eyes. The rare romantic man and he was mine! I hoped he'd enjoy the note I'd left inside his laptop. I figured he wouldn't find it until he opened it to try and do some work.

> *I love him. I trust him.*
> *He trusteth me alway.*
> *And so the time flies hopefully,*
> *Although he's far away...*
> —Barry Cornwall

XXOOJ

I called Antonio when we landed. He was about ten minutes away, driving Poldi Porsche and would meet me outside baggage claim. With the perfect timing of Richard's universe, he pulled up just as I came through the doors. By the time I reached the curb, he was there to take my bag, but not until I gave him a hug.

"Welcome home, Signorina," he said with a broad smile as he popped my suitcase into the trunk. He opened the door for me and moments later we were pulling back out into the traffic.

"The afternoon rush is starting. Do you mind if we take the coast and come back along Sunset? This would be good because there is something I want you to see." Antonio's attention was focused on the thick knot of cars looping the terminal.

"You're driving. Your call. It would be nice to see the beach."

I got my wish, a somewhat extended view of sand and surf—and all the buildings in between—as we slowed in the traffic along the coast. I didn't mind. The top was down and it was a beautiful afternoon.

As we turned off PCH and slowly made our way up Sunset, I mentioned to Antonio that I was happy he'd chosen that route. I agreed the views were much more interesting than crawling along on the crowded freeway.

"The scenery is about to get much more interesting," he assured me with a certain air of mystery.

"Really?"

The light turned and the line of traffic stopped. Antonio gestured to the left and up, waiting to see my reaction.

GOOD GRIEF! Talk about gobsmacked! A giant billboard rose above the buildings, displaying that necklace photo of me in super size! It was Giano's ad, the same as the double spread in the magazine only much, MUCH bigger!

I burst out laughing as I scrambled for my phone, then undid my seatbelt and got up on my knees to snap some pictures. My folks were going to be as surprised as I was. I wondered if Richard knew.

"I don't think so. You will have to ask Hunter." Antonio was laughing and the light turned.

"How long has that been there?"

He shrugged. "I don't know, but my uncle called and told me that I should surprise you by driving by."

I punched up Giano.

"Cressibella! Have you returned to us?"

"I have and your nephew has just driven me past a very large version of my face."

"Ah! So beautiful, no?"

"Well…surprising, certainly."

"You have just been with the boy. Has he allowed you forget you are a beautiful woman?" Giano asked with theatrical dismay.

"No. He is still as kind and loving as ever."

"This is good. But remember: if he ever fails you, you have only to call."

I laughed. "I shall remember, believe me. Any chance I can take you to lunch tomorrow?"

"I would be honored."

"Good. I'll call in the morning and we can make our plans." I thought I'd better get home and talk to Marie and Steph to find out what was going on before I made a firm commitment.

"Until then, Bella."

STILL LUCKY

Thursday, September 19

Note of the day:

...I pace around hungry, sniffing the twilight,
hunting for you, for your hot heart,
like a puma in the barrens of Quitratue.
　　　　　　　　—Neruda, *Love Sonnet XI*

Do you know where Quitratue is?
I do! XXOOJ

    I pulled out all the stops on Thursday for my meeting with the Ice Cream Boys, going extreme don't-fuck-with-me mode, head to toe. Whoever the meeting was with should know off the top who they were dealing with. If they were expecting a mousy computer nerd who spent most of his/her (did they know?) time in the basement staring at a monitor, I intended to disabuse them of that notion at first glance.

    I wore my black jeans that fit me like body paint ($80 not $600!), a white silk blouse and the natural raw silk blazer with my swan prominently pinned to the lapel, my new platinum bangles, my old CZ earrings (keeping with the white metal theme!) and a killer pair of stilettos Mark had convinced me to buy on our last shopping trip. I picked up the teal mogul bag Richard had given me and my briefcase with my laptop and I was ready for whatever the morning brought my way. I even decided to drive Poldi. (I knew Richard would be pleased and I needed some wind in my hair to put me in the proper frame of mind.)

    I arrived about eight minutes early and was immediately escorted into the office where Ben and Jerry were waiting. They both stood up as I came through the door, looking a little uncomfortable. I suspected they were wondering if Richard had told me about their call to him.

    I took a seat (before they could invite me!) and immediately put my sunglasses in my purse and pulled out my nerd glasses. I was careful not to seem too friendly. I wanted to remind them that I was a potential meal ticket and deserved to be treated with respect. The energy tended toward frosty on my side. I couldn't read them right away, beyond the fact it was obvious they were feeling a bit skittish.

"Good to see you CJ," Ben said.

"Thanks. What can you tell me about today's meeting?" I asked, jumping beyond the social chitchat. I could see this surprised them. "Am I correct in thinking these are the same people who were here last week?"

"Yes, " Jerry said. "They decided to give it another shot."

"I assume that was after you told them it was your error and not mine?" I said bluntly. Might as well let them have a good look at the playing field before we met the other team. (Sports analogy? Say what?)

"Yes," Ben jumped in. "We took complete responsibility for your absence."

"Good."

"So what can you tell us about your meeting with Peter Norton?" Jerry asked, with just a hint of needling in his tone. It was a parry to my opening. Fair enough. But I found that interesting. Was he trying to insinuate I had deceived them?

"I was in New York for the Black and White event at MOMA where I had a chance to introduce myself to Peter, and over the course of the evening he became interested in the project. I had brunch with Peter and Gwen the next day and discussed it in depth. He seemed genuinely intrigued so I left him with the promotional PowerPoint you're using. If he wants more information about the financing, I expect he'll get in touch with you. His interest seemed to lean toward helping me make contacts for capital."

Ben and Jerry exchanged a glance that I couldn't interpret, but I could feel the tension ease a bit.

They went on to explain that the meeting was with a corporation that was interested in buying the project. If it sold as is, I would be required to stay with the project for a term to be negotiated and to be available to work with the teams. The length of my involvement, the sale price and method of payment, what specifically would be required of me and other miscellaneous details would be worked out if they made an offer.

The men told me an agreement had been signed protecting my

proprietary rights and so I could answer any questions without fear that my ideas would be stolen. And they expected the meeting today would involve a lot of in-depth questions about me, my vision and details of the way the portal was designed, any limits and how it might be expanded even further. They also said the principals just wanted a chance to meet me and get an impression of who I was, if I knew what I was doing and if they could work with me.

I laughed. "Is that all?"

Ben and Jerry seemed greatly relieved and they both smiled, though just a little. I wondered then, if it might be the potential buyer who was intimidating them and not me.

"Are you concerned that I might not make a good impression?" I asked.

"No," Jerry was quick to assure me. "We have no doubt that you're up to the interview. We just want to stress that these folks represent a pretty significant interest and could be an even better solution for you than working with investors to get the project off the ground yourself."

"So which route do you think would be the best?" I was interested to hear what they thought.

I'd always imagined the project would be mine to build into a major player on the Internet. I knew it would take years and I was well aware that the learning curve, especially when it came to hiring a team, would be steep, but I'd looked forward to it. That was all before I met Richard. Now I found myself wondering how that would fit into our life. I hadn't really done much thinking about it yet, content to see how things developed and make my decisions when they were in front of me, rather than trying to anticipate all the possibilities in advance.

Ben said, "That will be totally up to you, if and when the opportunities present themselves."

The phone rang, letting us know the group was ready for us. As we walked down the hall to the conference room, it occurred to me to ask whom the meeting was with.

"Google," they both answered at the same time.

41

Vitamin Sea

Still Thursday

The meeting ran long and I had to speed to get home so Antonio could drive me to the airport. He was waiting for me with my bag in front of the house. I was glad I'd packed the night before, just in case this happened. He popped my carry-on in the trunk and we traded seats in Poldi and took off.

While I waited for them to call my flight, I gave Richard a quick call.

"There's my mogul," he said when he picked up. "How'd it go?"

"Well..." Where to begin? "I feel like a bit like I've been water-boarded!"

"Really? That bad?"

"No, actually. But I spent three hours being grilled relentlessly by six people I've never seen before."

"I bet they were appropriately stunned to find such genius so beautifully packaged!"

"Aw....ya love me, huh?"

"Yes, ma'am. Never doubt it."

"Well, glad I can count on it." They called my flight. "I've got to go," I told him. "Shall I give you a wake-up call?"

"Yes, please. Five a.m. my time. You can give me a warm start to the day and then we should have a chance to talk while I'm on the treadmill."

"I'll be there. I love you, Handsome."

"Travel safe, Sweetheart and tell your family I apologize again for delaying your visit."

STILL LUCKY

I opened my laptop and spent most of the flight carefully reviewing the morning. Ben and Jerry had given me an audio of the meeting, which they'd recorded for legal reasons. I made extensive notes, trying to get a handle on what Google's concerns were and if I had addressed them completely.

The Google people had been friendly and seemed open, but their focus was laser-like when it came to the discussion. The thing that pleased me was that what they asked made it obvious that the original PowerPoint had explained the scope of the project successfully and so their questions addressed details on everything from programming structure to my thoughts about expanding into broader coverage of the subject matter. It had exhausted me, but at the same time I'd found it exhilarating to be with six people who spoke my tech language fluently. (Ben and Jerry did more observing that speaking, and I detected a bit of awe in their eyes when I said goodbye!)

Finally, I closed the computer and spent the last forty minutes of the flight just dozing.

Gran picked me up at the airport in Daddy's car and gave me a long hug after I put my bag in her trunk.

"So good to see you! How was New York and that hunk of yours?"

I laughed as I got in to drive. "I have lots of pictures to show you. It was flat out amazing!"

"So you still love him, I see."

"Yup. More than ever. I can't wait for you guys to meet him."

"Any idea when that might happen? He FaceTimed me last night, but I want to see him up close and personal!" she said.

"Just remember he's mine! And actually, we plan to come in about three weeks, if it works for Mom and Daddy. You'll still be here won't you?"

"I'm here for the long haul, until your father's ready to be on his own and can convince me he's running at 100%. And he's been great, by the way. His doctors are amazed at how well he's doing."

"Your dietary influence, right?" I knew she was being very strict with what she fed him—he complained to me but his evaluation of his meals was delivered tongue firmly in cheek. I knew she was sure nothing but healthy and organic food would find its way onto Daddy's plate. Gran was determined to give him all the nutritional support possible while he healed.

"Absolutely. He's not always excited about the menus I concoct, but he's doing as he's told." She spoke those words with a degree of satisfaction.

"What would any of us do without you, Gran?"

"I don't intend to give you a chance to find out for another half-century at least!" She said sarcastically. Then she threw her head back and laughed.

"Good. I'm counting on that." She had me laughing, too, and I felt the tension of the day melting away.

My father's rate of recovery seemed remarkable to me. It had only been two weeks since I'd seen him and the difference in his appearance was amazing. He looked and sounded great and was moving around pretty well.

The four of us had a great dinner—well, three of us did—and really what Gran put on Daddy's plate looked pretty good to me, too. He wasn't unhappy about it. I was convinced my presence made up for any culinary limitations imposed on him.

I shared the New York stories with them and ended with the picture of my billboard on Sunset.

"OMG," Gran said. "Does the mean you're officially a celebrity?"

"Yeah, right. Like a Kardashian. Famous for doing nothing!" I laughed. "Fortunately, nobody knows who I am, so the paparazzi continue to ignore me, which, by the way, suits me fine."

My mother was studying the photo on my iPad.

"It's beautiful. So nice to see you as the woman you really are and up there for the world to appreciate."

"Think you're just a bit prejudiced?" I asked.

"Nope. That's a completely unbiased opinion."

"And I second that emotion," Daddy added.

Then we discussed Richard's visit and made our plans. I was so looking forward to them meeting him in person and seeing the two of us together. I knew they would love him almost as much as I did! How could they not?

After dinner I left them with the pictures and went out to the patio to give Richard his wake up call.

When he picked up he said, "Lark or nightingale?"

"I fear it is the lark, my Prince. Are you ready to begin your day?"

"Can I help you begin yours?" he asked.

"Sadly, no. We just finished dinner and I'm sitting out on the patio. I'll offer what encouragement I can but I fear it may be a bit subdued."

"This morning I think heavy breathing and a little verbal encouragement will make quick work of it. I was dreaming I was making love to you when the phone rang."

"Tell me about the dream," I said softly. I swear it only took the sound of his voice to dampen my thighs!

"We were at Giano's. On the balcony. It was a warm night and you had insisted on a soft serve dessert. You had me in that marvelous mouth of yours, but I pulled you to your feet and scooped you up and carried you to the bed. I lay you down and stood there, just looking at you. You're so beautiful, Sweetheart. You reached for my cock, urging me to join you...and then the phone rang."

I'd closed my eyes, imagining his scenario.

"My hand is still on you. Can you feel it?"

"I can."

"Then come closer and give me one more taste before you let me feel you inside me."

I gave him some juicy sounds and heard him groan.

"God, I love your balls," I said breathlessly.

"Wanna feel them against your ass?"

"Yes, please..." I followed that with the little gasp he knew so well. "Fuck me, Richard," I whispered.

I heard his breathing shift.

"Come for me," he said.

I made the appropriate sounds and heard him come.

"You feel so good," I said softly.

He gave a little snort. "It's a good thing we both have such vivid imaginations."

"The very best. But you make it so easy, my love."

"Ditto," he said. And then he paused. I sensed he was still stroking himself.

"Did you save a drop for me?"

"Yes."

I made appreciative noises. "You are delicious."

"I feel the same way about you. Only a few more weeks and we'll be together again."

"I'm counting the days."

For a minute or two, we were just quiet together, and then I said, "Do you really feel like talking while you work out?"

"I do. I want to hear all about your meeting, how your folks are doing and if our plans suit them. And today's the day you tell me where we'll be spending my birthday."

"But it's only Thursday," I whined. Actually I'd decided, but I wanted to tease him.

"My birthday, my time zone. I'll FaceTime you in about fifteen minutes."

"How do you do that?" I asked when he appeared on my screen, just jogging away.

"What? Run?"

"No. Carry on a conversation without sounding breathless."

He laughed.

"And laugh," I added.

"Practice. Have you tried it? You can probably do it just as well as I can."

"I'm pretty sure I'm not there yet."

So I told him about the meeting, including what had seemed to be their main interests as far as the questions were concerned. He had a few questions of his own and then I mentioned I had a recording.

"Do you want to share it?" he asked.

"Of course. I don't know how interesting it will be for you. There's a lot of tech talk involved."

"Need I remind you I'm a Trained Professional?" He was pretending to be offended.

"Oh no, I remember that quite well. You've demonstrated a myriad of examples."

"Good one. Do you know that in classical literature 'myriad' was a unit of ten thousand?"

"You see? There it is again. I rest my case," I said with no small amount of satisfaction. "Wait…that *was* my case!"

"Er…uh…guess it was."

In an effort to trick me, he quickly changed the subject.

"So tell me where I'm spending my birthday."

"Not so fast. Family first," I insisted.

"OK. Let me switch to cool down and get my calendar."

The treadmill slowed and he picked up his iPhone."

"First, tell me if you think a visit now is too much of an imposition. I know your father is easing back into some teaching and he seems to be doing really well, at least via FaceTime. But you're up close and personal. How does it look from there?"

So sweet. "Aw." I blew him a kiss, which he deftly caught. "Daddy's doing great. Amazing to me, but I'm so happy. Gran is managing his care schedule with an iron hand and is feeding him up on healthy, healing organic food. His doctor is very impressed. All that to say they are thrilled they'll finally get to meet you. So it's a go for the dates we discussed: arrive on the 4th, leave on the 9th. Do you want me to do the plane tickets?"

"I'll take care of the plane and a car, I have more frequent flyer miles than a person needs, so might as well use 'em. Can you find us a hotel?"

"Sure. Just so long as you remember this is Walla Walla and not New York or Paris. The accommodations may be a couple of notches lower than what you're used to."

Richard was suddenly quiet. "Seriously?"

"What? Why?" I was confused

"I do spend time in pretty luxurious surroundings, but I hope I haven't given you any reason to think I'm a snob."

I could hear this really bothered him.

"My Prince, I would never think that of you! You would be the last person to complain if we had to stay at a Super 8. I know that. I have a feeling that you, like me, would be happy even in a tent, as long as we were together. Though let me state for the record that sleeping on rocks is not my idea of a good time. That's more Steph's bailiwick. And after enjoying this summer's outstanding housing, I'm not sure she'd look forward to a sleeping bag any time soon. Maybe if Michael was in there, but…"

"Just checking. And yes, anywhere we're together is fine with me. Pick a place that you like and make the reservation."

"Okey dokey. And since you have your calendar, I want to schedule some photos of you and us with the photographer that took those really beautiful ones of me."

"Are you trying to lure me into the wicked world of porn?" he said with some amusement.

"No. I was thinking more of things suitable for friends and family. You're so beautiful, I just want to catch you while you're so in love with me."

Richard burst out laughing. "Well, I suppose I need to meet the person who took those pictures. They are exceptional, if somewhat unconventional. So how much time do you think we need?"

"Let's say four hours."

He offered me two choices of days and I told him I'd see what I could schedule.

"Now. My turn," he said firmly. "Where exactly are we going for my birthday?"

"I'm leaving that up to you…"

Before I could finish he sighed and said, "Cress…"

"Wait. I have some requirements. First warm weather, second, warm ocean, preferably at least eighty-two degrees. Then I would like it to be very private. Just the two of us; you, me, no distractions besides each other."

For a minute he didn't say anything. "Are you sure?"

"There is one caveat."

"And that is?"

"If there is something you'd rather do, someplace you really want to go, someplace you can't wait to show me—that you'll choose that instead."

STILL LUCKY

After long pause he said, "You never cease to surprise me."
"Good!"

Monday, September 23

Note of the day:

> *It doesn't interest me what you do*
> *for a living, I want to know*
> *what you ache for,*
> *and if you dream of meeting*
> *your heart's longing.*   —Oriah

No need to dream, I found him! XXOOJ

On Monday Ben called and asked if I could be available for a teleconference from Walla Walla the next day at ten. Google had more questions for me. I was surprised, but Richard had listened to the meeting and felt there was some serious interest on their part, so of course, I agreed.

When the time came there were just two people besides Ben and Jerry, a man and a woman, neither of which had been at the first meeting. They left me no time to wonder if that fact was significant. They immediately launched into questions about implementation strategy on two specific aspects of the program. They were coming at it from a different angle and had reached a dead end. I led them down the path I'd intended and they saw immediately what my strategy was. It was interesting to watch their expressions change as the light went on. We were done in less than forty minutes. I was thinking so far, so good, but I wasn't looking any farther ahead. No sense borrowing trouble!

42
The Elves Return

Wednesday, September 25

Note of the day:

> *At any rate, that is happiness.*
> *To be dissolved into something complete*
> *and great.* —Willa Cather, *My Antonia*

> Sounds like two people I know!
> XXOOJ

When I came home on Wednesday Marie told me there was a surprise waiting for me upstairs. Hmmm… I had her come up with me, knowing from her expression that she was anxious to see my reaction.

When I walked into our closet I was expecting to find something sitting on the island. There was nothing there, not even my fancy tray with my lily of the valley perfume. I looked at Marie in confusion and she urged me on, beyond the island where I noticed a wide pink ribbon with a big bow across the mirror at the far end, an envelope dangling from it. Marie's smile was so broad that it reduced her eyes to sparkling half moons. She gestured with a nod of her head and I walked over and opened the envelope.

STILL LUCKY

Sweet Juliet,
    Thought you'd appreciate a place
to keep those hot pants and other
new acquisitions as they arrive.
        Soon! XXOOR

Then I noticed a very fine seam running down the center of the mirror. I pulled the bow from where it was taped to the glass and the ribbons dropped to reveal two knobs. I pushed and nothing happened.

"They slide," Marie prompted.

Sure enough, they were pocket doors and smoothly slipped away to either side. You know what I'm going to say next, right? Gobsmacked for sure! Behind the doors was a mirror image of Richard's closet but done in light wood, including an island with a white marble top veined in a shade of creamy sand color that matched the wood perfectly. Sitting on it was an arrangement of pink roses and lavender, like the one he'd left for me in New York. Beside it was my tray with my perfume.

My things were carefully arranged in various cubbies and hanging areas, my shoes looking lonely on a rack designed for ten times as many. My long gowns had their own special section with glass doors. The rest looked pretty bare but it was simply beautiful. I pulled some of the drawers in the island, (already holding my things, carefully folded and arranged by color courtesy of Marie!) The drawers were just like Richard's, one with the lined sections for jewelry. Knowing him, I was sure he intended to fill the many empty spaces for me over time. He'd already made a good start.

After staring in stunned silence as I took it all in, I turned to Marie.

"How on earth did this happen without me knowing?"

"Bit by bit when you were gone. Do you remember asking me what they were doing on a day when you parked in front of the house and noticed the workers?"

I did remember. I'd come home to find some activity on that end of the house. Marie had told me they were changing the access on the storage area that ran through all three floors. Beyond that I hadn't been aware of the work going on. I'd never given it another thought.

"What was this space before?" I asked Marie.

"It was used for storage but I believe Monsieur Richard always hoped someone would share the house with him. It was a second closet in the original plans."

I glanced at my watch. I would have to wait for Richard's wake up call to thank him.

Steph was with Michael so I shared my New York photos with Marie over dinner. We talked about the house there and the people I'd met. She had some great stories. We sat together on the balcony with an espresso until 8:00 p.m. when I went upstairs to call Richard.

I was trying to think of how I wanted to start his day. He deserved something special, not only for the closet but because I felt bad that I hadn't had much to offer while I was with my folks. With Daddy home now and Gran there, plus the therapists and home health people in and out...well not much privacy for the sort of elaborate scenarios we'd been enjoying. And though I knew Richard didn't mind, I sort of felt like I'd been neglecting him.

I punched him up on FaceTime.

"Richard!" I said in a loud whisper.

"What?" he whispered back, his eyes still closed.

"The elves have been in your house!"

He rubbed his face. "It's OK. They work for me."

I stifled a laugh.

"Good morning, Sweetheart," he said with a smile. "What did the elves do this time?"

"They built me a closet just like yours, only mine's prettier."

"Good. I told them to make it special."

"It is beautiful, my Prince. And most important, I now understand why you have so many nice clothes."

"And that would be because...?"

"First, with closets this size there's a lot of space to fill. Second, my old clothes look pretty sad in among my fancy new things."

"Be still my heart! Does this mean you are finally ready to shop without resistance?"

"It could happen," I warned.

He laughed. "If all the encouragement you needed was an empty closet, I would have called in the elves months ago."

"Uh…it's a process. But I am making progress."

"You are indeed. Can't wait to see how you fill that space."

"Well, 'fill' may be a little strong…" I said doubtfully.

Richard yawned and stretched. "I've been missing you. See?" Eager to change the subject, he turned his phone toward his erection, which was in morning hardwood mode.

"Ahhhhh…" I said with a sigh. "I've missed you. And I'm sorry for neglecting you while I was with my folks."

"I don't feel neglected. We do what we can, when we can. It's enough."

"So how can I best please you this morning? I'm afraid I haven't had time to plan anything. I'm hoping we can have a few hours together soon."

"I'm booked pretty tight these last few days, making up for the New York detour. We'll have to save it for when I get home. It's only five more days, Cress. We can run a simpler program in the meantime."

"Is that computer-speak for my benefit?"

"Unintentional, but if you like it, I'm sure I can find a way to learn more."

"I'm sure you can. But meanwhile, what will you have this morning?"

"Where's Zoor?"

I took my key from the nightstand and went to unlock his. There was my fine friend, just waiting for some appreciation.

"Uh…if you're thinking of penetration, I really need to warm him up. Getting 'cold-cocked' isn't much fun."

"I was thinking more of your mouth. Maybe if you think of him as a Popsicle…"

"Yummm…those orange ones that are all creamy inside?"

Richard laughed as I set my iPad on the bed against a pillow and I slowly slipped my elastic-top dress down and off. I put both hands on my head and gave him a little sinuous belly dance turn.

"Beautiful," he said.

"I want to watch you," I said as I repositioned my tablet and framed Zoor and his balls so they came into the picture from the side.

It looked for all the world like he was standing next to me. I gave Zoor's lovely head a big lick.

Richard groaned. I played to the camera like some cock-sucking porn girl, though my pleasure was genuine. (The women in porn never look to me like they're enjoying themselves, no matter how many faces or noises they make!)

"Cress..." he breathed.

"Wait. I want some balls, too." I pressed Zoor's shaft to the side and tongued his balls and then took them both in my mouth, rolling them around slowly. It was amazing how lifelike those Neuticles felt.

I kept an eye on my screen. Richard was stretching his scrotum and fondling his balls. Me, I was dripping. I loved watching him as much as he loved watching me. I was wishing I'd grabbed Bob when I got that key!

I released Zoor's balls slowly and gave them a parting tickle with my tongue before running it slowly back up. When I got to the top, I lapped as I wrapped one hand around him and stroked him slowly.

Richard was ready to come, I heard his breathing shift and his balls tightened up and I took Zoor deep and worked him as I watched Richard's hand mimic my mouth. He had a towel ready but held it so I could watch him come. I loved that pulsing as he ejaculated. I could imagine clearly how it felt—it was always exciting to me. My lover was so hot!

I pulled Zoor out of my mouth and continued sucking gently at his head, adding some extra sound effects for my Prince's benefit. I circled my tongue and smiled.

"Delicious!" I assured him.

He moved the camera up to those beautiful grey eyes and said very matter-of-factly, "Well, if the whole computer portal thing doesn't work out, you can always set up a sex chat room. Probably make as much money. Lord knows you'd be busy."

"Might work as long as it was one way and I didn't have to watch them. And then I'd always be thinking of you...so... Nope, I'd rather just serve you, Handsome. Let me be your private dancer?"

"Absolutely. I'd hate to have to share you, Sweetheart, even long distance."

"You're in no danger. I can't imagine wanting anyone but you." I smiled.

STILL LUCKY

Thursday, September 26

Note of the day:

> *Whatever our souls are made of,*
> *his and mine are the same.*
> —Emily Bronte, *Wuthering Heights*

I started my day Thursday, determined to accomplish a lot. The pressure was on with Richard coming home next Tuesday and then us leaving Friday for Walla Walla.

He woke me at five, but he was on his way into a meeting and expressed his regrets at being unable to wake me properly. I forgave him and went immediately to the gym and worked out for all I was worth. Trying to make up exercise time is fruitless and I had trouble pulling my two rungs on the salmon ladder. I swore I'd try it two or three times a day between then and Richard's return. Ji would come tomorrow and I'd see if he had any tips that might get me to three rungs in time.

After my laps and a shower, I took my coffee and granola and yogurt to my office to try to get my calendar organized. I called Steph and made a lunch date, after which she would take me to the studio to see the new pieces. I called Giano to see if I could meet with him later in the afternoon. I had an idea of something I wanted for Richard's birthday.

Ben and Jerry settled for another teleconference, even though I was back in L.A. The news was that they'd heard from Peter Norton, who told them he was putting together a funding proposal on behalf of several interested parties. He expected to have it in another week. Nothing yet from Google. They assured me this was not unusual.

I reminded them of my upcoming travel dates. I would be in Walla Walla the following Thursday but available via Skype if they needed me, though I asked that they let me know in advance. I wouldn't know about the week after that until Richard gave me our travel info.

I was making progress! It was good to be back at my desk and feeling like I was getting things done.

I made an appointment with Seiji and we talked a little about what sort of pictures I wanted of Richard and of the two of us together. He asked if I'd mentioned his work to Richard and I told him I'd only described his talent so as not to spoil any presentation he may have planned for the future.

"And he really loved the shots you did of me," I assured him.

"Do you think it would be a good time to ask him for an appointment?" Seiji said. "When the two of you are here, I mean."

"Actually—and this is coming from someone who's clueless about how these things work—it might be a good idea to have a few of your pieces around the studio, you know, like you were trying to decide on some arrangement or something. I can't imagine they won't catch his eye and then you two can take it from there."

"Great! CJ, I can't thank you enough. And also I owe you some thanks for the connection with Chris at Universal. She's great to work with."

"Good! I have yet to meet her in person, but I'm looking forward to it."

Everything on my office list taken care of, I opened the door to find Marie, Antonio and a man I didn't recognize clearing the furniture from that corner of the living room. My expression of surprise brought a smile to Marie's face.

"What?" I asked.

"I assume you must have had something to do with this," she said.

"This what?"

"Monsieur Richard is having a piano delivered this morning. I hope it means he has decided to play again?"

"Yes!" I said, clapping my hands together. "Did you ever hear him play, Marie?"

"*Non*. But Monsieur Louis used to watch the videos of him in the competitions when he was a boy. These I saw. It always made me sad that he no longer played."

"I think he will play now. He played for me in New York."

"Ah…" Marie said with a knowing nod.

And suddenly I knew what to get Richard for his birthday! As much as he valued my company, I felt something additional was in order and now I knew just what it should be.

Antonio had left Miyuki parked in front for me. (Yes, I was becoming braver about driving one of Richard's pretty little cars!) There was no need to deliver any more quotes to Mark. The New York excursion left us with a surplus, but I needed some shopping guidance, so before I left I punched him up.

"Hey, CJ. Welcome home…again. I seem to be saying that a lot these days!"

"I know," I said, laughing. "And I'm afraid it's going to get worse before it gets better." I gave him a quick overview of our planned visits to my folks and then the mystery location to celebrate Richard's birthday."

"You little jetsetter, you," he teased. "How are you holding up?"

"I'm embarrassed to say I'm sliding right down a well-greased chute into this life of the rich and famous like it's where I belong. It's fine as long as I don't stop to think about it."

"Good to hear you're adjusting. The boss isn't always the easiest guy to keep up with," he admitted.

"Somehow, he makes it seem easy, at least when we're together. But today I need some advice. I want to get Richard a candelabra for his birthday."

There was silence on the other end of the phone.

"Are you there?" I asked.

"Yes. It just caught me off guard. Seriously, a candelabra?"

"I know, but trust me, he'll get a kick out of it. Still, it's not something I've ever had to think about buying and I'd like it to be special, you know, not the standard silver or crystal wedding gift sort of thing. I was hoping I could find something unusual, maybe sort of sculptural or modern or…gee, I don't know."

Mark laughed. "The store you want is called Flame. It's amazing. Everything from regular candles to things that hold them—single candleholders, candeliers (for the uninitiated those are the ceiling fixtures that hold candles instead of lightbulbs!), menorahs—and on up to the latest and greatest for indoor and outdoor fireplaces and firepits. Plan to spend some time, the place is an adventure ."

Mark gave me the West L.A. address and I thanked him and said goodbye, promising to send a photo or two if I needed help. Then I called Steph.

"How's my favorite artist?" I asked when she answered.

"Looking forward to a consultation with you. I'm getting a little nervous about the return of your Magic Man."

"Can't wait to see what you've done and assure you you're a genius. Is there any chance I could come now and we could go to lunch after?"

"Sure. I'm sort of having a studio clean-up day. I'm going to have to move out of here in a few weeks."

I'd forgotten Steph only had the studio space until the middle of October!

"Oh dear, we'll have to talk about that. Any chance you can take the afternoon off? I have to go hunting for Richard's birthday gift and I could really use an artistic opinion."

"Like you, opinions are something I have plenty of!" Steph laughed. "And today is a great day to get out of here. So come on down!"

My friend Stephanie never ceased to amaze me. In the month since I'd last seen her paintings, she had accomplished an amazing amount of work. Steph was no slacker, and even if Richard wasn't crazy about what she'd done—and I couldn't in any way imagine such a thing—he wouldn't be able to accuse her of not taking full advantage of the amazing opportunity he'd given her.

The beautiful botanicals had continued to evolve, becoming a little more abstract without losing the core essence of the plant she was capturing. (Where was my Trained Professional when I needed him and his words?) And the colors! Her paintings hit me in the same visceral way that my beautiful window painting did. Just gobsmacked! It was wonderful to see them all together, in order of creation. It was easy to trace the evolution.

"Well, you mouth is hanging open, I take that as a good sign," she said as she waited for my reaction.

"I don't know what to say," I admitted when I turned to her. My eyes were filling with tears.

"Uh, oh," she said. "I hope this doesn't mean you feel sorry for me and my lack of talent."

I had to laugh as I gave her a big hug. "I am so happy for you! To create all this...Steph...I don't know how you do it, but it has to be so exciting. To bring such beautiful things out of thin air..."

"Couldn't have done it without you, you know," she said when I finally let go.

"Hardly..."

"If you hadn't ensorcelled the good Dr. Hunter, I never would have had this opportunity."

I cracked up. *"Ensorcelled?"*

"OK, should I say seduced him with your hot body and wicked, wicked ways?" she offered.

"I'll admit that the enticements I offered may have procured summer housing for us, but it was your amazing talent that resulted in him giving you this space."

Granted, I'd made the introduction, but Richard's generosity was all his own. He was the one who asked if I would like having Steph live at the house with me for the summer. It was her work that had impressed him enough to extend the offer of the magnificent workspace. And my amazing lover had been the one who helped her decide to take a shot at a serious art career when she wobbled on the edge of indecision.

Before she could demur again, I asked about the calendars. She took me by the shoulders and turned me to face the other wall where eight smaller pieces, all the same size, were lined up. I moved closer to get a good look at them. It was easy to see why Mark had thought an entire year would make an impressive presentation when hung together on a gallery wall.

We spent a few minutes going over the months, laughing over the abstract way she had captured particular events. They were all there, from the beginning of our last semester at U.C.L.A., a couple of disastrous dates (one with a guy who had artistic aspirations—and no talent—to the night she met Richard, and the explosion of vibrant colors when she met Michael at our graduation party. Of course most people wouldn't see the connections, not knowing the events of her life, but anyone could see there were events and could interpret good from bad.

"Obviously I've got a few more days left in this month. And then three months to go, to finish out the year. Wonder where I'll be painting those last two."

She sounded a little sad.

"Do you know for a fact that you have to be out the end of next month?" I asked.

"Well, no. I haven't said anything to Mark. But that's the agreement I signed."

"I bet you'll be able to stay if they don't have it reserved for a visiting artist. If they do, we'll find you a space. I have Magic Man's bottomless AMEX card. The world is ours!"

Steph laughed. "How 'bout you take me to lunch with that piece of plastic and tell me what we're doing this afternoon?"

We grabbed lunch and then went to see Giano.

I was wearing my swan pin, which Steph had noticed without imagining it was really diamonds. I pulled the pearls from my purse because I wanted a simpler pair of pearl earrings to match. The fancy pair Richard had gotten for me were over the top for everyday (and no, a fabulous diamond swan wasn't!) and I intended to wear that swan quite a bit, with and without the necklace.

Naturally Giano noticed the pin, even as he greeted me with a hug and double kiss.

"The boy has been shopping for you in Paris, has he not?"

I laughed. "He has," I said as I reached into my purse for the necklace. "My swan goes on the pearls, too. I need some simpler earrings to match them. Richard got a pair for me in New York but they're too much for daily wear. I'd like something small and simple."

"May I?" he asked, gesturing toward the pin.

"Of course," I said, removing it and handing it to him.

Giano invited us to sit, taking a seat across from us at one of the little tables. He took a loupe from his pocket and examined the swan.

STILL LUCKY

"*Squisito!*" he whispered. He handed the pin back to me, saying, "I have only seen the photo of this piece. The designer is my friend Jean Marc Retoulier. I must tell him how happy I am this piece has found a home with you."

As Giano disappeared into the back, Steph leaned over and said, "Those are diamonds?"

Her expression was shock mixed with just a bit of horror and I had to laugh.

"Apparently. Richard said he saw it in the window in Paris and had to get it for me. That whole Leda and the swan thing." I'd told Steph the story of the swan connection when Richard sent that gold bracelet with the image.

"And you're wearing it casually?"

"You assumed it was rhinestones when you saw it, didn't you?"

"Sure. Guess I'll have to take a second look at what you're wearing in the future. Does it make Richard nervous that you're sporting it like costume jewelry?"

"Nope. I was horrified when he gave it to me and told me this one was mine, not borrowed. And then I realized that if it had been fake, I would have loved it just as much and would have really wanted it. I'm trying hard to adjust to these new circumstances. It's not easy, but baby steps...!"

Steph just shook her head. Then Giano returned with a tray of pearl and diamond earrings, some even simple enough for me! I ended up with a pair that were just single pearl studs that matched the necklace, each with three tiny diamonds at the top of the setting.

Steph was perusing the exquisite displays in the wall cases while I talked to Giano about what I wanted for Richard.

"I'm thinking of a small heart, flat-ish but three dimensional, not too much bigger than a quarter. I want to give him something he can carry in his pocket with his change. And I'd like it to be engravable, somehow. if that's pssoble."

"Ah," Giano said, and he disappeared again, only to return a moment later with two trays full of charms, all hearts, gold, silver, enameled, plain, and fancy with gems.

"These are to be worn on a necklace or bracelet, but I can modify any of them if you see something, you like."

I finally settled on a heart that was red enamel on the front, puffed a little, with sort of a net of silver lines with tiny gold beads where the lines intersected. The back was plain silver and flat.

"I can remove the bail, leaving just the little heart. What do you wish to have engraved?" He handed me a piece of paper on which to write the words.

Where'er you go, my heart goes with you, XXOOJ

I told Giano our plans and asked if I could pick it up next Thursday. I wanted to take it with us to the mystery location. I would save the candelabras for when we got home.

"And I want to put the heart on my Visa. The Amex for the earrings and something for Steph."

I treated Steph (via Richard of course, but I was pretty sure he wouldn't mind!) to a bangle bracelet with little amethysts (her birthstone) scattered all the way around. I wanted to celebrate her uber-productive summer. I didn't even bother to wonder if I was getting seduced by the idea of not looking at price tags. It was certainly less stressful!

Flame was everything Mark had said and more! Who knew what had happened in the candle-fire world since I'd last bought any candles? I realized I really had to get out more! We spent a couple of hours perusing the offerings and I finally narrowed it down to three choices.

"And why have you decided to give him a candelabra?" Steph asked.

"You're just wondering about this now?" I laughed.

"I was going to ask, but you know I sometimes find your reasoning inscrutable."

"Really?" I asked, innocently.

Steph sighed. "Does this mean you're not going to tell me?"

"When we were in New York, I asked Richard to play the piano for me. Long story short, he played a Liberace version of chopsticks that my dad used to play for me when I was a kid."

"And?" she prompted.

"And...when I was leaving the house this morning, Marie and Antonio were making space for a piano in the living room. Richard had asked them to bring one in. I assume it means he will play more in the future and I thought a candelabra would make him laugh." When she just shook her head, I added defensively, "He's not the easiest person to shop for, you know."

"And yet," she said, "You always seem to find the perfect thing."

"Not perfect yet. I can't decide. What do you think?"

I was down to a sort of French antique-looking (and maybe it was, if the price was any indication!) piece that was mostly black with gilt trim and the figure of a thinly clad woman holding a garland over her head with holders for three candles.

There was a set of three silver plated ones, each holding two candles. The bottom was a looped tube that curled up and around. You could use them individually or arrange them together in different combinations. The third choice was a sort of four legged, very modern thing that held two candles. What I liked about that one—*those* because I was thinking of three or four—was that they were shiny and came in gold, silver, hot pink, purple and orange. They reminded me of Jeff Koons' balloon pieces. I thought maybe since the New York trip, Jeff's work and the return to the keyboard were connected that might amuse him.

"I think you should eliminate the antique-y one. It doesn't really fit with the living room décor, in that the living room is more modern and sort of...I don't know...sort of neutral," Steph said. "I know the house has antiques mixed in, but I don't favor this one."

"Good point," I agreed. "The colored ones have the Koons association and if I got the pink, purple and orange, it would pick up the colors in that painting on that end of the room." I looked to Steph for confirmation.

"True. But the silver ones are really beautiful, and you could probably use them for other things if you wanted to."

She was right.

"When in doubt, go for beauty!" I gave her a high five. I handed her one, took two more and headed for the flameless candles. I was fascinated by the ones with the little wavering flame piece. They were SO real looking and eliminated the need to remember to blow them out! (My handsome lover and I did get distracted now and again!)

43

Home Again, Home Again

That same night

After dinner I retired to the library for Richard's wake-up call.

"Good morning, Sweetheart," he said sleepily when he answered.

"My Prince! Show yourself," I demanded, so he would turn on his camera, which he did with a click. I air-kissed my phone.

Richard laughed.

"So what have you been up to?" he asked.

"Spending your money," I answered casually.

"Good," he said with a stretch and a yawn. "Should I ask on what?"

"I drove Miyuki to pick up Steph, took us to lunch and then a little visit to Giano."

"Really?" He sounded genuinely surprised.

"Yup. I got a simple pair of pearl and diamond earrings to wear with my fabulous necklace and swan when they're pretending to be fake. And I bought Steph a bangle bracelet. I guarantee you will be stunned by what she's done. Can't wait for you to see it."

"Can you schedule a visit to the studio before we go to your folks? I imagine Steph will be anxious to know what I think."

"Already on the calendar."

"I have a few things to add, too. Can I call you from the treadmill?"

"Of course. You know I enjoy watching you sweat."

For a minute he just looked at me.

"I love you but, honestly, you are a little odd," he said.

"*Moi?*"

"*Toi*," he confirmed.

I gave him a very distressed expression. "Is your interest waning, Mr. Hunter?" (I saw the love in his eyes. I wasn't really worried.)

"Nope. I become more fascinated by the hour."

"Good. I'm not sure I could back away from living the high life at this point."

"I doubt you'd have to. Your bank account is bound to be expanding very soon."

"Oh, goody! You can be my official Boy Toy."

"It's the job I was born for," he said with conviction.

"I would never argue that point. And we could go on…but I'm wondering what I might do for you to start your morning."

"Ummm…I think a hand job would do me today. I need to get moving."

"Do you want my help or is it a DIY project?"

Richard laughed. "Give me your hand," he said.

"Here, " I said reaching toward the phone. "Wrap your hand around mine and show me what you want me to do. And let me watch," I added.

He made quick work of it. I was impressed.

"Well that was short and sweet. How do you do that?" I asked.

Richard laughed. "Years of practice."

"Do you masturbate?"

"What? I assume you didn't have your eyes closed just now. And you may recall your 'study' awhile back."

I sighed. "I know. But I mean regularly. Even when we're together?" It was something I'd always meant to ask him. He seemed to have so much control regardless of the situation. He could go for a very long time, or come pretty quickly, as he'd just done. "I'm just curious, wondering if it was a long term training thing."

Richard got out of bed, taking the phone with him, then setting it on the chair as he pulled on his shorts for his workout.

"I usually masturbate twice a day, even when we're together. It gives me more options and keeps everything working properly. I want to be sure I don't disappoint you." He smiled and zapped me.

"As if you could. Have I mentioned how much I love you?"

"Not yet, but give me about five minutes and I'll FaceTime you back from the laptop on the treadmill. I look forward to hearing you expound on that very subject."

With a click he was gone

When he called back, I requested an explanation for the piano.

"Explain? Well, it a musical instrument that creates sound by the striking of hammers on strings, all via a keyboard," he said quite earnestly.

"Fascinating," I replied sarcastically. "Actually, my query was focused on the beautiful instrument that arrived yesterday and now resides just outside the door to the library." I pointed toward the living room.

"Oh, *that* piano. Actually, it's been in storage. I thought you might want me to play for you while you work."

"Yes!" I shouted as I jumped up out of my chair and did a little happy dance.

Richard was laughing.

"Sweetheart, there's no way I can tell you how much it means to me to have my music back. I doubt it would ever have happened without you."

"Nah...you would have realized you were only punishing yourself for no reason and found your way back to it on your own."

"Maybe, but thanks for sparing me all those wasted years."

"You can thank me by filling our house with music."

For a moment he didn't say anything.

"What?" I asked.

"You just said 'our' house."

I couldn't read him. Was he happy or annoyed?

"Should I have said 'your' house where I'm likely to spend the rest of my life? And by the way, I'm assuming you're not going to kick me to the curb any time soon. After all, I do have my own closet now. It's certainly worth fighting for!"

"Cress, it just made me really happy to hear you call the house 'ours.' I'm very glad you feel that way."

"I told you, I think you've finally turned me. I'm into the lifestyle now. 'Not sure I could find my way back out."

"No need to try. But there is a need to look at our schedules again. Have you got your calendar?"

And so it was back to business, trying to work in all the things that had to be done between his homecoming and us leaving again for Washington.

Tuesday, October 1

Last Note in Paris:

He is the happiest, be he king or peasant, who finds peace in his home.
—Johann Wolfgang von Goethe

That goes for Princes, too! XXOOJ

Richard's flight was due to land at LAX at 9:40 p.m. on Tuesday night. I was trying to think of some special way to welcome him home. I pondered going to the airport in my *You Can Leave Your Hat On* outfit. Antonio told me that Richard had instructed him to pick him up, but that I was welcome to come along. (He told me it wasn't a good idea to change Richard's plans without permission!) And then I thought maybe I should just be waiting in the bedroom in my server outfit. But his flight was non-stop and eleven and a half hours long, so I had no idea what sort of jet lag he would be dealing with. Would he want sex, dinner, or sleep? Or maybe all three? Me, I was looking forward to a serious hug! Beyond that, anything my Prince wanted was good with me.

So that's what I was thinking about that afternoon as I was lizarding on a chaise by the pool. I was very pleased with myself having done two rungs on the salmon ladder that morning in what I imagined was pretty perfect form. (Ji had convinced me that performing two perfectly for Richard would be more impressive than three not-so-perfect attempts.) I was dozing when I heard a splash.

"Hey, Steph," I called out, not bothering to open my eyes. "You're home early."

She didn't respond, probably didn't hear me, so I drifted off again. Next thing I knew cold water was dripping on me!

"Hey!" I said, laughing as I sat up, expecting to see Steph.

"Hey, yourself," Richard said with a smile.

"My Prince!" I squealed. "What are you doing here?" I asked, taking the hand he offered.

"I live here. At least I used to," he said as he pulled me against his cold wet body and gave me a kiss.

I was laughing, so happy to find his arms around me despite the chill.

"I'm hoping you still do. You're just the guy I want to share this magnificent house with…especially if you're good in bed and can play the piano."

"Well, we'll see about that. You can let me know if I'm what you had in mind, later."

"Can't wait to study your qualifications."

He laughed and kissed me again.

"So you caught an earlier flight?" I asked as he took my hand and led me upstairs.

"Yup. I left at 10:45 this morning and after eleven and a half hours landed at 1:00 this afternoon. At least we beat the traffic home, though I did have Antonio take me by your billboard," he said with a quick kiss to my cheek. "Just beautiful"

"All thanks to you, Magic Man."

"I had nothing to do with it," he said, sounding surprised that I attributed my super model fame to him.

"Really? If Giano didn't love you, I never would have met him. If you hadn't taken me to the event, I never would have been modeling that necklace. And without you, I never would have had that billboard-worthy expression for the camera to catch."

He smiled at me as we went into the bathroom. When he reached to dial up our friend Zarathustra I told him I'd pre-programmed the music for him.

"Good, then I guess we'd better get you out of this suit and into the water so I can hear what you selected."

He kissed me, at the same time untying the string around my

neck. Gently, he peeled down both sides of the bikini top and took a moment to admire my breasts. He cupped them gently and let his thumbs caress my nipples before his eyes returned to mine.

"I've missed you, Cress."

"I've missed you more," I said, stepping closer and slipping my fingers into the waistband of his trunks and running them slowly back and forth, just at the top of his pubic hair. I slid my hands around to the back as I pressed myself against him and slowly eased the elastic down over that perfect round ass of his, pausing to give him a squeeze.

We were kissing and Richard unhooked the back of my top and dropped it to the floor. His hands glided down my back, and into my bikini bottom, squeezing me just as I was squeezing him.

I laughed and stepped back, pulling out the front of his trunks and looking in.

"See anything you like?" he asked with a smirk.

"You betcha! Let's get your suit off and see if we can work with that."

Richard snorted and I slipped his trunks down and got on my knees to help him step out of them. That lovely tumescent cock of his was in my face. I smiled up at him and stuck out my tongue, giving him a couple of light strokes across the tip and then a quick suck that startled him.

"I think we'd better get in the shower," he said, taking my elbows and helping me to my feet.

As the water came on and reached the proper temperature The Supremes began to sing *I Hear a Symphony*. Richard pulled me into his arms and we danced a bit. As he swung me around I grabbed the shower gel and squirted some across his shoulders and started to rub it into his chest and belly with one hand, the other still on his shoulder. He kept dancing, one arm around me, but open so I could continue to soap him. I stroked his soapy penis that was more than ready for business. He pulled me against him and slipped between my legs, sliding back and forth at the top of my thighs in time with the music.

"Are you going to tease me or fuck me?" I whispered against his ear.

He grabbed my bottom and lifted me, settling me down on him in one smooth move as my legs wrapped tightly around his hips. I squeaked a bit at the suddenness of it and he laughed.

"FYI, I chose 'fuck'," he whispered into my ear as he eased me against the water wall, balancing me as he ran his hands down the front of my body. Then he grasped my hips firmly and began to stroke me.

God! It was so good to feel him inside me again as he skillfully led me into that rolling orgasm with the water cascading around me.

"I love watching you come," he said as he continued moving,

"Come for me, Handsome, I want to feel every pulse. I love you so much!"

And he did, his eyes never leaving mine. We were both grinning like fools.

"Joy?" I asked as he relaxed and moved more slowly.

"Absolutely. It's so good to be home." He held me tightly for a couple of minutes before setting me back on my feet.

As we dried each other I asked if he was thinking about a nap.

"I can't even imagine how confusing the time thing must be for your body," I told him. "I can leave you alone if you want to sleep."

"If I sleep now I'll be wide awake about the time you're ready for bed. I'm thinking more like a nice glass of wine with a cuddle in the library." He kissed my cheek.

"Your wish is my command, my sweet Prince." I gave one of his nipples a quick lick, which cracked him up.

"Have you always been so oral?" he asked as he followed me into our closets.

I turned back with a frown. "That's the second time you've mentioned it. Am I overdoing it?"

"Only an idiot would complain," he said. "I'm so grateful, but I'm also curious."

I slipped into one of my elastic top dresses while Richard pulled on those dangerous grey sweats. What an incredibly beautiful man!

"Cress?"

I realized I'd been distracted by his physical perfection.

"Sorry. Oral. Well, I've always been willing to engage in a little cock sucking, especially since I expect a little oral action in return—turnabout being fair play and all," I said as we started down the stairs. "Though I have to say it's not always as nice as it should be—either way." I shook my head. "But with you, it's different. I'm simply compelled to devour you!"

Richard laughed.

"Seriously!" I insisted. " I don't know how to describe it. I want my mouth all over you. Of course you are delicious, as I've told you many times. And I love that gorgeous cock in my mouth in all its manifestations. But I have to keep myself from using my tongue on every part of you from your hair to your fuzzy cheeks, to those beautiful abs, your ass, your balls, the backs of your knees, your ankles, and I haven't done any serious toe sucking yet.... You have no idea the amount of restraint I exercise when we're together."

Richard was shaking his head as we reached the bottom of the stairs.

"If I'm going to be your Boy Toy, please feel free to do with me as you will. I have a little request of my own before we go to see your folks." He added a wink.

"Can't wait!" I said, wondering what new delight he had in mind.

"First some wine." He kissed me and headed for the kitchen as I turned toward the library.

We were at the table on the balcony, enjoying our wine and the fading light in the sky when Steph joined us. Richard stood and pulled out her chair before giving her a hug.

"Welcome home," she said.

"It's very good to be back. I hear you have a lot to show me tomorrow," he told her as he poured her a glass of wine.

"I certainly do, I'm just hoping you like it as much as we do."

"And if I don't?"

He said it with a perfectly straight face, which I could see unnerved Steph. For a moment she looked stricken and then realized it was a little cosmic test. She smiled.

"Your loss, I guess. Someone out there is bound to recognize my greatness!"

Richard smiled broadly, nodding as he raised his glass. "To your greatness!"

Richard was tired and we made an early night of it. We made love quietly and I held him as he fell asleep, his cheek pressed against my heart. When I carefully turned away from him, he reached out and pulled me against him, settling with his chest pressed against my back. So much nicer than my pillow. Warmer, too!

That delightful nudge woke me and made me glance at the clock, assuming it was the middle of the night. The clock said 4:00 a.m. and I smiled.

"You're early my Prince," I said.

"More time for us," he whispered with a kiss to the back of my neck.

"Does this mean I can play a bit?" I said turning my head.

"Boy Toy reporting for extended wake up call," he said rolling onto his back, arms thrown wide.

"Hmmm..." I said sleepily. "Well, let me see what you have on offer."

I flipped the covers back, exposing his very hard penis. It was still dark but the ambient light from the landscaping gave me a clear view.

"Oh, my," I said, as I slowly slipped my hand around his cock and pulled him perpendicular, but when I released him, he snapped back against his belly with an interesting thud. "I'm not sure I can work with that," I said skeptically.

"Try," he suggested rather pointedly.

"Hmmmm...." I mumbled as I straddled his thighs.

I slipped both hands under his scrotum and gently massaged his balls with a thumb on each, working in circles. Richard was watching me. I just smiled and returned to my study of his genitals.

I tugged his balls down, then pressed them up against his cock as I eased his legs apart and settled on my stomach between them, perfectly positioned to tease my tongue against that little spot behind his scrotum. I alternated my tongue and my finger pressing him there, assuming it was giving his prostate a little wake up call. Something was happening because my Boy Toy was making some soft sounds of pleasure.

I wiggled up a little farther, smoothing his balls back down and running my fingers up his cock. Richard wrapped his legs around me, running his heels slowly back and forth under my buttocks. I tried to stand his cock up again but it was very stiff and tight to his belly. I didn't want to hurt him.

"I don't know, Handsome, I think you're either going to have to play doggie, or…wait…"

Richard chuckled, awaiting my next move.

I turned and straddled his belly, facing away from him and he groaned as if I weighed a ton. It made me laugh as I leaned back and scooted forward until the tip of his cock was touching a very wet portion of my anatomy. I held him and rubbed him up and down my folds, massaging my clit, very slowly.

I felt his hands on my hips, urging me closer.

I spread his legs, putting my feet between them so I could slide down onto him. Richard groaned. I pressed his legs wider as I spread my own and lay back against his chest. He wrapped his arms around me, one just below my breasts, the other across my pubic bone, cupping me, his fingers on my clit, and feeling himself at the same time.

He began stroking me, setting his own pace as his hips moved beneath me. I couldn't move on my own and it was glorious to just lie there and have him fuck me! I had one hand over his and with the other I reached up behind his neck.

"You beautiful girl," he whispered against my ear. "You feel so good."

"So do you," I said breathlessly as his speed increased.

I came suddenly and cried out even as he followed with sort of soft grunt, that changed to a breathless "Oh!" He was motionless for a few moments and I felt that wonderful sensation of the pulse of his ejaculation in time with the beat of his heart.

We stayed that way for a few minutes, his fingers moving gently over my skin, tenderly massaging my breasts, sliding up and down between my legs where we were still joined.

Finally he said, "I think I know what you mean when you say you just want to devour me."

"Kinda hard for you to do much with that skilled mouth of yours in this position."

"True. But if there was just some way to absorb you, just totally take you into myself... It's an odd sensation."

"But one I understand completely," I said. "Maybe it's like that twin soul thing you sent me way back when. The quote from the sci-fi book."

"I remember," he said.

"Maybe we're just one soul, split into two on this plane and desperately trying to become one again."

Just then the alarm buzzed. He never set the alarm.

"The alarm? Really?"

"I wasn't sure if I'd oversleep and we have a big day ahead of us."

"Are you telling me I need to move?" I asked.

"Probably. I'm not sure I could get us both on our feet in this position."

"Try," I dared.

Before I knew what was happening he pulled me tight against him, swung our legs to the side of the bed and stood up. I was so surprised I started laughing and lost what was left of him. I turned to him and threw my arms around his neck.

"Magic Man, indeed," I said, with a kiss to his fuzzy cheek

44
Celebration

Wednesday, October 2

My handsome lover was suitably impressed with my perfectly executed (if I do say so myself!) exhibition on the salmon ladder that morning, so I was feeling great as I drove to Steph's studio about ten minutes ahead of Richard and Mark. I was hoping to have a calming effect on her if she needed one.

"Yoo-hoo?" I called out as I came in the door. "Any great artists here?"

"Just one," Steph replied. "Come here and tell me what you think." She was standing in the center of the room, looking at the row of botanicals. "I've arranged them more or less in the order I painted them, thinking it shows the transitions as my style developed. Now I'm second guessing myself and wondering if arranging them by color across the spectrum would be more impressive."

"You know I'm not the person to ask, but I like seeing where you've been and where you're going. Richard might be more impressed looking at it from that angle."

"Good," she said. "I left the calendars like they were the other day when you were here. I think they make more sense chronologically."

I agreed and asked if she was nervous.

"Yes. Of course, but even if Richard doesn't feel my work is right for his gallery, I think it makes a pretty impressive presentation. I'm convinced I can get a show somewhere."

"Good girl!" I said and gave her a hug.

"The biggest problem is where am I going to store all these if I have to be out of here in a few weeks?"

"I'm sure Richard will give you warehouse space—you can certainly have what I'm using. I need to get it cleaned out, anyway. I know he won't leave you high and dry, no matter what he thinks of your work."

Just then we heard a car pull up in back. By the time Steph got to the door, a second engine shut off.

"Are you ready?" Richard asked as he came in.

Mark was right behind him and they were both smiling. I think I may have been more nervous than Steph was, but I really don't know why. She was right: If her work wasn't right for Richard, there was no doubt she'd find a gallery.

"As I'll ever be," Steph assured him. "Just promise me you'll give me an honest opinion. No blue sky."

He laughed. "Don't worry. Business is business." He put his hand on her shoulder and I saw her wobble just a little. "Show me."

Steph led him back and gestured toward the wall of paintings. Richard looked from them to her and smiled.

"You've been busy," he said.

"Had to make hay while the sun was shining on this space."

Richard's eyes were glued to the paintings and he moved closer, Mark following to stand just behind him while Steph hung back with me.

My phone rang, and I turned away, walking back toward the door so I wouldn't disrupt the proceedings. It was a FaceTime call from "M. Hunter."

Curious, I accepted, wondering if it might be Robert despite the "M." Instead the face on the screen was a woman that I realized must be Richard's mother! I ducked into the studio's bedroom. As I closed the door I could see Steph looking at me with concern, but I shook my head to let her know everything was OK.

"*Madame*?" My voice wavered a little which annoyed me. Confronted by the Dragon Lady herself, I certainly didn't want to appear weak!

"Miss Bailey, please forgive me for disturbing you."

She was a beautiful woman. It was easy to see that she was a major contributor to Richard's genetic perfection.

"Please, call me CJ. Richard is here, do you need to speak to him?"

"No, it was you I was seeking. And you must call me Madeleine."

"Thank you," was all I could think of to say. My mind was whirling, trying to imagine why she'd called.

"I was going to write to you, but I wanted to introduce myself since Richard (she said *Ree-chard*) has failed to do so. I feel it is very important to tell you in person how grateful I am that you have encouraged him to return to the piano."

I smiled. Not so much the Dragon Lady, after all!

"I can't really take credit. As I said to him just yesterday, I'm sure he would have come to it on his own."

"It has been many years, so I do not know how long it might have taken had you not been there to influence him."

"I don't know what to say."

"No need to say anything," she said returning my smile. "You have made my son very happy and I just wanted to let you know that I'm more grateful than you might imagine. He is such a good boy and he deserves the best. It seems he has found that in you."

"He is wonderful, Madeleine, truly. I'm sure you're very proud of him. And thank you for saying such nice things."

The love she had for Richard showed in her eyes. Why was everyone afraid of her? Mee-Cha was right, Richard's mother was obviously direct, but that was something I understood.

"I sincerely hope that we will have the opportunity to meet in person very soon," she said. Her tone left no doubt that it would happen

"Thank you. And thank you for calling. I'm very pleased to meet you. You've raised some exceptional men in Robert and Richard and I look forward to meeting Cybelle and Grégoire, as well. I hope it won't be too long before we can get together."

"*Au revoir*," she said as she signed off.

I went back into the main room and rejoined Steph.

"Everything OK?" she asked.

"Yup. It was Richard's mother."

Her eyes widened, a question behind her look.

"Tell ya later," I said, turning my attention to Mark and Richard as they moved along the wall of paintings, stopping to comment and discuss—*sotto voce*, mind you.

"Any clue what they're saying?" I asked.

"No, but this much discussion must be a good thing…at least I hope it is!"

"It has to be," I agreed. "If he didn't like them, I think it would have been obvious by now." I put my arm around her shoulder and gave her a squeeze.

We watched as they reached the end of the line of canvasses and Mark directed Richard's attention to the other side of the room where the calendar paintings were displayed. Richard was obviously surprised. As he crossed the room, Mark signaled us to join them.

Richard smiled broadly at Steph. "All those botanicals weren't enough?"

"You know how it is with us creative types," Steph said. "When the muse arrives, you have to dance with her."

"Give him your rundown on these," Mark said.

Steph launched into the idea behind the first one and led him through the months of the year. When she finished, Mark talked about his idea for them to be hung all on one wall in a block.

Richard turned to Steph, took her hands and pulled her close enough to kiss her cheek.

"Congratulations. Your work is outstanding! I'd be honored if you'd allow us to represent you."

She pulled her hands from his and threw them around his neck for a big hug, that he returned with a laugh, as he lifted little Steph off her feet.

"Is this a good time to ask if I can have the studio a little longer?"

"Probably," he replied as he looked to Mark.

"Stakoulik won't be here until January 11. It's wide open," Mark said. He was grinning, too.

"Then it's yours until the end of December," Richard said. "I want to see those calendars finished."

Steph turned to me for a high five.

"Can I take you all to dinner tonight to celebrate?" Richard asked.

"I'll check with Michael," Steph said, "I'm sure he wouldn't want to miss it."

"I know Sam's free," Mark said. "We'd love to join you."

Richard glanced at his watch. "We need to get back to the gallery. We'll be in touch about time and place for tonight."

STILL LUCKY

I walked to the door with Richard, behind Mark and Steph.

"Is everything, OK?" he asked. "I saw you got a call."

"Oh, it was nothing," I said nonchalantly. "Just your mother FaceTiming me."

Richard's eyebrows shot up in surprise.

"I'll tell you about it when you get home this afternoon." I gave him a quick kiss on the cheek and he was out the door.

I turned back to Steph. "Looks like all this rich girl practice is about to pay off!"

Richard took us to Melisse for dinner. I don't even know where I could begin to describe the event—and believe me, that's what it was! Sinceriously, it was the most amazing dining experience of my life and word girl though I am, this is so beyond my descriptive abilities that I can only suggest you go online and read about it, see the pictures of what we ate and turn green with envy. (Or make a reservation for yourself and prepare for something fabtastic!)

It was a wonderful evening with friends. We dined through many courses and multiple wine pairings over the space of three hours as we celebrated Steph's triumph and Richard's return. We added toasts to a lucrative new account Michael had bagged and a recent promotion for Sam. I could only claim "some interest" in my project. I hadn't shared the details with anyone but Richard, not wanting to jinx what seemed at that point to be my own good fortune.

Richard talked about Steph's work and gave her a serious Trained Professional evaluation—which Mark added to—before suggesting a February show date, which struck her as a suitable way to mark her twenty-fourth birthday. It left Steph glowing. Really, the evening couldn't have been more perfect.

On the way home I was holding Richard's hand between gear shifting, mesmerized by the lights of the traffic and suffused with a feeling of immense gratitude, not only for lacking nothing (my usual mantra) but for another magical evening, courtesy of the man I loved and our friends. I couldn't understand how I could be so lucky, but I was thankful for all of it.

"Thank you, my Prince, for another magnificent evening. It is impossible to explain how grateful I am for your love."

"Ditto," he said with a squeeze of my hand before he downshifted as the line of cars slowed for a red light.

When we stopped, he turned to me and smiled.

"Interested in a little spa time when we get home?" he asked.

"Yes, please." That sounded like a great idea. I was already feeling so happy and relaxed that hot water would just put a cherry on top of the whole night.

He handed me his phone so I could start the water heating for us.

"I need you to tell me some things about your mother," I said as I punched the screen.

"Like...?"

"Things she likes or is interested in. I want to drop her a note thanking her for introducing herself and I'd like to add a touch of something she'll appreciate."

"I'm still surprised she called you. That's not like her," he said.

"Well, from what you've told me, you haven't had any serious girlfriends for her to try to make a connection with...unless of course there are a few you forgot to mention?"

Richard chuckled. "No girlfriends. I guess you're right. How could I know how she would act with a woman I was interested in?" He looked over at me. "Good call."

"How is she with Robert's wife?"

"They seem to have a good relationship. Maman is not a...a warm person. As I told you before, she's reserved. Not cold, mind you, she just seems to hold herself back when she interacts with people. Some people think she's a snob, but that's not it. I think my father's infidelities hurt her deeply, though I never saw anything overt— no fighting or arguments. There just seemed to be love missing from her life.

"When I was young I tried very hard to please her. That's how the piano started for me. She wanted it, and I wanted to make her happy. Of course then I loved it, and it consumed my life. And I loved Maryse. I'm afraid my concerns for my mother fell by the wayside in those years."

I could see this bothered him.

"She must have been very proud of you."

"Oh, she was. But as I got older, my father made more demands on her time—he required her as a hostess for his business concerns—and she didn't attend as many of my performances." He paused for a moment.

"It's fortunate you weren't an only child," I told him. "She still had Cybelle and Grégoire to fill her life."

He looked at me and smiled. A little sadly, I thought.

"Maman wasn't too hands-on with any of us. We weren't ignored, but there was staff to deal with us, private schools, in my case a career. I think what my mother valued most in her life was her relationship with my father. By the time I was twelve she must have decided she'd had enough and as I told you, they divorced when I was fifteen. I think he broke her heart."

I put my hand on his arm. "I'm so sorry. My parents—well, you'll see when you meet them—still love each other very much. Despite their careers, their relationship is the center of their lives." And then I laughed. "At least that's my take on it. They're like us, Handsome. Very, very lucky."

"Very lucky," he said with a smile as he turned into the driveway at the house.

"So what about the man in your mother's life now? Henri, is it? You said he wants to marry her."

"The consensus among the siblings is that she does love him and it's pretty obvious that he's crazy about her, but we all feel that she's holding herself back. Cybelle thinks she's afraid of being hurt again. I honestly don't see enough of either of them to have a real understanding of their relationship, but I can say they both seem happy. Maman seems to think it's enough, so who am I to judge?"

"Not your circus, not your monkeys?" I suggested.

Richard laughed. "Exactly."

"So tell me what sort of photos you were thinking of for tomorrow?" Richard said as he extended his hand to help me down into the bubbling heat of the spa.

"Hmmmm…." I closed my eyes, enjoying the sensation as the

water engulfed me. I stood in the center of the deeper end, the water just covering my breasts, and let my arms float free while Richard settled himself on the seat along the edge. After about a minute I joined him. I kissed his cheek as I sat down and let my legs float up.

"Pictures?" he prompted.

I looked at him blankly and then refocused.

"Well, I'm thinking we should have a few different shots, you in a tie and jacket, in some sexy silk sweater, maybe that cashmere hoodie with no shirt, jeans for sure."

"And why do you want these, again?"

"Because you're beautiful. Something for my art collection."

"You told me for friends and family," he reminded me.

"If I recall that was my response to you accusing me of leading you down the slippery slope into porn…you know, that place where you keep telling me I have a rosy future."

Richard laughed and put his arm around me, pulling me closer.

"What I said was that your sexual skills would guarantee you a lucrative career. And honestly, it is really about the delight you express so freely in things sexual between us."

I sighed and rolled my eyes. "I keep telling you: you're delightful, hence my delight. A simple equation."

Richard just shook his head.

"But seriously," I continued, "I would like a couple of shots of us together. I want to see the same look on your face that I have on that billboard."

He gave me that exact look, an expression so full of love that my eyes began to fill.

"Yeah, that one. I want to see if Seiji can catch it. But apparently you can produce it at will, so the shoot should go quickly."

"And I'd like a photo of you with your short hair," he said. "Are you still loving it?"

"I am. I'm not looking to grow it out any time soon."

"Good," he said.

That surprised me. "Why good?"

"I loved your hair long, don't misunderstand. But I have to say I enjoy seeing more of your beautiful face when you're sucking my cock."

I pretended to be scandalized as I splashed him and started to get up, but he laughed and grabbed for me, spun me around and pulled me onto his lap.

"And what about me?" he asked. "Shall I shave?"

He rubbed his fuzzy cheek against my breast and got me laughing and wiggling as I attempted to break free. As I squirmed I felt some movement below. I stopped and gave him a squinty-eyed appraisal.

"Is this an inducement to intercourse, sir?"

"Do you need an inducement?" he asked.

"Yes," I said seriously. "Kiss me and let me think about it."

And he did. And he kept kissing me, finally shifting me a little to free his erection. Lips still joined, I got to my feet and pulled him along until I could position him on one of those convenient pillar seats. This got us both laughing because I was trying to see where I was going while kissing him and the lip-lock-eyes-open thing created some very odd visuals.

I pushed on his shoulders and he sat.

"Still wanna fuck me?" I asked.

Richard surveyed our surroundings critically and with a sigh said, "Might as well, there doesn't seem to be anything else going on."

He sounded so bored I cracked up. And him telling me I had all the acting talent! I also noticed he was stroking himself and fondling his balls. I was standing in front of him, just out of reach.

"There's probably something worth watching on TV," I suggested reasonably. "Shall we go check it out?"

"Nah. But would you come a little closer and turn around?"

I smirked. "Having trouble getting in the mood?" (Hardly! He knew I could see he was more than up to the job!)

"I'm just not sure I remember how this goes. Come here and let's see if it comes back to me. I heard someone say it's like riding a bicycle."

"Really?" I said, trying to keep a straight face as I turned my back to him.

"I guess we'll find out."

He put his hands on my hips and made a show of getting me in exactly the position he pretended to be looking for.

His hands slid up and moved slightly forward, his fingers teasing the undersides of my breasts for a moment before slipping back down to my waist. His thumbs caressed the spots where my Dolly Dimples would be if I had them. (Damn! His were so perfect!)

"I seem to remember that somewhere around here…" He began to caress my buttocks, squeezing gently and working his hands in circles, very slowly.

"Yes?" I whispered, absorbed in the sensations. If we hadn't been in the water I would have been very wet on my own!

"There was some sort of way to…" Richard was giving a really good performance as a man who was trying very hard to remember how to do something. What a guy! I stifled a giggle.

His hands moved down a little as he grasped my thighs, his thumbs running back and forth along the curve of my bottom, that special place that I loved to have him touch me.

"I like the shape of you," he said clinically.

"Thanks."

"Maybe…"

One of his hands moved to my hip, the other burrowed between my legs tentatively. His fingers moved, seeking entrance but tapped here and there as if he wasn't exactly sure where his target might be. Finally, he slipped the tip of his finger into me.

"Oh!" He sounded surprised. Then after a moment of silence while he moved his finger around a little (just the end of it, mind you) he said. "Well, this isn't going to work." He sighed with dramatic disappointment and removed his hand.

I turned to face him, my own hands on my hips.

"And that would be because…?"

He was playing shy, not meeting my eyes. (He probably couldn't have managed to keep a straight face if he looked at me!) His hands were moving slowly beneath the water, stroking his penis.

"Well, I have this…this… It will never fit in there."

I clamped my teeth together and pursed my lips to keep from laughing.

"Are you sure?" I asked.

He reached for my hand and wrapped it around his cock.

"If my finger barely fits, how could I get this part of me in there?"

I began stroking him.

"I see what you mean," I said with great concern. "Still, I

have an idea." I took his hands and placed them around the base of his penis, holding him upright. I moved forward, straddling him, my breasts in his face. His brows arched in surprise, as if he had no idea they were there for his pleasure as well as my own.

"Are you ready?" I asked, putting both hands on his shoulders.

"I…I guess so."

"Now, hang on tight and don't move." With that, I slowly lowered myself onto him.

"Oh!" he said, as if it were a surprise.

He didn't move his hands, so he was only partially inside of me. He looked up at me in complete innocence, but I could see he was having as much trouble keeping up the ruse as I was.

"Uh, Richard…"

"What?"

"You can let go now."

"Are you sure?"

"I am. And you might want to suck on this," I said pressing my breast against his mouth as his hands moved to my bottom and I slid all the way down on him (accompanied by my usual gasp!) I began moving up and down.

"How does that feel?" I asked.

"It's all coming back to me now," he said with a growl.

He stood up and moved with me to the edge of the pool, bracing me against the wall and gaining some leverage to slowly push himself deep inside me.

"See?" I said breathlessly. "You fit perfectly."

"That's because you're perfect, Sweetheart. Never doubt it."

He kissed me, and kissed me some more. And more after that, as he stroked me off into that amazing place where my orgasms ebbed and flowed with the tide of love he brought me.

45
Spoiled Rotten

Thursday, October 3

Thursday morning after breakfast we threw a couple of changes of clothes into a garment bag and left for our photo shoot. Richard had his hair cut the day before (I loved it short and teddy-bear-fur-like!) and had trimmed his beard back a little so it was more just the five o'clock shadow thing. I knew he was indulging me with the photos, but he also said he needed some new headshots for publicity, so he wasn't really dragging his feet.

Seiji had taken my advice. When we arrived at his studio, there were six large prints from his series displayed along the wall where his big flat screen monitor hung.

I made the introductions and I swear Seiji wobbled a bit when he shook Richard's hand!

"Looks like you've printed some of your photos, " I said, moving toward the wall. The images were absolutely beautiful.

Richard followed me, equally intrigued.

"Seiji was working on this series when he took those shots of me," I explained to Richard. "But I see you've expanded it a bit," I said smiling at Seiji.

Richard began to discuss the work and while they talked I took our things to hang them in the dressing room. When I came back, Seiji had the flat screen working and was running through the photos, showing Richard the more distant shots that revealed the origin. I noticed that along with the female shots (that were me), the more distant shots still weren't identifiable. There was also a black body in the mix now.

"Is that Ji?" I asked.

Seiji smiled. "It is. Thanks so much for hooking us up. He's a great guy."

Richard gave my shoulder a squeeze.

I had to school my expression when that weird shot of the space between my toes came up. It was amazing. And Seiji had turned it so my toes pointed down (the tips of my actual toes didn't show, mind you) which made a sort of triangle shape of negative space pointing upward in the photo. (Do you think my Trained Professional's jargon may be rubbing off on me?) It reminded me of the arch at Window Rock in Arizona.

"We're going to be traveling for the next two or three weeks," Richard said to Seiji, "But I'd really like to talk to you more about these when we get back."

I could tell Seiji was thrilled, but he managed to keep a professional expression on his face.

"I'd really appreciate your input," he told Richard. "But I think we'd best get started on your shots."

Seiji took a lot of photos, working more candid than posed. We did a few of just Richard in a sports coat and suit coat and tie, for both his art and wine businesses. When it was the two of us, Richard was commenting to me softly as we went along, cracking me up and making it very difficult for me to keep a semi-straight face. Funny boy, my Prince.

There were a few changes of clothes: him in that silk sweatshirt, my favorite hoodie, a V-neck Tshirt, me in a matching Tshirt, a halter dress—I even brought that beautiful nightie from New York and got some of me in that and him with his shirt off in just his jeans. Richard made me take my shirt off for the last few shots, though he held me against him so I wasn't really exposed. There were even a couple of kisses Seiji caught along with the laughter.

Driving back to the gallery I had to ask what Richard thought of Seiji's work.

"I'm really impressed," he said. "Why didn't you tell me that you'd modeled for him?"

His tone was neutral, unreadable. He was busy weaving through the traffic so I couldn't see his eyes.

"How could you tell?" I asked, surprised.

He turned to smile at me briefly. "I'd recognize your toes anywhere, Sweetheart. You have very singular feet."

"What?"

"Your feet—they're exceptionally well formed."

I cracked up. *"Well-formed?"*

Richard laughed. "You always tell me I can't see myself as I am. You, apparently, can't see your feet." He gave me a quick wink.

"They're just feet," I insisted.

"You need to start taking a closer look at other women's feet. Bunions, toes squeezed to a point by fashionable shoes…there's nothing wrong with any of those things, it's just that your feet are sort of…pristine."

"Must be my lifelong aversion to uncomfortable shoes and my lack of concern for fashion."

Richard shook his head. "Must be. But the question was: why didn't you mention modeling for Seiji?"

"First, he wanted to approach you professionally when he had work to show you. He intended to ask Mark to see if he could get an appointment. Then when he did my photos, we decided on a trade and that's how I had credit for his efforts today. And I did get a confidentiality agreement with him to protect you from the scandal of my intimate poses." When Richard didn't say anything, I asked if it bothered him.

He gave me a look. He was smiling. "Hardly. I like hanging out with a supermodel."

"Well, this supermodel likes hanging out with you."

I dropped Richard at the gallery and took his car (Poldi) with a plan to pick him up in the afternoon. I had lunch with Steph, then stopped by to pick up my little heart from Giano. He wasn't there, but it was ready and waiting for me. Then I went home to pack.

Richard called at 4:00 p.m. to say he wouldn't be ready to leave work for another two hours.

"Want to pick me up and I'll take you out to dinner?"

"Perfect," I told him. "I'll let Marie know."

"See you then, Sweetheart."

Over dinner Richard told me he had decided we'd take Giano's jet to Walla Walla.

"La-dee-dah," I was my reaction.

He chuckled. "Anything to cut our travel time. I've had enough commercial flights for awhile."

"Does that change our departure time?"

"I'll talk to Giano later. If anything, I imagine we could go a little earlier, have more time to get settled before we go to your folks."

And that's what we did.

We had a smooth flight with Captain Santorelli at the controls and arrived around noon.

My folks weren't expecting us until four-ish so I took him to Brasserie Four, thinking he'd appreciate the wine selection and the French food, which was, by the way, delicious!

We drove around a little so I could show him the lay of the land and then checked into our suite at the Marcus Whitman.

"I was thinking," Richard said as we unpacked, "If you wouldn't mind staying with your father tomorrow, I'll ask your grandmother if she wants to go with me to the vineyard. She could do some wine tasting while I have my meeting and it would give me some time to get to know her better."

I just stopped what I was doing and looked at him.

"What?" he said when I didn't respond. "I know she likes wine, she told me so in one of our online conversations."

"She does. And I know she'd be hugely flattered by the invitation. What made you think of that?"

"You said she'd been basically running your father's rehab and that she was doing a spectacular job. I thought she'd enjoy a break and I didn't think you'd mind standing in for her. Was I wrong?"

I walked over to him and just stood there.

"Are you ever wrong?" I asked, very seriously.

He burst out laughing. "Oh, yes," he assured me. "More often than I like to admit."

I gave him a squinty look of speculation. "If that's true, you hide it well."

He pulled me into his arms and gave me a big hug.

"You see?" he whispered. "I have you completely bamboozled. With luck I'll be able to keep you that way."

I pressed myself more tightly against him.

"I'm looking forward to some of that bamboozling when we get back to the room tonight."

"Me, too, " he said with a quick kiss to my cheek as he eased me away from him. "Right now I think we'd better get going. I don't want to start off on the wrong foot by being late!"

Are you nervous?" I asked as we came up the walk to my folks' house.

"No. Should I be?" Richard seemed surprised by my question.

"No, of course not. Just curious."

"Well, I do feel as though we've already met. I've spent some time online with all three of them."

He nudged me (I had a wine bottle in each hand!) and gave me a quick kiss on the cheek.

"Don't worry, Cress. I'll be on my best behavior," he said as I rang the bell.

I gave him a skeptical look just as my mother opened the door and we stepped into the entry.

"We're heeeere…" I said. Gran came up and took the wine bottles from my hands as I put my arms around my mother and gave her a hug.

She turned to Richard and wobbled, big time, the minute their eyes met. He caught her with his free hand, having transferred the champagne he was carrying to the arm that was holding the flowers.

"See?" I said, laughing.

Gran had set the wine on the hall table and pushed her way forward. She gave Richard an appraising look and managed to resist the wobble, but she staggered a bit as she took a step closer.

"It's about time," she said sternly, quickly adding a smile.

"It certainly is," he agreed, taking her hand and kissing her cheek. "These are for you," he said handing her the flowers. "Just to let you know how much we appreciate all the work you've been doing with Matt."

"And what about Matt?" Daddy asked from behind Mom.

"Better late than never," Richard said as he moved toward him.

Daddy took his hand, smiled. "And not a moment too soon. I was beginning to think I'd have to hunt you down in La-La-Land.

"I promise I'll always be easy to find," Richard assured him.

Daddy's smile was broad as he gave Richard a bro hug.

"Come in, come, in, " Mom said while she and Gran took our coats and ushered us through to the family room.

I got Richard and Daddy settled and then shooed Mom out of the kitchen so I could help Gran with the flowers. As she brought the vase over to the island where I was trimming the stems, I nudged her with my hip and said, "Well?"

She took hold of my shoulders and turned me to face her. Deadly serious she said, "You are the luckiest woman on the planet." She burst into a big grin and threw her arms around me. "I am so happy for you! If anyone deserves such a special guy, it's you. Don't forget how fortunate you are that I'm not twenty years younger!"

"Gee, and you only just met him." I couldn't stop smiling.

By the time Gran and I had gathered the champagne glasses and brought them and the bottle to the family room, Benny and Jetz had discovered Richard and inserted themselves into the circle of his energy. Benny was purring on his lap and Jetz had stretched himself along the back of the chair, rubbing his face against Richard's short hair. Richard was unfazed and was petting Benny, adding an occasional scratch at the base of his tail, which sent the cat in an ecstatic arch as he gazed up at Richard, enraptured. (Probably very similar to the way I look at Richard!)

"Well, I see you've passed the final test," I said nodding toward the cats as I set the tray and glasses on the table.

Gran handed Richard the bottle. He took it, and gently popped the cork with no explosion. And somehow without disturbing the cats.

"What?" he said handing the open bottle back to me so I could pour. He must have noticed my expression of surprise.

"Just wondering how you did that without an explosion of cats."

Richard chuckled. "Trained Professional, remember?"

My family probably didn't get the inside joke but they were all smiling.

"Forgive me for not standing," Richard said, gesturing with his glass to the furry new parasites he found himself hosting. "To CJ's nearest and dearest with sincere thanks for agreeing to share her with me. I have so looked forward to this day and many more to follow in your company."

We all drank to that. As the conversation continued I watched Richard interact with my family and the cats. I realized I'd never seen him with any animals. Like everything else, he just took it in stride, but he seemed to be enjoying the cats' attention. The cats, like me, were in love.

After dinner Daddy went to the piano to play for us as he usually did. Mom always said she enjoyed doing the dishes while he made music for her. But Richard chased her and Gran out of the kitchen, saying we'd do the clean up. I looked at him in surprise.

What?" he said. "Don't you think I know how to wash dishes?"

"If a tree falls in the forest…" I began.

He laughed. "Well, you're here to see it, so observe. Why don't I rinse and you load the dishwasher?"

"Fine," I said, still skeptical.

Like everything else, my Trained Professional was skilled and efficient at kitchen clean up and we had everything taken care of pretty quickly, albeit with some laughter, nudges and quick kisses on our part. Occasionally, I looked up and saw my family watching us. (This included Benny and Jetz, sitting patiently on the island, their eyes glued to Richard!) I could only grin in response. I knew how they felt!

We returned to the couch and continued to listen to Daddy play. It was a comfort to see routine of the house restored. Richard put his arm around me and I relaxed against his shoulder.

"So Kate," Richard began. "I was wondering if you might like to come with me tomorrow. I need to visit one of our wineries and you could do some tasting while I have my meeting. CJ and I think you'd enjoy a break and she can stay with Matt."

I could see Gran was both surprised and flattered.

"I'd like that," she said with a smile.

We didn't stay late. It had been a big day for Daddy and a long day for us.

We were in the shower, Richard soaping my back when I started giggling.

"What?" he asked.

"I just realized that you have spoiled me rotten."

"Good. Precisely what I intended."

I was still laughing.

"I just this minute realized that whenever I'm not showering with our friend Z or one of his cousins, I miss it." This struck me funny and I kept laughing. How absurd!

Then Richard was laughing. "I know exactly what you mean. And especially when we're together. We can still dance," he reminded me as he took my hand and spun me around and into his arms. "But it's not quite the same, is it?"

"Only this part," I said pressing my soapy-self against him. I kissed him.

We continued dancing slowly, if only to the sound of the running water.

"This part won't change, Sweetheart."

"Good," I said, putting my arms around his neck and my cheek against his shoulder as we continued moving slowly, like two teenagers slow-dancing at the prom.

He clasped his hands at my lower back, but then they slowly parted so he could grab my bottom and press me more tightly against him.

"Mister Hunter, are you attempting to bamboozle me?"

"Actually, I was hoping I was succeeding," he said, slipping his penis between my legs.

"Well, something is happening," I admitted.

"Shall we get out and see if we can figure out what it is?"

"I believe I have a pretty good idea."

He reached to turn off the water.

"Me, too," he said as he took my hand and helped me out of the shower.

Richard handed me a towel, took another for himself and began drying me. There was kissing.

46
Busted

Saturday, October 5

Richard and Gran took off Saturday morning for the winery, Mom had gone to work, still playing catch up, but she was hoping to be back in time to join us for lunch. While Daddy and I took his morning walk together around the neighborhood, he caught me up on the local gossip and changes in the residents. I was impressed by how easy (if a little slow) the exercise seemed for him and how robust he looked.

When we got home, he went to work on some lesson plans while I made us some coffee.

"So, I hear you're cleared to leave the house," I said when I brought him a cup in his office.

"I am. Shall we go out and paint the town to celebrate Richard's visit?" he asked, swinging around in his chair to face me as I curled my feet under me on the couch.

"Not sure about the painting part, but Richard wants to take us all out to dinner if you feel up to it."

"I do. And if you can distract your grandmother, I might be able to order some serious food." He laughed.

"It hasn't really been that bad, has it?"

"No. I hate to admit it, but if I'm honest I think I have to attribute my speedy recovery to her no-nonsense oversight. She's a remarkable woman." He winked. "But don't tell her I said so."

"She's amazing. The fact that she could take time off from running the foundation to come here is a blessing in itself."

Gran was the founder of a Seattle non-profit organization that sponsored musical theater productions involving inner city teens and young adults in all capacities from actors to stagehands to musicians. She was hands-on, managing the projects and seeing them through to performances. She'd even put together a touring company to promote the work and raise finds. I was hoping that her time with Richard today might convince him to help her find more donors. I hadn't mentioned it to him, just said she worked with creative kids in Seattle.

"Is your boyfriend likely to help out her foundation?"

"He has a lot of connections and can probably hook her up, if she asks. I'm glad they have the day to get to know each other better. And, by the way, it was his idea."

"He's a pretty amazing guy," Daddy said. "Much as I hate to admit it."

"You don't really hate to admit it, do you?" I was curious. I knew he liked Richard, that had been obvious from the time they'd started FaceTiming, but now that he'd met him, I wanted to know what he was thinking.

Daddy rolled his chair over to the couch and took my hand.

"Of course I don't. I couldn't be happier for you, Seachange."

A brief note: Seachange became my nickname when I started talking and couldn't say CJ, I told people my name was Seachange and it had stuck! Mom had trained herself out of using it since I'd grown up, but Daddy had occasional lapses when we were together.

"Richard is everything you said he is, and more. It's obvious how much he loves you and he sure seems to be exactly what he looks like: a smart, talented, serious guy who knows what he's doing in the world and who does it well. It doesn't hurt that he's rich, not to mention painfully handsome." Daddy shook his head. "He's also got a great sense of humor and I can see how much fun the two of you have." He gave me a long serious look. "I couldn't ask for a better life partner for you." He leaned forward and kissed my cheek. "So when are you two going to get married?" he said casually.

"Daddy!"

"Well? It's the next step, isn't it?"

"Is it?"

"Of course. Has he asked you?" He was frowning.

"I'm not interested in getting married. Besides, we've only known each other a few months. Things are just fine as they are."

He looked at me seriously for a minute and then rolled back to his desk.

"OK. Just as well, I probably couldn't afford your wedding to a millionaire, anyway."

I cracked up. "If I ever decide to marry Richard, I'm sure you won't get stuck with the bill. You will have to walk me down the aisle, though."

"Just say the word and I'll be there, attired in whatever clothing you select. Are you thinking royal-style top hats or tuxes?"

"I'm not thinking anything! Do I honestly strike you as the Bridezilla type?"

"Uh…no. But Richard's family also has money and there may be certain expectations," he said, looking doubtful.

"Hey!" I said, with a laugh. "Watch my lips: I have no plans at the moment to marry Richard. If that changes, you'll be the first to know. I promise. Now can we change the subject? Where do you want to go to dinner?"

Mom came home just before lunch, bearing takeout from A Wing and a Prayer, my father's favorite local barbeque. As she set the yummy smelling bags of food on the island, Daddy took her in his arms and gave her a passionate kiss.

"I love you more at this moment than I ever have," he assured her.

"Well, they say the way to a man's heart is through his stomach," she said with a wink at me.

"There are several other organs involved along that route to a man's heart," he said in a husky whisper while nuzzling her neck as he continued to hold her.

"Matt! Your daughter is right here!"

He looked over at me. "I have a feeling our Seachange is fully cognizant of the road map." He released Mom and rubbed his hands together in anxious anticipation. "We need to send Kate out more often so I can get some food meant for a man and not a rabbit!"

Mom reached over and pinched his cheek. "I admire some of those rabbit-like qualities. They do you proud."

We were all laughing as Mom pulled some plates from the cupboard while I opened the bags and set out the food. I had a feeling that my folks were having sex again and things were getting back to normal in Walla Walla.

Richard and Gran came in about 4:00 p.m., laughing.

"Looks like you two had a good day," I said as I joined them.

They looked at each other and cracked up.

"Uh, let's just say that if you ever decide to cast me aside," Richard said, "I'll be chasing after Kate."

"Let's hope that's sooner rather than later," Gran said.

"*Why there's a wench! Kiss me, Kate!*" he said, quoting Shakespeare and before Gran knew what's happening, he bent her back and kissed her quickly on the mouth.

It caught her totally off guard, but when she was upright again, her cheeks were pink. I couldn't remember ever seeing my grandmother blush!

"Watch out when he starts going Shakespeare. It can get dicey. Exactly how much wine have you two had?" I asked, hands on hips and shaking my head.

They looked at each other and laughed again.

"Okay," I said abruptly pulling her away from Richard. "Time for a breathalyzer."

I pressed myself against him and gave him a deep kiss, which he returned enthusiastically, his hands against my bottom, pulling me tight. I was pleased my lover passed the test. There was no evidence that alcohol was involved in his high spirits.

"What's going on out here?" Mom asked as she and Daddy joined us.

"Richard seems to be rethinking his devotion to me and considering Gran as a alternative."

"You should know better than to let my mother loose on a handsome man!" Mom said shaking her head.

We all laughed.

STILL LUCKY

After dinner Mom and Gran did the cleanup, unaccompanied by the piano because Daddy was talking to Richard about his students and the work he did with them on individual piano performance. His enthusiasm was contagious and though I had heard his stories many times, I never tired of listening to them. Richard was equally interested.

"Despite the students I've sent on to prizes and acclaim, none of them have ever been able to match a performance I saw back in the '90s. I have a recording. Would you like to see it?"

"Sure," Richard said.

"Seachange, would you get the CD for me? It's the first one on the left."

I went to the bookcase, retrieved the disc and popped it into the CD player. Daddy had the remote.

"I swear to you, this is the most remarkable performance I've ever seen. And there's still a part of this piece I just can't figure out the fingering on, no matter how much I watch this."

I'd seen it many times over the years. I remembered Daddy going away—I was only six at the time—and how happy and excited he was when he came home. And he was right. The young man's skill and concentration were phenomenal.

"You're going to love this," I said to Richard with a squeeze of his hand.

He gave me a quick kiss.

It was recorded with Daddy's hand held video camera, (later transferred to disc) but he'd done a pretty good job, complete with close-ups. He'd always intended to share it with his students.

The scene began with welcome speech in three languages— French, Russian and English announcing the final round of the 1996 Moscow piano competition.

Suddenly, Richard gripped my hand tightly and I could feel a wave of...of I'm not sure what—it almost felt like shock... I looked at him but his eyes were glued to the screen.

The contestant was announced along with the name of the piece that would be played. And suddenly I felt a wave of recognition as I heard the name "Richard Chasseur." Sure enough, as the serious young man took the stage and bowed, Daddy had moved in for a close up. It was Richard!

It took Daddy a little longer to make the connection, but he turned to Richard with a look of astonishment. Richard smiled weakly as his younger self sat down at the piano and began to play.

It was just then that Gran and Mom joined us.

Mom laughed. "My apologies, Richard. He inflicts this on as many people as he can."

"Well, it's certainly worth watching," Gran added. "So much talent and so much beauty in one package!"

Then, at almost the same moment, and with the aid of another close-up on the fifty-inch flat screen, they both stared at Richard.

"Richard?" Gran said.

He looked at her and smiled with a shrug of his shoulders.

"I won it," was all he said.

We continued to watch in silence until it was over. Then all eyes were on Richard, waiting for an explanation.

"You told me you'd played years ago…" Daddy said. I could tell he was having trouble understanding why Richard had avoided sharing the extent of his involvement with the piano in the course of their online communications.

Richard took a deep breath. "Well, that was almost twenty years ago. I was fifteen then and when I was eighteen I gave up the piano and came to the U.S. for college. I didn't touch a piano again until a few weeks ago when CJ and I were in New York."

Mom was sitting on the other side of him and she turned to him and put her hand on his shoulder.

"What happened? A gift like that is not something you just throw away."

"It is if you're a foolish kid trying to punish yourself by denying yourself one of the most important pleasures in your life."

His tone made it clear that he wasn't willing to discuss it.

"But you've started to play again?" Daddy said.

Richard smiled at me and lifted my hand to his lips.

"CJ can be very persuasive."

"It didn't take much persuasion," I insisted as I kissed his cheek. "He told me he'd do anything for me, so I asked. He's a man of his word."

Richard chuckled. "I'm still having trouble explaining to her what it's meant to have her give my music back to me."

In an effort to lighten the mood I added. "Not only does he play but we can do a duet. Wanna see?"

They all laughed (being familiar with the extent of my musical talent!)

"This I gotta see," my father said.

I pulled Richard up from the couch and led him out into the sunroom where the two baby grands were interlocked so Daddy could face his students. I'd rigged up a video connection with cameras and monitors on both keyboards so each could see what the other was doing without Daddy having to get up and down.

I sat between Richard's legs, just as I had that night in New York, and flexed my two pointer fingers to warm them up. My family laughed. He kissed my cheek in encouragement and I began my first public performance. Richard came in on cue and continued with his Liberace homage.

When we finished we were all laughing. Daddy was shouting "Bravo!" and Gran offered some piercing whistles along with all the applause.

47
The Bard Runs Deep

That night…

Richard told me about his day with Gran on our way back to the hotel.

"She's every bit as extraordinary as you've told me she is," he said. "And what a life she's led. I see where your free spirit genes come from."

"Isn't she amazing? I'm sure I'd be a completely different person if she hadn't been such a big part of my childhood. My parents were still in school when I was born and Gran lived with us and helped out with me."

Richard chuckled. "I loved her story about your mom's name."

"You mean the Shakespeare references? Beatrice from *Much Ado About Nothing* and Adriana from *Comedy of Errors*. She says that describes her unwed-motherhood to a T. Did she also tell you she named herself?"

"No, she slid right over that one. Was it part of her hippie rebellion?" he asked.

"Yup. I don't even know what her real name was. She started calling herself Katherina—for *Shrew* of course—and Rosaline."

"For *Love's Labor Lost?*"

"Exactly! She had an abusive childhood and left home at fourteen. When she turned eighteen she changed it legally.

"It must have been hard for her," he said, shaking his head. "I can't even imagine a girl on her own at that age, though I know there are plenty of them living on the streets these days. Where did she go?"

"In some ways it must have been a little easier on runaways then. The drug culture seems to have been more benign in those days. Gran found a commune outside of Boulder, Colorado." I had nothing but admiration for my grandmother and her independence. As Richard said, a remarkable woman.

"She brushed it off when she told me the story," he said. "In those days it was still scandalous to be a single mother outside the hippie community."

"It was," I agreed. "But she was also very determined. Was she impressed by your knowledge of the Bard?"

"Naturally," he said smugly. "Being a Trained Professional..."

I laughed. "Don't start."

"As you wish," he said with a nod.

"What? Now it's *Princess Bride*?" I asked as he parked at the hotel and came around to open the door for me.

"I like the sound of that," he said with a laugh.

I rolled my eyes. "The movie or are you hinting again?"

"That's for me to know and you to wonder."

"Listen Mr. Trained Professional, before you get to feeling too frisky, I want to talk about the piano business."

"Are you thinking of going into retail? Musical instruments or just pianos?" he asked innocently.

"Oh, no you don't," I said as we got into the elevator. "How do you feel about your secret being exposed tonight?"

Richard looked down, feigning surprise as he checked his fly.

"Funny boy. I'm serious."

He took me by the shoulders and got serious, himself.

"Relieved. And your folks were great about it." He kissed me, then smiled. "But really, how weird is it that you father was in Moscow that year? And even stranger that he videoed it and has watched it all these years."

"The universe must have wanted me to find you. It started early exposing me to your beauty and talents." I slipped my hands in under the front of his jacket and ran my fingers lightly over his chest, teasing his nipples through his shirt. "How 'bout you demonstrate some of those talents for me?"

He pulled me closer. "And which talents are you interested in, specifically?"

"Come up to my room and I'll show you."
I'm right behind you," he said as the elevator door opened.

We got out of the shower and were standing at the window looking out at the view of Walla Walla. We were naked, Richard standing behind me, his arms around me, his lips moving lightly over the side of my neck. He'd dried me off, but that spot between my legs was already starting to drip.

"It's not exactly our view in New York, is it?" I asked.

"No reason it should be. I like it here. It's a nice town."

"Maybe it's just the company you keep?" I suggested.

He gave me a squeeze. "No doubt a big part of my assessment."

I turned to face him and caressed his cheek as I put my arms around his neck.

"I'm so glad you came."

"I'm planning on coming again, if you're interested," he said before giving me a long lingering kiss. "Maybe you'd like to join me?"

"Yes, please," I said softly when we came up for air. "Is soft serve an option?" I asked as I pressed myself closer to see if he was starting to get aroused. "I need a taste of you."

"Best hurry. You can't keep a good man down."

I laughed and led him to the bed and sat him down as I dropped to my knees. I pulled him a little closer to the edge of the mattress so his testicles could hang over as I spread his knees. I couldn't keep from smiling. Such a lovely sight!

"Uh...Sweetheart, I enjoy being admired and all, but if you want to start from scratch you'd better get a move on."

I looked up at him with a smile as I began to fondle his balls. I leaned closer and teased the end of his cock lightly with the tip of my tongue. Richard groaned. I gave him a tiny suck as I stretched his scrotum down. Taking just the head of his cock between my lips, I ran my tongue around and around him and heard some sharp intakes of breath from my lover.

Richard leaned back on his hands, pressing forward in an effort to move farther into my mouth, but I backed up a little, foiling his efforts. He was no longer flaccid and quickly growing, so I quite suddenly gobbled all of him that I could, ran my tongue around and around him and then released him suddenly. Richard moaned very softly and I glanced up to see him smiling.

I smiled back as I released his balls and moved to take them into my mouth, one at a time, rolling my tongue around first one and then the other, leaving his cock untouched as it twitched and grew. I knew he wanted me to touch him, to wrap my hand around him, but I was enjoying a little bit of torment.

I let his testicle slip out of my mouth very slowly and ran my tongue back and forth from one to the other, teasing, bouncing them lightly, but leaving his cock straining for attention. I placed my hands on the tops of his thighs and pressed them farther apart, keeping my thumbs moving in deep caresses. Then I paused while I took a moment to study my Prince's equipment in all its marvelous perfection.

"What?" Richard said softly.

I noted he was a little breathless.

"You are soooo beautiful..." I took the base of his cock between my thumb and forefinger and lightly ran them up, paused, and moved back down again. I knew he wanted me to take a firm hold on him, but I continued to stroke him that way, with just two fingers.

I leaned forward then, sliding my body over his to move up and give his nipples some attention. Richard leaned back onto his elbows, his head thrown back, eyes closed as he rubbed his penis against me. I arched myself away from him and he groaned.

"Sweet Juliet, I have saved more than a drop for you. I beg thee, take it."

I just smiled up at him, while I continued slowly nibbling at his nipple.

Richard sat up suddenly, put his arm around my waist, picked me up and before I realized what had happened, he had me on my back in the middle of the bed. He hesitated then, just for the moment it took me to laugh and throw my legs around him. (Remember those superb manners?)

It was my turn to squeal as he entered me, one of those instant orgasms that happened so rarely. He stroked me hard and deep as I hung on tight, feeling his need as plunged into me—and mine as I moved with him. This time when he came, he kept moving through his ejaculation, quick strokes with a series of staccato moans. Those sounds sent me into another pulsing orgasm of my own.

Richard continued moving as he whispered, "Sweet Juliet," before covering my mouth with his.

"Can I have a taste now?" I whispered.

"Only if you'll share," he answered, easing away from me.

I happily turned around, moving over him and quickly taking his cock into my mouth and offered him my juicy (and no doubt cum-filled) cunt for his own enjoyment. We proceeded enthusiastically until our heart rates slowed, his cock softened and I'd had enough orgasms to consider myself GTF. With a nuzzle to his sticky pubic hair, I moved off of him, turned around and collapsed beside him.

Richard smiled and pulled me close for a sloppy "us" flavored kiss.

"You and those snakes," I said, rubbing my hand around in the mess on his face.

He laughed. "Gimme some cuddles before we go back to the shower."

"If you insist," I said as I threw my leg up over his hip and pressed myself against him.

When we came back to bed, all fresh and clean, I crawled in next to him and gave him a kiss.

"I am so grateful you're not one of those men whose penis is so sensitive after orgasm that it can't be touched. I'd miss that part of what we share."

Richard chuckled. "You can credit Maryse for that. She convinced me that the afterplay is as important as the foreplay. I really feel sorry for people who don't realize that. Recreational sex is fine, but when it's someone you care about, it's a very special place to continue sharing. I cherish it. It would be a shame to not be able to have you touch me then."

"You'd be surprised to know how often I bless Maryse. I know she's in a large part responsible for how kind and caring you are."

"And what a stunningly excellent lover I am?"

I kissed him and he laughed.

"That, too."

He gave me a squeeze. "Everything that's excellent about the way we are together is because of you, Sweetheart."

"Wow...she must also have taught you how far flattery will get you!"

"Well..."

"Good thing I love you so much, Charming."

"Good thing," he agreed.

Sunday, October 6

Sunday, Richard spent most of the day with Daddy, trying to work out that section of the piece my father had never been able to conquer. Richard was having trouble remembering it exactly, but once Daddy got him going, helped by my cameras and monitors, they started making progress. Daddy was in heaven and I could see Richard was enjoying himself as the fingering slowly came back to him.

We had a great dinner out, relaxed and full of laughter. Gran didn't say anything about my father's menu choices, though Daddy kept watching her out of the corner of his eye until his plate was served.

On Monday morning, after a sweet wake-up call, Richard presented me with a small box, a card, a kiss and a "Happy anniversary, Sweetheart."

"Richard, you have to stop this," I said shaking my head.

"I thought we'd already established that wasn't going to happen."

"Yahbutt...." I whined.

"Open the box first," he said, ignoring my objections.

I untied the bow and found two narrow cuff bracelets inside. One was engraved with *I Love You More* and the other with *I Love You Most*. They were silver in color but very lightweight.

"Now open the card. It may be the best part."

My Prince, the Trained Professional, had apparently made

the card himself. It had a red heart on the front with yellow lines like rays coming out from it all the way around, drawn and filled in with a marker, and inside it said:

> *There are darknesses in life and there are lights, and you are one of the lights, the light of all lights.*
>
> *Happy Anniversary, Light of my Life!*
> *XXOOR*

There was a piece of paper folded in the middle. It was a receipt for "Two aluminum bracelets — $48."

"My Prince!" I exclaimed with delight, "Have you discovered that the best things in life may be cheaper than you thought?"

He laughed. "I've discovered alternatives to the marketplaces of the one percenters. It seems that they can bring just as much pleasure to the woman I love as Barsanti and Cartier."

"Equal, for sure, though I love everything you've ever given me. Each gift has been special, expensive or not."

I put the bracelets on and gave him a big kiss.

"What's the quote from?"

"Well, I liked the words but hesitated to add the attribution."

"Because…?"

He swung his arm up and across in front of him as though hiding his face behind a voluminous cape. With a Carpathian accent he said, "Bram Stoker's *Dracula!*"

"Seriously? How did you find it?" I asked.

"Being a Trained Professional…" he began.

I raised my eyebrows at him and he relented.

"Okay, I Googled 'Love & Light'."

I stared at him for a moment. "How sweet of you to think of me that way."

"Well, I think of you many other ways, as well.

"Care to elaborate?"

He gave me a quick kiss on the cheek. "After our workout."

STILL LUCKY

That morning we went to the fitness center at the college. My folks had gotten us passes, but I'd forgotten to ask about the hours. They didn't open until 7:00 a.m. so we spent a half an hour jogging through the campus with me as tour guide before hitting the weights.

Back at the hotel we both tackled our computers. I'd had the hotel bring us a second desk for our "parlor" (that's the hotel's word, not mine!) so we each had workspace. Richard, naturally had more work to do that I did. My project was still up in the air, just waiting for something to happen.

We went to the house and I left Richard with Daddy and took Gran shopping.

"So where shall we go?" I asked as we pulled away from the curb. "I've got a piece of plastic that bills to Richard and it's burning a hole in my pocket. The day is ours and the sky's the limit. New winter clothes, fancy jewels, home decor?"

"I really need some clothes for the upcoming funding meetings," Gran said. "No need for Richard to pay, but I'd love to have you help me make the selections."

So off we went to Macy's where we found a number of things for Gran and I even found a few things for myself. I got sneaky and gave the salesgirl my card in advance, so when Gran got ready to pay she was told it had already been taken care of!

On the way back to the car I explained Richard's theory of spending money. All Gran could do is shake her head and smile. I also told her I would have put it on my card if Richard hadn't insisted—just as my own thank you for all the help she'd been to Daddy.

"It's been a joy," she laughed, "Though don't tell your father I said so. Despite all our teasing back and forth, I know how much he and your mom have appreciated it. And he jumped into my program with both feet. We've all seen the results. I couldn't be happier."

"Are you missing much back at the foundation?" I asked. She'd been in Walla Walla for almost seven weeks.

"No. Suzanne is doing a great job and we're in touch daily. We meet online with the different departments when we need to." She laughed. "I'm not sure how I should feel about them getting on so well without me."

"Do you miss it?"

"Funny you should ask…" She paused and took a deep breath. "I've been thinking about that a lot lately. I'm feeling a little antsy, like the time may be coming when I should find something else to do."

That really surprised me, and I said so.

"Well, so much of what I'm involved with these days is fundraising and honestly, I don't have the personality for it. I automatically assume that anyone who isn't impressed by what we do is an idiot, which to be honest, doesn't go over very well."

I cracked up. "Did you talk to Richard about funding?"

"I did and he said he'd see if he could make some connections for me."

"He is absolutely amazing," I told her. "You may be surprised by what he comes up with."

48
Leavin' On A Jet Plane

Wednesday, October 9

We flew home on Wednesday afternoon, courtesy of Jet Giano. I pestered Richard a little, trying to figure out where we were going for his birthday, but he launched into dissertations on the desirability of surprise, the need for spontaneity, and even had the audacity to ask me to explain why I felt the need to be so controlling. (He was kidding, and was enjoying teasing me.)

I insisted that I needed to have a clue so I could pack.

"No need. Marie packed for us and our luggage has already been sent on ahead."

That shut me up for a minute.

"But what if she forgot something I might need?"

"Seriously?"

(OK, I admit that the chances of Marie not performing the tasks assigned to perfection was a stretch.)

"Well," I said with a sigh, "I guess I won't know until we find our gate at the airport.

"Or not." His expression was smug.

"What does that mean?"

"I think you'll just have to wait until tomorrow."

I relaxed and dropped it. I was pretty sure I could get a clue from what was missing from my closet. More the fool me. When we got home I found most of my things were gone, everything from bikinis to some of my sweaters and my parka. And one of those first fancy dresses I'd bought before the San Diego gala, one I hadn't worn yet. A variety of shoes were missing, too, sneakers to stilettos. A lot of my jewelry was no longer in the little compartments where things usually nested. Including my fabtastic swan!

"At least she left me something to wear to my meeting tomorrow!"

Richard just laughed at me!

Thursday, October 10

That Marie! She refused to respond to my sneaky interrogation questions at breakfast the next morning. I accused her of only pretending to be loyal to me while her boss was gone, and the minute he returned, becoming his co-conspirator. Marie merely offered a series of Gallic shrugs. I pretended to be annoyed, but they both knew how much I was enjoying the deception.

Richard left to take care of some last minute things at the gallery and I was off early to see Ben and Jerry.

Mandy, their receptionist, escorted me into the conference room, but no one was there. I poured myself a cup of coffee and pondered the bagels. Actually, I was about ten minutes early, but the men joined me just a few minutes later.

"Good morning," Jerry said as he came in. He was smiling. He was also carrying two rather fat folders. "Welcome back. How's your father doing?"

"Excellent. His recovery's ahead of schedule."

"We're happy to hear it," Ben said. "We have some good news for you."

I looked at them expectantly. Jerry took one of the folders and opened it.

"As we told you, Peter Norton has connected with a venture capitalist who is offering an initial investment of $500,000 for a 30% share with an option for first additional funding in twelve months."

They went on to explain exactly how the funding worked with

respect to how much of the company I would be losing to investors as we progressed on our way to an IPO.

We had discussed this several times over the course of working together, but they went into detail with speculative numbers. I turned off the part of my brain that felt like I was watching my project slip out of my grasp as my share of the profit pie got smaller and smaller. It helped when they explained that as my percentage got smaller, the pie was likely to get a lot larger.

They moved on to projections, which they assured me were conservative. The numbers didn't sound anything like conservative, but I kept my mouth shut and listened, only occasionally asking for clarification. After about an hour, Jerry finished his presentation, closed the folder and pushed it toward me.

"Everything is in there. The offer is good for thirty days so take some time to go over it in detail. And call if you have any questions."

I glanced at the second folder and then at Ben.

He smiled. "We have an offer from Google. They want to buy you outright. There are many negotiable parts to the offer such as how long you would continue with the project while working with their people until it's ready to launch, work time requirements, physical locations where you would work, vacation time, how the offer amount would be paid out and so forth. As I said, these are all negotiable, so while you're going over it, make notes about what your optimal choices would be, and if you choose to go this direction, we will negotiate on your behalf."

They both went into more detail, gave me scenarios of different choices and what they would mean. They explained the consequences of breaking any part of the contract, what options Google would retain, what interest I could negotiate to retain, if any. It was a lot to take in.

Ben pushed the second folder toward me along with a flash drive that had the digital versions of both offers.

"They fully expect give and take on the offer, so don't hesitate to make your wish list a big one. We can always back off but it's hard to go the other direction."

"You've certainly given me a lot to think about." I said. "What you haven't mentioned is the amount of the Google offer."

They looked at each other and smiled broadly.

Jerry said, "$350 million."

Well, *that* gave me plenty to think about on the way home! You might imagine that I would have been screaming with joy and too excited to drive, but very much to my own surprise that wasn't the case. Frankly, I didn't know what to think.

As I've previously I mentioned, for the last six years I'd assumed I'd move to funding and then begin setting up my company, doing everything that entailed, from finding commercial space to hiring. In my dream scenarios, I even imagined partnering with someone like Google, but still being there, running the show myself.

On the other hand—and despite the amount of investigation I'd done—I'd never before really seen, in a black and white version, how much of my company I would lose to venture capitalists— some of course, but I never realized it was likely to be such a big percentage. Ben and Jerry had been very clear about that, but they also showed me the projection numbers, which could eventually dwarf Google's offer.

The Google offer boggled my mind. The numbers were just too unreal. The price was huge, and to walk away with so much…but then it wasn't really a case of walking away. I would have to commit to work with the team for a specified amount of time, probably several years, so maybe that would help me feel like I was still involved without the capital-raising headaches.

And then there was Richard. My life had changed in a thousand ways. There was so much we planned to do together, so how would accepting either of those offers affect our relationship?

It was a lot to think about and, frankly, I wanted to think on my own and understand my feelings before I presented the options to Richard. I really wanted his input because I knew he'd be able to look at both offers from all sides and help me see the advantages and disadvantages. I was also confident that he wouldn't attempt to influence me.

I just wasn't ready to go there. And I knew he'd understand, but I didn't want to have anything create a cloud over our trip. So, like Scarlett, I decided to think about it tomorrow, after we arrived at our mystery destination.

STILL LUCKY

We left the house at 4:00 p.m. with nothing but our laptops, passports and some odds and ends in a shared carry on. It was very freeing to trust that Marie had sent anything we would need ahead. Richard had laughingly assured me that we were not venturing into the jungle in a dugout and would therefore be able to buy anything she might have missed.

Imagine my surprise when Antonio dropped us in front of Giano's little jet where Captain Santorelli was waiting for us. When we boarded, he introduced us to our co-pilot Arabella Bonelli (Girl Power!) and our steward (Really? A steward?) Stefano Fera.

"Is Jet Giano turning into a habit?" I asked.

"Well, it was a way to keep you from knowing our destination."

"Maybe you need to think of getting one of these little numbers for yourself," I suggested.

"I've been thinking about it. Or maybe asking Giano if I can buy an interest in this one."

"Seriously?"

"I have to talk to the accountants—you know Chasseur International, Chasseur U.S., or for the gallery."

"Lah-dee-fuckin'-dah!"

Richard laughed.

After we were airborne, he asked if everything was all right. I looked at him in surprise.

"Are you kidding? A mystery trip with the man I love—what more could a girl ask?" I kissed his cheek.

"Cress, what aren't you telling me?"

I could see he was serious. He was also worried. I wondered if I could buy a poker face with my impending fortune.

I sighed and decided to confess.

"Ben and Jerry had two offers for me this morning."

"And…?"

"I can't decide what to think."

"Were the offers disappointing? Less than you expected?"

He took my hand as if a physical connection might make it easier for me.

That made me laugh out loud. "Nope. Quite the opposite."

"Then congratulations!" He gave my hand a squeeze. When I didn't react he added, "So what's bothering you?"

I looked at him. He had shifted to Dr. Hunter mode. I could see it and it made me smile.

"Ah, the good doctor is in."

He laughed. "Available day or night to certain patients. House calls made, complete with exceptional bedside manners."

"Exceptional manners in bed and out." I gave him a serious kiss.

"Maman would be proud."

"Oh?" I said brightly. "Want me to email her and let her know?"

"Uh...probably not. It's sort of a TMI thing."

We continued the banter for a few minutes as I noticed how skillfully he was adjusting my mood for me. *What a guy!*

Long story short, he convinced me to give him an overview of the two offers. He explained that laying the information out on the table would let air and light into the situation and we could then have an open discussion whenever the mood suited us. I wouldn't have to muddle through it on my own.

As usual, he was right.

Feeling much lighter, I happily leaned my head against Richard's shoulder and promptly went to sleep. I woke about an hour later and looked out the window. Nothing to see but clouds picking up the colors of the sun that had, or must have been about to set. I couldn't decide if that made me think we were going east or west.

"See anything?" Richard asked with a smirk.

"Clouds," I said brightly, as if my curiosity wasn't influencing my response.

"Would you like a glass of wine, Sweetheart?"

"Yes, please."

Stefano appeared and took Richard's request.

"Uh, how is it that we have a steward this trip?" I asked.

"Long flight. I thought you'd appreciate some dinner."

"I see. And what's on the menu?" It was bound to be more impressive than the usual packet with three peanuts!

"Patience," Richard said smugly.

I sighed and gave up, which is what he'd been trying to convince me to do all along!

49

Here Comes the Sun

Early Friday, October 11

It was ten minutes to eleven by my watch (L.A. time) when we landed. Richard was keeping my phone and since I had no idea where we were, I had no way to guage local time! (And the crew was mum!) No terminal was visible as we came in for a landing and I could see only a pair of headlights in front of the hangar where we stopped. A dark line of trees showed beyond the chain link fencing, but that was about it.

The door to the cabin opened and Richard gave me a quick kiss and got up, asking me to wait just a minute. I could see him on the tarmac, shaking hands with a man who was standing in the light from the headlights of a white SUV.

Richard returned and escorted me from the plane and introduced me to Leonardo, who would be driving us to our destination. The air was warm and humid but the smell was more airport than anything else. No clue there. So into the SUV we went after bidding our crew goodbye.

Once we left the immediate vicinity of the airport, it was very dark. The road we were on was paved but narrow, and the only thing I could see to either side was thick foliage.

Richard and Leo (as he'd asked us to call him) carried on a general conversation that gave not one clue to where we were or where he was taking us. I said I'd given up the struggle but now that we were—I assumed—almost at our destination, I was once again on pins and needles, anxious to have the mystery revealed.

We slowed at a formidable pair of iron gates supported by sturdy pillars, one of which had a bronze plaque that said *Beaujeu*. Leo rolled down his window, flipped a card into the slot and the gates swung open.

"Your first clue," Richard said.

"And that would tell me...what?" I gave him an eye roll. He deserved it!

"The name of the place we're staying," he said with a perfectly straight face.

Another quarter mile and I could see lights lining a circular driveway with just one little white car parked there. Leo pulled up to the front of what seemed to be a very large house. There was no sign of any other people, so I was thinking it couldn't be a resort. There was a solid plastered wall that must have been eight feet high stretching to either side of the wide entry and disappearing into the thick shrubbery, so despite the landscape lighting, there were no windows to be seen.

We followed Leo, who carried our single bag up four wide stone steps to the double doors.

"For the house and the car," he said handing Richard a set of keys. "The light panel is to the right just inside the doors. You will find a book of information and the house remotes on the kitchen counter. Don't hesitate to call if you have any questions." He wished us a happy stay and left us.

We watched him go and then Richard turned to me with a smile. "Are you ready?"

"More than ready." And I was. Enough with the suspense!

The doors swung open and when Richard flipped the switch we were treated to a scene right out of the pages of *Architectural Digest*! The wide entry where we stood had a huge vase of exotic fresh flowers on a table in the center. Beyond it and several steps down was a large living area with multiple couches, everything white with the color accents all turquoise, including the area rugs. The floors were whitewashed plank and very shiny. Overhead, the beamed ceiling was also white and featured a huge chandelier crafted like a chunk of a coral reef and surrounded by four ceiling fans. A wall of plantation shutters ran across the far end of the room.

"Wow!" I didn't have another single word available.

"Exactly," Richard agreed as I followed him across the room.

He went to the shutters and folded them back exposing a large window wall that looked out on a covered terrace, then a few steps down to another terrace with a lighted pool. Beyond that, darkness. It was cloudy, so no moon to shed any additional light.

"What's out there?" I wondered aloud.

"I guess you won't know until morning." He chuckled and pulled me into his arms.

"Whatever it is, I'm thrilled to be here to see it with you."

"Ditto," he said and then he kissed me.

Things heated up quickly until Richard eased me away from him.

"Do you think you can manage to distract me and push my curiosity about where we are to the back burner?" I asked, as if I actually questioned his abilities. "If not, I'll never be able to sleep."

"Let's find the bedroom," he suggested, "and I'll give it a try."

We stepped up onto the next level where the dining room was—a big glass-topped table and a dozen chairs. I had to walk over and take a closer look. The glass was supported by a metal sculpture of fish swimming through sea plants. The rug beneath it was waves in shades of turquoise and white, matching the patina of the base and giving the impression of water. The chairs with high backs were white. It was beautiful.

The kitchen was large, with a big island—white stone of some kind—high on one side making a breakfast bar. Sitting on it was the book Leo had mentioned along with a bottle of Chasseur Champagne and two glasses.

"Would you like some?" Richard asked.

"I'd rather wait and celebrate tomorrow." I stepped closer to him and slipped my hand down to caress his cock. "I have something else in mind at the moment." It was obvious that he did, too.

Richard took my hand and led me around the corner, past a fancy powder room, to a pair of double doors. To the right, a wide hallway revealed more doors along the left side. The right side, toward the driveway, was all windows with dimly lit foliage between them and the front wall.

"How big is this place?" I asked. It seemed to go on forever!

"Six bedrooms plus the master."

"Do we need so many bedrooms?" I was sort of amazed.

Richard laughed. "No. But I chose it for the location and the ambiance, not the number of bedrooms."

He opened the French doors to another exquisite room. On the right wall was a large four-poster bed, complete with mosquito netting that was looped around the turned posts. The end wall and the left wall were shutters, covering more windows, I assumed. On both sides of the bed were doors. The nearest revealed a closet, where all our things, delivered earlier, seemed to be hanging or arranged on the shelves.

Richard left to get our bag and I went to explore the bathroom. *Oh my!* The large (Yay!) shower and the huge tub were on the outside wall—again, all windows. A flat screen TV above the tub offered the opportunity to watch a favorite movie—or probably the stock market, considering the people who were most likely to spend time there— while soaking.

"What?" Richard asked as I came out of the bathroom with a big smile on my face.

"Big shower with a Baby Z!" I said gleefully. "We can make our own music!"

He slid his arm around my waist and pulled me close for a kiss, then whispered against my ear, "How about some horizontal tango?"

I laughed. We continued kissing as we began undressing each other. We did it slow and sexy, his fingers moving over my skin, leaving me breathless. Suddenly, an image flashed into mind of that night when we came back from Santa Barbara, the first time he'd taken me from behind.

I must have made some sort of noise because he stopped kissing me and looked at me, a question in those beautiful eyes of his.

I smiled. "I was just remembering..." I said as I unbuttoned his pants and unzipped his fly.

He waited, his thumbs moving slowly back and forth over my nipples. I pushed his pants down and found he was wearing silk boxers. I loved the feel of his hard cock under the slippery fabric and as I caressed him, my train of thought got derailed by the weight of him in my hand.

"What were you remembering?" he asked.

"That night we came back from our day in Santa Barbara."

"The first time I took you from behind on the bedroom floor?" he asked.

"Exactly. How can you remember that?" I was actually surprised. I had been prepared to tease him through it, though I knew he would do anything I asked.

"Seriously?" he asked. "You know how much I enjoy seeing you from that angle…seeing us, that way. And…" he said with a slow kiss. "You remember, so why wouldn't I?"

"Fancy another go?" I said, giving him a squeeze.

"Your wish is my command." He kissed me again, pressing me tight against him, my fingers still wrapped around his cock.

"A taste first," I said, dropping to my knees.

I brought his penis out through the fly but continued to fondle his balls through the silk as I teased and sucked at the tip. I looked up to see him smiling.

"Are you ready?" I asked.

"You tell me," he said, emphasizing the obvious.

I eased the boxers down so he could step out of them, then stood up to kiss him again. His hand slowly moved down from my breast and into my bikini panties, his fingers moving gently, exploring familiar territory. Familiar and very wet. His other hand pressed me against him as the tip of his finger began moving in slow circles, just barely inside me. All I could think of was the overpowering urge to spread my legs and encompass all of him.

"Maybe it's time to take these panties off?" he suggested.

It was a question but the answer was obvious. At the same time I didn't want to lose his fingers. He hesitated, forcing me to choose and ease myself away from him. I quickly slipped the panties down and kicked them aside.

"Where?" All I was thinking was now…please…now!

He gestured toward the end of the bed and I quickly crawled onto it and positioned myself on all fours, thinking he'd join me. Instead he grabbed my hips and gently pulled me back to the edge of the bed. I looked around but he was staring at the spot I most wanted him to be, while his hands gripped my bottom and his thumbs worked in circles.

"You are so beautiful," he said softly, just before he bent to taste me.

And then my Magic Man's magic tongue began to work its own magic. Lord, talk about a Trained Professional! I closed my eyes and arched my back, angling my clit a little closer to his mouth. He immediately provided some quick tongue action—rubbing side to side and up and down. I caught my breath, ready for an orgasm, but then he changed tactic and gave me a few long, slow laps, stopping for a suck where the juice was.

"Your little penis is really hard," he said softly.

I was in no mood for subtlety! "Ya, think?" I said sarcastically. "Maybe if you gave it a few good sucks…"

"If I did, would you come for me?" His fingers continued their gentle teasing.

"Who knows? Maybe you should try it and find out." I could barely breathe. I lowered my shoulders, moving my other end higher, begging him to do it.

I squeaked in surprise when he gave me a little nip on my bottom, but before I could say anything, his fingers began running up and down both sides of my clit in the same way I stroked his cock. Moments later his mouth found the tip of me and he did suck.

My orgasm exploded, but I held myself still, hoping he wouldn't stop. He didn't and I began to feel that lovely wave action start to build. He continued to stroke and suck at me as my thighs trembled with pleasure. Small cries of ecstasy escaped my throat and then he was inside me, and I cried out at the magnified sensation. He went deep, stroking me slowly as one hand came around over my hip to keep fingering my clit.

Richard must have sensed that I couldn't take much more and he eased back, putting both hands on my hips as he moved more quickly. I felt like it would be the easiest thing in the world to dissolve into a puddle of sensory overload, but I didn't want to miss anything!

He huffed with a little moan as he came and pulsed, even as I continued to pulse, myself. And then, just has he had that night, he separated us, turned me over, slid me up farther onto the mattress, and was inside me again. It was so swift and seemed to be so effortless, a girl might think he'd rehearsed it!

"Smooth move," I said in surprise. "Tell me you haven't actually spent time practicing that."

Richard pressed tight against me and laughed.

"I haven't spent time practicing that," he said. "But if you think it needs work and are willing to assist…"

My turn to press against him as I laughed. I wasn't ready to lose him (and frankly, from what I could feel he wasn't going anywhere just yet.)

"The move is perfect, but I'm happy to assist whenever you feel the need."

He kissed me, and kissed me some more.

"I love you Sweetheart," he said with a smile.

"I love you most," I reminded him.

50
Playing House

In the Morning

I felt Richard get out of bed but happily rolled over and snuggled even deeper into the luxurious featherbed and went back to sleep. No interest in waking up yet, I was still blissed-out from the night before.

Sometime later I felt his lips brush my cheek and heard a whispered, "Good morning, Sweetheart."

I turned toward him, my eyes still closed as I reached for his cock, expecting my morning wake-up inducement. The shock of finding him flaccid prompted me to open one eye and give him a speculative look.

"Ummmm…what happened to my incentive to greet the day with a smile on my face?" I asked.

Richard laughed. "It's still available, but I had a feeling you might be too distracted to give me your full attention."

That opened my other eye and I realized the room was full of light. He had folded back the shutters and let the outside in! I quickly sat up to see what was actually out there and was literally stunned. I jumped out of bed and rushed to the French doors leading to the terrace and threw them open to the warm daylight.

Richard was laughing as he got up and followed. "See what I mean?"

There were various pieces of outdoor furniture—couches and chairs—and several glass dining tables with chairs on the level above the pool. Down a few steps, the pool itself and more lounges and potted plants. At the far end was a stone-faced cooking area that looked amazing. But beyond that low hedge that had marked the edge of visibility the night before, lay an endless expanse of ocean, beginning in a light shade of turquoise that graduated to a deep blue on the horizon.

"It's everything our window painting is, and more!" I squealed with delight. A moment later I turned to him and threw my arms around his neck with a big kiss, then took his hand and led him outside. (We were both naked, mind you, but then I didn't see any sign that there was anyone else in the vicinity and Richard didn't hesitate.)

I went down our broad steps to the pool level where I realized that it was an infinity pool. If you were in the water it would seem to blend into the ocean and had been painted a shade of turquoise that matched the nearest water perfectly. I couldn't wait to experience it for myself. Without any curiosity about temperature, I dove in and came up laughing, my lover beside me.

We swam to the ocean side where I discovered a sort of crenelated two-layer shelf where you could either stand or sit. We chose to stand, staring out at the sea.

The beach below was beautiful! White sand, stretched in both directions for quite a way before being hemmed in by rocks. Very private and picture postcard perfect.

"So are you ready to tell me where we are?" I asked. "My guess is Paradise."

"It certainly looks like it but it's actually called Provençal Island."

"Never heard of it," I confessed, "But I'll never forget it!"

"It's privately owned. There is a small harbor and private yacht club on the other end of the island, and the little airport where we landed."

"And you found it, how?"

"One of Umberto's and Cybelle's clients."

"So all you rich people DO know each other!"

Richard laughed. "Sure. When your money comes through, I'll introduce you around." He kissed my cheek. "Hmmmm…I just realized I'm not sure I want to share you."

"If you could magically provide me with a cup of Marie's coffee, I'd be willing to promise you you'd never have to. Unfortunately, Marie is far away…"

"And a pot of her coffee is waiting for you in the kitchen." He turned me to him, hugged me tightly and growled in my ear, "So you're mine, all mine!"

Laughing, I pushed him away. "So do we have staff?"

With a look of dismay he said, "Do you honestly think I'm incapable of making a pot of coffee?"

I gave him a speculative look. "I don't know, let's find out!"

I pushed away and swam toward the steps. As I got out I realized I hadn't brought a towel.

Behind me, Richard said, "On the chaise."

Sure enough, two fluffy turquoise towels were waiting. I picked one up and tossed him the other. I went in through the living room and was treated to the delicious aroma of brewing coffee. It actually did smell like Marie's!

Richard grinned as he poured me a mug full and pushed the tray with the cream and sugar (and a sunny yellow hibiscus blossom) to me.

I was impressed. Apparently he'd been a busy boy while I'd slept the morning away.

"So be honest, with me," I said seriously, "Has it always been your secret desire to be a butler and now you've given yourself the opportunity as a birthday gift?"

Richard smiled as he returned the French press to its own little hotplate. He looked at me as he took a sip.

"My secret desire has always been to find you and to love you the way you deserve to be loved."

"Really?"

"Really," he assured me quite seriously. "So how am I doing?"

"Can I answer after I see what you're offering for breakfast?"

He shook his head and moved to the refrigerator, opening the double doors and beginning to look through the contents.

"Looks like we have eggs, bagels, croissants…there are some muffins…" he picked up a plastic container and shook it, "granola, yogurt—flavored and plain—and a large selection of fruit…"

"Jam for the croissants?" I asked.

"Guava, apricot and blackberry. There's some cream cheese, as well." He turned to me, awaiting my order.

"Croissants, butter and apricot jam, please," I said, trying to keep my face straight. I wondered if he would heat the croissants.

Not to worry, my Trained Professional could also operate a microwave, and he delivered warm croissants and the requested butter and jam just a couple of minutes later. I buttered half of one, added some jam and offered him the first bite. He took it with a smile and let me lick the overage from his lips. He expressed his gratitude with an apricot-y kiss.

"Now are you ready to tell me how I'm how doing?" he asked.

"So far, so good," I said nonchalantly. "But your performance will have to be reviewed on a regular basis."

"Promise?"

"Company policy," I assured him.

"And what company is that?"

"J'Adore."

"I see. And what exactly does J'Adore do?"

"We specialize in providing the Three C's for select clients."

Richard was enjoying the improv and, I suspected, hoping to trip me up. More the fool him. I'm the word girl!

"And the three C's would be…?"

"We pride ourselves on offering Care, Consideration and Companionship." I licked jam from my fingers with some very suggestive tongue action and reached for another croissant.

He leaned in to whisper against my ear, "Sounds like prostitution to me."

"Not at all," I insisted professionally. "Our client list is very exclusive—and I admit rather short. They are looking for long-term, intimate relationships with a single partner. The people we contract with insist on True Love, nothing less."

"I see," Richard said as he poured more coffee into my mug. "That may be a problem.

"Oh?" That surprised me. "And why would that be a problem? You seemed to be so interested in the position a minute ago."

"This may surprise you," he said, all sincerity, "But I'm a one woman man. I'm afraid I would be unable to make my amazing self available to anyone but the woman I love."

I had to smirk at the "amazing" part—even if it was true!

"I see," I said with a sigh. I was quiet for a moment and then looked up brightly. "Would you consider the position if I were to offer you the exclusive assignment as my lover?"

He regarded me for a moment. "Well, no offense, but I would have to have an in-depth explanation of what was required...you know...to decide if I was interested."

"Really?"

"Really. I mean, you're beautiful, but for that sort of commitment I would need some...well, shall we say 'more intimate' exposure before I could accept the position."

"I see. If I can find my appointment book..." I looked around the countertops as if it might be there. "I'll see if I have an opening for you."

"I know you have at least two," he said as he stepped very close to me.

"And those would be?"

"Let me demonstrate," he said reaching for my towel. He hesitated, his eyes seeking permission (as if he needed it!)

I spread my arms and let him unwrap it slowly. He let it fall around the stool but he didn't touch me.

"One of them would be here," he said as he ran his finger along my lip, urging my mouth open.

I yielded and he leaned forward and gave me a kiss, starting slowly and then probing my mouth gently with his tongue. He wasn't touching me, the only point of contact was our mouths. It was all I could do to remain in my seat. When he finished the kiss, he smiled.

"And the other opening?" I asked as if I hadn't a clue.

He placed his hands on my knees lightly and spread them apart. Again, his one hand being the only point of contact, he slipped it between my legs, between me and my barstool, and then raised his finger to slip into me.

"I see..." I said with an involuntary gasp. "And how would you utilize these two openings?"

"Would you like me to demonstrate?" he asked innocently.

"I believe I would."

Richard offered me his hand and I took it as I slid off the stool. When he turned toward the bedroom I reached for his towel, which fell to the floor. I followed him, admiring his perfect ass.

When we reached the bed, he tossed the covers back and urged me to sit on the edge of the mattress, which I did primly, wondering how far he wanted to carry our little game. Never a dull moment with my Prince!

"So, is that the best you can offer?" I asked with a glance at his penis, which was only just beginning to stir.

"No," he said. "I was waiting to test the compatibility of my cock and your mouth. There's always the possibility that one or the other of us might not be suited for such activity."

"Really?"

"Yes," he said with a sigh. "It may be hard to believe, but some women don't enjoy having a man's penis in their mouths."

"No...that can't be true!" I said in mock horror.

"It's true. And some women just go along because it's expected. I require more."

"Such as?"

"I expect the woman I love to love all of me, just as I intend to love all of her. Would you care to see how you feel about it?" He lifted his half erect cock and offered it to my mouth.

"Hmm..." I said, reaching out tentatively for a little suck. "Well, that's actually quite nice. Can I have more?"

"Please," he said, releasing himself.

I reached for him and stretched him down then raised him to my mouth again, and began a round of tongue gymnastics. After all, I had to prove to him that my commitment to J'Adore was total. Then I suddenly took as much of him as I could manage and gave him some swift head and some hand action on his shaft while I stroked his balls. That surprised him, but his cock shaped up fast.

I continued to stroke him as I looked up with a pouty lip. "You're too big now, I can barely get you in my mouth."

"That's alright, we still have that other spot to try. Let me show you."

He urged me into the middle of the bed. Richard was doing an amazing acting job and I was getting a kick out of his efforts.

"You realize this part of the interview counts for fifty percent of the evaluation?" I warned him.

He was kneeling between my cocked legs, hands on my knees. "Explain."

"Well, the numbers are flexible," I said very analytically. "It depends on the candidate, but generally it's 20% on manners, 40% on intelligence, 20% on appearance, 40% on sense of humor, 50% on sincerity and 50% on sexual skills."

"Uh… any chance of making extra points by helping you with your math?"

"None," I said with confidence.

Richard sighed, attempting to keep a straight face. "Well, I guess I might as well go ahead with this part of the process."

"Might as well," I agreed.

He smiled as he spread my knees wider and put his skilled tongue to work. After delivering two Triple O's (that would be Outstanding Orally-induced Orgasms) he proceeded to the penetration section of the evaluation. As you can probably imagine he achieved the highest possible score.

Afterward, I lay in his arms, enjoying the light kisses he scattered over my cheeks.

"So, tell me, how did I do?" he asked.

"You have passed with flying colors. And how do you feel about me after this additional exposure."

"You, Sweet Juliet, are the girl of my dreams."

"Good. Then there are just two more questions to conclude the interview."

Richard smirked, waiting.

"What time is it and where the hell are we?"

Richard bust out with a huge guffaw, which dislodged him. Then he rolled onto his back, still laughing.

"There is no way to explain how much I love you!" he laughed.

"Yeah, yeah. Answer my questions."

When he finally caught his breath he reached over to his nightstand and picked up his phone, which he'd evidently reset.

"It's twelve minutes past noon and we are in the general area of Turks and Caicos in the Caribbean."

"Thanks. Just like the phone, I have to orient myself on the planet. Sort of an internal GPS thing," I explained.

"Of course."

"And now I want to explore. Care to join me?"

51
Consultation

Still Friday

I found a brightly patterned sarong—three actually—in the closet, and three more of the short ones for men. So we attired ourselves in island wear and proceeded to inspect the house, starting with the bedrooms. They were all beautifully decorated, each having a little private outdoor area and its own spacious bath with Baby Zs! At the end of the hallway, a door on the front side of the house opened on a well-equipped gym.

Off the kitchen, another door led to a breezeway and to a little two bedroom house that we decided must be for staff when needed. Back in the main house and on the far side of the living room was a large room, the front portion being a TV area that could be shut off from the library section by folding doors. The ocean end of the library had lots of books and art as well as three desks, but I was most excited to see the baby grand piano (white to match the décor!)

"Was this your request?" I asked, inclining my head toward the piano.

"Nope. But I'm happy it's here. I thought you might want some musical accompaniment to your deliberations about your offers."

That remark sort of stalled me. I hadn't even thought about them since I'd given him the overview on the plane.

"I'm not ready." I know I was frowning.

"No problem. I'll play and you can dance for me, or sing along, or swim. Whatever you like."

I smiled. "Want to go down and take a closer look at the ocean?"

It was so much fun being alone with Richard, sort of playing house in Paradise! He was so easy to be around and seemed to be enjoying the experience as much as I was. We did as we pleased, eating, sleeping and napping whenever the mood struck us.

We ran on the beach early in the morning after that first day, came back for a swim and a shower and then had breakfast. That became our routine. Our kitchen was well stocked and we grilled our fish or steaks in the evening, ate salads and fruit, things suited to the tropical climate. Whichever of us felt like it, did the dishes. He was certainly easy to live with, even without Marie orchestrating behind the scenes. It was a bit of a surprise, but I should have known that Richard would have thought these were things he should be able to do for himself, and consequently had taught himself to do them well.

On Sunday Leo returned with his wife, Angelina, and they changed the bedding and our towels, brought groceries and did general tidying up. They worked unobtrusively and efficiently and didn't disturb us at all.

Richard and I had agreed to limit our computer time to a couple of hours a day, max, mostly around his schedule. I spent the bulk of my "work" time reading through the proposals and making notes. I did email Ben and Jerry a couple of times with questions. While the legalese of the documents was tedious, I did understand it. There was just so MUCH of it. I wanted a read-through before I discussed it with Richard. He was reading it, as well, and making his own notes but withholding comments for the time being.

After a very relaxed wake up on Monday morning, I announced I was ready.

"What? Again?" Richard laughed.

"In your dreams, " I said with a smirk and a poke to his ribs.

He grabbed me and pulled me to him, nuzzling my neck and

saying, "I may be down but don't count me out!" Then he started tickling me.

"Nooo….!" I cried, trying to squirm away from him.

He gave me a quick kiss on the end of my nose and released me. I threw myself across the bed and stood up, attempting to regain my dignity. (What dignity?)

"Today's the day I'm ready to discuss the offers. But right now I need to get to that sand!"

After breakfast, we settled ourselves on opposite couches in the living room, looking at each other across the big glass coffee table. I even put on my nerd glasses to indicate I was in business mode—not as obvious when I shifted as when my Trained Professional did!

"Where would you like to start?" Richard asked.

"I don't know. I think I have a good basic understanding of the two offers, but I have no clue how to make a decision."

"Do you feel any inclination, one way or the other?"

I thought about that for a minute, trying to see if I had missed anything in my own admittedly confused analysis.

"I don't think so. Maybe if I back up and explain my thought processes, you'll understand where I am."

I half expected a smirk but Richard was focused.

"Okay," I began. "From the time I first conceived the idea, I thought it would be a really fun project to undertake academically. Then, as the concept changed and grew and continued to expand, I became convinced it had legs. As my mental picture of the possibilities grew, I fantasized about it making me rich—all this, mind you, with no actual concept of what making astronomical amounts of money would really be like."

"Do you understand what that would mean now?"

"No, not really. Google's offer boggles my mind, but I expect that if they value it so much at this stage, the potential worth must be far beyond that."

"Valid point," was all he said.

"I always thought I would move to funding and then be faced with setting up the company, doing the hiring and overseeing the project to IPO status. That was when I imagined I could consider a dollar amount followed by too many zeros."

"So you imagined putting the company together and running it while it became a working portal?"

"I did."

"Did you like the idea of the management part of what that business would be? Managing people, tracking expenses, meeting with funders and lawyers—keeping up with everything that goes into coding and such things? And forgive me, you know I'm not familiar with that aspect of your work. I'm asking if you thought you'd enjoy running the show while you grew the business. To me it seems less creative than what you've done so far. I want to understand what part of the work you enjoy the most."

I thought about that for a moment—for probably three minutes, in fact.

"I think it's the creative part I like the most. It's been hard work, too, but I've always enjoyed the problem solving aspect of moving ahead. I probably enjoyed the creative part of imagining what it would be like when I got funded, maybe more than the reality of it, which is now coming out of the shadows."

Richard smiled. "Did you consider the possibility of selling out at this stage?"

"It never occurred to me until Ben and Jerry mentioned it. You and I discussed it then."

"I remember. So it sounds like you had a pretty good plan going with moving into funding, but no scenario for the early-buy."

"Exactly. But there's another factor in the picture now."

He looked at me expectantly.

"You."

"I hope you're not going to tell me that you met me and now want to give up all your dreams to become my love slave?"

Somehow he managed to keep his face straight as he said it. I couldn't.

"Not quite, though it does present a certain amount of temptation. No, not ready to give up my dreams, but our relationship is very important to me and I have to consider it. It wasn't a factor until quite recently."

"Cress, we both have our work and it doesn't seem to have

had a negative effect on either of us. I have to continue doing what I do and I've always assumed you would succeed with the project and continue with it in some capacity. I hope you know I would never try to keep you from doing something you love."

"I never thought you would. But what I love doing is you. And us. Now, suddenly, I have to look at what either of these choices will mean. I'm afraid that both of them will curtail our traveling together next year—maybe for several years. Frankly, I don't want to miss out on time with you."

"Thank you, Sweetheart, you know I feel the same. So, let's come at this from a different direction. Will you try a little relaxation exercise for me?"

"Sure." I was interested to see what he was up to.

"Get comfortable and close your eyes."

He led me through the breathing and relaxation, just like our meditation CDs.

"Now, I want you to imagine that you have completed your obligations to the project. You've either sold it or IPOed it—it doesn't matter which—and you have a vast amount of money at your disposal. The project has left the nest and you now have few, if any, responsibilities to it."

I had to work at that, especially the "vast amounts of money" part. Nothing came to me and after several minutes I said, "Honestly, the money thing is a big issue and I just am clueless. I see myself sitting in a big pile of it, looking confused."

"We'll talk about the money later. So now, crawl out of your pile of money and walk out the door of the room. There is a long hall in front of you and at the end is another door. Walk toward it. When you reach it, you will open it and step through and find yourself five years in the future."

He gave me some time, then said, "Now what do you see yourself doing with your time?"

"All I can see is us, here together, just like we are now."

"Good," he said. "But I have to get back to work so what are you going to do?"

I know there was a long pause because I couldn't see anything. Then all at once I saw myself walking along a street, West-Hollywoody but nowhere recognizable. I turned into a building, went through a medium-size lobby and up a wide staircase to a sort of mezzanine level. I was describing this to Richard as I went, slowly, looking at things around me and telling him about them.

I came up to a glass door to an office. There was writing on it.

"What does it say? Richard asked.

It took a moment before I could read it.

"You won't believe this." I didn't believe it.

"Tell me."

"J'Adore."

"Just J'Adore? Not J'Adore Products, or J'Adore Clothing or something to indicate what the business is?"

"Nope. Just J'Adore in scripty gold lettering on the glass."

"Go through the door. What do you see?"

It was a nice office, very tasteful decor, and there was a young woman sitting at the reception desk. She looked up at me and smiled and said "Good morning, CJ." I went farther into the building and into what I somehow knew was my office. Nice! Lots of glass. I was relaying all this to Richard.

Then a young man came in and said, "'Morning, Boss." His name was Adam. I don't know how I knew that, either.

"Ask Adam what you do at J'Adore," Richard suggested.

I asked Adam to describe the scope of the company. Oh, my! I wasn't going to share that with Richard! I became quiet.

"What does he say?"

"Uh…we're sort of a multi-level company with our fingers in a few pots."

I could tell Richard was aware that there was something I wasn't telling him.

"So, are you successful? Ask Adam how the business is doing."

"Up 300% over last year!" I said gleefully.

"Well, I think its time for you to come back from your very successful future. So take a deep breath and follow my count down to number one, when you'll be back in the Caribbean with me."

When I opened my eyes, he was watching me.

"Well, the point of that was to see what you might be doing after the project has flown the nest. It sounds like you're still on a creative roll, yes?"

I tried not to grin. "Yes."

"Do you want a break?" he asked. "I could use a cup of coffee."

"Let me get it," I insisted as I headed for the kitchen. I couldn't trust my transparent face and I didn't want to get into a discussion just yet about my future business endeavors. The problem I wanted to finish tackling was those two offers.

52
An Idea

Still Monday

We spent the rest of the morning making a pros/cons list for each of the proposals, with Richard reminding me that Ben had told me to ask Google for the moon when it came to the portions of the offer that invited negotiation.

That dream list fell on the pro side with Google. These were things like a two week break every four weeks, not starting until March first, a workplace within a thirty minute commute. (Richard reminded me that Google had several "campuses" in the L.A. area, which I'd forgotten, despite touring one while I was doing my undergrad work.) I also decided that, ideally, I would finish my commitment to them within three years. After that, if they needed me, they'd have to contract me as a consultant.

Believe me when I say that all this seemed quite fantastical (not really fabtastical) to me. I was so grateful that Richard was there to ask the questions that kept me focused on the possibilities each of the offers.

Dropping the discussion for lunch, we talked instead about Richard's museum project and what the demands on his time might be for that. Of course it was too soon to even know if it was a go. He'd already planned another trip to New York before the end of the month for more meetings with Peter

After lunch I asked him if he'd take a walk with me on the beach and talk to me about money. He gave me a kind of funny look.

"I'm referring to the money Google would give me if I choose them. I have no concept of those numbers, at least as far as what they would mean in my life."

"I'm hoping they'd mean you wouldn't throw me over for someone with more of it," he said in mock seriousness.

"Nope. Money or not, I intend to keep you and continue to make you believe you want to keep me, too."

"You're doing a pretty convincing job, so far," he said with a very sweet kiss.

With that we gave each other a generous dose of sunscreen, grabbed our sarongs and headed for the beach.

"So what's a girl to do with $375 million dollars? " I asked as we walked along the sand. "I assume IRS will be standing in line for an awful lot of it, but I imagine whatever they leave behind will still be more than enough to keep me in pocket money for the rest of my life."

Richard gave my hand a squeeze. "Ben and Jerry will help you with that, but if you decide to take the Google offer, I'll hook you up with Ari Marx. He's my guy in New York who handles all the structure for the family's joint concerns and for me. He can give you a second opinion. And we can also try to get Robert to come over and meet with us for a third perspective. There are ways you can hang on to most of your money, and leave yourself some to give away."

"Are you angling for compensation for your outstanding service, Mr. Hunter?"

"No, but I'd be interested to hear what you think I'm worth."

"Far more than Google has in their account." I emphasized that with a kiss, which turned into more kissing as the tips of the little waves tickled our toes.

I thought about pulling off his wrap and dragging him into that inviting water for a salty wet one, but I wanted more financial info first.

"So, really. Give me some concrete examples. What can I do with all that money?"

"What do you want to do? What have you always thought you'd do if you had the money to do it? Are there institutions you believe in? Things you admire? The High Line would be happy to receive a donation."

That pleased me. "That would be fun. But how much? What do you give them?"

"We give them $50,000 a year as a family—siblings and Maman."

That got him a kiss on the cheek. "Very generous. You are so good. But it would take a lot of fifty-thousands to dent my possible bank account."

"Think of the things you want to support. How about Kate's foundation? And your folks—you could do small things for them—pay off their mortgage if they have one, new cars when they need them. And what would they like to see most in their departments at the college? Do they need a new theater, or a new wing of something? You could establish a scholarship fund or two."

I thought about those things for a few minutes as a whole new world of possibilities began to open up.

"How could I do something for Steph? Beyond just writing her a check, I mean."

"I'll give you the talk about giving money to friends when the time comes. But there are lots of other things that might help her with her career. She's going to need studio space after the end of the year. You could buy a building, remodel it—say for studio space and offices for yourself or to rent. Then you could give Steph a lease for some set period of time for a small amount. I suspect she'll have a pretty sizable bank account of her own after her show in February. There are lots of ways you can help her when you know what it is she really needs."

"I'd have to decide how much would keep me for the rest of my life and set it aside where I can't touch it."

"Sweetheart, that amount of money can be invested and provide a large income for you to fund your next project and continue doing good things for the rest of your life and far beyond it. You'll have the opportunity create a legacy that can easily outlive you."

I pulled down my sunglasses and frowned at him.

"Do you know something I don't?"

He laughed. "Not about your lifespan. I'm not worried about

that, I'm sure it will be a long one. And you don't seem to be the type to blow a fortune unless you finally decide to go for those $600 jeans and never wear a pair more than once. And even then…"

"I told you, no $600 jeans, EVER. Period!"

"Whichever proposal you accept, you'll have everything you need and the ability to share it for the rest of your life. It's a magnificent gift, Cress, one you've worked very hard for, for a long time. And one that will let you create a great deal of good in this world."

We tabled the financial discussion for the day and while we ate dinner by candlelight on the terrace—the salad I made and grilled fish and fresh corn courtesy of my Magic Man—I was thinking about the next day and exactly how to celebrate his birthday.

"So my Prince, will you allow me to take you to the yacht club for dinner tomorrow night to celebrate your natal day?" I'd read through the "house" book and gotten the info on the yacht club. It looked pretty nice. I'd already made the reservation.

"I'd like that. I was going to suggest we check it out at some point while we're here."

"Good! They're expecting us at 7:00 p.m. I understand dancing is a possibility." I added with a wiggle of my eyebrow. "Now, tell me what else I can do to make your day special."

"Well, actually…" He stopped there.

I waited. "Are you going to tell me?"

Richard grinned. "Tomorrow night."

I rolled my eyes. "Seriously? I hope you're not going to make a habit of this surprise and suspense thing. I'm not crazy about it."

"Really? You seem to be enjoying this one," he said gesturing toward the ocean.

"I LOVE this! You know I do. But if you'd told me we were going to a private island—and nothing more—I would have reveled in the anticipation. I would have found enjoyment in imagining what was to come."

"And what if you imagined something like this and it turned out to be a little grass shack on the beach without plumbing?"

My turn to laugh.

"First, I was previously incapable of imagining anything at all like this, and second, you don't seem to be the type to go for primitive experiences. And…if I were in a little grass shack with you, it would still be wonderful, even if it was just a tent. After all, we'd still have the ocean."

"Uh…just a minute. I distinctly recall you saying you had no desire to sleep on rocks."

"Ah…that's true. But you said 'beach' so it would be sand, wouldn't it?"

"I yield," he said with a smile.

Richard left the table, went into the house and returned a few minutes later, holding something behind his back. I looked up at him, waiting. He smiled, and with a flourish, deposited Zoor on the table in front of me, where he stood tall and proud.

I squealed with delight, immediately picking him up and giving him a quick lick and a suck before cradling him against my chest like a baby. Richard caught his breath.

"How did you sneak my old pal into the luggage without me noticing?" And then, suddenly I had a horrible thought. "Please tell me you didn't have Marie pack him."

I'm sure it was the look on my face that made him laugh!

"I slipped him into the carry on."

"Good thing we flew Air Giano. I'm not sure what the TSA folks might think seeing him on an X-ray!"

"It might make their day," Richard suggested.

"Maybe," I said, kissing Zoor affectionately. "I'd really hate to have anyone besides you and me handling him, though."

Richard sat back sipping his wine. He was looking at me. And with a smile so sweet it would melt your heart. (It melted mine.)

"What?"

"Just thinking what a wonderful woman you are."

"Wonderful enough for you to play for me if I do the dishes?"

"At least that wonderful. And who knows, maybe wonderful enough for a special dessert."

"Ooooh, I like the sound of that," I said with a wink as I stood up and bent to kiss him.

STILL LUCKY

Richard played while I cleaned up our dinner debris, Zoor observing from the center of the island. It made me laugh. Finally, I took him to the bedroom and put him in the drawer of Richard's nightstand. I had no idea what he was planning on doing with Zoor, but that kind of anticipation was exciting!

I made myself comfortable in the library and just watched Richard play. He was so focused on the keyboard, so intense and yet it was almost as if he was glowing. There was passion in his playing, but I also saw how profound his love for his music was. I was so grateful he'd returned to it and found it impossible to imagine how he had managed to keep himself—and for so long—from something that gave him so much joy.

53

Birthday Boy

Tuesday, October 15

I woke and slipped out of bed at 4:35 the next morning. Richard stirred when I got up, mumbling, "Everything, OK?"

"I just had an idea—need to go write it down. Go back to sleep and dream of me."

He reached blindly for my hand, gave it a squeeze, and with a smile on his face, rolled over and snuggled into his pillow.

I went quietly into the closet, wrapped myself in a sarong and got his gift out of my purse, then went across to the library and the desk where my computer sat. I opened the drawer and took out my notebook. Tucked between the pages was a pile of little notes I'd made for Richard to help celebrate his birthday.

I put one under the lid of his laptop for him to find when he took care of work that afternoon, another on the piano keyboard, closing the fall over it so he'd find it whenever he decided to play. In the kitchen I set our mugs on the counter, a note and his gift next to his. Returning to the closet, I slipped the last note into his running shoe, went in the bathroom, gave my teeth a quick brush and added a spritz of my perfume.

I paused a moment before getting back in bed, just to admire my lover as he sprawled across the sheets on his stomach. He was getting browner and his tan lines were disappearing. We did spend some time sunbathing in the altogether each day, and had managed to do it without getting burned. Lucky us!

I crawled across the bed and planted a gentle kiss on his lovely round bottom. That resulted in muffled laughter from his pillow.

"Yeeeessss….? Something you need?"

"It seems a good time to wish you a happy birthday," I said reasonably.

"Does it?"

"Turn over and we'll see."

Richard rolled onto his back with a smirk. To my surprise, his cock didn't seem prepared for a wake-up call.

"Er…maybe not," I said with exaggerated disappointment.

He glanced at the clock. "It's not five yet."

"What, your penis is like a cuckoo? Or would that be cockoo?"

"Noooo. But usually, I can combine the normal morning erection with an opportunity to introduce you to the day."

"Would an inducement lead to an early response?"

"Always worth a try," he said with a perfectly straight face.

"Oh, goody!" Immediately, I straddled him, setting my wet self down just above the base of his cock. I smiled and gave his nipples a pinch.

"Good morning, my Prince! *Buon Compleanno et Bon Anniversaire, mon amour, mon homme doux, coeur de mon coeur.*

"*Tu sens merveilleuse,*" he said softly, as his hands moved to my hips.

"I have a man who buys my perfume for me."

"What else does he do for you?"

"He makes me very wet," I said, emphasizing that as a fact.

His hand moved lightly over my belly. "How does he do that?"

"Just by the way he looks at me."

I leaned forward and gave him a quick kiss, followed by many little kisses all over his face. His hands ran lightly down my sides, coming to rest on my bottom, gently squeezing me.

"Tell me how he is when he makes love to you," Richard said, with a raw expression that surprised me. I wasn't sure what was behind it.

"You mean besides perfect?"

"Yes."

"It's something I don't really understand," I said, in a very scholarly tone of voice. I was explaining all this while spreading kisses over his face, throat, and shoulders and giving his nipples an occasional tongue tickle.

"He seems to have a sixth sense for what might excite me at any given moment. He tells me he listens to my heart and that's how he knows exactly what to do, how to lead me to a place where I feel both so loved and so full of love that's it's as if we really do become one person." I kissed him again and smiled. "And that's not to mention that every time we make love my orgasms are as varied as I can ever imagine them being. He's taught me new paths to those experiences and seems to truly enjoy my pleasure as much as his own. " I paused and smiled. When he said nothing, I asked, "More?"

"More," was all he said.

Suddenly, I flashed back to the night when he'd asked me to tell him how I saw his body. It felt a little bit like that.

"My lover can make love to me even from halfway around the world. I can come just at the sound of his voice. Sometimes I have those wonderful aftershocks from a single thought of something we've shared. And you know what's best of all?"

"Tell me."

"He loves to play with me. "

Richard smirked.

"No...not in that sense, though he seems to enjoy that, too. What I mean is, he's playful. I recently relaized that I feel like I've spent most of my life looking for playmates. I'm here to assure you they are very few and far between. It is so wonderful when someone can make you laugh or..."

I'd been conscious of his erection for a minute or two, so as I said that, I rose up, quickly positioned him, and in a smooth move came down on him. He gasped in surprise.

"...or," I repeated, "make that sound!"

I leaned forward again, giving him the opportunity to stroke me at his own pace as I ran my finger over his lips. His arms tightened around me.

"Happy Birthday Richard René Louis Hunter. I love you!"

" I love you most," he said as he kissed me.

STILL LUCKY

The note in his shoe said:

The half life of love is forever.
—Junot Diaz, *This Is How You Lose Her*

How long do you have? XXOOJ

After our run, and another birthday fuck in the shower—do you think it might have been because I did a Marilyn impression as I sang *Happy Birthday* to him?—Richard came to join me in the kitchen. He saw the box and note on the counter.

"Happy Birthday, Handsome. Am I being redundant?" I asked, as I filled his mug.

"Nope. Feel free." He smiled at me as he sipped his coffee.

"Are you going to open that?"

"This?" He picked up the box and shook it. "What is it?"

"Seriously?" I said in exasperation.

Richard laughed and untied the bow. I had purposely re-boxed the little heart so he might not know it was from Giano. He took it out and held it in his fingers, running his thumb over the texture on the front. Then he turned it over and read the inscription.

He stood up and came around the island to kiss me. "There is nothing on this earth I value more than your heart."

"Well, now you have it. And you can carry it with you in your pocket with your coins. You'll see it every time you reach for change to pay someone."

"How do you think of these things?"

"I admit it's not easy to find a gift for the man who has everything. But a girl's gotta do what a girl's gotta do."

The card said:

It isn't about the material things or pride or ego.
It's about who your heart beats for.—Hafiz

Mine beats for you! XXOOJ

479

"Ditto," he said with a smile.
"Now what shall I fix you for breakfast?"

After lunch Richard asked if I could go with him to New York.

"I'm going to meet with Peter. You could talk to Ari about the money and if you can go, I'll see if I can set that appointment and also have Robert come over to meet with you."

"When is this?" I couldn't remember exactly what day he was leaving, and my phone and calendar were in my purse.

"A week from Friday. Then back to L.A. on following Tuesday."

"Sure, I'd love that. I can meet with Ben and Jerry on Thursday to discuss some of the details, but I don't have to make a decision until November 10th. At least I assume that's how it works? If I take Google, I say yes by their deadline and then we negotiate? Or do we have to have a revised offer by then?"

"Give the Ice Cream Boys a call and ask them. I'll go see what I can organize with Ari and Robert."

The note in Richard's laptop was addressed to Handsome:

The Earth would die
If the sun stopped kissing her.
—Hafiz, *The Gift*

I know how she feels! XXOOJ

"I'll never stop!" Richard called from his desk.

Marie had packed my flowered halter dress, no doubt aware of how often I wore that style when Richard and I went out. She may also have remembered I'd worn a halter dress the night we met—after all, she had washed it for me that first day! She's also included a pair of my splits. I didn't know if I should be embarrassed or grateful that she would think of such things! Of course, she was French...

Richard was wearing a natural color linen short sleeve shirt and a pair of khaki Bermudas. He had great legs—have I mentioned that before? At any rate, we were off, Richard driving us in the little white Fiat convertible that came with the house.

The marina and yacht club were at the opposite end of the island, maybe three or four miles south of the airport. We left at 5:00 p.m., wanting to have some time to explore before we lost the light. The road was unpaved so we took our time and enjoyed the lush scenery. It was dense foliage, tropical, with spots of color in the blossoms here and there. Occasionally there was break, and we could see the clouds coloring as the sun edged toward the sea.

And then, suddenly, we found ourselves in a circular drive in front of a modest-size low building. It was smaller than I'd expected. By the time Richard had shut off the engine, a young man in a crisp white uniform was opening my door for me.

"Good evening Miss Bailey, Mr. Hunter. We're so pleased you could join us. You may leave the car here. Our guests all arrive via water and it is currently a shoulder season for us, so there are not too many people here tonight. It will perhaps make your evening all the more enjoyable?"

By then we had reached the double glass doors which Enrique (he was wearing a name tag) opened for us. We stepped into the vestibule and he moved ahead of us.

"This is a private entrance, used only by the guests from *Beaujeu*," he explained as he led us down a short hallway. When he reached a pair of smoked glass doors at the other end, he handed Richard a plastic keycard. "You may use this to access this entrance during your stay. There is another in the book at the house."

He pushed a panel on the wall, the doors opened and we stepped out onto a magnificent mezzanine with a balcony overlooking the main floor of the yacht club, which must have been at least sixty feet below.

No wonder the entrance had seemed so small! First, it was private, as Enrique had explained, and the club was built into the cliffs on that end of the island. The building's architecture was interesting, making you feel almost as though you were standing in the bottom of a huge ship, looking toward the bow, which was all glass that met in a point and framed the view of the horseshoe-shaped bay. The marina itself took up the left hand side. The right side was a beautiful white sand beach.

"Is this Umberto's design?" I asked in wonder.

"It is. Beautiful, isn't it? Shall we go take a closer look at the marina?" Richard asked.

"Yes, please," I said, as he took my hand and we walked down one of the two curving staircases.

The main level was very much like a luxury hotel lobby, only very large. Multiple seating areas were scattered across the space, interspersed with extravagant tropical flower arrangements, but most prominent was the view, even more impressive from there, where the widows soared high above us.

To the left was a row of small shops, looking like what you might expect at a resort: clothing, books and magazines, gifts, cigars—they looked very expensive and I was thinking I might have to come back and see if I could find something for Steph.

The bar and the restaurant were to the right, and as we approached the terrace, we could see that tables extended onto a deck out over the sand.

Outside, we walked in the opposite direction, along the boardwalk that led to the slips. There were only six boats of varying degrees of luxury, but all obviously very expensive. The largest yacht was at the far end and we stopped to admire it. It was magnificent. I know nothing about boats, but it was big and white and so sleek it looked like a space ship!

"Is this what you sailed off to Corsica on?" I asked Richard.

He laughed. "Hardly. That was a sailboat, and a very nice one, but nothing like this."

"How much do these things cost?"

"Why? Are you making plans for all those millions?"

"Nope. I'm just curious. This sort of thing is so beyond my ken that if I'm going to become one of you, I think I should have a vague idea of how your world works."

"Well, I'm not into yachts myself, but I have been on a few.'"

We stopped about halfway down the length of the boat. I could see Richard estimating the size.

"I'm guessing this is about 160 feet. Five decks above the water and it looks like there's a helipad on top. I'd guess somewhere between forty and sixty million."

"For a boat???" I said rather more loudly than I meant to, which attracted the attention of a man in a white uniform, who was working above us. I waved, hoping he hadn't heard me. He smiled and waved back.

I turned to Richard and said more softly said, "Really?"

"Well, as I said, I'm no expert. But we can go yacht shopping sometime if you'd like to see what they're like inside. It's actually pretty amazing."

"If that's the price tag, I really would like to see one, just for fun."

He gave my hand a squeeze. "Maybe we'll meet the owner tonight and get a look at this one. And I expect we can get you aboard something in our travels next summer. A sailboat to Corsica, anyway."

Of course that required some grateful kissing of my Prince, which he participated in enthusiastically.

We sat in the bar and talked with some other guests as we watched the sun set. It was entertaining to see how Richard went about engaging with the others, a little chitchat and before I knew it they had joined us at our table. There was an older couple, with whom we exchanged some Italian, though they both spoke perfect English. Three brothers, who looked to be in their late twenties and early thirties, were from Oslo. Richard found things to talk about with all of them, and while I didn't have a great deal to contribute, he always made sure I was included. I really enjoyed seeing him in that setting, how easily he adapted to the group, and how interested he was in what the others were doing and how their paths had crossed.

We had a delicious dinner, just the two of us, and afterward were lured back into the bar by the music. A few more people were there—I counted fifteen besides us—and my Prince took me in his arms and danced with me. What a guy!

When we took a break, the waiter delivered an iced coconut

concoction called a *Sorbet Bay* that Richard had ordered for me, with a light hit of rum. (I wanted to be sober so I could fully appreciate the plans he had for me and Zoor.) The drink was wonderful and more like a coconut smoothie than a cocktail. Perfect!

One of the Norwegian boys, Amund, came and asked Richard if he might have a dance with me. Richard, of course, deferred to me, and soon I found the other two, Finn and Ingvar, attempting to fill my dance card. Richard danced with a couple of the ladies and then I saw him back at the table, watching us. He was smiling, so I kept dancing.

My phone was in my pocket and when it vibrated, I excused myself and went to the edge of the deck to answer, unable to imagine who might be calling. I felt a flutter of anxiety, hoping Daddy wasn't having problems. But it was an iGram from the Birthday Boy of *Kiss You All Over*. I looked up to see him watching me and got a blast of that energy when our eyes met. I rebuffed another invitation from Finn as I crossed the dance floor to rejoin the man whose thoughts seemed to be mirroring my own.

"Ready to go home?" I asked.

"Are you?"

"I am. I'm anxious to find out what you have planned for me and my not-so-little friend.

54
There's Something About Mary

Tuesday night

"So do you want to tell me about your plans for me and Zoor?" I asked on our drive back to the house.

Richard glanced at me. "Are you sure you really don't want to be surprised?"

"Honestly, I'd rather savor the possibilities. I'm not sure a 'surprise' involving my sizable friend can be guaranteed to be pleasant."

Richard laughed. "I understand, but you do know I'd never do anything you weren't into? I'd never hurt you, Sweetheart."

I leaned over and kissed his cheek. "I know that. I'd honestly prefer a general idea what you have in mind."

"Alright. I suppose it might be better to tell you ahead of time. Actually, I've been trying to decide how to present my fantasy."

"Ooooh! Fantasy! I like the sound of that!" I gave his thigh a squeeze. "Tell me."

Richard smiled. "Well, you know how much I enjoy watching my cock slip into you."

"I do. And you know how much I enjoy the sensation. I wish I could see it, too. It's the part of porn I find the most stimulating."

"Porn?" he said in surprise.

"Sure. I watch it sometimes. And that's a discussion I want to have with you one of these days, but right now I want to hear more about you slipping into me."

Richard gave me a look I couldn't quite read.

"Well, I was hoping you would indulge me by sucking my

cock while I have an intimate view of what that penetration looks like. My surrogate cock and your cunt, viewed from close-up. I find the thought of that very exciting."

"So do I, my Prince. A threesome! Two cocks and one girl , but no other man in my bed. You, my Trained Professional, are very creative." I slid my hand to his crotch and was surprised to feel his erection. ""Hmmmmm…you do like that idea."

Richard laughed.

When we got back to the house, Richard chose to do some kissing as he helped me out of the car. I was more than willing. I loved kissing him. (Perhaps that's been obvious?)

He pressed me against the car, his hands moving over my breasts, then gently scooping them out of the halter so he could fondle them. My nipples stood up and saluted, even before his thumbs skimmed them.

"Mind if I take you right here?" he breathed against my ear.

"I'm yours, anywhere, any time, my love." I took one of his hands, guiding it toward the hem of my skirt. He didn't need a map, and his fingers moved smoothly up under the fabric and found my splits.

"*Déjà vu?*" he said, not unexpectedly.

There was only one response: "All over again," I breathed as his finger slipped into me.

We both groaned.

"Please fuck me, Richard."

"As you wish," he whispered, as he pinned me against the car with his hip just long enough to turn and unzip his fly.

One arm slipped around my waist and lifted me just a bit, his other hand positioned his cock, but he hesitated. I didn't know why, I didn't care.

"Please…"

Oh, the relief! We both made a sound expressing our pleasure at being joined again. Richard made short work of the encounter, but held me tightly afterward, seeming reluctant to disengage.

He put his hand against my cheek and smiled, then gave me a slow, lingering kiss before releasing me.

"Does this mean there may be soft serve available for dessert?" I asked as we walked hand in hand to the door.

"It does indeed," he assured me.

We took a nice slow shower, washing each other tenderly and with more kissing than talking. I had put Zoor in a sink full of hot water to warm him, and he was up to temperature by the time we'd dried each other.

"Are you enjoying your birthday, my Prince?" I asked as I gently dried Zoor, gave him a quick tongue tease before passing him to Richard.

"The best birthday of my life, Sweetheart," he answered with a kiss, before leading me into the bedroom.

We got into bed and he reached for me to pull me close.

"You need to keep Zoor against your body so he won't cool off. I'll enjoy your fantasy more if there isn't a chilly willy to break the mood."

Richard chuckled and placed Zoor between us, which made me laugh.

"That's an interesting sensation," I said softly as I snuggled against both of Richard's cocks, one firm, the other ready to be dessert.

I put both my arms around his neck and rubbed my face against his cheek, enjoying the feel of his little beard and inhaling the smell of him.

"How can you smell so good?"

"How can I be so lucky to love a woman so perfectly suited to my pheromones?"

That made me laugh. "She's the lucky one."

He found my mouth and ran his tongue over my lips before giving me a deep kiss. I teased his tongue with mine, reminding him what was about to happen to his cock.

"I think you'd best gobble up your next course before it's too late."

"Oooh...I don't want to miss dessert!" I slid myself down along his body, running kisses over his abs as I went, and slipping one hand behind him to cup that perfect round ass of his while the other teased his nipples. I squeezed his bottom and nuzzled his pubic hair, ran my tongue down his penis and then, as he'd suggested, I gobbled him up. He caught his breath.

He quickly exceeded my capacity and then Richard insisted on a taste for himself. Without releasing my hold on him, I turned around and presented my dripping self to his face. I didn't know if he would go right for Zoor or what he had in mind. I put my mouth on him again, just as he applied his clever tongue to me.

I had just started to focus on one of his balls when he said, "Are you ready for your other friend?"

"Yes, please."

Then everything happened at once. Zoor slid into me slowly, but the testicle I was sucking jumped with a life of its own! I heard a groan and Richard ejaculated in several strong bursts that shot up and rained right back down on my head!

I laughed. "A little excited are we?"

"Oops…" came from the other end of the bed, followed by a deep belly laugh.

Neither of us was deterred. I tongued him and sucked, seeking my Juliet drop, and Zoor stroked me with the same skill his fleshy counterpart always exhibited. It didn't take me many more of those strokes to come, myself and when I did, Richard removed Zoor and extended my orgasms with his mouth. I was feeling like it was more my birthday than his.

When we'd both slowed down he gave me a light slap on my bottom and said, "Come here you beautiful girl, I want a kiss."

I eased myself off him and turned, but remained on my knees, both hands on my hips as I looked down at him.

Richard cracked up. "You look like Cameron Diaz with her new hair gel."

"Yes. Well, we all know there's something about Mary. You'll forgive me if I jump back in the shower."

"I'll join you," he said getting up and wiping a hand across his mouth. "Every time I talk to snakes…"

We'd given Zoor a wash, too, and Richard set him on his nightstand as we got back into bed. He pulled me close and kissed the top of my head as I snuggled against him.

"I apologize for that. You got me a little too excited."

We'd both thought it funny.

"Me or Zoor?" I asked, squinting suspiciously.

"Well, it's obvious the two of you together are a force to be reckoned with."

"Are you thinking you'd like to give it another try?"

"Not tonight. But yes. I enjoyed the experience."

"Uh…yeah. Maybe a little too much."

"You're so beautiful, and that was a whole new angle on our lovemaking. Does it bother you that I found it so exciting?" he asked.

"You know, you told me once that you'd be happy to be my science project. I extend the same offer to you. Curiosity and experimentation are all part of it, as far as I'm concerned. You haven't balked at any paths my enquiring mind has led me down so far, and I'm open to yours."

"Must be why I love you so much."

"Is that why you love me? I've often wondered…" I teased.

"Well, I'm in no hurry to figure it out. What fun would that be?"

"Exactly!"

On Thursday morning Richard let me know that he would be tied up all afternoon with online meetings.

"I'm sorry to be breaking our two hour rule, but I need to take care of some business with Mark and Ari."

"No problem. I was thinking I might head back over to the Yacht Club. I wanted to do a little shopping and see what their market has to offer. I'll take off after lunch, if that's okay with you."

"Perfect. And do you have Seiji's number? I want to see if we can get together next week before you and I have to leave again."

I clapped my hands together. "Great! I love his work and I'm so happy you do, too. He'll be so excited!"

Richard smiled and gave me a quick kiss. "Who knew you'd become an artist's agent?"

"No agenting for me. I just wanted to be sure you didn't miss some spectacular talent. And speaking of talent, have you thought about which of Steph's paintings you're going to take for your studio rent?"

"I thought we'd choose something together. Do you have a favorite?"

"I love this new work and I'm torn between the calendars and the botanicals. And who knows what she may create between now and February?"

I took the little Fiat—Richard informed me it was a pristine classic 1985 Spider though it looked for all the world like a brand new car to me—and headed back to the Yacht Club.

I strolled along the boardwalk toward the slips, this time looking up at the rocks that sheltered the bay. There were maybe two dozen smaller structures scattered at different levels among, and set into the rocks, all with glassy sides facing the sea. Apparently these were intended to provide visitors with accommodations if they chose to spend some time off their boats. (Honestly, for $50 million, wouldn't you think everything imaginable would be *ON* the boat?)

I returned to the shops in the main building. It was fun to see what the one percenters were likely to be buying and I confess I was appalled by some of the price tags. (Really? Four THOUSAND dollars for a PURSE?!) I couldn't help wondering if it would eventually cease to bother me—and secretly hoping I could maintain a certain amount of practicality despite my pending wealth.

I bought two little paintings by an island artist. They were miniatures with the actual canvas area only about three by three inches, though the wide coconut-wood frames made them closer to nine by nine. The one for Steph was an impressionistic pink hibiscus and for myself, I chose a slightly more abstract sea view—horizontal lines of color starting at the bottom with sand and then going through the varying shades of blue for sea and sky. It reminded me a little of the big window painting at home. It seemed I might be developing a thing for the ocean.

I couldn't resist getting Richard a bracelet that was six medium brown, twisted leather strands, bound in the center by three gold curvy bands that looked like waves to me. It was expensive, but I so loved to see him with something around his wrist and he seemed to enjoy wearing the pieces I picked out for him from his own collection. I wanted him to have something special from this trip.

There was a nice (if pricey) market there, too, so I picked up some thick lamb chops—flown in from New Zealand, I was informed. (I suspected I paid for their first class ticket!) I also got a pretty little chocolate *gateau*. Okay, that was primarily for me, but I thought if I stuck a candle in it, I could convince Richard that it was a belated birthday cake! Got a box of little candles, too!

55

That Money Shot

Friday, October 18

It was our last night at Beaujue. We'd had a simple dinner of red snapper with a papaya salsa and a spinach salad. I was curled up with Richard on the couch in the library while we enjoyed our wine and watched the stars come out.

"So was this trip what you had in mind when you told me what you wanted for my birthday trip?"

It couldn't be more perfect for me," I assured him. "But at one point you said you wanted to go somewhere and see it through my eyes. I'm not sure this seclusion was what you had in mind."

"You're right, this isn't what I was thinking of when I decided to let you choose. I admit I could never have imagined what I would see through your eyes here, and yet it turns out to be a gift far beyond my imagination."

I turned to look at him. I must have been frowning because he reached to smooth the space between my brows with his thumb before kissing that spot.

"Then you're not disappointed?"

"Nope," he said with conviction.

"Help me out here. What's the gift then? Seeing me look at the ocean for a week can't be very surprising. I think we both see it pretty much the same way."

"It's not the way you look at the ocean. It's the way you look at me and seeing myself through your eyes."

I sat up and just stared at him. He was serious.

"Uh, isn't that what mirrors are for?"

He laughed. "I've told you what I see in the mirror. You've assured me that I'm missing a great deal when I study my reflection. I think, after this week I can see a little more of what you see."

"And that would be?" I prompted.

"A man who pleases you, a man whose love you accept with your arms and your heart wide open. A man who lights you up from the inside when you look at him."

"The man I love," I concluded simply.

"Exactly."

I sighed very dramatically. "I suppose this means you'll be all puffed up and full of yourself now."

Richard chuckled and nuzzled my ear as he whispered, "Well, it's safe to say that a part of me is bound to puff up now and then, but it's you I want to be full of me."

It was my turn to say, "Exactly."

We had an uneventful flight home on Saturday and then immediately began taking care of things that needed doing before we left again for New York on Tuesday. After more than a week of relaxation with little that had to be done, I was having some trouble getting back in the groove. We'd kept our 5:00 a.m. schedule (complete with preferred wake-up routine!) on the island and with Richard's urging, I found myself back on the treadmill on Sunday morning. I only managed one rung on the salmon ladder—with Richard's help— and was determined to give it another shot that afternoon. That was a skill I didn't want to lose! You-Know-Who gracefully ascended and descended as if he'd just been at it the day before.

"Show off!" I mumbled grumpily.

That made him laugh. "I've been doing this for four years, Sweetheart. When you have that much time under your belt, you'll be able to maintain it, even if you take a week off."

I offered a doubtful look and a pouty lip, which he kissed before heading for his turn on the treadmill.

At lunch I decided to ask him about the salary he'd been paying me all summer. I still felt funny accepting money for doing nothing as the resident IT girl at the gallery. I did have some ideas for their system but hadn't had time to do anything about it.

"You know that generous salary Christina's been depositing in my account weekly?"

"Don't tell me you're angling for a raise," he said, perfectly serious, albeit with that telltale twinkle in his eye.

"Hardly. And I assume you'll tell me it's my money and I can do whatever I want with it."

"Yes."

"Well, I was thinking of using it to pay off my student loan. My debt is modest by most standards and I have enough now. I'd kind of like to go into this pending world of solvency debt-free."

"I understand. Is there a problem? I can give you more money if you need it."

"No!" I said firmly.

"You can pay me back when your bank account explodes, if that would make you feel better. I thought we were clear about my position on finances."

"I am—we are," I said with a modicum of frustration. "And I even understand it. I just haven't quite fully integrated into my personal zeitgeist yet."

He sat back and just looked at me. "Really? *Personal zeitgeist*?"

"Yes," I answered defensively. I wasn't angry, and I knew he was teasing me, but it was frustrating. Everything was just sort of building up to what felt like a huge change in my life, one I still wasn't comfortable with. While I was trying to give that thought the attention it deserved, I imagine my expression must have been a dead giveaway, because Richard was just staring at me.

"Am I going to have to explain the Koons Inflatables to you again?" he said sternly.

It took a minute to register, then I remembered the hilarity of that discourse and burst out laughing, all irritation forgotten.

"It's not funny, you know," he said, putting his fork down and giving me a look that added gravity to his words. "Jeff's work is a serious contribution to the lexicon of contemporary art. Why the lobster alone, when considered from several perspectives…"

STILL LUCKY

Before he could finish I launched myself from my chair and into his lap, putting my hand over his mouth. He frowned, but continued talking, his words muffled under my fingers.

"No!" I cried, tears of laughter beginning to fill my eyes. "Please, I can't take it."

Finally he stopped talking, and then I felt his tongue moving slowly over my palm. The teasing strokes became kisses. I removed my hand and gave him my mouth.

No much later we were on a plane to New York—not Jet Giano this time, but comfortable first class. (I admit I was really looking forward to *that* perk of a full bank account!) We had a flash drive from Seiji that he'd given to Richard when they met to talk about his work. I was anxious see the pictures, but wanted us to look at them together and the time in the air was the perfect opportunity. And not only did we get to see photos, but Richard's meeting with him had resulted in a show for Seiji scheduled for April, following the artist who was already on the calendar to follow Steph. I was so excited for Seiji. His work certainly deserved to be seen.

"I have to thank you again for introducing us," Richard said as he dug his laptop out of his briefcase where it was traveling next to mine. "You have a great eye."

"*I only have eyes for you...*" I sang softly.

Richard laughed, shaking his head, then gave me a quick kiss on the cheek. He plugged the drive into the computer and opened the file. For the next thirty minutes we reviewed the photos, and—not to be vain or anything—they were fabtastic! As we looked at the shots, it took me right back to that morning, and how much fun we'd had. There was even one picture of Richard—in his sports coat and tie for one of his business headshots—completely cracked up, bent over and laughing.

"Do you remember what you were laughing at?" I asked.

"Do you?"

"Probably something I said, but I don't recall what it was."

"I believe you were mumbling something about regretting leaving Zoor at home and wondering if it might be a good idea to have him peeking out above my belt. You were acting like a stylist, going on about the advantage of displaying assets and so forth. And then you suggested we could just go for the real thing and let everyone think it was just a joke."

Hard as it might be to imagine, I blushed!

He looked at me, surprised. "Really? NOW you're embarrassed?"

"Well, it sounds more scandalous when you tell it." I was grinning as I remembered. "And Seiji didn't hear what I was saying. He just told you to smile. And I think he said it was 'the money shot.' That's what made you laugh when his words sort of went along with my commentary."

He just looked at me. "As I believed I've mentioned many times, you're really something, Miss Hot Pants."

That earned him a kiss.

We continued to sort through the pictures, putting them in three files: Perfect, Really Good, and Less Than Perfect. There were far more in the "perfect" file than there should have been, including that amazing shot of my Prince with exactly the same look of love that I had in Giano's ad. And there were several of the two of us that I thought our friends and family would really appreciate. I found myself wanting one of those accordion-fold-out things grandmothers have, I wanted to fill mine with pictures of the two of us, never mind just sharing them on my iPhone. Seeing us together made me feel every bit as lovely as Richard kept telling me I was.

"Now can you see how beautiful you are?" I asked.

Richard just smiled.

I appropriated the laptop, pulled a flash drive out of my purse and popped it in. I opened the file and chose the picture I wanted to show him. It was my favorite from our sojourn on the island. Richard was naked, kneeling on the sand, hands on hips watching the waves. His outstanding round bottom and a hint of dangly bits showing through his spread legs—well, it was just perfect.

I turned the screen toward him. And he burst out laughing.

"When on earth did you take that?"

"That's your birthday shot, or one of them. Your mother loved it."

"My mother?"

"Yup. I knew she'd appreciate an update on the bottom she diapered so long ago."

Richard was just shaking his head.

We proceeded to share the other pictures we'd taken on the island, many of them when the subject wasn't aware. We had a lot of fun remembering.

The following Tuesday, October 29

When we were safely airborne on the way home New York, I turned to Richard and said, "So, holidays."

He looked at me, waiting for me to elaborate.

When I said nothing, he sighed dramatically and pretending a great deal of patience said earnestly, "Well, holidays are certain days of the year when various things are commemorated or celebrated. Holidays began as pagan cultural rituals and…"

"Have you always been such a smartass?"

"*Moi?*" he replied innocently.

"*Toi.* Forgive me for assuming that we are now so deeply attuned that a simple one-word clue would allow you to ascertain the subject and intent of my brief inquiry. Obviously, I was mistaken."

"Obviously," Richard said, dryly.

"So to rephrase…" I continued, "What do you usually do over Thanksgiving and Christmas? Do you go to Paris? Do you have your friends come to your house for turkey?"

Richard smiled and dropped the pretense of confusion.

"I usually go to Paris for Christmas and New Year's. Obviously, my family doesn't celebrate Thanksgiving. I sometimes get invited to join a group of friends, but for the past few years I've just stayed home and shared some turkey with Marie. She tends to either have her nieces come at Christmas while I'm gone, or she goes to New York. She and Antonio sometimes take turns being at the house for the holidays and we have a couple of people who can stay if we're all out of town."

"I was thinking of proposing…" Before I could finish, Richard interrupted me.

"I've told you the answer is yes. Just say where and when."

I gave him an eye roll and a loud sigh of exasperation.

"I was *going* to suggest that maybe we could go to my folks for Thanksgiving. Of course they want us to come, but I didn't know if you had other plans."

"I'd really enjoy that. I'm thankful for you and your family, so why not celebrate that together?" He kissed my cheek.

"What about Giano? Do you know how he spends the holiday? Does he have family here besides Antonio?"

"As far as I know Antonio is going to be with his girlfriend's family in San Diego. Let's call Giano when we get home and see."

There was an idea that had been floating around in the back of my mind for a while that I hadn't mentioned to Richard. Suddenly, it seemed like the perfect time.

"Do you think Giano might like Gran? Ever since I met him, the thought keeps coming and going that I should introduce them. Or does he already have a lady friend that you've neglected to mention?"

Richard just gave me one of his unreadable looks.

"What?" Was I really so far off base? "I know you love Gran, why wouldn't Giano?"

"Tell me, is matchmaking yet another one of your skills."

"I think maybe you're the matchmaker here. Look at Steph and Michael."

Richard shook his head. "That was one hundred percent Mark's doing. I knew Michael but never thought about him for Steph until I saw them together at the party." Richard squeezed my hand. "In my own defense I have to say I was pretty much focused on you and making sure you knew how amazing we were together."

I tried to laugh, but it came out as more of a snort. "As if I were clueless." But he hadn't answered my question. "Well?"

"Well what?" replied my usually much more focused lover.

"What about Gran and Giano?"

"A match made in heaven," he said with a smile, "Just like this one. And the best part is that I know they've already Skyped, because I asked him to talk to her about the Foundation."

"You never told me! Why hasn't either of them said anything? Does he like her?"

Richard laughed at my enthusiastic questions and the speed at which they were presented.

"I believe Giano's comment was '*bellissima*' and I think he also threw in 'magnificent creature' accompanied by some admonitions about hiding her from him all this time. He said it was easy to see where you got your beauty. Actually, I could tell he was pretty excited, so I suspect he will be more than pleased with an invitation. We might even be able to hitch a ride on Jet Giano."

That's exactly what we did. We flew Jet Giano up to Walla Walla the Tuesday night before Thanksgiving. I tried to keep a straight face as Giano attempted to hide his excitement. I have to say it looked to me like he might just be a little nervous about the upcoming face-to-face with Gran, which really surprised me. From the first time we met on that magical night when Richard took me to *Les Miz*, Giano struck me as a very sophisticated man of the world, charming and kind and a very astute businessman. Getting to know him had only confirmed that impression and added his outstanding taste and amazing artistic skills to his list of attributes. At any rate, his behavior made me wonder if maybe he'd been spending a little more long-distance time with my grandmother than either Richard or I was aware of.

Shortly after take off Giano said to me, "So Cressibella, what have I done that would cause you to keep your incredible *nonna* a secret from me, a man who adores women and worships the magnificent among them?"

"You must forgive me," I said, playing along. "I naturally assumed that a man as handsome and charming as yourself would have a long line of enchanting ladies to keep him company. How was I to know you were seeking love?"

"There are women and there are goddesses. The women are plentiful, goddesses rare. Your Katherina is a goddess..." he said, as he shook his finger in my direction, "...and I remind you we are all seeking love. The two of you are blessed to have found it."

"Uh, Giano, can I give you a piece of advice?" I asked, changing the subject in order to slow the dramatic torrent of words he was channeling in my direction.

"But of course, Bella. You, too, are a goddess, and what fool would dare to ignore the words of a goddess?"

"My grandmother might not be impressed by your flattery. A softer approach may get you further in the long run."

Giano threw back his head and laughed. Hard. For a moment I wasn't quite sure what had struck him so funny. I looked at Richard, who didn't seem to know, either.

When he finally recovered, Giano wiped the tears from his eyes and said, "This is true, but it is also something I have already learned. I believe at one point her exact words were: 'Cut the crap, Barsanti. Either you're interested in the Foundation or you're not'."

Richard and I both cracked up. That sounded like Gran. And it made me think that maybe she'd been onto something when she told me she'd been thinking of retiring. If she was treating a potential donor that way, it might be a good idea to at least put someone else in charge of fundraising!

I was pleased that Giano seemed so smitten and wondered what Gran was thinking. When I'd FaceTimed her after we got back from New York and asked about Giano, she'd been evasive. Hmmmm…I was sure it was going to be interesting to see those two together. I was still convinced there was a chance they were pretty evenly matched and if that proved to be the case, anything could happen!

There was a four-door Mercedes waiting for us when we landed and Richard drove us to the Marcus Whitman. Jono was at the front desk when we arrived, a special favorite from our first stay. He remembered us and greeted us warmly.

Richard introduced Giano. Jono had done his homework.

"Welcome, Signore Barsanti. It is an honor to have you stay with us. I've admired your ads for some time and I recognized this lovely young lady from one of the recent ones.

"It is my good fortune that she agreed to model for me. The photograph captured a remarkable moment."

"*Amore?*" Jono said, with a wink at me.

"*Di preciso!*" Giano said conspiratorially, delighted that Jono had noticed.

Jono sent a bellman for one of the shiny brass carts and loaded our bags himself, then accompanied us up to our rooms in the tower while giving Giano a little hotel history that he'd shared with us on our first visit.

We had the same room we'd had last time. Jono had even noted my previous request for two desks and had them already set up for us. I took a moment to let my family know we'd arrived and made arrangements to meet them for breakfast at the hotel in the morning at 8:00.

We were both tired. Richard had had some sort of a last minute situation to deal with at the gallery that had caused us to be about a half hour late to meet Giano. Not being on time was something that really annoyed Richard, but Giano was unconcerned when we finally arrived at the airport.

My own day had also been a bit on the frantic side. I'd spent more than an hour on the phone with the Ice Cream Boys discussing some of the contract negotiations. That had also required a call to Ari for an answer to what I'm sure to him seemed like another of my endless questions, though he had been gracious and taken my call immediately. I'd even called Robert earlier to confirm the line of thinking I was pursuing. I knew we'd all be both glad and relieved when my future was signed, sealed and delivered. I just wanted to be sure I was keeping a close eye on those ducks of mine, to be sure they were lined up perfectly!

I hadn't told my folks and Gran anything about the deal with Google. They believed I was still waiting for a funding offer, though I had mentioned there was some serious interest. And that was true, wasn't it? Besides, my family's concept of the dollar amounts involved in selling my project were as modest as mine had been in the beginning.

I was approaching the negotiations pragmatically, and not allotting any time to spending fantasies. Plenty of opportunities for that, if and when the final papers were signed. (Can you tell I was not quite ready to believe it was all actually going to happen?) Richard was respectful of my approach and avoided the subject unless I asked for his input. I will confess that in the back of my mind I was thinking what a magnificent Christmas gift the mere fact of my success would be for my family.

So, as I said, we were tired. By mutual, if unspoken, agreement, we passed on sex in the shower and settled for mutual soaping and a modest amount of kissing. When we crawled into our luxurious bed and each other's arms, it was with a sense of relaxation and contentment. And yes, the exquisite sensation of skin on skin led to a low key session of lovemaking that sent us off to sleep with smiles on both our faces.

56
Gratitude

Wednesday, November 27

At 5:00 a.m. my lover woke me in the way I'd come to expect (and enjoy!) and then we went for a run over to the college, around the campus and neighborhood. It was still dark, but the streetlights provided adequate illumination and we weren't the only people getting an early start on the day. The sky had grown light by the time we returned to the hotel with the sun creeping toward the horizon.

We went down about a quarter to eight and to the room near the rear entrance to the hotel, where a fire was already burning in the fireplace. That was also where a baby grand piano seemed to be begging for Richard's attention. He sat down at the keyboard and I settled on one of the couches to enjoy the music he made while we waited for Giano and my family.

As he played, a few people stopped to stand and listen. One couple took a spot on the other couch. Then Giano arrived and sat down beside me. I could tell he was shocked.

Without taking his eyes from Richard he said softly, "When did this happen?"

"On our trip to New York, before his birthday."

He turned to me then. "But why? How?"

"A man may do surprising things for love," I said with a wink. Then I leaned over and gave him a kiss on the cheek.

Giano took my hand and brought it to his lips. I thought I saw the hint of a tear in his eye.

"You are an angel sent straight from heaven, Bella. A gift to the boy…and to me."

Before I could respond, my family arrived. Richard saw them and brought the piece he was playing to a conclusion, accompanied by applause from us and a handful of other guests.

Richard got to them first. "Ah, the beautiful Kate," he said as he kissed Gran's cheek. "And her equally lovely daughter." Mom got a kiss, too. He was giving Daddy a bro hug when Giano and I reached them. He turned to introduce Giano.

"Allow me to present my good friend and second father, Giancarlo Barsanti."

Giano first shook my father's hand, and startled us all by quoting Pertuchio.

"I am a gentleman of Verona, Sir, that hearing of Katherina's beauty and her wit, her affability and bashful modesty…" He paused to wink at Gran. *"…her wondrous qualities and mild behavior, am bold to show myself a froward guest."*

Richard smirked and said, "Well, he *is* from Verona."

We cracked up as Richard continued the introductions. I had my eye on Gran, noting her responses. She couldn't take her eyes off Giano, who kissed my mother's hand and pronounced her as beautiful as her daughter.

When it was Gran's turn, Giano kissed her hand, too. "Ah, the astounding Katherina." Then he quoted: *"Good morrow Kate, for that's your name, I hear."*

Gran smirked and he continued.

"You are even more magnificent…how do they say it now?… up close and personal!"

Everyone laughed. I was amazed to see Gran blushing! (That makes twice. Remember that kiss Richard gave her after their day at the winery?) If you knew Gran, you'd know how unusual it was. It seemed both she and Giano were smitten. Yay LOVE!

As we walked toward the restaurant someone's cell rang. The tone was the beginning of the *Les Miz* theme. (*Do you hear the people sing?*) We all looked at Gran.

"Sorry," Gran said. "I thought I'd turned it off." She pulled her cell from her bag and glanced at the caller ID. "I apologize. Get a table and order me some coffee. I'll be along in just a minute."

By the time the coffee came, Gran joined us. I could see from the look on her face that she was upset.

"Everything OK?" I asked.

"It was Suzanne. We've got a crisis and I need to go to Seattle. The flights are all overbooked, of course, with the holiday, so I'm going to have to drive. Damn! With luck I can still be back in time for dinner tomorrow, but I'm afraid I won't be much help in the kitchen."

"Can you wait 'til after breakfast or shall I drive you home now to get your car?" my mother asked.

"*Signore*," Giano broke in. "Please allow me to be of service. My plane is at your disposal. I would be honored to escort you to Seattle."

My family turned to Giano, all three of them surprised. Richard and I looked at each other, making an effort to hide our smiles. He reached for my hand under the table and squeezed.

"It is nothing," Giano assured them. "The flight, I believe, is less than an hour. So you can stay and enjoy your breakfast, no?"

"Gran, say yes to the nice man," I urged.

She looked around the table. We were all smiling. She shrugged her shoulders.

"Yes."

"*Bene*," Giano said with a smile. "So it is settled. Do you need to return to your daughter's home to collect your things?"

"No. I have everything I need in Seattle. We can go from here, if that's convenient."

"Very well. If you will excuse me for a moment, I will make the arrangements."

Giano left our table, I presumed to let Captain Santorelli know the plans had changed.

"What have I gotten myself into?" Gran said. She looked quite surprised by the sudden turn of events.

"Takin' care of business," Daddy said nonchalantly, hiding his own smile. "You need to get to Seattle and Signore Barsanti has generously offered his assistance. Problem solved."

"Come, Kate," Richard chimed in. "If you play your cards right you can return with a donation for the foundation."

"Richard!" I was shocked.

He laughed. "I merely mean you'll have a chance to give

Giano a first hand look at your facility. If somehow your considerable charm fails you, surely your work will impress him."

Gran narrowed her eyes at my Prince. "I'll have you know that the day has yet to come when my charm fails me."

Richard smiled and raised his water glass to my grandmother with a toast.

"To the charming Kate, may your problems in Seattle be easily solved and your return to us swift."

Everyone joined in and a minute later Giano rejoined us.

"It is arranged. We will leave at 10:30, so let us enjoy this meal."

When we'd finished a sumptuous and somewhat leisurely breakfast from the amazing hotel buffet and were heading toward the parking lot, Giano turned to Richard and said. "I will take the car, yes? You can arrange another rental?"

"Of course." He handed Giano the keys.

"Wait," Gran said as she reached into her coat pocket and pulled out her set. "Take mine. You can ride with them to the house and then take it wherever you need to go."

"If you're sure you don't mind?"

"I suspect I can trust you with Cosette."

Richard laughed. "I'll do my best to take good care of her. I only need to run out to the winery for a meeting. After that I expect to be underfoot at the house."

"Ha!" Mom said. "There will be work, Mr. Hunter."

We waved them goodbye and headed for Mom's car.

"OK," I said as we all got in. "Spill it! What's going on with Gran and Giano? I saw Gran actually blush when he kissed her hand."

Mom and Daddy both laughed.

"We wish we knew," Mom said. "There have been FaceTimes and phone calls, but she's being very secretive. Saturday there were flowers. I suspect there's a lot going on besides fundraising. Did he say anything to you?"

"I only found out they'd been in touch when I asked Richard about coming here for Thanksgiving. On the flight up Giano called her a goddess, and he cracked up when I suggested he take a less effusive approach with her. Apparently, she'd already schooled him regarding her lack of tolerance for bullshit."

My parents laughed.

"Well, I wish him luck," said Daddy. "Like you, Seachange, she's a handful."

"I beg your pardon!" I said indignantly. "I'm not a handful, am I, Handsome?" I said that last bit seductively, leaning over to run my tongue around his ear, ending with a big wet kiss on his cheek.

Richard snorted. "Uh…I can honestly say I love nothing more than having my hands full of you."

"Richard!"

"Are you sure you're not Italian?" my father asked from the front seat.

When we got home, Richard took Gran's Subaru and went to his meeting. Mom and I stood in the kitchen, contemplating a division of labor since we were down one pair of hands.

"How about I do the dressing and you start the giblet gravy? It won't hurt to have all this done before tomorrow," I suggested. "Then we can move on to the pies."

"We can leave a few things for your grandmother, when we know what time she'll get here," Mom added. "And we can always push dinner later, if we need to."

And so we started.

I loved Gran's dressing and made it often myself, or at least I used to when I was still cooking for myself and Steph. I would have to make some for Marie and see what she thought. It was so great with anything—pork chops, chicken, Cornish game hens, and of course turkey. It was mostly a sage dressing recipe (bread, butter, chopped celery, chopped green onions, sage and thyme) but Gran added chopped Brazil nuts and cayenne pepper. It was so yummy I was happy to eat it right out of the bowl. (Exactly why I'd volunteered!)

We got the pies in the oven (two pumpkin and two pecan) then stopped for a lunch of Mom's homemade tomato soup with a green salad and garlic bread.

"So what do you think?" Daddy asked us while we ate.

"Will they be back tonight or will Kate stay and take advantage of a handsome man with his own jet?"

"I hope she keeps him overnight," I said, raising an eyebrow. "Giano's pretty special and he's already calling her a goddess."

"Uh, oh. I hope he doesn't become disillusioned." Daddy shook his head.

"Matt! Stop trying to pretend you don't know what an incredible woman she is," Mom scolded.

"I'd never argue with that, but she is a bit..."

Mom's eyes narrowed.

"She's a bit of a challenge," he finished.

"Like Mom?" I asked innocently.

"Like Mom, and her daughter," he agreed.

We all laughed.

"Well, Richard seems to enjoy the 'challenge' and no matter what you say, I know you do, too." I told him.

"Wouldn't have it any other way. There is nothing on this earth I'd trade her for." He leaned over and gave Mom a quick kiss. "I suspect Mr. Hunter feels the same way about you."

Richard came back a little before three, carrying a case of wine with a large bouquet balanced on top. I rushed to take the flowers and deliver a kiss.

"How was your meeting, Handsome?"

"Successful. I'd like to take you out there one of these days." He set the wine on the floor and took me in his arms. "How go the preparations for the feast? It smells wonderful."

I pointed to the pies cooling on the island. "We're holding our own, despite the fact that Gran has abandoned us."

He kissed me and gave my bottom a quick squeeze. "Any word from our jetsetters?"

"Nope, we were wondering if they'd come back tonight, or tomorrow."

Richard smiled. "I'm betting tomorrow. Giano is probably in heaven for having a chance to spend time alone with the magnificent Kate. Do we know what the crisis is?"

"Nope," Mom said. "I expected her to text by now with an update, but haven't heard a word."

We were all wiggling our eyebrows at each other and then we burst out laughing.

Mom put Richard to work retrieving the big turkey platters and candle holders from the top shelves in the pantry, then asked him to wash them with a wink at me. She and I got out the good china and the silver and added it to Richard's wash pile while Daddy started drying.

Richard's phone toned *O Sole Mio* and he quickly dried his hands and pulled it from his pocket. He answered in Italian and told Giano he was putting him on speaker and suggested he behave as he set the phone on the island. We all gathered around, anxious to hear the latest.

Giano laughed. *"Buon pomeriggio, miei cari amici!"*

"Yeah, yeah," I said. "How's the 'taming' going?" I asked.

"Hearing her mildness praised in every town, her virtues spoke of, and her beauty sounded—Yet not so deeply as to her belongs," he quoted.

My folks looked at each other in surprise.

"Giano, you surprise me," Richard said.

Giano pretended to be offended. "Do you think I am unfamiliar with the works of Signore Shakespeare?"

"No, we think you are besotted with the magnificent Kate," Richard replied.

"Ah well, I confess it is true. And can you blame me? But enough about my joy at this turn of events. Katherina has informed me we will be here until 10:00 a.m. tomorrow and should return to you by noon. She has suggested I ask you to move the meal to 5:00 p.m. so that she may still assist with the preparations. We should be there no later than 1:00 p.m. If that changes I will call again."

"Giano..." I added before he could hang up. "I expect her to return with her cheeks like the blush of a pink rose."

He laughed. "Believe me, Bella, I will do my very best! *Ciao!*"

We all looked at each other.

"I guess that answers that question," I said. "Now we have to wait for the next installment!"

Richard took us to dinner at T Maccarone's and we spent a good part of the meal concocting scenarios involving what Gran and Giano might be up to. It was hilarious since one of Mom's included Giano being drafted to play Sky Masterson in Sunday's upcoming production of *Guys and Dolls* with Gran as Sarah. Pretending to take the suggestion seriously, we all admitted Giano would look sharp in a fedora, Richard assured us Giano had a good baritone and we concluded he might just be so entranced with Gran that she could talk him into it. As we stretched out the concept, Daddy and Richard agreed, straight-faced, that they could provide music for practice, and Mom was sure she had a script in her office.

It was a great evening. After we took my folks home and were on our way back to the hotel Richard said, "I think I understand what you mean about the playfulness you and I share. You obviously get the inclination from your parents."

"And how do you come by yours?" I asked.

"You know, I'm not sure. Max was a good playmate when we were in school, but it was kind of just between the two of us. I doubt anyone considered me much of a funster in those days. I was still bottomed out from Maryse."

"But your gallery folks all have a sense of humor. You seem to enjoy them and I know they enjoy you. They adore you."

"They're a lot of fun, but we do more superficial joking, not the kind of complex back-and-forths you and I just seem to fall into naturally."

"You know how happy I am about that," I said giving his hand a squeeze.

"Me, too."

The next morning Richard dropped me at the house, picked up Daddy and they left for the college so Richard could get a tour of the music department.

I showed Mom the trick I'd stolen from Martha Stewart of making a pattern under the turkey skin out of sage leaves. Then we stuffed the bird, an impressive twenty-pounder. The balance of the dressing was in another pan to cook outside the bird.

"What are we going to leave for Gran?" I asked as I started chopping mushrooms to go in the string beans while Mom was slicing the sweet potatoes..

"She can do the Waldorf salad and we'll make her mash the potatoes. Beyond that, I think we're good."

Daddy and Richard followed Giano and Gran in the door a little after noon. Remarks were made as they came in that I couldn't catch, but everyone was laughing and sure enough, Gran's cheeks were pink.

"*Buon lavoro, Giancarlo! Bravo! Come una rosa rosa,*" I whispered to Giano with a wink.

When Gran got her apron on, she tried to pretend everything was normal but I noticed some really pretty earrings that looked to me like the work of a certain jeweler I knew.

"Nice earrings, " I said casually. Much to my own surprise, I managed to keep my face straight as her cheeks colored. Wow! Something was definitely going on!

"'The silly man insisted and I could hardly say no."

I just looked at her.

"Hey!" she said in a whisper, "Who knew I could manage to get a little of this for myself at this point in my life? Let me enjoy it!"

I gave her a big hug. "Isn't it the best?" I asked as I kissed her cheek.

When we were all finally seated at the table, which was groaning under a lavish variety of dishes, Richard made sure everyone had a glass of wine, then stood to propose a toast.

"I want to express my sincere thanks to Bea and Matt, and of course to the magnificent Kate, for including Giano and me in this very special celebration. To share a meal with people you love is time spent in the company of angels in disguise. Let us enjoy this little piece of heaven."

We all drank to that.

"So happy you could join us," Daddy said. "And we have a little Thanksgiving ritual we hope you'll consent to participate in. We go around the table and express what we are most grateful for in this coming together of friends and family."

Daddy reached for my hand on his right and for Gran's on his left and we all joined hands around the table. Giano kissed both Gran's hand and Mom's as he took them.

"Having survived a rather extraordinary experience recently, I'll begin," my father said. "I am filled with gratitude and deep appreciation for everyone here today. For my beautiful and endlessly patient wife and for her mother, who, despite my comments to the contrary, I credit with the speed of my somewhat miraculous recovery. You know I love you Kate. I always have.

"I am so thankful that my beautiful daughter has at last found a man who is worthy of her love and obviously shares the depth of her commitment. And to Richard, for his kindness and generosity which seem to us to be boundless. Welcome to our family, and thank you again for everything.

"And to Giano, you my friend are already considered a part of this family...uh...like it or not! Welcome, and may you return to spend time with us often."

Daddy turned to Gran, who smiled and looked around the table before she spoke.

"This moment might well be the happiest of my life. I am so grateful to be here with the people I love, my wonderful daughter and this husband of hers who loves her every bit as much as I do. Thank you Matt for being one of the very best of men. My beautiful granddaughter—I'm so grateful that you're moving into the amazing life you deserve. And that man sitting next to you, he sees you for the extraordinary woman you've become and even seems to appreciate some of your...uh... more *interesting* quirks."

We all laughed and Richard planted a quick kiss on my cheek.

"And as to this handsome Italian sitting next to me," Gran paused and gave Giano a long, penetrating look. "So far, so good."

Giano laughed loudly at that, then took his turn.

"I must thank you all for making me feel so welcome. To Matt and Bea, *mille grazie* for welcoming me into your home. This is the perfect family for my Riccardo, who, like the beautiful Cressida, deserves the very best. I believe they have found that in each other." He turned to look at Gran. "And to Katherina, who has stolen my heart. I pray that you will never want to return it."

I could see him give her hand a squeeze, just as her cheeks were coloring. (Again!)

"Well, I'm not sure I can follow that, but I'll give it a shot," my mother said. "I am so grateful to be in the company of people who love so deeply and share a generosity of spirit that, frankly, boggles the mind. For Richard, who loves my daughter and makes no bones about it, and for CJ, who continues to live her life with integrity and a sense of humor. I'm grateful everyday for my husband who loves me still, and never let's me forget it and for my amazing mother, who has stepped in and helped with my life challenges whenever I've needed her and has somehow maintained her own fierce a sense of humor. I assure you all this was no small accomplishment! And lastly, to our new friend Giano, who is a citizen of what CJ calls Richard's amazing world...welcome. Thank you all for being here today."

Then it was Richard's turn.

"It is really difficult for me to find the words to express the depth of the gratitude I'm feeling at this moment. I think everyone at this table knows how much I love CJ, but it might be hard for you to understand what finding her has meant to me. The fact that you, as her family, have welcomed me into your lives with open arms means the world to me. I promise you that I will do everything in my power to see that she is happy. To be here today with you and with Giano, the father of my heart, is something I will always treasure."

That got him a kiss on the cheek! And then, finally, it was up to me.

"Who knew we'd all become citizens of this man's

extraordinary universe? Speaking as someone who signed up early on, it is the very best place to be. As proof, witness the fact that I am here, sharing this magnificent meal with the people I love most in this world. Gratitude is a feeble word for what I'm feeling, but true, nonetheless. May we share many many more years together as we are now, hand in hand in love."

We all dropped each other's hands at that moment and lifted our glasses. Unprompted, in unison we said, "To love!"

STILL LUCKY

We hope you've enjoyed this book. It is the second in the Lucky Girl *trilogy, the first being* Lucky Girl.

If you want to find out what's next for this amazing couple, the answers will be found in Book 3, YOU.

Reviews & Recommendations are greatly appreciated.